SKETCHING
LITCHFIELD LAKE

TRACY BROEMMER

Theresa Broemmer

Sketching Litchfield Lake

by

Tracy Broemmer

Women's Fiction/Suspense

Published by Tracy Broemmer

2nd Edition edited by Lexie Broemmer

Cover Photo: Deposit Photos

Cover Design by Redbird Design

Thank yous to Dawn
& Kim J

And a special thanks to Lexie
-It's nice to have another writer in the house now,
a like-minded person who loves to talk about characters like they're
real people. Thanks for hashing out the ending of SLL with me.

Chapter 1

TREVOR

black water
black water lapping at his shoes
his boots
why was he wearing boots?
black water
gray black sky—
a shiver climbing his spine
the water's warm
warm and black

Trevor Gerhardt gasped awake. His heart was going to explode. Jesus Christ, he was having a heart attack. He was going to lay here and die. What if no one even found his body? Like, for days?

Bright, garish yellow light streaked the ceiling. Trevor stared at that light, wondered who in his family would be waiting for him on the other side. His heart still pounded; he could feel it in his neck and his chest and toes and fingertips. Hurt, though. His chest hurt, and he was still panting, trying to catch his breath. It was stifling in this fucking room. The air was stagnant.

Like the lake water.

The thought drove him off the bed. His foot caught in the damp sheets as he scrambled to get up. He tripped, hopped a couple of steps, and crashed into the wall by the window. The drapes shifted under his clenched fist and that streak of sunlight grew wider and brighter, and Trevor squeezed his eyes shut against the sharp pain in his head.

"Jesus, Trevor."

Shit. He wasn't alone. Heart still beating too fast, he bent at the waist and rested his hands on his knees. Gulped in air, but it was fetid and hot, and it stuck in his lungs, draped over his ribs like syrup.

"Shut the curtains."

He stood up straight. Glanced at her as he rounded the double bed. On her stomach, her right arm up under her pillow, she watched him as he scratched his way down over his stomach and his dick. Dishwater blond hair matted to her head, she narrowed her eyes at him and turned to face the other way on her pillow.

Shit. He forgot her name. Who the fuck was she?

He left the door open as he lifted the toilet lid.

"Really?"

He ignored her. Felt somewhat better as he flushed. He wasn't one to look in the mirror often, but the bathroom in this apartment was so small, his nose was almost pressed up against the mirror as he washed his hands. His hair was smashed against the side of his head, too, and his skin was pasty white, and there were still drops of sweat on his forehead. He parted his blood red lips and looked at his teeth. Dropped his gaze to the sink. Saw his toothbrush. A pink toothbrush lay by his.

His heartbeat finally slowed; he was beginning to catch

his breath. The room almost tilted as he turned to go back to the bedroom. She rolled over and stared at him. He hated that. He hated the way she stared at him in the mornings.

The thought startled him.

She snorted a sarcastic laugh.

"You forgot me again, huh?"

Trevor rubbed his hands over his head as he crossed the room to the bed and lifted his knee to sit down beside her. Flat on her back now, right arm still over her head, she stared at him boldly.

He watched his hand as it moved, as if it had a mind of its own, to touch her. Cover her small breast. He met her familiar gaze. Moved his hand over her, but not the way she liked it.

"Mallory."

"Jeez, Trevor, really?" She flinched when he lifted his ass from the bed and yanked his underwear off. She didn't like it like this. She'd told him that once, and he didn't mean to hurt her. But in this sleep-dream drunk stupor, he was rough, and he yanked her panties down just to her knees. She'd give it to him. She always did, but she didn't like it. She opened her legs for him, and he drove into her hard and fast.

She held on to him, fingernails scraping his shoulders as he pumped his hips over hers. He'd looked at her face once, when he did this to her, and he'd seen a mix of boredom and pain and wondered what *he* looked like when he was like this. Since then, rather than look at her, he'd buried his face against her neck, smelled the remains of the night before—whether that be perfume, sleep sweat or sex—and rode her hard until he came inside her.

The first time he'd done it that way, they'd panicked. She hadn't been on the pill then. Whatever happened between them, he sure as fuck didn't want a kid right now. He sure as hell wasn't daddy material; he wasn't sure she was mother material. She'd gotten the pill, even after she'd told him she didn't like it this way, that it hurt and he was a slob and a jerk, and so now at least when he fucked her like this, a three minute thing that left him shaking and spent and drove the goddamned nightmares out of his head, he didn't have to worry about getting her pregnant.

"Least you remembered my name before you fucked me this time."

He flopped over to lie on his back, breathless and sweaty again, and watched her roll away from him. She climbed out of bed and stalked to the shower. She could be prickly on a good day. Pissy and mean when he started her day like this. She turned the shower water on and then turned to look at him.

"What?"

He huffed out a deep breath and raised his hands. Dug the heels of his hands into his eyes.

"You want coffee?"

When she didn't answer him, he propped himself up on his elbows to look at her. She was leaning against the door-frame, the shower water running behind her. It would take a while for the water to heat up. Time enough for him to do something for her. He did that sometimes. After he mauled her, he would touch her. The way she liked. If he did that, if he made her come, she'd give in, get over it. They wouldn't have to bitch at each other the rest of the day.

He sat up. Stared at her nude body. She was a waif, all bones and hard angles. Tiny hips, small breasts. She was good in bed, and he loved the dirty things she said when she was excited, when he made her come.

Didn't have time today. He had to move. Coffee. Canvases. He needed more canvases. He had to paint. Fuck it, he should just paint now. Still had one canvas left. He could do without the coffee if he started painting now.

Maybe he could capture that weird sliver of light over the black water if he started right now. Never mind that he had nine other canvases with that same black water and that same strip of light lined up against the wall in the other room. Maybe this time he could get it right.

"You're such a dick." She rolled her eyes and ducked back into the bathroom.

Chapter 2

HANNA

The rain started slowly. She felt it on her face first. Just a tiny drop of water, like a kiss, on her cheek. And then she'd felt it in her hair. Almost felt good at first, like when Bowie ran his fingers through her hair. But then the gentle drops of rain turned into big splashes on the pavement, and her hair was dry and then damp and then soaked. She watched where she stepped as she jogged.

So much for weather forecasts. *Sunny and hot today*. The last time she'd checked the forecast—she'd looked at her phone before she left the house—there had been sunshiny icons all across the screen. Bowie would get a kick out of this, Hanna showing up at home soaked like a stray dog out in the rain. If Sylvi were napping, Bowie might even kiss her when she came inside. Tease her about wet t-shirt contests— thank God those days were long gone—and most likely he'd strip her wet clothes from her right there in the kitchen and maybe press her up against the wall (the high-top table was out of the question) and make love to her.

Sylvi wouldn't be napping. Not at four-thirty in the afternoon. Hanna waved at a car as it crept by, appreciating that the driver had slowed in order to not splash rain water all over her. Then again, she was pretty sure she couldn't get any wetter.

The crashing music in her earbuds was a perfect backdrop to the summer storm that had rolled in so suddenly. She switched it up every time she used her iPod, but most of the time, she relied on hard rock or even heavy metal to get her through a workout. Her spin class had been floored the first time she'd blasted them with Royal Blood.

She stepped in a puddle as she turned to jog up the driveway. Looked at her Nikes with regret. She'd only had them a month, maybe six weeks. She hated when her running shoes got wet. She slowed to a walk as she entered the two-car garage. Just what she needed—to slip on the wet cement and fall. She'd just recovered from a broken finger; it was still a little stiff. Her mom had reminded her she'd just turned thirty, and she might possibly have some arthritis in her finger. Hanna had nodded at her mother with a frown. Thanked her for that reminder. The party had been great; Bowie had pulled off a hell of a surprise. Being thirty *now*? Not so great.

"Mommy, it's storming!"

Sylvi, blue eyes and sweet smile, ran into the kitchen as Hanna stepped inside and closed the door behind her.

"Just raining." Hanna shook her head. Sylvi's initial excitement during storms was always quick to become anxiety, so Hanna and Bowie had learned to downplay those storms as much as they could. She toed off her left shoe and let it drop to the black and tan rug in front of the door.

"Mommy, you're wet!"

"Yep, Mommy's—" Hanna cringed as Sylvi threw herself at her and wrapped her arms and legs around Hanna's legs. "Well, now we're both wet, silly girl."

Sylvi giggled as Hanna leaned over to peel her daughter off her.

"Where's Daddy?" she asked as she kicked her other shoe off.

"Daddy is right here," Bowie announced. Hanna, hopping now on one foot so she could peel her wet sock from the other, looked up and grinned at her husband. "It's raining."

"Got that." She nodded as he handed her a towel. Their eyes met over Sylvi's head—just three, she was short, so they had several years left of looking at each other over the top of her—and Hanna laughed softly when Bowie arched an eyebrow at her.

Towel in one hand, she changed feet and pulled her other sock off.

"Hungry?"

"Kinda." She whipped her tank off over her head, ignored Bowie's lecherous grin and rubbed the towel over her wet hair. Her sports bra was just as wet as her tank, but she wouldn't take that off out here. Not with Sylvi standing between them. She leaned over and rubbed the towel down her bare legs. Stepped around Bowie and slipped into the small laundry room off the kitchen.

"Guess who called while you were running?"

Hanna decided she wouldn't tell him she was actually just jogging. Maybe if she would've picked up her pace sooner, she wouldn't have ended up soaked and freezing.

"No idea." She shrugged. Looked down at her bra and shorts. She would toss them all in the washer together, but she didn't want to walk through the house nude with Sylvi following her around.

Bowie grinned. Stroked his fingertip from the hollow of her neck to the top of the bra. She laughed and rolled her eyes. Bowie's grin was worth more than any drug, for any need.

"Sam."

Hanna shook her head at him. Saw Sylvi peek her head around the corner behind Bowie.

"C'mere, munchkin." Bowie held his hand out to Sylvi in invitation.

"Sam who?"

"We made sketti," Sylvi informed Hanna as Bowie lifted her to put her on his shoulders.

"Good grief, Sylvi!" Hanna grabbed her feet and gave her a gentle squeeze. "How'd you get so tall?"

Sylvi giggled.

"Real spaghetti." Bowie nudged her barefoot with his toe. Hanna laughed and then sighed and shook her head. If he was feeding her real spaghetti, not whole grain or spaghetti squash, he expected something in return.

"I'm hungry," she admitted.

"Go warm up. Take a shower. I'll get your stuff and wash it for you."

She leaned in to kiss him. "Love it when you talk dirty to me."

"Mommy, kiss Sylvi!"

Hanna trailed noisy kisses up her chubby leg.

"Sam who?" Hanna looked back at Bowie over her shoulder as she moved back around him to go take a quick shower. "That guy from the gym?"

Bowie's turn to look confused. Hanna watched him run through a mental checklist of people they knew from the gym. He shook his head no as he reached up to lift Sylvi off his shoulders.

"Are you wet?" Hanna asked her. "Do you need to put on dry clothes?"

"Nope."

"Sam Collins," Bowie announced.

Hanna frowned and shook her head. "Sam who?"

"Sam Collins," Bowie repeated. "From school."

"Oh my God!" Hanna shrugged and shook her head in disbelief. "How in the world would I have guessed Sam Collins? What the heck did he want?"

Bowie followed her back to the kitchen where she hesitated. Took a deep breath and smelled the garlic.

"Did you fix garlic bread, too?"

He smiled and raised his eyebrows.

"What'd he want?" she asked him again.

"I dunno. Just…said he was in town. Asked if we wanted to meet for a drink."

"Really?"

"Yeah. Why?"

"Well…that's weird."

"Why's it weird?"

Hanna snatched one of Sylvi's carrots from her snack plate. Sylvi grinned at Hanna when she glanced at her.

"I dunno," Hanna said around a mouthful. "We haven't seen him in, like…three years."

"Nine," Bowie corrected her quietly.

She looked up, met his eyes.

The sudden quiet between them was extra loud. Hanna heard one of Sylvi's shows in the living room. Apparently, Sylvi did, too, and she ran through the kitchen to stand in front of the TV.

"So. You and me? We're gonna meet Sam for a drink?"

"Sam and Neelie."

"Neelie?" Hanna whispered. "Seriously?"

"I mean…we don't have to. I didn't give him an answer yet."

Hanna swallowed the last of the carrot, coughed when it got stuck in her throat, suddenly a little sick to her stomach. Bowie laid his hand on her shoulder.

"You're freezing," he told her. "Go take a shower."

She looked up at him. Puckered her lips when he leaned over to kiss her.

"This spaghetti's the bomb, by the way," he called after her.

She considered flashing him, but again, she chose to behave in case Sylvi happened to look away from the TV.

"So am I," she reminded him. Bowie's laugh was hearty, contagious.

"Holding you to that."

"Totally okay with that," she answered as she turned away.

Once in the bathroom, water running, she peeled her wet bra off, not without a lot of work. The damned things were hard enough to squeeze her boobs into or out of when they were dry, pain in the ass when they were wet. She dropped it to the floor, shimmied out of her shorts and underwear and then stepped into the shower.

Sam Collins? Why in God's name had Sam Collins called Bowie? And what the hell was Neelie doing with him?

Chapter 3

TREVOR

Still wasn't right. He'd painted this damned scene at least twelve times now, and it still wasn't exactly what he was seeing in his head. In his dreams.

Nightmares.

He hesitated, brush in his hand, as he studied the spot in the black water where the shadow would go. A stroke of pale gray just there, near the shoreline. But he couldn't paint that swath of pale gray yet. What the hell was he missing? What was missing from this damned painting?

Trevor ducked his head to the right and wiped the sweat from his face on the sleeve of his vintage Mountain Dew t-shirt. Jesus, it was hotter than hell in here. The damned window unit was blasting away with lukewarm air, blowing it into this huge combo living room and kitchen area. Couldn't even keep up with this one room; no wonder it was so fucking hot when he and Mallory tried to sleep.

He hadn't showered. Kind of regretted that now. Mallory had been quick enough, he supposed. She wore heavy black eyeliner every day, but she rarely took the time for more makeup, especially when she was only going to work. But he'd been impatient, and while she was in the bathroom, he'd grabbed his jeans from the floor by the bed and started to put them on. Decided underwear might be necessary since he'd just balled her and he was still a mess, so he grabbed the pair he'd taken off to do her and put them on before the jeans.

Mallory had found him shoveling nearly dry cereal into his mouth—they were almost out of milk, and Trevor thought the Sugar Smacks he'd eaten had tasted a little funny, even though the milk was only two days past the date—studying the succession of paintings. Every one of them the same black water. Each of them just a tiny bit different. None of them right.

She'd rolled her eyes. Told him he had a problem. Told him he was disgusting. Trevor set his brush down on the card table where he kept his supplies and rubbed his eyes. Tried to remember if she'd said anything else before she'd walked out. No kiss goodbye. No *goodbye*. She was just gone.

Once she'd walked out, he'd muttered to himself that she could move out and fuck herself. But he'd never say that to her face. As blunt as she could sometimes be, he liked her. *Well*. He'd liked her well enough before this obsession had gripped him, and he'd suddenly been driven to paint this black water. And the gray shadow. And the shoreline.

He wasn't stupid. He wasn't a catch by anyone's stan- dards. Mallory, outside of this squalor where she was currently living with him, was hot. Smart. He'd met her at Rewind, the music store where he worked. Seen her there with her friends, and something about her flower-print dress and her combat boots had driven him fucking crazy. Or maybe it was the hat she wore. The gray wool cloche hat. Jesus, he'd asked her to wear it once when he fucked her. Turned him on more than her tits.

Not that anyone would hear him complaining about her

tendency to hang out topless, if not nearly nude, when she was at home.

The faded green t-shirt was sticking to his back. Each time he wiped at the sweat on his face, he got a whiff of the sweat in his shirt. He was beginning to disgust himself. He'd shower. A cool shower. And get out of the place for a while. Take a walk around the block. It was entirely possible it was cooler outside than it was in this apartment.

Yep. He'd shower. Take a walk. Find something to eat and then work on the painting again. He didn't have to go in until five. Plenty of time. He sighed and nodded. Took his black horn-rimmed glasses off and tossed them down on the table. Grabbed the collar of his t-shirt and yanked it over his head. Tossed it on the floor and then unbuttoned his jeans and dropped them next to the shirt. Small piles of dirty laundry dotted the scuffed, faded hardwood. Trevor sniffed the air and decided it was time someone did laundry. The whole bedroom was beginning to stink.

The cool water felt good on his sweat-slick skin. He washed his hair quickly and then, as he dragged a washrag and a bar of soap over his body, it hit him. Why the painting wasn't working right. He'd jumped in too fast. Hell, he'd never been much of a painter. He'd always been an *artist*, but he hadn't become obsessed with the acrylic paints (didn't even know the difference in acrylic or oil or watercolor) until he'd started having that dream. He'd jumped straight to paints, because he'd been obsessed with the color. He'd been desperate to find the distinct colors of the water and the shadow and the fescue at the shoreline.

He fished in his drawer in the chest he and Mallory shared. Came up empty-handed and then pulled on a pair of semi-clean jeans. Zipped up carefully, made a mental note to throw some whites in a basket and run downstairs later to the cellar and throw them in the washer. Bare-chested and barefoot, he scrounged around in the refrigerator until he found a piece of bologna and cheese. Slapped both on a piece of stale bread and tore off half of it for his first bite.

He had to sketch it. The pond. The lake. Whatever it was. It would come to him once he started. Once he got the contours right, the depth of the water and the way the lights hit it and the shadow, all of that would come to him. He shoved the second half of the bologna sandwich in his mouth and then rinsed his hands off in the kitchen sink. Mallory had done the dishes last night, so he grabbed a clean glass and then poured some orange juice for himself. Eyes on the canvases again, he took a swallow and then sputtered and nearly choked. Spit the juice in the sink and picked up the carton to check the date on it. *Jesus.* May 19. Almost two weeks old. He rinsed the glass out and then took a drink of tap water to swish away the taste.

Leaving the open carton on the counter, Trevor shivered again as he crossed out of the corner kitchen and into the living area. He picked up his glasses, accidentally smudging the left lens with his fingers, and put them on. Pain in the ass. He could hardly see now.

He stood for a moment and stared at the unfinished paintings. The canvases seemed to mock him. What the fuck was missing from each and every one of the pictures? Some of them were so unfinished, that only the black water was pictured. He wasn't concerned about the dock or the trees on the west side of the water or the house or even the trampled grass near the shoreline, just past the wild fescue. It was something in the water itself.

At least he had sketchbooks. Jesus, he had sketchbooks out the ass. Several of them were full. Pictures of sunsets, buildings, flowers, trees, comic book characters. Pictures of women. Women in business attire, formal attire. Nothing. He'd been careful which books Mallory had seen. She didn't mind most of the pictures he'd drawn. Not even of the other women he'd been with. But she hadn't seen the pictures of women in full sexual poses. Only the ones he'd drawn of her.

He hurried back to the bedroom and pulled his latest book out from under the bed. Grabbed his charcoal pencil from the table in the living room and then sat in the straight-backed yellow vinyl-covered kitchen chair. Scooted it nearer to the window, felt the tail ends of the air from the window unit. The lighting was somewhat better by the window, though they kept the shade pulled to try to keep it cooler.

His hand flew over the page in big bold strokes. The water. The body of water was first. Always the focal point. Of the nightmare. The art.

Why, though? Pad on his lap, right hand pressed over it to hold it in place, he shoved his fingertips up under his glasses and rubbed his eyes. Why was it a nightmare?

Warm, black water.

He curled the fingers of his left hand around the book and let his right hand go. Watched as he drew the strokes that would translate to color, to lights in the paintings. He stopped once, overwhelmed by the details in the sketch, thought he heard his cell ring. Decided he didn't hear it, that if he did, there was no one he needed to talk to—Mallory never called when she was at work—and continued on the sketch.

Chapter 4

Hanna

Women fell in love with her husband every day. Mostly, she found it amusing, and often, she would stand to the side and watch women of all ages fawn over him, watch him squirm under their stares (sometimes flirtatious, sometimes downright smoldering). She always made sure he knew she was watching, because that made him squirm more. Though Bowie was friendly and generous with his smiles, and though she trusted him without question, she got a kick out of teasing him about his legion of female fans, and now and then she called in sexual favors to make up for them. Not that he minded.

She was in plain sight today, but the two girls—couldn't have been a day older than eighteen—who had him cornered didn't seem to notice her. Hanna was bent over the front counter, looking at her class reservation list. She peeked at Bowie from under her blond bangs. Smirked when he shot her a look of desperation. Longish blond hair and deep blue eyes, he looked like a surfer right here in the good old land-locked state of Illinois. She'd teased him a lot when they were younger, still just friends—they'd known each other several years before they'd started dating—about fate's mistake, depositing him in Illinois when he was clearly a California boy.

Mostly, when she teased him, he rolled his eyes or shook his head. And reminded her that she was a blue-eyed blonde and maybe she, too, belonged in California. They'd wanted to honeymoon there, but the flight was expensive, and the wedding itself was expensive enough, so they'd road tripped it to Florida. Told themselves they'd make it to California one day.

Back sore from leaning over the counter, she stood up straight. Saw the little redhead touch Bowie's arm as the girls giggled and thanked him again for the *awesome* workout. Bowie watched them go and then turned to Hanna.

"What?" he asked with a grin.

"I'm starting to think you like their attention."

"Nope." He moved to stand on the opposite side of the counter.

"You do turn thirty next month," she reminded him.

He lifted a shoulder in a lazy shrug. "Just because you turned thirty already doesn't mean you're wiser than me."

"Oh, that's low, Bowie White." She shook her head.

"Yeah? And what is my punishment going to be tonight?"

She tapped her pencil on the calendar and narrowed her eyes in thought. "I think Sylvi and I want ice cream tonight."

"Yogurt?" He shook his head. "Really? I was hoping—"

"Ice cream," she repeated.

He blew her distinction off with another shrug. "I was hoping I was going to have to help you shower later or something."

"You could do that, too," she agreed. "I mean, it was an *awesome* workout."

Bowie flashed his white teeth in a quick grin.

"I think you're jealous."

Hanna pretended to consider his words again. "Yeah, I wouldn't mind having an eighteen-year-old body again."

Bowie made a show of leaning over the counter to check her out.

"Yeah. You're hot, Han. Eighteen. Thirty. Forty. You make me—" Bowie stopped talking when the gym door opened and one of their clients walked out. Claudia Jackson rubbed her face with a towel. She noticed the two of them at the counter and offered up a smile.

"Thanks, guys," she called as she walked out of the lobby area. Hanna and Bowie stood in the same spots for a moment, heard the main door open and close, and then looked at each other again when they were alone.

"She didn't look good," Hanna mumbled.

"She told me she's just coming off a nasty flu."

Hanna cringed. "Yuck."

"Told her to take it easy today. Treadmill, maybe."

"Great." Hanna tapped her pencil again. "Maybe we should go sanitize everything."

"I'm sure she did." He stood up straight. One of their main gym rules was sanitizing all equipment after using it. Hanna had taken a sinus infection home once when Sylvi was an infant. She and Bowie brought Sylvi with them to work, nearly every day but she was usually isolated from the clients.

They couldn't be sure, but when Sylvi ended up with an ear infection not long after Hanna's sinus infection, Bowie had gone germophobe (well, that had actually started twelve years ago) and posted signs on every flat surface in their gym that all equipment was to be sanitized after each and every use.

Hanna knew that Bowie would go in and wipe down the treadmill Claudia used anyway. Just to be sure. If he wasn't sure which machine Claudia had used, he'd wipe every one of them down. She supposed his obsession with cleanliness and health was a little over the top, but then again, everyone dealt with things in their own way. At least Bowie's obsession was positive.

"Did you ever call Sam back?"

Bowie had pulled his phone out, and he was scrolling over something. She reached to tilt it so she could see it, too. Rolled her eyes when she saw it was yet another article about boosting metabolism. Bowie eyed her silently for a moment, and she held her breath waiting for him to lecture her for the eye roll.

"No." He set his phone down and looked back at her. Rubbed his hand over his messy hair. "You didn't say if you wanted to go or not."

Hanna wasn't sure if she wanted to go. They hadn't seen Sam in several years. In the beginning, it had seemed important. All of them staying in touch. Now it all seemed kind of distant. Hanna wasn't sure she wanted to dredge all that stuff up again. Wasn't really necessary anymore, and she wasn't sure she wanted Sylvi involved in any of that.

"I don't know," she said quietly. She felt Bowie's gaze on her as she settled into the chair behind the counter. She reached for the adding machine on the desk and tapped the keys absently.

Sam Collins had been Bowie's best friend all through high school, even before high school. She'd liked him. When they were younger.

"We don't have to." Bowie's voice was gentle. Hanna lifted her eyes to look at him. Thought of their first kiss. That she'd been surprised at how soft his lips were. How tender the kiss was.

Bowie, a little lanky for the spot—Hanna thought—had been the star quarterback when they were kids. Had a hell of an arm, hell of a spiral. Hell of a head for the game. And then he'd had a hell of an injury and blown his knee out when he was a senior. He'd recovered, but the college scouts passed him up, and he'd decided physical therapy was fascinating, and here they were twelve years later, married, with a precocious three-year-old and a livelihood that both supported and depended on good health and longevity.

Sam and Neelie had been at their wedding, though not together. But now, they didn't talk about Sam. Or the others.

Hanna wondered if Bowie missed him. Them. Davis had come home a time or two years ago, and Hanna was friends with Peyton on Facebook. Although on the computer a lot (more than Bowie would like), Hanna didn't spend much time on Facebook, and Peyton hadn't done anything other than change her profile picture in the last year and a half.

She hadn't seen Trevor. Ever. Since.

Didn't think Bowie had, either, but she didn't even want to bring it up to ask him.

"What's he doing with Neelie?"

"He married her."

Chapter 5

PEYTON

Peyton Kelly flipped the light off and pulled the door to the workroom closed. Locked it and then dropped her keys in her bag. Bellamy had turned the lights in the showroom down. Peyton considered stopping to check the cases. Make sure the jewelry was put away and the display cabinets were locked. But Bellamy was good at what she did. The cases were locked, the register balanced. She'd probably get down on the floor and lick it clean if Peyton asked her to. Especially now.

Which is probably why Peyton felt weird about everything. The sudden uncertainty. Checking locks. Making sure the lights were off. Checking to see that the break room was clean. Her issue was with *Bellamy*. Not her job performance.

A wave of heat hit her as she opened the front door. Peyton looked around the empty parking lot as she turned back to lock that door, too. Her long legs—the heels made them look longer—ate up the asphalt as she hurried to her red Juke. She still got a little thrill each time she saw it; she'd only purchased it recently, and it still had the new car smell.

The thrill wasn't enough to make her feel better, though. She set her bag in the passenger seat and started the car. Even though it felt like it was seven hundred degrees in here, she shivered when she turned the A/C on and the stuffy warm air blew straight at her face. She tilted the vents up a bit and sat for a moment. Her phone had buzzed earlier, when she'd been working on the new *Always* bracelet design. She hadn't answered it. Hadn't so much as looked at it.

Still didn't want to look at it.

She rested her head on the back of her seat for a second. She'd thought she was done making mistakes. *Well. Those* sorts of mistakes. The kind a girl might make when she's eighteen. Learning life. Finding herself. Not something a professional woman did.

When the air blowing full force out of the vents finally cooled a bit, she put the car in reverse and backed out of her spot. She half-expected a car to be there. Someone watching her. But the lot was empty. She made an immediate left out of the lot and then a right onto Broadway.

She'd have a drink when she got home. *Well.* That was one thing she *didn't* need. Clarity was good. She hadn't had a drink in almost two weeks, even though she'd gone home from work every damned night craving the taste. Wine. Wasn't like she often hit the hard stuff. Wasn't like it was a bad thing that she liked wine, was it? Cabs were usually her favorites, but she loved the buttery finish of a good chardonnay. The numb feeling that washed over her once she'd had too much of whatever it was she was drinking.

That scared her. Drinking to get drunk rather than to savor the taste. That and what she'd done. Two weeks ago. *That* scared her.

Maybe she needed to get out more. She loved her loft apartment. But as lovely as it was—still new, and decorated just as she liked with odds and ends furniture and knickknacks and lots of books—it was still empty and sort of big for just one person.

Getting out more wasn't fun for just one person, though. She hated sitting alone at a bar. Might as well advertise: *Lonely and desperate*. Almost the same grabbing lunch by herself. No lecherous looks or roaming hands or drunk guys trying to buy her drinks. But women—in groups of twos or threes—looking down their noses at her. *Look at that poor woman, all by herself.*

Maybe if she hadn't messed things up in her last relationship, she would at least still have friends. She hadn't realized when she'd ended it with Brion that she would lose all of her friends. They'd all apparently blamed her for the break up (who else was to blame?) and sided with him, and now and then Peyton saw Brion out with some of those friends.

She tapped her fingers on the steering wheel as she slowed to a stop at Twelfth and Broadway. The silence in the car was almost overwhelming, but she kind of preferred it. The music they played at the store every day, though mellow —sometimes to the point of narcolepsy—gave her a headache. The quiet drive home was usually enough to soothe it away.

Her phone buzzed again. This one was a phone call, rather than a text. Didn't matter. She had no interest in talking to anyone. Not right now. She was driving, anyway. If it was important, the caller would leave a message.

Maybe she'd go for a walk. With her figure, people probably assumed she worked out faithfully. She pursed her lips as she drove, tried to remember the last time she'd worked out. It'd been at least five years. She'd gotten lazy with Brion; that had probably been the beginning of it. She'd stopped playing tennis with him. Turned down his suggestion that they take golf lessons together. Stopped fucking him, but then that had nothing to do with fitness and everything to do with boredom.

At Eighth, she turned left and accelerated to Maine. Pulled into an open spot and climbed out of the car. She reached back in for her bag and then swung the door closed. Beeped the locks and crossed the street. Her loft was above The Pink Daffodil, a women's boutique, and now and then, she slipped inside to have a look before going upstairs. Some nights, like tonight, the boutique was already closed.

Her heels clicked on the stairs as she climbed. No hurry. Not in these heels. And not in the physical shape she was in. She pulled her keys from her bag as she neared her door. Thought of Hanna White. *Jesus.* Talk about a Barbie Doll. She and Bowie probably did push-ups while they fucked. She used to stalk her on Facebook, but not for well over a year. Only so much love one person could take.

She missed Brion. Why was hindsight twenty-twenty?

Her home phone was ringing as she stepped inside. She shut the door and leaned against it. Squeezed her eyes closed. Maybe she should ditch the landline. She rarely used it. Nine times out of ten, it rang when she had a headache (like now, though usually she had a headache because she was hungover), and so it was annoyingly loud.

She kicked her black heels off and crossed the hardwood floor barefoot. Looked at the cordless on the end table by the sofa. Nothing on caller ID. Useless as far as Peyton could tell.

It continued to ring as she walked away. Dropped her bag on the granite counter. Moved on through the kitchen, because she could hear the wine in the rack calling her name, and unzipped her gray pencil skirt. Slipped it down and stepped out of it. Grabbed a pair of athletic shorts—oh, she could look the part—and hurriedly put them on. Avoided looking at her bed, because it was still daylight, and she could actually see it, and seeing it made her remember that stupid thing she'd done a couple of weeks ago. She kept her back to the bed as she unbuttoned her blouse and slipped it off her shoulders. Dropped it in her dry-cleaning bag and then pulled a 2012 James Taylor concert t-shirt on.

She wasn't particularly hungry, but she decided if she ate, she might be less likely to cave and drink. Barefoot still, she turned music on. She kept an iPod dock in the kitchen, but she had speakers in other rooms. Brion had hooked them up for her even after they broke up. She selected something new wave, something instrumental and then gave herself a mental shake. She wasn't at work. She changed it to David Bowie and then started pulling lettuce and peppers and cheese from the refrigerator for a salad. And then she wondered just what the hell she thought she was accomplishing from not drinking. Did she really plan never to drink again in her life? *No.* So, did it matter if she sat at home now and drank a bottle of wine? *No.*

She left the salad items on the counter and selected a bottle of cabernet sauvignon from her wine rack. Opened it with ease and breathed deeply as she poured herself a healthy glass. This was okay. She was alone. Who the hell cared what she did when she was alone?

Emboldened by the wine, she decided to check her phone.

See what exactly Bellamy had to say.

The phone call had come in from an unknown number. She hoped it was a wrong number, and not Bellamy using someone else's phone. For more than one reason. The texts— two of them—were indeed from Bellamy.

Sold the Stars pendant this morning.

And

Brion was in around noon looking for you.

.

Chapter 6

TREVOR

James Mercer's voice usually soothed him. That's why he'd chosen to play The Shins when his shift started. But he'd already paced the whole damned store at least seven times, and he'd only been here an hour.

An hour? Seriously?

He glanced at the oversized, black-faced watch on his left wrist. Shit. He'd only been here an hour. Trevor smoothed his hand over his neck and then dragged his fingers back around and ran them over his mouth.

This was fucking killing him. Mallory just might pack up and move out. Not that he'd blame her. Not now. This obsession had him by its teeth, and he was helpless. He'd moved on from the dreams to just not sleeping. Mal had suggested he see a doctor. Earlier today, as he was getting dressed—he'd done some laundry, so he was wearing clean clothes, and he had to admit it felt good—she'd just randomly suggested he see a doctor.

Trevor had buttoned his khaki skinny jeans and reached for the beanie he often wore to work. Mallory gave him shit about it, especially when it was hot enough to fry eggs on the sidewalks, but he liked it. Worked with the music scene and the kids he talked to at the store.

She was eating a peach—like an apple—and there was juice dripping off her chin, and she'd just said, "Trev, maybe you should see a doctor."

But that hadn't been the worst of it. He'd hesitated as he reached for his keys. Actually considered it. But then he'd wondered who he should see.

"What? Like a sleep study or something?" he'd asked her.

"Like a shrink," she'd answered simply. And she'd taken another bite of the peach, and more juice had dripped down her chin, and even though it pissed him off that she'd suggested it, he'd kissed her. Flicked his tongue over her chin and tasted the peach, and then he'd left without another word.

"How ya doin'?" He offered the couple that wandered into the store a smile. Watched them for a few seconds and then moved a few steps away from them. Probably they weren't seriously interested in buying anything. Seemed like only hardcore music people actually bought old vinyl records. Sure, they had some CDs, but Trevor was into the vinyl albums.

Mallory thought he needed a shrink. That freaked him out. Why did he need a shrink? Okay, yeah, he was messed up. But it had only just started a few weeks ago. Right? He glanced at his watch to check the date. Yep. He didn't recall the night the nightmare got him the first time, but it hadn't been longer than a few weeks. Before that, he'd been normal. And try as he might, Trevor couldn't figure out what had triggered the dreams. The obsession with that lake.

He wasn't afraid of water. He'd never been on a swim team, but he knew how to swim. He'd gone swimming and

fishing in ponds and lakes. He'd waterskied. He liked boating. The obsession made no sense to him.

A shrink might be able to make sense of it, though. Not
that he wanted to admit to Mallory that she might be right.
And not that he *wanted* to see a shrink. He'd figure it out in
time. Just had to hang in there. Maybe he'd take Mal out
tomorrow night. He was off. They could grab dinner out,
maybe. See a movie. He'd been a dick to her lately. He knew
that. He'd just see if he could fix things and then get it under
control. Maybe he could just tell her the dreams had stopped.

"Is there anything specific you're looking for?" Trevor
wandered back down the aisle toward the couple. The girl
was young; she looked even younger than Mallory. She also
looked as thrilled to be here as Mallory usually was when he
brought her here. Mal loved music, but she had no interest in
looking at it, shopping for it, browsing and finding something
good. Choosing what to listen to. She used to tease, when
they'd first started dating, that she'd found her personal DJ in
Trevor.

"Just looking," the girl answered as the guy—flipping
through the letter *S* in the vinyls—said, "Yeah, do you have
any Glass Tomboy?"

Trevor stared at the guy for a half a second, wondered
why he might be looking for Glass Tomboy in the letter *S*.
When the guy looked up at him and raised his eyebrows,
Trevor answered with a curt nod.

"Should." He led the way back down to the G's and
flipped through them until he found the band.

"Awesome. Thanks."

Trevor nodded and wandered back to the counter.
Slipped in behind it and rested his butt on the utilitarian
stool—uncomfortable as hell—and folded his arms over his
chest. Was the guy just lazy? Didn't care to look in the G's?
Or had he been looking for something else? Trevor's eyes

roamed the store. Wondered if playing The Shins had given the guy a subliminal message to look in the S's. Almost chuckled at the thought.

He shifted his eyes to look at the couple again. They were talking now, laughing softly about something. Trevor felt a little stab of jealousy. Not of the girl. Hell, he had Mallory, didn't he? It just seemed like for-fucking-ever since he and Mallory had done anything normal. Like shop for music. Okay, that didn't count, since she wasn't a music shopper. See a movie. It seemed like forever since they'd seen a movie together.

They smoked a joint together now and then, though it'd been a while on that, too. Had sex a lot, but not good sex. *Well*, Trevor wasn't complaining, but he'd found Mallory taking care of herself on more than one occasion lately, because he'd been so self-absorbed, he hadn't paid enough attention to her needs.

He glanced at the couple again. Hated feeling skittish. Probably a lot to do with the dream. That stupid lake. But there'd been a shooting on this end of town about a month ago, too. Trevor wondered if all the retail places—lots of antique stores and boutiques and home interior places on Maine—were all feeling a little nervous about shady-looking customers. Not that this couple was shady-looking. Just odd to look in the S's for Glass Tomboy.

Trevor sighed when he realized he was doodling on the back of someone's abandoned takeout receipt. He dropped the pencil when he saw the lake and the dock. Rudimentary drawing, but still, he knew what it was. He crumpled the paper up and tossed it behind him in the trashcan. Picked up the pencil and started fidgeting with it again.

"Find what you needed?" he asked when the couple approached the counter. The guy was carrying two Glass Tomboy albums, and he was reaching for his back pocket.

Trevor froze, totally expecting to have a gun pointed at his face at any second. Blew out a quick breath when the guy pulled out a brown leather billfold and then took three twenties from inside.

"Cool place." The guy looked around appreciatively as Trevor scanned the barcodes on the albums. "Is that Mylo Bekis' guitar?"

Trevor took the money the guy handed him and looked up over his shoulder at the shiny silver electric guitar that had indeed been given to his boss by Mylo Bekis.

"Yeah." He nodded. Made change and handed it back to the guy. "You know Bekis Kiss?"

"Oh, yeah." The guy thanked him for the change and put it back in his billfold. "Hell, yeah. They were, like, phenomenal about ten years ago."

Trevor nodded. "My boss knows Mylo."

"Damn." The guy looked shocked.

"What're you drawing?" The girl—she wasn't as young as Trevor had originally thought, he could see that now in her eyes—leaned way over the counter to look at another piece of paper he'd started doodling on. The back of a purchase order this time. "That's incredible," she said with an excited laugh. "Kinda looks like the lake at Baxter Lodge."

"Like what?" Trevor looked at her and then looked back down at the paper. Mallory would love *this*. He was drawing shit when he wasn't even aware of it now. When he was having conversations with other people. He dropped his gaze when the girl pointed a bright pink nail at the dock he'd drawn. A building behind it.

"The lake at Baxter Lodge. In Barronville."

He shook his head. "Never heard of it."

"Barronville, Indiana?" The guy tried this time.

"Nope."

"Are you an artist?"

"Yeah." He nodded in answer to her question. "Yeah, I am." He wouldn't tell her this damned lake and dock and house had sidetracked him for the past couple of weeks.

"Wow." She nodded. "That's impressive."

"Do you ever show your work?"

Trevor looked at the guy and wondered if he was serious. If it was possible he was still going to get shot tonight before these people walked out.

"I've had a few things at a gallery down the street."

"Awesome!" The girl grinned. "We just moved here, so we're like…trying to get to know the place. Where to find music and good food and stuff."

"Great." Trevor offered them a sincere smile. "Welcome to Tamarack."

"Thanks." The guy reached over the counter to shake his hand, and Trevor hoped he missed the way he flinched.

Maybe Mallory was right. If he kept acting like this in public, he might lose his job or end up in the psych ward. Maybe he should just bite the bullet and call someone. Then again, his insurance was shit. And what if a shrink told him he'd been molested by a babysitter or something when he was five? He'd rather just leave that bone buried.

What if he could just get a huge-ass piece of paper and draw the whole goddamned scene out—a whole forest of trees around the house and the lake and just see what the hell he came up with?

Other than possibly losing Mallory, it seemed a lot less risky. And cheaper. Which meant it was the only option.

Chapter 7

PEYTON

"Hey."

She was glad she'd stopped at two glasses last night when she nearly walked into Brion Mitchell on her way out of the stairwell. She'd decided to go for a walk this morning before going to work. They opened at nine; it was just seven-thirty now. If she'd had just one more glass of wine, she might not have made it out of bed at this hour for a walk, and Brion might have knocked on her door and got her out of bed, and she might look like hell instead of alert and sort of good enough to run into an ex-lover.

"Brion." She nodded. Stepped around him to get outside. Felt the sun already blazing like the fires of hell. Decided they might all die before the July and August heat and humidity got here.

"Where are you going?" Dressed for the office in gray trousers and a pink button-down shirt, he looked like a dad who'd come to give his kid a what-for. Except Peyton didn't look anywhere near young enough to be his daughter.

"For a walk."

He raised his eyebrows, obviously surprised by her answer.

"I came in yesterday."

She nodded. "Bellamy told me. I'm sorry I missed you."

"I doubt that." He shrugged and rested his hands on his hips. "Listen. Do you have that first edition copy of *Lonesome Dove*? That Larry McMurtry book? Remember? My dad gave it to me for my birthday a few years back?"

"Yeah, I remember." Already sweating, Peyton lifted her shirt collar and wiped her mouth with it. "But I don't have it."

"You have to have it," he argued. "Because I don't."

"You had it in a box of donations—"

"No, I didn't. I'm sure you have it."

Peyton took a deep breath. She didn't have the damned book. Period. She knew damned well Brion had put the book in a box of books he'd donated to a fundraiser book sale a few years ago. She'd asked him about it when he did it. He'd been in a pissy mood, and probably, he hadn't paid attention to her when she'd asked him—he rarely paid attention to anything she said—and he'd given it away.

She could send him up to the apartment and let him look to his heart's content. But she didn't want to. This was her apartment. *Hers*. And even though she had nothing to hide—well, nothing he would find if he went up right now to look around—she didn't want him rifling through her things.

"I don't have it, Brion."

"Well, come upstairs with me so we can check."

"I'm going for a walk."

"That can wait—"

"Actually, it can't. I wanna go for a walk, and I have to work today."

"What's the sudden urge to exercise?"

She wouldn't even say it was an urge to exercise. She just needed fresh air.

"What's your sudden need for the book?"

"Jesus, Peyton. Gimme a break."

"Come back later if it's that important."

"Can't you just look—"

"Not gonna waste my time looking for it. You got rid of the damned book."

Typical Brion threw his hands up in frustration. She watched him turn his back to her and strut back to his car. How was it that she couldn't see what had attracted her to him in the first place, but she could still miss him? He unlocked his Explorer, climbed in and the SUV roared to life. Peyton watched him drive away without a backward glance at her.

He was arrogant. She'd seen that as confidence when they'd first met, and she'd needed it. Maybe she'd hoped it would rub off on her. They'd had three good years. But somewhere along the way, Peyton realized she was fed up with being talked down to. Tired of Brion treating her as if she wasn't quite as intelligent as he, not quite as cool, good-looking—you name it. Brion had it; Peyton didn't.

When the sex got stale—after all, according to Brion if she didn't like it, it was her fault—she'd decided there was nothing left. They hadn't had those fun, witty conversations in months. No fun dates. No tender moments.

Brion had acted so shocked, so desperate when she'd ended it. What the hell? He couldn't have been enjoying their relationship any more than she was. She'd chalked it up to damaged pride, and then she'd watched her friends—one by one—pull away (always too busy) and end up hanging out with him.

Not true friends, she'd decided. Still, it hurt.

She walked at a fast pace. Tamarack Square was busy at this hour. No farmers market today, but there were still a lot of people just strolling around. Moms, pushing babies and toddlers in strollers. Older ladies and older men, clustered together on park benches, sipping coffee. Peyton was as much a coffee addict as the next, but not outside in a park when the temperature was pushing eighty at 7:52 in the morning, and the humidity was so bad, she felt like she was wearing a wet, wool blanket around her shoulders. She'd wait until she'd showered, and she'd grab a cup on the way to work.

Well, she wouldn't. She'd done that a couple times lately. Only to find Bellamy pouting because she'd made coffee. For Peyton.

She had to do something about that. About Bellamy. No idea what. But *something*.

Peyton found herself thinking about Hanna and Bowie White again as she walked around the square. She and Hanna had been good friends in school. They'd grown apart; well, they'd all grown apart after school, but Peyton had kept up with them through the years—she'd see them now and then on a date or at the farmers market. She'd stalked Hanna's Facebook page. Spent long minutes looking at the snapshots Hanna posted from their wedding. Peyton had been stung that she hadn't been invited. At that point, they'd grown apart, but they'd been friendly when they'd parted ways. Her envy had grown through the years so much that Peyton felt only contempt when she thought of them now.

Sam and Neelie had been at the wedding. She didn't think Davis had, but she'd seen a snapshot of him on Hanna's wall. Not that it meant anything. Or maybe it was Bowie's wall. Hard to remember. Peyton didn't post much at all on Facebook, because she didn't want anyone from her past snooping through her life now. But she was certainly one to do the snooping, to click and click and click and find herself looking at someone's sister's nephew's neighbor's graduation pictures. She'd seen a sort of recent picture of Davis Buckley somewhere.

They all looked good. At least, the last time Peyton had gone looking at pictures, they'd looked good. But on the surface, so did she.

Trevor.

Trevor Gerhardt.

Peyton snorted as she walked. What the hell was he up to now? God, she hadn't thought about him in years. He'd sort of dropped off the face of the earth. Nobody had any pictures of him on their Facebook page. Then again, he'd been kind of quiet, stayed to himself, mostly. Probably, he'd found a job at IBM or something, or he was writing computer code and developing cutting edge technology, and he was rolling in cash, and he probably had some hotshot runway model for a wife. Probably lived on the West Coast or something. It'd figure someone like him would end up doing better than the rest of them.

She didn't care. She looked up as she neared the door to the stairwell at her apartment, half expecting to find Brion back. But there was no one around. She pulled the door open and peeked into the boutique as she did so. They weren't open yet. She liked the orange scarf in the window, though. Decided she might have to go in over the weekend and check it out.

She sort of jogged up the steps, and then she was out of breath, and she had to stand there and gulp in air while she unlocked her door. So, things kind of sucked right now. Life was a little slow, a little boring. She considered that for a second, stepped inside, and then shut and locked the door. But maybe boring was okay. After what had happened a couple of weeks ago. That was…Peyton shrugged and shook her head. She didn't even know what to call that. Other than a huge regret.

Still, she'd never been one to seek comfort in the past, and she wasn't about to start now.

She turned the taps in the shower. Stripped down and then stopped to look at herself in the mirror. Small mirror. All she could see was her face. There was a nice glow to her skin right now. Probably just the exertion from walking after zero activity in ages. But still, it was nice to see something other than the normal tired face and the simple brown eyes.

Her mind wandered to Eden as she stepped into the steamy water.

Chapter 8

Hanna

"So." Hanna closed her eyes. She was so sick of the documentaries on health and illnesses, disease. So tired of living in a gym. She and Bowie had a great house; they just spent so little time here. Just once, she'd like to curl up with him on the couch and watch the latest blockbuster movie. She couldn't remember the last real movie they'd seen.

She got it; Bowie wanted them to be healthy. He wanted to raise Sylvi to be health-conscious. Yeah, it was nice that they could usually fight off a cold easier than the next person, but now and then, one of them still got the sniffles. They weren't bionic, for God's sake.

This was Bowie's push back at the past. She got that, too. God, did she get it. *But really?* They weren't fighting the flu. Or AIDs or cancer. All of Bowie's no-nonsense eating and fitness routines weren't going to change anything.

Neither was her addiction, but she didn't want to think about that now. Eyes still closed, she raised her eyebrows when Bowie skimmed his fingers up over her bare legs. Sylvi had been down for over an hour now. She was out cold.

Hanna was certain of that, because if she were awake, she'd be demanding a story or a glass of water or half a banana. Sylvi White didn't lie quietly and wait for sleep to take her. She never had.

"What?" Bowie's voice was a little gruff. Hanna wondered if he was tired or if something about her faded college t-shirt had turned him on.

"Are we doing this?" She stretched her arms over her head and turned her face away from the TV. She was tired. She could go to bed now and sleep until noon.

She treated him to a lazy smile when she heard him chuckle.

"I'm good with doing this."

She opened her eyes as he slipped his fingers inside the waistband of her shorts and tugged gently to slide them over hips.

"Not what I meant."

No, but if Bowie wanted to play in her shorts, she wasn't going to stop him. In fact, she lifted her hips to help him and then sighed as he smoothed his hand up her inner thigh.

"No?"

She closed her eyes again.

"Huh-uh."

"What'd you mean?"

"Are we..." She moaned softly when he traced his fingertips low over her belly. "Having drinks with Sam and Neelie?"

"I told him we'd meet them tomorrow night."

"Hmm."

"You don't want to?"

She shifted again, straightened one leg and drew the other knee up higher, eyes still closed.

"I don't know."

"Why don't you wanna see them?"

"Just…"

She felt like he'd drugged her. Then again, Bowie *was* her drug. The first time they'd done this, taken their clothes off and discovered each other beyond the years of friendship they'd shared, Hanna had felt hungover for the next week.

"I dunno know, Bowie." She rolled her head slowly on the arm of the couch. "It's just…it's been so long since we've been around them. Just feels weird."

"I wanna do it, Han."

Arms still stretched above her head, eyes still closed, she grinned when he slipped his fingers inside her.

"Me too," she agreed.

He laughed softly. She felt him move, felt his weight shift on the couch cushions.

"I wanna go out tomorrow night. I'll get a sitter."

It was rare for Bowie to *want* to go out. Have a few drinks. Bowie rarely drank, and when he did, he could nurse one beer to make it last hours. She wasn't really too excited about seeing Sam and Neelie, but the idea of going out with Bowie was a little bit exciting. Dressing up—at least in nice jeans (sometimes Hanna felt like she was in workout clothes for weeks at a time)—and heels and putting on makeup and having dinner and a drink and maybe even dancing with Bowie sounded great.

His fingers were doing things to her right now that might make her agree to dinner with the devil. Or worse yet, a five-mile run first thing in the morning.

"Okay." She nodded. Opened her eyes and reached for him.

One thing about Bowie's sometimes ridiculous workout routines and healthy lifestyle. She'd bet she had a better sex life than anyone else she knew who'd been married ten years. Bowie often wore her out. Though he always pleased her, there were times when she wanted to fake it just to get it done. And then sometimes, he could still go another round. And sometimes another.

She'd reminded him once, not long ago, that sleep was important to health, too. He'd laughed, and then later that night, he'd dragged her from sleep to slip inside her and make slow, gentle love to her.

Now, on the couch in the light of the TV, he let it happen quickly. Probably because they were right out in the open, and though it wasn't likely, Sylvi could wander out and find them. When they made love in their bedroom, the door was always closed and locked.

"Where are we going?"

His head on her chest, her t-shirt bunched up under his cheek and her bra pushed to the side out of the way, Hanna played with his hair. She'd told him once she'd leave him if he ever got it cut. In school, he'd worn it long enough to pull it back in a ponytail. It was shorter now, but it still fell to his shoulders.

"Well, we could do the kitchen, but I think the bedroom might be a little—"

"For drinks," she said with a soft laugh. "Where are we going with Sam and Neelie?"

"Mm." Bowie turned his head and kissed her collarbone. He was generous with kisses and kind words, and now and then when Hanna'd had a particularly bad or long day, she'd wonder just what his deal was. He was too good to be true. Most of the time, she relaxed in that knowledge, loved him right back.

"Sam suggested NineTen."

Hanna mouthed the word *wow*. *NineTen Big Fat Hen*— sounded like a pretty dumbass place, really. But it was one of the more upscale bars in the area with low lighting and sexy, jazzy background music. Backroom, upscale drug deals and high-dollar drinks. She didn't know that for a fact, the part about upscale drug deals, but she'd heard some stories that made her wonder.

Still. She'd go to NineTen for a drink. She'd smoke a joint with Bowie again if he wanted to. He wouldn't. Those days were long gone. She'd never tell him how much she missed them. And she wouldn't change a thing. Especially not Sylvi.

"That okay?" Bowie lifted his head to look at her.

"Yeah." She shrugged and nodded.

Bowie nibbled on her chin.

"You ever think…" He stilled his mouth. Breathed over her lips. "You ever think about it?"

She opened her mouth to answer him. Tried to decide *how* to answer him. What he would most want to hear. Did *he* ever think about it? He'd say no, but he did. Hanna knew Bowie thought about the past every damned day.

The same way she did.

"No." She ran her fingers through his hair. Shook her head. No sense in dredging up bad memories. Precisely why she'd been hesitant to agree to seeing Sam and Neelie in the first place. "Do you?" She played along, watched his eyes while he considered his answer.

"Why would I worry about the past?" He smiled against her lips. "When I have everything I could ever want right here?"

She smiled her agreement. She did have everything she could ever want right here in this house. A good, happy marriage, a faithful, loving husband, and an adorable little girl.

But she still thought about the past. She'd never learned to bury things quite like Bowie had.

Chapter 9

MALLORY

She felt a little guilty now for being so mad at him. Dinner would have been enough, but then he'd suggested a walk by the river. Well, first he'd suggested a movie, but the late show didn't come on until after ten, and Mallory was tired. She knew Trevor would never make it through a movie that started that late. Not right now.

The walk by the river had been nice. They'd passed a few people as they walked; a few joggers and a gang of guys going into a bar, but mostly they'd had some time alone. Funny, because Mallory wouldn't have said they needed alone time so much as she needed Trevor's attention. But being outside, alone together, seemed to soothe him, which meant he was attentive to her.

It was still warm, even the breeze that lifted the ends of her hair from her shoulders was warm, but the harsh heat had let up when the sun had gone down. They'd held hands as they walked, and though Trevor hadn't been talkative, he'd listened to her talk about work, and the book she was reading, and she knew he'd been listening, because he questioned her a couple of times about the book, and they laughed a few times over stories she told about work.

She'd hoped, as they climbed the wooden stairs to his apartment—well, she supposed it was *their* apartment now, as she'd pretty much moved all of her things here from her old place—that they'd sit together for a while in the living room. Start a movie at least. Smoke a joint. Make love. Trevor used to be generous with her in bed, but with the dreams and that obsession with the water, he'd become so surly and selfish and angry. God, he seemed to be angry all the time.

That hadn't happened. But he'd crashed. They'd sat together, and they'd made out a little and then he'd just lay back on his end of the couch. Stared blankly at the TV. Mallory had gone to the bedroom and slipped out of the blouse and bra she'd worn for dinner. Unbuttoned her jeans and then gone back to the living room to find him dead to the world. She'd leaned over him, shaken him gently, even straddled him on the couch to see if he'd open his eyes, but he hadn't.

He'd gone from the dreams—all she knew about the dreams was the water, the black water on the twelve canvases lined up against the wall right now—to not sleeping. She couldn't be sure, but it seemed like Trevor had gone a few nights with no sleep at all.

She'd covered him with a blanket, put a pillow beneath his head, though that had been a bit of work. He was so deeply asleep, she couldn't get him to lift his head at all. She'd ended up just kind of stuffing it under him, hoping he'd rouse himself just enough to realize it was there and pull it into a comfortable position. Then, she'd turned the lights off and gone to bed.

Thought about the paintings he'd been stewing over for weeks now. None of them were finished. All of them seemed to be exactly the same, but there was almost nothing to them.

A blob of black water. A tree. The hint of a dock on one. His drawings were more detailed. She'd glanced at them the other day when he'd gone to work.

She'd suggested he see a shrink. Pissed him off. But she still thought it was a good idea. Trevor Gerhardt was too much for the life he was living right now. Even if she weren't with him, she'd think that. He was smart. Book smart. Clever, too. Too smart to be selling music at Rewind. He'd gone to college; he'd told her that much. But he'd never been very specific about his grades or what he'd studied. But after living with him for just a few months, Mallory could see he was better than how he was living.

Tired, but not sleepy, she turned to her right side. Smoothed her hand over his side of the bed. The sheets— she'd changed them just the other day—were smooth and cool. Couldn't even pull his pillow in to snuggle with since she'd taken it to him. She closed her eyes, but they popped open almost instantly. She wasn't interested in sleep. Flopped over to her back. Ran her hand down over her bare stomach, but she stopped at her lacy underwear. She didn't want to do that, either. She wanted Trevor's hands on her.

He was afraid. Of the dream, yes, of the water. But he'd blanched at the mention of a shrink. Like he knew there was something horrible buried somewhere that a shrink would dig up. It had taken Mallory hours to forget that look on his face. Even now, she could call it up with absolute clarity. Not *exactly* guilt. But fear. She got it. No one wanted to see a shrink. No one wanted to ask for help, to invite someone inside his or her head to poke around. But for just a moment, when he'd looked at her like that, Mallory had wondered just who the hell Trevor Gerhardt really was.

She'd moved here from Des Moines, after school. She'd moved here to share an apartment with a friend. Kelly had gone to the big nursing school here, and she was now a nurse at Tamarack Memorial, and so Mallory—jobless and lease up in less than a month—had moved to Tamarack to share an apartment with her high school friend. She'd been here nearly two years when she met Trevor at the music store. She and Kelly and a girl she'd gone to nursing school with had grabbed pizza at a little place on Maine Street and then wandered down the street a few blocks and found the music place.

Trevor, skinny jeans, black hipster glasses and gray beanie, had caught her eye immediately. Not love at first sight, because Mallory didn't think it existed. She wasn't even sure about it now, if she loved him. But she *liked* him a lot. Most of the time. She'd like him a lot more if he, if *they,* could figure out the root of the dreams and the sleeplessness and the obsessive sketching and painting.

To that end, she rubbed her eyes and then climbed out of bed. Maybe because she'd been in the bed alone, her skin was a bit chilled. She grabbed one of Trevor's t-shirts from his drawer and pulled it on. Padded back out to the living room. He was still on the couch. Hadn't moved. The pillow still hung mostly off the end of the couch, just a corner of it sort of under his head.

She'd left the TV on. Not wanting to wake him, she settled on the floor by the canvases. Studied them. No good. In the dim light from the TV, the canvases all looked the same. She knew there were vague differences in some of them, but in this light, she couldn't make out a thing. With a glance over her shoulder, she climbed to her feet again and turned on the floor lamp in the corner of the room.

She took the ancient laptop they shared and carried it back to the spot on the floor. She sat again and booted the dinosaur up. Moved to her knees and then reached blindly over the card table while the laptop powered on. Grabbed a fistful of papers and then sat down again, legs folded in a lap in front of her.

She flipped through the sketches. Again, each of them was almost the same as the last. Much more detailed—right down to the ridges in the tree bark—than the paintings. He'd said he'd started with the paintings because he'd needed to find the colors. The colors in the dream had been more important than anything else. Somehow, Mallory doubted that. Maybe the colors had been vivid, and maybe they'd prove to be important. But how could color be more important than substance?

What the hell did she know? she wondered. She didn't have a degree in dream interpretation. She hadn't studied psychology. She didn't know a damned thing about art, only that Trevor was certainly a gifted artist and he'd been in the middle of drawing a comic strip when suddenly he'd been compelled to throw it all to hell and start painting black water.

She set the sketches aside and focused on the laptop. Typed black water into the search bar. And waited.

It was a long shot. But then again, wasn't Trevor's obsessive sketching and painting a dream a long shot as far as trying to interpret something and chase the demons out of his head?

Chapter 10

PEYTON

She'd driven to work, angry with Brion just for showing up. Just for that damned condescending attitude of his. The way he'd demanded she go up and look for that damned book, when she knew damned well she didn't have it. What the hell did it matter now, anyway? Why did he suddenly need the damned book? Unless it had just been an excuse to come knocking around again. Check on her. Peyton wasn't sure why Brion would suddenly decide he needed to snoop around her life. Jesus, she didn't even go out anymore. She couldn't remember the last time she'd gone out.

Head already pounding, she unlocked the door and stepped inside and out of the heat. Another two minutes in the humidity, and she would wilt. The smell of coffee hit her as the door drifted closed behind her. At the moment, nothing but the coffee mattered. Not even Bellamy. Peyton glanced at her sleek navy Michael Kors watch and saw they had another ten minutes before they opened, so she turned the key in the lock again and then headed to the back of the store.

She mumbled a hello to Bellamy as she entered the break room. Set her keys and purse on the table and slipped her phone from her purse to glance at it. Fully expecting to find a missed call from Brion, she stared at the screen, puzzled by the unknown number.

"What's up?" Bellamy asked from her place at the counter. Peyton glanced up at her and wondered if she was guarding the coffeemaker. If she intended to make Peyton talk to her before moving out of the way and giving her access to the mugs and the coffee.

Peyton wasn't in the mood for it. Not after the run-in with Brion this morning. She shook her head and looked back at her phone. Probably Brion calling from an office phone at work.

"You look upset about something."

She dropped her phone back into her purse and then picked up her keys and dropped them in, too.

"I am upset about something," Peyton grumbled. She decided she wanted her phone and dug it out of her bag again. Stuck it in her back pocket—it was Saturday, and the jewelry store was hers (and her brother's, but he'd up and moved a month ago, so for now she was calling the shots) so she'd worn jeans. Skinny leg jeans and navy flats and a pink blouse that just missed fuchsia. She'd pulled her dark hair up in a high ponytail, but already pieces of it had slipped out to frame her face.

"What's wrong?" Bellamy tried again.

"Brion is what's wrong." Peyton finally gave Bellamy her full attention. She couldn't miss the disappointment sweep over the girl's face. Deciding to push her advantage, Peyton picked up her purse and dropped it in the bottom drawer of the filing cabinet they kept in the break room for personal items.

She stepped up to the counter, indifferent to Bellamy, and

reached around her to open a cabinet. The blonde moved a few steps down the counter and watched Peyton grab a mug and pour her coffee.

"What's going on with Brion?"

Peyton took a drink of the strong, hot coffee and then followed it with a deep breath. Closed her eyes and waited for the moment that the tension in her neck and shoulders eased, as per pretty much any coffee commercial ever. *Nothing*. She sighed and opened her eyes. Thank God, Bellamy wasn't staring at her anymore. But the way she was picking at her nails now was almost worse.

"Showed up at my place earlier." She shook her head. "Demanded that I go up and help him look for some book that he claims I still have."

"Go up?" Bellamy lifted her head. Peyton resisted the urge to roll her eyes when Bellamy's eyebrows shot up in question. "Were you out?"

Peyton turned her back to her and walked out of the room. Bellamy was asking if Peyton had gone out last night. If she was just getting home earlier when Brion demanded she go upstairs with him to find his book.

"Went out for a walk this morning," she answered, knowing without looking that Bellamy was at her heels.

"What book is he looking for?"

Like that mattered to Bellamy.

"A first edition of *Lonesome Dove*." Peyton sipped her coffee again. She leaned into the workroom and flipped the light on. Turned and almost ran into Bellamy. She cringed and cradled her mug so she wouldn't spill coffee on either of them. "He swears I have it. I know he had it in a box to donate when we were living together."

"Ouch." Bellamy laughed softly. "Probably worth something."

"Sure it is," Peyton agreed. "But I don't have it. If I did, I'd give it to him."

Peyton stepped around Bellamy again and wandered out to the showroom. Bellamy flipped the lights on as Peyton walked around the display cases and admired the precious gems. Her father had owned the place first. He'd been a jeweler, started as a bench jeweler at a store on the north side of town. Peyton and her brother admired the craftsmanship and liked the study of gemstones, and it had been a natural thing for them to take over the store when their father retired and her parents moved to Arizona.

Behind her, Bellamy cleared her throat. Peyton felt hunger stir, and even though it was still early, and she was just on her first cup of coffee, she fantasized about sending Bellamy out on a bacon cheeseburger and onion ring run. Wouldn't happen. For one thing, she wouldn't use Bellamy that way. No way would she string her along like that. And besides, she needed a cheeseburger of any sort and an order of onion rings like she needed a hole in her head or another twenty pounds on her butt.

"Are we ever gonna talk about it?"

Peyton flipped the key in the lock and pulled it from the front door. Made a show of watching the cars fly down Broadway. Others turning onto Broadway from Thirtieth. She took another drink and turned slowly. Felt Bellamy's eyes on her, but she didn't look at the girl. Not yet. Wasn't just that she wanted to discourage this particular conversation or any future *things*. She was embarrassed. Ashamed. And she'd give anything to go back in time and change what had happened.

"No." She finally looked at Bellamy. The girl was pretty, no question. Peyton wondered now how real that doe-eyed innocence was. If it was a practiced look or if Peyton had really done something bad two weeks ago.

"Why not?" Bellamy averted her eyes. Peyton watched her open the register and count out the drawer. Noticed her start over twice. Shoot her a glance and then start over a third time. It was simple. They started with a hundred dollars of change. Should be the same as any other day. Bellamy was flustered.

"Because I don't want to," Peyton said simply.

"If I were a guy, would we talk about what happened?"

Peyton, mug at her lips, stopped in front of the counter and blinked at Bellamy.

"It shouldn't have happened." She shrugged. "Nothing to talk about."

"Why?" Bellamy abandoned the cash drawer, let her hands rest on it, and stared at her.

"We had too much to drink—"

"Peyton, I wasn't drunk—"

"Well, I was." Peyton raised her eyebrows.

"You're not interested?"

"No. I'm not." She shook her head and walked away. Part of her felt guilty. She didn't want to hurt her. Hell, up until it happened, she'd liked Bellamy. She *still* liked her, but she didn't want to be *involved* with her. Part of her wanted Bellamy to decide to quit and walk out right now. Chances were, they wouldn't run into each other often. Tamarack was a good-sized town. If Peyton tried, she could avoid the girl.

"You liked it."

Peyton sighed. She turned at the door of the workroom and stared at Bellamy, who stood with one hand on the counter and the other on her hip. She worried her lower lip with her teeth. Peyton had a flash of memory, those lips on her neck, and looked away.

"I was drunk," she said softly. "Yeah, okay, it was…" She shrugged. Not so drunk that she didn't remember exactly what had happened. The kisses. The roaming hands. Waking up next to Bellamy. The orgasms that had ripped through her and left her boneless and sated. Couldn't lie about that, but that didn't mean she wanted it to ever happen again.

"So, you're saying I took advantage of you? When you were drunk?"

Peyton took a deep breath and lowered her head. Rubbed her forehead with her free hand.

"No. I'm not. But I'm telling you I'm not interested, Bell. It shouldn't have happened. I'm sorry it did."

She looked up when she heard Bellamy sigh.

"'kay." Bellamy nodded.

"Look, I'm sorry. I like you. You're a good friend."

Even those words felt wrong now. A little bit dirty. She and Bellamy had been okay friends. But more than that, Bellamy was her employee. Bellamy was younger; in fact, at the moment, Peyton was hard pressed to say exactly how old she was. Of age, certainly, but still.

"No, it's okay." Bellamy shrugged. "I...um..." She shook her head, and Peyton felt a rush of guilt for hurting her. She wished Bellamy would have waited until closing time before forcing this conversation. Then again, Monday would come soon enough, and they'd still be here together. Not alone, which almost made it worse. Having to pretend in front of other employees that everything was normal.

Peyton waited until Bellamy was out of her line of vision, back at the cash drawer, before she ducked into the workroom. She set her mug down and pulled her phone from her pocket again. The missed call from the unknown number bothered her. No one ever called her. So, who was this trying to get a hold of her?

She considered calling her brother. He'd hired Bellamy, but he probably didn't know her much better than she did. Would she be the kind of person to cause Peyton trouble?

Phone calls? Sexual harassment lawsuit? Would it progress from there?

Peyton rolled her eyes. She was being ridiculous. First of all, she wasn't going to call her brother, because there was no way she was going to give him an inkling of what had happened between herself and their employee. Second, one unknown caller and a one-night stand with an employee didn't have to have anything to do with each other.

Chapter 11

HANNA

She'd waffled on her decision all day, but she hadn't told Bowie that. She couldn't even be sure what her objections were to seeing Sam and Neelie. It just seemed like a bad idea to go digging in the past. Sure, they'd had good times, but there was other stuff buried, too, and Hanna didn't want any of that to come up.

But Bowie was excited about this. No sense in bringing him down. And it was harmless, really. What could one night hurt? Bowie's mom was all set to keep Sylvi for them; in fact, she was probably more excited than any of them, having her only granddaughter over for a sleepover. Hanna and Bowie were going to have dinner at the Pier Mississippi, a restaurant where Hanna could indulge in something unhealthy and Bowie could order grilled fish to his heart's content. Not to mention it was just a sexy place on the riverfront, on the southern part of town featuring romantic lighting and music. And after dinner, they'd meet two old friends for a few drinks and go home. Where they'd have the house to themselves all night.

What could go wrong?

Hanna cringed. She knew the hard way that just about anything could go wrong at just about any given time. They all knew that. *Still.* This was going to be fun.

"You look good enough to eat," Bowie announced as she walked on stiletto heels into the kitchen. The skinny-legged jeans made her legs look even longer, and her black blouse hid the weight she'd gained since high school. Okay, so really, thanks to Bowie's constant harping, she hadn't gained more than five pounds in twelve years. Maybe seven. But still, the black gave her confidence, and she had to admit (at least to herself) that she needed it right now. She'd put big, loose curls in her hair and played up her eyes with some heavy mascara and eyeliner. Neelie Collins had always had big, beautiful green eyes. Hanna had pulled out the big guns to make up for her ordinary blue.

"Yeah?" She grinned and arched an eyebrow at him. "Maybe later, you could put your money where your mouth is."

"I'd rather put your boobs where my mouth is," Bowie said with a shrug.

"That works." She nodded. When he turned to open the back door, Hanna took the opportunity to check him out. The way his white button-down shirt molded his big shoulders. The way his tight jeans cupped his ass. She'd like her hands there, but she would wait. Bowie's mom had already picked Sylvi up—they were headed to the mall for a shopping spree before they had dinner (Hanna wondered what Bowie's mom would feed her)—so the two of them climbed into the Highlander together.

"Weird." Hanna glanced at the backseat and then looked at Bowie.

"What?"

"Not having the munchkin back there."

"It's quiet." Bowie nodded his agreement. "She's a chatterbox."

Hanna laughed softly. Bowie put the SUV in reverse and backed out of the driveway. She covered his hand with hers as he backed into their street and reached up to hit the button on the garage door opener.

"Your hands are cold."

Eyes on her window, Hanna felt him looking at her. Trying to gauge her mood, no doubt. She'd written another blog post today, and that had helped calm her nerves a little bit. She didn't tell him that, though. Bowie hated her blog. When she'd first started it, he'd called her *Nancy Drew*, which had rubbed her the wrong way. When she told him so, he'd switched it up and called her *Trixie Belden* for a while. She didn't like that much better, but she kept her mouth shut, and eventually, he got tired of teasing her. She'd been tempted to remind him that they were dealing with the past in their own ways. Bowie was obsessed with life and how to live larger and healthier. Hanna was obsessed with death. But reminding him of those differences and the memories they were both running from might mean talking about it. And who the hell could run from something at the same time they talked about it?

"Nervous?" He squeezed her hand gently.

She answered with a tiny nod.

"Why?"

Hanna looked at him now. Tried to put a few words together to form an answer. A bullshit answer to get him off her back. That thought made her feel a little guilty, because she loved him, and she should be willing to talk to him about anything. He was her husband, for God's sake.

Blank, she only shrugged.

"It doesn't bother you, does it?"

Hanna twisted toward him in her seat. "What?"

Bowie shrugged and nodded his head side to side. "All that stuff. From when we were kids."

She frowned. Bit her lip. Wondered just exactly what Bowie was talking about. Pretty sure he wasn't talking about Eden, because she was more than just stuff.

"I mean…Neelie and I sorta dated for a while…but…" He shrugged again, and Hanna felt a rush of heat in her face. No, that didn't really bother her. She wasn't particularly jealous thinking about her husband *sorta* dating Neelie back in the day. On the other hand, that whole thought process left her uncomfortable for an entirely different reason. She stared out her window, rather than meet his eyes.

"Han, we hooked up…like…once. Wasn't a big deal. For either of us—"

"No, Bowie, it's okay." She shook her head. Counted to three. When she thought she had the blush under control, she turned her head a little to look at him. "We were both with other people before we started dating."

He nodded uncertainly. She realized if she was okay about him dating Neelie when they were kids, he might start poking to see why she was so uneasy about tonight.

"I mean…" She licked her lips and raised her eyebrows at him. "You don't still…have feelings for her, right?"

Bowie drew back, as if she'd hit him. She took a quick breath and hoped she hadn't gone too far playing the part of the jealous wife. Honestly, it *didn't* thrill her that Bowie and Neelie had been together, even if it was only once. What wife ever wanted to know who else her husband had fucked? Especially if it was someone she knew. Someone she'd once been good friends with. She'd known before he told her, anyway. Just weird to actually discuss it with him. But she wasn't a saint, either, so she had no room to talk.

"Of course not," he said quietly. "I never did. We were just friends."

Hanna shrugged and nodded and turned to look out the windshield. She stared blankly at the jewelry store on the corner as the SUV zipped down Broadway. Peyton Kelly's father had owned the place. Hanna wondered if he still did. She hadn't seen a commercial for the store in ages; Bowie rarely had regular TV on. The signage out front still said *Kelly's Emeralds and Gems*, but that didn't mean anything. Someone could have bought them out and kept the name for recognition. Kelly's had a lot of loyal customers.

"Peyton Kelly still around?" she asked and thought Bowie might think her question was totally random.

"Yeah." He let go of her hand and turned the volume up on the stereo. Hanna felt a little stitch of nausea in her gut when she heard the Jennifer Lopez song "Jenny from the Block." "I saw her a coupla weeks ago."

"Yeah? Where at?" Hanna tried to focus on Bowie and not the song. Wasn't even the song so much as the era.

"Frontier Market," he answered.

Hanna shrugged her lips. Who knew Peyton was a health nut, too?

"Did you talk to her?"

"Nah." Bowie shook his head. "She was leaving the store as I parked."

"What's she look like these days?"

"Pretty much the same, really."

"Hmm."

"What *hmm?*"

"Nothing. It's just weird that she lives here, and we never see her."

"Call her."

"Didn't say I *wanna* see her," Hanna said softly, "just weird that I never do."

Bowie hit the bank on the way to the riverfront and surprised her when he grabbed a couple of hundred from the

ATM. She wondered just how much he planned to drink. The thought made her a little queasy, and she was still stewing about it eleven minutes later when Bowie made a right off Third and crept down to Front Street.

"What?"

She looked at Bowie in surprise when he cut the engine. Looked around, surprised that they were in the lot at Pier Mississippi.

"Nothing. Why?"

"You're frowning."

Hanna reached for his hand, stilled it as he smoothed his fingertips over her eyebrows.

"I'm fine."

"Han, I love you." He dropped a sweet, soft kiss on her lips.

So, he was back to thinking she was upset about Neelie. Maybe she should be, if he was putting this much energy into promising her there'd been nothing between them. But she couldn't doubt him. She'd never doubted the way they felt about each other or Sylvi. Everything else, *maybe*, but not their family.

"I know, Bowie." She pulled his hand to her mouth, pressed her open lips to the palm of his hand. "I love you, too."

Chapter 12

HANNA

Neelie Collins had changed. Hanna did a double take as she and Bowie stepped into NineTen. Moderately busy at eight on a summer Saturday night, she and Bowie did a quick search of the dimly lit room. She noticed a couple at a high-top table near the bar, looked away, and then realized the guy was standing up. When she looked back, Sam Collins was striding toward her husband, arms out to give him one of those *bro* hugs. Hanna stood beside him; it was impossible to miss the big grin on Bowie's face and the way he slapped Sam on the back with sincere enthusiasm.

She tore her eyes away from them and looked back at the woman at the table. Surely there was some mistake. That woman was not the Neelie she remembered. Her friend Neelie would be wearing tight jeans and a slinky tank top and spiked heels and tons of makeup on her gorgeous face. The woman at the table might have resembled Neelie, the way a ghostly ancestor might have worn someone's features in an old black and white photo.

"Hanna."

The woman at the table smiled and lifted a hand in greeting, and Hanna cocked her head to study her, wondering just who the hell she was. But then Sam let go of Bowie and reached for her, and it took all of Hanna's concentration to sort of hug him and sort of hold him off and still make it seem like she was thrilled to see him.

She wasn't.

Years of buried memories, feelings clawed their way up her throat, and for a second, Hanna thought she might be sick. Sam managed to pull her against him and rub his hand up over her back, and though it was appropriate, Hanna's skin crawled like it was covered with maggots.

Her eyes met the strange woman's—Neelie's?—and so she had to smile, and then Sam kissed her cheek as he released her, and Hanna couldn't hold the shudder back. Sam pretended not to notice, but when she looked at Bowie, she saw the uncertain look on his face. She flashed him a fake smile and mumbled something about getting a chill coming inside from the heat. He nodded, and then Sam took her hand, and Hanna swallowed hard again, hoping to push the linguini she'd just eaten back down, and followed him to the table.

He was talking about how good it was to see them, and Bowie was right behind her, and Hanna squeezed her eyes closed for a moment.

You can do this. Suck it up.

"They haven't aged a day, Neelie," Sam said as they joined her at the table. Up close, Hanna could see the woman was indeed Neelie, but she looked completely different. She wore a sundress, for one thing. The only dress Hanna had ever seen Neelie don was a prom dress their senior year, and it had looked more like a legwarmer, it was so tight and short. Her dark hair fell in loose waves around her shoulders, and maybe she wore mascara, but her face was the most natural

Hanna had ever seen it since they were twelve, and they'd started wearing makeup.

"Hanna." Neelie slipped off the stool. She was shorter than Hanna, even with the heels—not stilettos at all but cute wedges with crisscrossing straps of blue that matched the flower print of her dress. "You look great!"

Again, Hanna felt herself enveloped in an embrace that wasn't particularly welcome. Neelie smelled like spring, and Hanna wondered if she'd discovered the fountain of youth and found that it not only turned back time but doubled as a perfume. Neelie Collins looked great, and Hanna felt a flash of discomfort. She'd dressed all wrong for this. Whatever Neelie had been twelve years ago, she certainly wasn't now, and Hanna backed away and shot Bowie a look of fury. If only he had just said no.

She almost laughed at herself, and then Sam was asking her what she wanted to drink. She glanced at Neelie's glass and wondered if she was drinking straight vodka or water. Sam's Old-Fashioned glass was nearly empty, but it appeared he was drinking the hard stuff. She glanced at Bowie and hoped like hell he didn't decide he needed to order whatever Sam was having.

"Martini?" Bowie asked her. She nodded, and she knew he'd get her a chocolate martini, but still she worried about what he would order. Sam flagged down a waitress and when she appeared, Bowie asked for a draft Sam Adams and a chocolate martini. As Hanna had assumed, Sam was drinking Crown and Coke. Apparently, some things never changed.

"So!"

Hanna slid onto the stool to Neelie's right and set her wristlet purse on the table before she turned her attention to her old friend. And it hit her again that some things did change. Sexy, say-anything Neelie, now looked sweet and feminine.

"What's going on with you guys?" Neelie reached toward her and touched the back of Hanna's hand. "God, it's been so long since I've talked to you."

Hanna nodded.

"Just." She shrugged. "I dunno, Neelie. The same old thing, ya know?"

"I don't, though. What is it? What's your same old?"

"Bowie and I have the fitness center." Hanna glanced to her right as Bowie and Sam settled in at the table, already deep in conversation. She felt the buzz of nerves in her chest, but she turned back to Neelie, determined to ignore it. "And…" She shrugged. "We pretty much live there. Take Sylvi there every day, so we're always together."

"Sylvi?" Neelie's eyes lit up.

Hanna glanced at Bowie and Sam again. Had they not talked at all in the past three years? How could they talk and Sam not know about Sylvi? Then again, how could they not know about the fitness center? Maybe they hadn't really stayed in touch. Bowie hadn't been able to tell her what Sam was up to these days. Only that he and Neelie were married, which could have happened recently.

"Our daughter," Hanna answered as she looked back at Neelie.

Neelie's big smile showed perfect white teeth. Hanna had a flash of memory of a thirteen-year-old Neelie, mouth full of braces.

"Ohmygod, how exciting!" Neelie, still touching Hanna's hand, squeezed her wrist now. "Do you have pictures?"

"Um." Hanna raised her eyebrows. "Of course." She picked up her wristlet and unzipped it to pull her iPhone from it.

"How old is she?"

"Three. Going on fifteen." Sylvi was safe territory. Hanna felt herself relaxing. She could talk about her daughter twenty-four seven if she found a willing listener. The waitress returned to their table as she searched her phone for the best picture of Sylvi. Far too many to choose just one, but she did: Bowie and Sylvi by the swing set in the backyard. As she held her phone out to Neelie, she offered the waitress a small smile and said thanks. Neelie took her phone, oblivious to the waitress as she switched out her glass for another. Full. Of water? Had to be water, didn't it? Ice water. Unless it was something mixed with Sprite, maybe?

"She's adorable." Neelie studied her phone with a small smile. "God, Han, she's a mini-you."

"She's a chatterbox," Hanna told her. "You can scroll through the pictures."

Maybe she shouldn't do that. Give this woman access to pictures of Sylvi. But then, Hanna had known Neelie for years before they'd lost touch. Might be Neelie would get sick of looking at the pictures, but this way she was getting a good idea of what Sylvi was like. Pictures of her at home, at her tumbling class at the center, in her cheerleader costume last Halloween. Hanna didn't know what pictures were even on there, but they were all of Sylvi.

"Do you guys have kids?" Hanna asked.

Neelie lifted her eyes from the phone and then raised her eyebrows. Hanna felt a jolt at the first real look at her old friend. Neelie handed her phone back to her. She took a drink from her glass and then rested her hand on her belly.

"We will," she said with that new, stranger's smile. Serene. God, no wonder that smile was wigging Hanna out. Neelie had always been daring and bold and yes, even obnoxious, at times. This serene woman was a total one eighty, and Hanna was both curious and appalled. "I'm due February tenth."

Hanna had almost picked up her drink, but she hesitated, hand hovering by the glass. Honestly, she'd never pictured Neelie married. Absolutely *when hell freezes over* married to Sam Collins, and the *world-ending sort of hell freezing over* pregnant. The old Neelie had no patience for kids. The old Neelie wouldn't be able to stay faithful to anyone and would laugh in Sam Collins' face when he proposed to her. What the hell had changed her?

"Congratulations." Hanna hoped her smile was sincere. She was happy for her, for them. Really. Just confused. She felt like she was at the bus station trying to board the wrong line as her own bus left her behind.

Neelie dropped her head back and treated Hanna to the wicked, hearty laughter from the old days. Hanna felt a rush of relief at the familiar sound, but it was gone just as quickly. Was Neelie messing with her? Were she and Sam bullshitting Hanna and Bowie? Maybe they weren't married? Not expecting a baby together?

Hanna finally picked up her drink and took a big gulp. She'd had two glasses of wine with dinner. Not enough to feel like she was moving at half-speed and the rest of the room was on warp-speed. As she put her glass down, her eyes swept over Bowie and Sam again. Bowie was talking now, but she couldn't really hear him without leaning closer.

She looked back at Neelie. The diamond on her left hand couldn't have been fake.

Neelie was grinning at her when she met her gaze again.

"Thank you." She turned the brassy grin down a few notches until it almost looked like a shy smile. Hanna stared at her silently and finally smacked her lips together.

"I gotta ask," she finally said, and when she realized she'd said it out loud, she wondered if maybe she had had a little too much to drink already. Decided it didn't matter now and plunged ahead. "How? How did..." She shrugged and glanced at Sam.

Neelie raised her eyebrows when Hanna looked back at her. She took a deep breath and then offered a helpless shrug.

"I don't know, Han. It just…it just hit me one day right between the eyes. He makes me happy."

"Happy." Hanna smiled, but she was suddenly drained. The track lighting around the bar and the ceiling was giving her a headache. She blinked and looked around the room at large. With her back to the door, she hadn't realized the place was filling up. There were no more empty tables. Even the black leather, low-slung couch at the far end of the room was occupied.

"I know, right?" Neelie nodded when Hanna looked back at her.

"Happy's good," Hanna agreed. She wanted to hear more. Now that she was here, and Neelie was sitting here with her, she wanted to hear more. To hell with the lighting and the headache that throbbed just behind her eyes and the pounding music that seemed louder now than when they'd walked in and made her lean forward, strain to hear Neelie.

She wanted to know what Sam Collins did to make Neelie happy. She wanted to know how each of them was dealing with death. Maybe morbid curiosity. Maybe she just wondered if she and Bowie were doing it right.

Chapter 13

TREVOR

"It was nice."

Trevor, on the floor in front of the paintings, used his forefinger to push his glasses back up his nose. He glanced at Mallory, curled in the corner of the couch. The smile she gave him over her book was soft and sweet, the same one that had drawn him to her in the first place.

"Last night." She tilted her head to rest her face on the couch cushion. "It was nice." She shrugged.

He hadn't dreamt last night. Maybe he'd passed out from exhaustion. When he woke this morning, his body cramped sideways on the couch, he'd hurt from head to toe. A crick in his neck. His shoulders were stiff. His hips ached, and his knees had popped when he'd stretched his legs. But he'd felt good. Not *stupid*. He didn't believe the dreams were gone. Something about it, the black water, was still teasing the back of his mind.

But last night *had been* nice.

Not just sleeping. But dinner with Mallory. Walking at the riverfront. Holding her hand. The way the summer heat had burned out of the day and left the air just pleasantly warm.

"It was." He nodded and looked back at the paintings along the wall.

When she didn't say anything else, he twisted on his butt to watch her read. After a few moments, she lifted only her eyes to look at him.

"What?"

"What're you reading now?"

Mallory arched her eyebrows and closed the book to look at the cover. She looked back at him curiously, obviously because he could see the title of the book.

"It's a biography about Vonnie Holt."

He nodded absently.

"The actress from that old TV show—"

"Comedienne," Trevor corrected her.

"What?" She glanced down at the book again and then at Trevor.

"Vonnie Holt. Comedienne," he mumbled.

"Right." She nodded. "She died last year."

"Ovarian cancer."

Mallory pursed her lips and studied him silently.

"What?"

"How do you know that?"

"I loved her show," he answered simply. "When I was a kid. And I know she died because I read tabloids."

"Oh, you do not!' Mallory laughed and rolled her eyes. "I've never seen you read anything but the TV guide on screen and the information bits in the video games you play."

He grinned. Shook his head. "I read tabloids when I'm standing in line at the grocery store."

"Mm." She nodded his way as if to give him a point.

"And I used to read."

"Used to read," she repeated. "And now you date a librarian, and you don't read."

"Sexy librarian," he corrected her.

She snorted.

"I'm sorry."

"For calling me a sexy librarian?"

He laughed and stretched his legs out in front of him.

"No. For crashing on you last night."

Her lips formed a silent O.

"I had other things in mind."

"Yeah?" She wiggled her eyebrows. "You could always do those other things...now..."

"I know I've been a dick..." Absently, he pushed his glasses up his nose again and then took a quick peek at the paintings. At the stack of drawings he'd set in front of him when he'd sat down earlier. "Well. Almost since you moved in—"

"Not that long."

He laughed softly when she chuckled, and he turned to meet her gaze.

"I'm not..." He bit his lip and then shrugged. "I'm not always a dick."

Mallory set the book aside and crawled to the end of the couch closest to him.

"I did some research last night."

Trevor cracked his knuckles and then bent his legs and hooked his arms around his knees. He stared at his bare feet rather than look at her.

"What kind of research?"

Mallory sighed. When he took a quick peek at her, she was staring at the wall, the paintings, actually. She'd looked at them before. In the beginning, she'd looked at them and studied them from all angles with him and even read articles on dream interpretation and come up empty-handed.

"I just started searching lakes. Ponds. Small bodies of water. Looking at images."

"And you had, like, what? Three million and sixty-two hits?"

She grinned sheepishly.

"Yeah. But I kept trying to narrow things down."

"Like how?"

"Um. Midwestern United States."

"I've traveled to both coasts, too."

"Yeah, okay, but I had to start somewhere."

"Find anything?"

"Not exactly. But I fell asleep on the floor. Woke up at, like, three and gave up."

He winced.

"But we could keep looking."

"And what if the water in my dreams is symbolic of the fact that I peed my pants in first grade when the teacher surprised us with a spelling test?"

"Did you?" She snorted and then covered her mouth quickly. Trevor let her sweat for a minute before letting her off the hook.

"Well. Not that I know of. But isn't that the point of dreams? To remind you of things you've forgotten?"

"Maybe." She climbed off the couch. "Some doctors say dreams are necessary to keep people from going crazy. Our brains need a rest.,"

"That's sleep. Not dreams."

"Still. Dreams are a byproduct of sleep."

Trevor watched her crawl toward him.

"Sex is a good release for our brains, too." She took his hands in hers and scooted to sit between his legs when he opened them for her.

Trevor let her lead. Let her ease closer to him. Touch his

lips with hers. Run her fingertips over his chin. Up over his jaw and into his hair.

"I've read that," he agreed as she drew his hand to her. Settled it on her hip.

"I think we should try it." She placed soft kisses over the trail her fingers had just touched. "Slow, easy sex."

Trevor wasn't sure it would work any better than the way he'd been fucking her after the nightmares, but she smelled good, and up close, her eyes were gorgeous, and his dick was rock hard and ready.

"We probably should." His eyelids drooped as she sucked his earlobe into her mouth.

Chapter 14

HANNA

It had been an okay night, and she'd admitted that to Bowie, both later that night when they got home and again the next morning when they awoke. Probably, when she'd said it late Saturday night when they'd tumbled into bed together, half-clothed and pawing at each other, she'd been just a little bit drunk. And maybe that's why she'd felt compelled to say it again the next morning.

It was okay.

And then they were in the kitchen, and Hanna was fixing omelets with egg whites and turkey sausage, and Bowie was squeezing fresh orange juice, and his phone buzzed. Hanna had been half-asleep, sort of paying attention to the omelets and sort of watching Bowie with the oranges and thinking she'd give ten bucks to forgo the freshly squeezed juice and have a cup of coffee. Or a glass of that old powdered juice her parents used to serve, for God's sake. When his phone buzzed, Hanna figured it was her mother-in-law calling to make arrangements to bring Sylvi home. She missed her girl; she was ready for Bowie's mom to bring her back.

Except Bowie answered the phone as Hanna plated the omelets and the sausage patties, and he wasn't himself. Wasn't the Bowie she knew, and the Bowie who'd talk to his mom about Sylvi. She eyed him suspiciously as he puffed up his chest and talked in a voice much louder than necessary about how it had been a great time and that he and Hanna were so glad he'd called.

Sam. Hanna rolled her eyes as she carried the plates to the high-top table over by the back windows. She snuck a glance at him as she went back to the counter to grab silverware and napkins. Bowie stared at the juicer as he spoke through a grin, chest still puffed up as if it made him feel tougher or more macho. She watched him as she sat down and cut her sausage patty in half with her fork.

Male posturing? Was that what it was? Why did guys do that? Did women do that? Hanna studied her omelet as she chewed. Yeah. Probably women did it, too. Maybe it sounded different, looked different, but yeah, she guessed women sometimes pretended to be someone they weren't. She swallowed a mouthful of the egg white mixture, felt it get stuck in her throat when she realized she'd done the same last night talking to Neelie. That if it had been Neelie who'd called her cell this morning—God, had they really exchanged numbers? —she'd be the one posturing right now. She'd be sucking in her stomach and laughing louder than was necessary, all to convince Neelie that of course they'd had a great time last night.

Thirsty, Hanna stood again and shuffled across the tile floor. She grabbed a glass from the cabinet and then stepped around Bowie to fill it with ice water. She took a drink and tuned in again to what Bowie was saying. She froze, glass still at her lips, and stared at him with a frown. He'd just said something about today. Cooking out. *Today.*

Dammit. He was inviting Sam and Neelie over. Today. To

cook out. Bowie shrugged helplessly and tossed his free hand up as if in surrender. Hanna sighed. Picked her phone up from the counter and carried it back to the table with her. She scrolled through her email as she ate. Not much there. Some ads. A few comments on her latest blog post. She'd written about Kady McGee this week, about the seventeen-year-old's car accident that had killed her and left her best friend paralyzed. Kady lived in Wyoming, but Hanna had found a news story about her online. She'd mused about teens and the dangers of distracted driving. It had been suspected by the local police that Kady and her best friend were racing a car full of boys when they ran off the road.

"Lunch today." Bowie set his phone down and turned his attention back to the juicer. "I'll pick up some chicken breasts. We can grill 'em. Have a salad."

Hanna stared at him blankly.

"Or I could get salmon? We could do it—"

"Bowie." She sighed. Rubbed her face and then propped her chin in her hand.

"What? You said you had fun."

"I did." She shrugged. "But seriously? One night wasn't enough?"

"Han, they're going back home tonight. Maybe it'll be another ten years before we see them again."

Home. Hanna racked her brain to remember where home was for Sam and Neelie now. Kind of hard to remember much through the haze from last night. No, she hadn't been bombed, but she'd had quite a bit more to drink than usual. Add in the loud music and the crowd of people who'd ended up pressed into the bar, and she'd probably heard every third word Neelie said.

Springfield, she thought. They were living in Springfield. An hour and a half drive and suddenly it seemed very likely that they would see Sam and Neelie again. A lot sooner than ten years.

"Do you think about her?" she asked softly. Was this going to become a new game? Asking each other if they thought about Eden, the accident? And then they'd both lie and go on with their lives?

Bowie, one hand on the top of the juicer and the other at the base, finger still pressing the power button, glanced at her. She figured he hadn't heard her. Turned her attention back to her plate.

The loud grinding noise stopped, and the sudden silence in the kitchen was almost palpable.

"Yeah."

Hanna looked up quickly, surprised that Bowie had heard her. Even more surprised that he'd answered her. They didn't talk about it. Sort of an unspoken agreement. Among all of them. But even in their marriage, all this time later, when they'd lost touch with everyone else (or so Hanna had thought), she and Bowie didn't talk about it.

She stared at him silently. Kind of wanted to push it now. To talk about her. And yet, Bowie had caught her off guard and she had no idea what to say.

"Just." He shrugged. Poured two tall glasses of juice. Hanna watched the pulp float in the glasses as he carried them to the table and sat down with her. "I mean…doesn't do much good to think about it, because we can't change anything."

"Exactly," she agreed. "So why are we hanging out with Sam and Neelie?"

"Hardly hanging out." Bowie rolled his eyes. "They're in town for a family thing. Sam's nephew got married Friday or something."

"Who gets married on a Friday?" Hanna frowned.

"Really?" Bowie shook his head.

"I just don't get why we have to do this. It's not like we're gonna change anything."

"No one's trying to change anything. We're gonna have lunch with them."

"After hanging out with them last night."

Bowie picked up his fork and started eating. It gave Hanna just a bit of satisfaction that his food had to be cold by now. She pushed her empty plate away and picked up her juice. Closed her eyes and took a drink. Pretended it was coffee. Whisky. Whatever might get her through the day.

"Sam said he talked to Davis a couple of months ago."

Whisky. Definitely.

"Great." She nodded. Offered Bowie an icy smile and slid off her chair. She didn't want to see Davis Buckley a million times more than she hadn't wanted to see Sam and Neelie again. It was the beginning of *something*.

"We could do salmon," he said as she carried her plate to the dishwasher. "And wild rice—"

"Whatever, Bowie," she mumbled as she all but slammed the plate in the bottom rack. "Whatever you wanna do."

Chapter 15

PEYTON

She leaned on the counter and watched Brion go through the book titles on her bookshelf. It was a second pass; he hadn't found what he was looking for the first time. She'd been home only fifteen minutes when he'd shown up. Barely time to get out of the dress she'd worn to work and into denim shorts and a black tank. She propped one barefoot over the other. Worried the toe ring on her left foot with the toes of her right foot. Eyed the open wine bottle a few feet away from her on the counter across the small kitchen.

"It's not here," he finally announced. She raised her eyebrows when he shot her an irritated look over his shoulder.

"You're kidding."

"Peyton, I need the book—"

"I don't have it."

He turned to her, hands on his jean-clad hips.

"You don't have any books anywhere else?" He looked around the living area and then back at her. "You used to have a shit ton of books at the house."

Peyton sighed. Fuck it. She wanted a glass of wine. Ignoring Brion's disapproving frown, she moved to get a glass from the cabinet with the glass door. She decided she might love this apartment more than she'd ever thought she loved Brion Mitchell. The wine, too. But then, hadn't she always known she loved wine more than Brion Mitchell?

"I don't have the book. There's a book on my nightstand if you wanna look at it. But I can save you the trouble. It's a Steig Larsson book. *The Girl Who Played With Fire*. Why the hell would I have your cowboy book, Brion?"

She poured herself a healthy glass of wine, licked her finger where it had splashed over the lip of the glass, and then pushed the cork back into the bottle.

"Why bother?"

"What?"

He swung his hand at her, at the bottle.

"Why bother corking it? You'll probably finish the bottle tonight."

"Fuck you."

"Did you sell it?"

Peyton snorted. She put the bottle down and took a drink.

"Yep. You got me. I sold your book because I needed some drugs."

Brion shrugged. "You clearly have an addiction problem."

"Clearly," she agreed. "You're just pissed because I chose the bottle over you."

Brion took a deep breath and turned his back to her. She watched him curiously as he wandered around her living space. Decided she wanted to fuck him. Not because she wanted him. But because the conversation with Bellamy was still stuck in her head. The conversation yesterday. The sex two weeks before. She needed to push that thought out of her head. She'd watched girl on girl porn with Brion, sure. Turned him on. Turned her on. Didn't mean she'd wanted to do it, for God's sake, though she did suddenly wonder what Brion would say if he knew.

"Why would I have put it in a box of donations?" He stopped pacing. Stood at the huge picture window at the back of her apartment. Great window. Shitty view. Peyton hoped they rethought some of the design when they redid the next loft apartment. Just because she had a great view of old brick buildings—some of them crumbling—and an alleyway complete with a dumpster didn't mean her neighbors should.

Wary, suddenly, of the bickering, she took a deep breath. Moved to stand behind the sofa. When he looked at her over his shoulder, she shrugged.

"I don't know. You probably set it down, not even realizing you did it. I did tell you," she said quietly. "And you didn't listen."

"And here we go." He hung his head.

"Just sayin'."

She folded her arms over her chest. Lifted her glass to sip from it. Had a flash of drinking wine here, on the sofa, with Bellamy. Laughing with her. The Italian food they'd eaten; their plates on the glass-topped coffee table in front of the sofa. The Civil Wars music on surround sound. The moment when their laughter suddenly had an edge, an awareness to it. The rush of heat in her belly when Bellamy had leaned in and kissed her.

No. She hadn't been so drunk she didn't remember it. But she'd had enough to drink to let it happen. To want it to happen.

"What're you thinking about?"

Peyton lifted her gaze to look at Brion.

"Do you have somewhere you need to be?"

He blinked at her. Laughed harshly after a moment of silence and then shook his head.

"Yeah. I'll get out of your hair."

"I don't want you to go." Ashamed of the need, she dropped her gaze.

"No?" He tilted his head in disbelief.

"No." She met his eyes again and unbuttoned her shorts. "I want you to stay."

Brion eyed her silently. Looked pointedly at the glass in her hand.

"How much have you had to drink?"

She shook her head. Took a few steps around the sofa and leaned over in front of him to set her glass down on the table. Before she could change her mind—after all, a few swallows of wine wasn't much in the way of liquid courage—she unzipped her shorts and shimmied out of them.

"I don't want you to talk." She reached for his hand. "But I want you to stay."

Brion's face twisted, like he was in pain. She tugged at his hand, pulled him toward the sofa.

"You don't wanna do this."

"I do." She nodded. "I need to do this."

She rubbed her fingers over his jeans, cupped him in her hand. Brion caught his breath as she hurriedly opened his jeans and shoved them down out of her way.

"Like this?"

She looked up at him and nodded. Turned to push him to the sofa. He sat, watched her slip her panties off—he looked puzzled, like he was watching a foreign movie and couldn't figure out what was going on—and then looked at her, wide-eyed in surprise when she straddled him and took him in.

"Peyton."

"No. You don't have to do that." She shook her head,

caught his hand when he touched her inner thigh. "I just need this."

"Why?"

Moving over him, remembering that she wasn't in love with him and hadn't been for some time, but liking the way he stretched her, the way he felt inside her, she watched him with hooded eyes.

"Are you complaining?"

"Can I at least get a little of this?" He tugged at the tail of her tank. Pulled it over her head when she nodded. She moaned softly as he unhooked her bra. Shrugged her shoulders to let the straps slide off. Rose up on her knees when he tossed it aside and threw her head back as he nuzzled her breasts, his five o'clock shadow scratching her nipples.

It felt good, but she didn't say so. Couldn't tell him that it felt good to have a man's mouth on her. Not that Bellamy had done anything wrong. In fact, Bellamy had made her come more than once. And she had to admit, it had been a hell of a rush, touching her, making her come.

When it was over and he'd come only seconds after her, Peyton ducked her head over his. Felt his hair on her lips. She was careful not to kiss him. She used to kiss his head, his hair, when she'd loved him. She didn't now. She panted, struggled to catch her breath. Felt Brion's fingers still on her breasts, still pinching her nipples. Half-repulsed by the feeling now, she almost slapped his hands away. But again, the thought of Bellamy's soft hands, the long nails and the rings on her fingers, made her want Brion's calloused hands on her.

"Jesus." Brion groaned. He flopped his head back on the sofa. Eyes closed, he was still breathing heavy. "What the hell was that all about?"

Her right cheek pressed to his, she shook her head.

"I feel like I just played seven minutes in heaven." He dropped his hands, fingers skimming over her belly.

"That's a stretch."

"You pulled my dick out and jumped on."

She pulled away from him, sat up, but she refused to meet his eyes.

"You think I'm gonna last ten minutes like that?"

"I'm not complaining." She shook her head.

She moved her eyes to look at him when he touched her where their bodies were still joined.

"So, was that a one-time thing?"

"I'm not in love with you."

He shrugged. "Can I stay? Take my clothes off?"

"No strings?" She arched her eyebrows in question.

"Promise. Just wild, casual sex."

She laughed softly. Nodded.

She closed her hand over his, though, and shook her head. If he was going to stay, they might as well move to the bedroom, so she could drive Bellamy out of there, too.

Chapter 16

HANNA

She hadn't admitted to Bowie that lunch with Sam and Neelie had been okay, because even though she'd sort of had fun, she'd had a feeling of dread winding through her all day and night and now even today again. She'd snapped at Sylvi this morning when she wouldn't sit still for Hanna to braid her hair. She knew Sylvi's crocodile tears were over the top; her daughter was spoiled rotten, but it still made her feel guilty.

She'd been a little absent-minded in spin class earlier, too. But then on the other hand, exercise was a good way to relax. Mentally. To chase ghosts out of her head.

It had happened. Of course, it had. Jesus, Bowie had to be lying to himself to think it wasn't going to come up. They'd grilled the salmon—Hanna liked it, she couldn't complain—and they'd sat on the deck, in the shade, and they'd made an afternoon of it. Sylvi had dazzled Sam and Neelie both, and Hanna and Bowie had both been those proud, obnoxious parents that smiled too much and too big while Sylvi sang her *ABCs* for them and talked nonstop about *McMath the Machine*. Neelie had been especially wowed when Sylvi counted to fifteen in Spanish.

But then Sylvi had fallen asleep on the couch while watching *McMath*—Hanna suspected Grandma had let her stay up too late the night before—and the adult conversation had turned to reminiscing. Talking about the old gang, the old times.

Hanna took a deep steadying breath now. Her hands were shaking. She stared at the computer screen—she'd sat down in the office with the intention of paying a few bills—but her mind was trying hard to be a million miles away. Or just twelve years away, actually.

She gave herself a mental shake. Thought about how cute Neelie had been in the white denim shorts and the pink button up blouse. Tiny polka-dots. Hanna would look ridiculous in polka dots.

Neelie had told Hanna about hooking up with Sam again, several years after the summer after graduation, after Hanna and Bowie's wedding. How she'd accepted a job in Human Resources at a hospital in the Springfield area and moved there. Found an apartment. Made a few friends at work and ended up running into Sam at a club one night, only to find out that he'd been living there since that summer.

They'd quickly rekindled their friendship—Hanna had been struck with disbelief there—and started hanging out. Going to dinner, movies. Watching ball games together—baseball, football, didn't matter—and then of course, they'd ended up spending the night together (no disbelief there on Hanna's part) and the sex had been good, and they liked being together and the next thing Neelie knew they were dating.

Sam was a financial advisor. Neelie still worked at the

hospital, though they'd decided they could live on Sam's salary for a while so that Neelie could stay home with the baby when it came.

Speaking of babies, they both wanted a boy. Hanna figured Sam wouldn't be able to handle having a little girl and knowing the things every boy would want to do with her as she got older. Sam had been *that guy* when they were younger. Hanna figured he'd hit on everyone in their graduating class. Who knew how many girls had actually slept with him?

And then Bowie had brought out three beers—apparently he'd bought a twelve-pack when he'd picked up the salmon—and he and Sam had twisted the tops off of theirs (Hanna wasn't sure she wanted one), and they'd started talking about Bowie and Hanna coming up to their place some night soon for dinner.

Hanna had opened her beer and taken a big swallow to fight the sinking feeling inside. They'd avoided this for twelve years. *Twelve years.* Even after their wedding—seeing Sam and Neelie—they'd all gone their separate ways again, and she and Bowie had avoided this, and now here it was again.

You couldn't outrun the past. Hanna knew that. *Cessation* was proof of that, wasn't it? Maybe she wouldn't have created a blog about death if Eden were still alive. But the blog, Bowie's obsession with health and fitness, their private fight against the past seemed a lot simpler, safer than four of them reminiscing. Six of them. Seven of them—there'd never be eight of them again—but seven was bad.

And Sam had mused about getting everyone together again. Hanna, sort of listening to Neelie talking about their spare bedroom that Sam was turning into a nursery for the baby, had expected Bowie to laugh Sam's suggestion off.

Sure, it had been great to see Sam and Neelie again, fun weekend, yada yada yada, but they were too busy, too much going on with the fitness center, too busy with Sylvi's tumbling class and her piano lessons (Bowie's idea) to make any honest attempt at getting the gang back together.

He hadn't argued. He hadn't said any such thing. In fact, he'd gone along with Sam's idea. Nodded enthusiastically. Said he'd like to see Davis again. That he'd seen Peyton a while back. And then Sam had said Davis was living in Camp Point—closer to Hanna and Bowie than Sam and Neelie, seriously less than a half hour away—with his son and that Sam knew for a fact he'd be up for going out.

Hanna rubbed her eyes and flopped back in her chair. She'd only finished one beer. And still, her stomach was sour today. Everything to do with the company she and Bowie were suddenly keeping. Again. Nothing to do with dinner or drinks or the salmon and beer. Some things were better left buried.

Hanna didn't want to expose Sylvi to their old friends. To the things better left buried. It was bad enough that she'd been around Sam and Neelie yesterday.

"You're slouching, babe."

Hanna rolled her eyes, but she sat up straight when Bowie leaned over the back of the chair to drop a kiss on her head.

"How was body pump?"

"Good."

She glanced up at him in time to see him tilt his head back and chug from a reusable bottle of water. Not only were they health conscious to a fault, they were incredibly aware of their carbon footprint. At the moment, Hanna wanted to shove her carbon footprint right up someone's ass. She couldn't decide if that someone was Sam or her husband.

"Sam text—"

"I don't wanna hear it." She settled her hands on the

keyboard and tapped out a few words. The printer in the corner behind her whirred to life and began spitting out their accounts payable ledger.

"What're you printing?"

"Accounts payable."

"Why?"

"Because I'm taking it home to work on it."

"Why?"

Hanna stood up, felt a weary sigh dredge its way up through her diaphragm and her lungs and then up her throat. "Because I don't feel well. And I'm tired."

"Really?"

She stilled her hands—she'd leaned over the keyboard again, to sign out of the accounting program—when she heard the wistful note in Bowie's voice. Slowly, she straightened and then turned to look at him.

"What?"

He grinned suggestively.

"What?" she repeated.

"Maybe..." He stepped toward her, apparently oblivious to the anger in her voice. She watched his hand as he reached forward and rubbed it over her stomach. "Think you might be pregnant?"

Hanna clenched her fists. And her jaw.

"What?" She lifted her gaze to his and stared at him. "What? You think that would be a good—"

"Han." Bowie's voice was that same gentle voice she'd fallen in love with all those years ago. "We talked about having another baby."

"We need another baby right now like we need to go digging in the past. Are you kidding me?"

She took a step back from him when he started to lift his hand. To stroke her arm. Or cup her face. Something sweet. She wanted no part of that right now.

"What does that mean?"

"What does that *mean*?" she repeated. "Bowie, I don't wanna do this. I don't wanna go to Sam and Neelie's for dinner. I don't wanna do this again. I don't wanna—"

"We're not hurting anything. They're our friends. What's the harm—"

"And I don't wanna get the whole goddamned gang back together. I don't wanna go out. I don't wanna see Davis—"

"So, what then? If we get together, you're just gonna stay home? Wait up for me?"

Hanna blinked at him, shocked that he would consider going out with all of them and leaving her at home.

"And if you think I wanna be pregnant now, with you and Sam trying to relive the good old days—"

"Hanna, Hanna, Hanna." Bowie shook his head. He was pissed now, too, but she didn't care. Maybe she backed down sometimes, not that they actually fought much, but she sure as hell wasn't going to back down this time. "We're not reliving the good old days."

"I don't even want Sylvi around them."

"Sam and Neelie?"

"Any of them!"

"You're being ridiculous—"

"I'm not being ridiculous!" she shouted. Bowie shot a nervous glance at the open office door. Hanna filled her cheeks with air and then let it out slowly. Lowered her voice, though she was trembling with anger. "When was the last time you visited Eden's grave?"

Bowie shot her a look that said she was being ridiculous and that her question only proved it.

"I don't visit Eden's grave," he snapped.

"Exactly! You guys have forgotten—"

"No one's forgotten!" he roared. "No one has forgotten Eden, Hanna, least of all me!"

Shocked by his outburst, Hanna stared at him silently. She raised her eyebrows and then, looking around the office, she nodded slowly. Grabbed her stuff off the printer and picked her purse up from the floor. Walked out without a goodbye.

Chapter 17

TREVOR

The dream had come back, of course. He was trying to hang onto his sanity, to the lifeline Mallory had offered him when she'd started the online search for images of lakes. Mostly, Trevor knew it was the absolute pie-in-the-sky *Hail Mary* of *Hail Marys,* but still, it was something. It was better than wallowing in his exhaustion and his growing frustration. Better than sketching the same body of water and the same dock over and over again. Better than banging his head on the wall over the paintings, trying to figure out just what was missing in the details of the black water.

Who was he kidding? It wasn't better than anything, because he and Mallory could grow old and die before they ever came across any images of the lake he was drawing. Hells bells, it could be something nagging at him that had nothing to do with a fucking lake or pond. It could be something dating back to grade school. It could be something from when he was a preschool kid or something. Seriously. Who knew? It could be that his body was being possessed by some water demon or something equally insane. The point being, whatever was driving this urge to sketch and paint a lake could be *anything*.

What had suddenly made it a bit more bearable was Mallory being involved. Rather than watching him toss and turn and lying like a lifeless doll beneath him when he pounded his anger into her, she woke him when he was dreaming. Talked him down. Held him. The sex was still sometimes violent and angry, but she participated fully, and it eased some of his guilt that even when he was harsh and rough with her, she was getting something out of it. And yeah, they were still studying the pictures and the paintings and still poring over the Internet to solve the mystery.

Trevor sang along with Blue Oyster Cult as he tapped his pencil on the glass counter. They'd been busy tonight. Weird how some days he didn't see more than three people, one of them being whoever was leaving work as he came in, and other days, like now, when he had three, four, even five groups of customers coming into the store. And buying things. He'd sold seven CDs today. Two of them had been cheap and in Trevor's opinion were crap, but no one had asked his opinion, and he didn't share it unless he was asked.

Right now, he let his eyes roam over the large sketchpad he'd picked up at the art store just four storefronts down. He had plenty at home, of course, always did. But he'd slipped into the store earlier, on the way into work, on a whim and grabbed the pad, and in between customers, he'd been scratching away. Not the lake this time. He'd decided he was damned good and well going to work on a comic strip. And he'd done it. He'd drawn a few cartoons, and then his attention had wandered, and he'd started sketching a caricature of his boss. Nothing vicious. Just for kicks. Just to keep his mind away from the black water.

After he'd sold another disc and a vinyl album, he paced the perimeter of the store. Picked up a few different albums and read the information on the back covers. He was interested in one of them (The Ramones) and the other (Beck) he had at home on disc.

The jingle of the bell above the door drew his attention. Couple of guys probably about seventeen. Trevor watched them closely for a moment. He remembered being seventeen. Wouldn't have dreamed of stealing anything, but that didn't mean he hadn't done some stupid shit back then.

"Hey, man." One of the guys noticed him watching them. Trevor gave the kid a nod back and then wandered the rest of the way around the store. Ended up back at the counter, hands in his pockets, eyes on the sketch pad. He reached for the pencil and bumped it, knocked it off the counter. Leaned over to pick it up from the floor and noticed it had teeth marks in it. He hadn't realized he'd been chewing on it, and on the off chance that he hadn't made the marks himself, he tossed it in the trash, and without looking, grabbed for another pencil out of the cup by the register.

"You guys give music lessons?"

Trevor looked up from the pad to find the taller of the two kids at the counter.

"Guitar."

The kid nodded. Trevor pulled a sticky note from a pad near the pencil cup and jotted down his boss' name and the store number. He'd found it easier to handle these questions this way rather than continue a conversation when he really had nothing to add.

"Thanks." The kid took the note, paused for a moment to read it—Trevor had careful handwriting, but you wouldn't know it from his signature on any of the artwork he'd been lucky enough to sell—and then tucked it in his pocket.

Trevor rested an elbow on the register and watched the guys slowly move back toward the front door.

His phone buzzed as the bell above the door jingled, and the door itself closed slowly behind the kids. Figuring it was Mallory, he reached to pull it from the back pocket of his jeans. She'd met her friend for lunch earlier. Mentioned that she might end up at the library, filling in for someone who had left on vacation. Trevor couldn't imagine that a library could be so busy that Mallory would have to cover someone's shift, but then he didn't frequent libraries, so what did he know?

He read. Hell yes, he read. Lots of music books. Biographies. Music theory. Art theory. Books about artists. Now and then he threw in a novel or two; he was especially partial to horror novels, and he sometimes read thrillers. Neither sounded appealing right now, being that he sort of felt like the main character in a thriller these days. He could imagine himself in a shrink's office, saying something about having that dream again and that would be the starting line and then the shrink would dig into his psyche and figure out that someone was stalking him and trying to kill him, or if it turned out to be a horror novel instead of a thriller, then maybe the shrink would figure out that it was indeed some sort of entity possessing him.

He glanced at the screen as he lifted the phone to his ear. Saw that it wasn't Mallory, but he had the phone at his ear before he processed the thought and so the male voice on the other end of the call threw him.

"Trevor?"

Trevor frowned and pulled the phone away from the side of his head. No help. Unknown caller. Someone not on his contact list, but someone who still knew him. And had his cell number.

"Yeah." He cleared his throat before he said into the phone, "Who's this?"

"Hey, man." The voice sounded vaguely familiar, but no names came to mind. "It's Sam."

Trevor stared blankly at the plate glass windows at the front of the store.

"Sam who?"

Chapter 18

HANNA

...Least of all, me...

What the hell had Bowie meant by that?

Hanna pushed her fingers up under her sunglasses and rubbed her eyes. She was dead on her feet. Since Sunday when Sam and Neelie had come for lunch, and then Monday when she and Bowie had fought at work, she hadn't slept well. When she did, the dreams were so bad, she wished she could stay awake.

She'd been playing hooky a little bit, though, from the fitness center. Kind of pissed her off that Bowie knew she just needed a little alone time, a little space. She wasn't exactly sick, but she was worn down and tired and still mad as hell about the whole *getting the gang back together* thing. *Well.* Mad as hell that Bowie had apparently decided he wanted to see the old gang, *with or without Hanna.*

She should get out of the SUV. People were probably staring at her. Wondering what she was doing parked in front of The Donut Hole, not moving. And God forbid someone recognized her car and reported back to Bowie that not only was she playing hooky, she was at a donut shop. She moved her hand and let her glasses drop back into place. Pulled her keys from the ignition and opened her door. Rather than take her purse in, she grabbed her billfold and then dropped her purse behind the front seat and climbed out of the car. She noticed her cell phone in the cup holder as she pushed her door shut. Decided she didn't care; she'd be in the place all of five minutes, maybe eight, and if Bowie needed her and called her in that possible eight minutes, he could leave a message.

As she walked, she aimed the key fob backwards at the car and hit the lock button. Once inside, she was happy to see only one person ordering in front of her. A few tables were taken, even at this late morning hour, but she scanned them quickly and breathed a sigh of relief when she didn't recognize anyone.

They'd made up. Sort of. Bowie had said all the right things: he loved her, didn't want to fight, and that of course Sylvi was more important than anything else. But he'd also said that he didn't understand what it would hurt to see more of Sam and Neelie, especially if they were settled down and expecting a baby. He'd also told her—and he'd had the big, pleading eyes of a little boy asking his mom to play cars with him—that he really would like to see Davis and Peyton and Trevor. That it might be fun. That it didn't mean they had to hang out with them all the time, but that it could be a fun way to mark the year they all turned thirty.

When Hanna had sighed, he'd known she was giving in. Promised her that seeing everyone wouldn't hurt anything. That nothing that had happened in the past would affect Sylvi and that nothing between them would change. Intellectually, she knew all of that. But she'd still felt dread creep up her throat, even while Bowie undressed her and made love to her. She'd wondered, too, if he was hoping she'd get pregnant every time they were together. She wanted another baby, yes. She wanted to give Sylvi a sibling. But if they were detouring to the past this summer, it certainly wasn't the time for a baby.

"Can I help you?"

Hanna jumped when the young guy behind the counter spoke to her. She blinked, realized the guy in front of her was gone, and it was her turn to order.

"Can I get a medium coffee to go?"

"No donuts?" The guy—obviously he didn't know who she and Bowie were—looked wounded. Hanna caught herself before she giggled.

"Sure. Gimme a half dozen donut holes."

He seemed somewhat mollified as he tapped her order into his cash register (apparently, she had to order a dozen real donuts to get a friendly smile) and then set about collecting everything for her. She paid with cash. Sipped her coffee as she hurried back outside to the car. Once inside with the door locked—she laughed at herself for the thought, as if someone she knew might see her and yank open the door and steal her breakfast away—she set her coffee in a cup holder and picked up her phone. No calls, no messages.

She sighed in relief that quickly soured to something like loneliness. She hated this. This wasn't how she and Bowie operated. They were friends as well as lovers. They'd been friends first. They talked everything out when something threatened to come between them. What really bothered her was knowing that it wasn't just Sam and Neelie suddenly showing up in their lives again that was upsetting her. She'd been feeling a little resentment toward Bowie lately just because of the tight hold he had on her and their marriage. He pretended, but really, he didn't see her as his equal. He ruled the house, the fitness center, and Hanna suddenly wanted to push back. To stretch her wings a bit. To take Sylvi to the movies or to the park when it wasn't on the schedule. She wanted to give Sylvi an ice cream cone instead of a cup of yogurt.

Wanting to push back didn't mean she didn't love him. She was crazy about him, and she hated feeling separate from him these days.

She started the car, backed out of her spot, and pulled out on Broadway, car headed east. Bowie listened to talk radio or audiobooks, but Hanna usually drove with the radio off. She liked the silence, and when Sylvi was with her, she liked to listen to her daughter's sweet little voice. Today, Hanna turned the radio on and punched buttons aimlessly, until she heard something appealing.

The Goo Goo Dolls had never been her favorite. In fact, if asked, she'd only be able to name this particular song, "Slide". But for the moment, it worked. She settled the white wax bag on her thighs as she drove and reached inside for a donut hole. They'd probably be a little stale by now, and she'd be sorry she even ordered them.

The first one was so sweet and so fresh, Hanna moaned a little bit out loud and then laughed at herself. She hadn't had a donut in years. She reminded herself to eat slowly. To savor the dough. Besides, if she slammed a half dozen donut holes on an edgy stomach that wasn't used to sweet stuff, she'd end up sick. She licked her fingers and then reached for her coffee.

The music changed from the Goo Goo Dolls to Pearl Jam. Again, she didn't know much of their music—sadly, she was most familiar with mashup mixes of any song that she used in her spin and aerobics classes—but she liked this song. "Last Kiss". She listened closely to the lyrics as she drove. Found herself thinking about Eden. Eden was always in her head. She kind of felt like it was Eden inside her that wrote

Cessations. But after seeing Sam and Neelie last weekend, she'd been thinking about her even more.

She looked around as she put the car in park. Surprised to find she'd driven to Kelly's on autopilot. Obviously, she was thinking more about Eden these days, more about the gang, if she'd just taken a comatose ride and ended up at Peyton's store. *Peyton's Place.* She laughed out loud at that. She should tell Peyton that, to change the name of her store to *Peyton's Place.*

She glanced at the plate glass windows, but she didn't look too closely. She wasn't ready for that yet. She'd just finish the donuts first. Take her coffee in with her. She'd have to think of an excuse for why she was here. Wasn't like she could just waltz in and start talking to Peyton like they'd just seen each other last Tuesday.

Her fingernails scratched the bottom of the bag. Disappointed, Hanna ducked her head to examine the inside. The donut holes were gone; she'd eaten every one of them. She took in a deep breath and crumbled the bag up. Set it on the passenger seat and told herself to remember to throw it away. Stared at it for a moment and decided she didn't care if Bowie saw it. If he knew she'd eaten donuts. She might even just tell him they'd been better than the sex they'd had last night.

She filed that away for thought. Grabbed her coffee. Twisted around to grab her purse from behind the seat and then put her phone in the outside pocket. Couldn't walk into a jewelry store without her purse.

She felt underdressed as she rounded the front of her car and stepped up on the sidewalk. At least she had denim shorts on and not spandex, but still. Odds were, Peyton would look professional sexy and make Hanna feel like a slob. Unless maybe jewelers didn't dress nice? Did they have to wear work clothes? Like, would Peyton be in the back working, designing stuff? Hanna tried to remember back to when they were kids, if she'd ever seen Peyton's dad come home from work.

A lick of heat stroked up the back of her neck as she pulled the heavy door open and stepped inside. Cool, dry air enveloped her and chased a shiver through her. Hanna let her eyes roam the posh interior. She hadn't set foot inside this place in a good thirteen or fourteen years, maybe. By the time they'd started driving, no one had much reason to stop in here. Peyton worked her shifts and then hurried home to change to go out with all of them.

She was a woman, so maybe it was natural to get caught up in the glittery, sparkling gemstones in the display cases. Her rings were gorgeous; Bowie couldn't have found anything more perfect for her, but she still loved to look at diamonds. Soft, instrumental music played from hidden speakers. Hanna forced herself to look around. Exchanged smiles with a young blonde showing an older man a pair of earrings. She wandered around a bit, eyes greedy for the jewels around her.

Wasn't practical for her to have expensive jewelry, other than her wedding ring. She spent over half her waking hours in spandex, sweaty and red in the face, and sometimes she even took her rings off when she was teaching. She wondered about Peyton. Did her fingers drip rubies and sapphires? Was she married? Was she still the gorgeous brunette Hanna remembered? Would she be pleased to see Hanna or not?

"Can I help you find something?"

Hanna looked up when she heard the deep voice. Still no Peyton, and this wasn't her brother, either. She was pretty sure. She had a flash of doubt, maybe they'd sold the store to someone else? And maybe she wasn't going to run into Peyton today after all? *Run into*. She felt the smirk on her lips, hoped the man in the white dress shirt with the crisp sleeves and perfect creases and the blue and silver tie didn't think she was being snotty.

Because what did Hanna White know about being snotty? Could a woman who lived in spandex, whose *go-to* clothing was made by Under Armor rather than DKNY, even be snotty?

"Um." She cleared her throat. Glanced over the man's shoulder and noticed a door at the end of a short hallway that said *Employees Only*. "Actually, I'm looking for Peyton. Peyton Kelly?"

The door opened as she spoke, and Hanna suddenly felt eyes on her. Not coming from that direction, though. Peyton appeared in increments, as she slowly pulled the door open. Eyes cast down at something in her hands, she didn't see Hanna.

Feeling the itch of someone looking at her, scrutinizing her actually, Hanna turned her head and looked around. Saw the blond girl staring at her. The girl looked away, back at the earrings she was trying to sell, but Hanna still felt the burn of her heated stare.

"Peyton." The man behind the counter turned sideways. "Hmm?"

"Someone's here to see you."

Peyton looked up quickly, saw Hanna standing there, and looked back down at her hands. Hanna raised her eyebrows. Did she not recognize her? Would she admit it if she did?

For God's sake, Hanna. You were best friends for years. You grew up with her. Of course, she recognizes you. You aged. Not like you went through witness protection and had the structure of your face changed.

Hanna felt the girl watching her again. Peyton finally looked up and flashed a smile at Hanna. She lifted a hand, as if to say *just a second* and then she walked over to stand with the girl and the guy and the earrings. She handed something back to the man, and Hanna decided maybe she'd been cleaning jewelry for him. She spoke with him for a moment, said something to the blonde, and then turned back to Hanna.

"Hey." Her voice was thick and buttery, just like it used to be. She was still tall, legs and legs and more legs until they ended at her thin waist. She was dressed in a pencil skirt and gray heels and a pale pink blouse, and Hanna had to swallow a mouthful of regret. Why had she come? Why had she come here to put herself through this?

Hadn't she and Bowie been at odds about this since that first phone call from Sam? So, what the hell was she doing?

Bowie had reconnected with his closest friend. Other than Hanna. Maybe she'd just wanted to do the same.

Maybe she'd been desperate to drum up someone else who was adamantly opposed to the lot of them hanging out again.

Chapter 19

Hanna White's body felt perfectly toned under Peyton's arms. It was a quick hug, thankfully; Hanna seemed as uncertain about it as she was. Hanna let her eyes roam a bit when they parted, as if she didn't really want to look at Peyton.

"You look great," Peyton told her begrudgingly. She *did* look great. Denim shorts. Not the Bermudas Hanna had worn all the time when they were younger. And not the kind so short that ass-cheek seemed to be part of the appeal. They were a nice fit. Looked cute with Hanna's royal blue sleeveless blouse and the cute flip flops she wore with them.

Being a jeweler, Peyton noticed Hanna's ring. Not one of their designs, but stunning just the same. White gold. Pear shaped diamond. Channel diamonds on the wedding band. The whole thing looked like it had set Bowie back a down payment on a house.

"Yeah." Hanna laughed softly. Peyton stared at her curiously. Wondered what that was about. What *this* was about. What was she doing here? Now? After all these years, why had Hanna White just shown up at the store? "You look—"

"Old?" Peyton grinned when Hanna met her eyes.

"Professional." Hanna offered a lazy shrug.

"Nice."

"I like it," Hanna insisted, tossing her hand out to indicate Peyton's outfit, or maybe the whole store or who the hell knew what?

"So." Peyton cleared her throat. "What's going on?"

"Um." Hanna raised her eyebrows. Peyton noticed her knuckles go white as she tightened her grip on her coffee cup. "I wanted to look at...something for...my daughter."

Peyton decided to pretend she didn't hear the lie in Hanna's voice.

"How old?" She patted her hip pockets but came up empty-handed.

"Three."

Peyton felt her smile falter just a smidge. Of course, Hanna and Bowie had a three-year-old daughter. She was probably a fucking princess with a pink pony at home and a spot secured for her at Harvard for when she was eighteen.

"Oh, wow." She nodded. "What're you thinking? Maybe a necklace? Or a charm bracelet, maybe?"

Honestly, Peyton thought fine jewelry for a three-year-old was a waste of money. She wouldn't say so to Hanna, though. She'd get around to the real reason she was here soon enough. And if Peyton made a sale off her hesitation, she'd take it.

"Here." Bellamy handed Peyton her keys as she led the older man to the register. Peyton nodded her thanks, but she didn't say anything.

"She'll be four in a few weeks." Hanna pursed her lips. "What do you think? Do you have anything..."

"Cheap?" Peyton arched her eyebrows. Hanna laughed softly. "Let me show you these."

Hanna rested her hands on the glass counter as Peyton

unlocked the cabinet. She noticed Hanna's glittery pink nails, the tender red hangnails on her left hand. Somewhat smug and a little bit curious, but not enough to ask, she leaned over just enough to reach in and pick up a charm bracelet.

When she set the little silver bracelet on the counter, Hanna stroked it carefully with a fingertip. Peyton remembered the friendship bracelets they'd worn in junior high. Hanna's had been blue and white; Peyton's pink and purple.

She gave herself a mental shake. Reached back into the display case and lifted a tray of charms.

"Sam Collins called Bowie."

A jolt of heat, of regret, shot through Peyton, and she almost dropped the tray. She steadied herself, took the tray out, and set it on the counter. Wondered if Hanna would give up all pretenses now or if she'd keep looking at the charms.

"When?"

Peyton winced when Hanna set her cup on the counter. She hoped it was empty. Hanna avoided looking at Peyton; instead she studied the charms like they were the answer to life.

"Coupla weeks ago."

Peyton stared at the top of Hanna's head. She wondered if she was still naturally blond or if she had to color her hair yet. She laid her hand over her stomach for a moment, trying to soothe it. The coffee Bellamy had made for her—Bellamy was still dogging her every step, as if she might wake up and realize she was madly in love with her—and the breakfast burrito she'd picked up on the way in this morning hadn't set well.

She moved her hand when Hanna looked up. Rested it on the counter. Resisted the urge to drum her fingers on the glass.

So what if Sam Collins had called Bowie? What the hell did that have to do with her?

"He and Neelie got married."

Peyton snorted and then quickly covered her mouth. Bellamy had taken care of Mr. Markwell, and now she was watching Peyton boldly. Tom Bockoven, her other sales person, had disappeared to the back of the store.

"Sam and Neelie?" She dropped her hand and whispered.

Eyebrows raised, Hanna only nodded.

"Oh, man." Peyton shook her head.

"That's not all." Hanna licked her lips and looked back down at the charms. "They're expecting a baby."

"Neelie." Peyton nodded. "*Neelie* is pregnant? And she's... going to...have it? Keep it?"

"I know, right?" Hanna agreed, again without meeting Peyton's eyes.

Peyton cleared her throat. She looked up as Bellamy walked by them. It hit her then. Bellamy was jealous of Hanna White, because Peyton was talking to her.

"Bellamy, this is Hanna White."

Hanna straightened up quickly and turned to Bellamy.

"Hanna, this is Bellamy Cooper."

Hanna and Bellamy exchanged somewhat stiff hellos. Peyton got it with Bellamy, but she wasn't sure what to make of Hanna's clipped tone.

"Hanna and I were friends in high school."

She noticed Hanna shoot her a quick look, but she didn't acknowledge it. Bellamy offered Hanna a tight smile and then excused herself and slipped by Hanna to get to the front door. Peyton watched her look around, like she was surveying the parking lot and then turn and head to the back of the store.

When she was gone, Peyton turned her attention back to Hanna.

"Are they living here? In town?"

"Springfield."

Peyton nodded slowly. Still no clue why Hanna had felt it necessary to come here and tell her this.

"Do you ever see anybody?"

Peyton shrugged. "I see you and Bowie now and then—"

"What? Where?"

"Here and there. The theater. Frontier Market."

Hanna opened her mouth to say something, and Peyton stopped talking. Waited for her to ask why she never spoke to them. Decided if she did, she'd tell her. She didn't speak because she didn't want to. The past was the past; they'd all moved on.

"I see her parents sometimes," she said quietly and when Hanna stared at her wide-eyed, she twisted her lips and sucked the bottom of her teeth and wished to hell Hanna would get the hell out and leave her alone. She didn't want to think about Eden. Definitely didn't want to think about her parents. They'd aged hard after Eden's death. They were a desperate looking couple, and seeing them made Peyton hurt inside.

Hanna nodded.

"Sam and Bowie..." She sighed. "Wanna get the gang together."

Something itched just under the skin of Peyton's neck and face. She figured she looked like a ghost, the blood draining from her face so quickly.

"Yeah?" She lifted one shoulder and smoothed her finger-tips over the glass. "We gonna go sit around her grave?"

She took small comfort in Hanna's pained expression.

"You don't wanna do it?"

"No." Peyton shook her head. "I don't. Ever."

"Good." Hanna nodded slowly. She tapped a puffy silver heart. "I'll take that and the bracelet."

Peyton stood frozen for a moment, trying to catch up with Hanna. Was she angry? Disappointed? Or was she *relieved*? Did she feel the same smothering dread at the thought of all of them being together again?

"Sure." She moved suddenly, and shattered the moment, and took the pillow the charm rested on from the tray. Hanna was careful not to look at her as she put the tray away, slid the back of the cabinet closed and locked it. She followed Peyton to the register. Handed her a debit card when Peyton gave her a total.

"Would you like it giftwrapped?" Peyton offered as Hanna signed the receipt. She held her breath, praying Hanna would say no.

"No." Hanna handed her the signed paper and left the pen on the counter. Peyton watched her pick up the coffee cup— if it wasn't empty, it had to be cold—and then she handed Hanna the small dove grey bag and thanked her.

Hanna offered her a quick, uncertain smile and thanks as she took the bag. Turned and beat a fast path to the front door.

"Han?" Peyton called before she could open the door. Peyton saw the way the use of her nickname hit Hanna between the shoulder blades. Slowly, the woman, once her best friend, looked back over her shoulder. "What's her name?"

"Sylvi."

Chapter 20

MALLORY

"And you don't know him?" Mallory called as she worked her fingers through her wet hair. The lukewarm water sluiced off her head and ran down over her back.

"Well."

Mallory frowned at Trevor's answer. She pulled the shower curtain back a bit and peeked out at him. He was flopped over the bed on his back. Mallory studied his bare feet for a moment and waited for him to explain.

"Well. What?" She finally got tired of waiting. Trevor lifted his head from the bed and looked at her over his bare chest, athletic shorts, and bare legs and feet.

"I know him," Trevor admitted with what appeared to be an attempted shrug. "But not that well."

Mallory considered Trevor's words as she let go of the curtain and ducked back under the water. She'd like a hot shower, but if she did that, she'd be a sweaty mess before she dressed for work. If she and Trevor were going to stick it out together, and really three months was too soon to know, she'd like to find a new apartment. Preferably one with functional air conditioning.

"So, what does that mean?" She picked up her shower gel —they'd been out of the coconut scent, her favorite, so this was lavender, and it was just okay—and squeezed some into her hand.

"I went to school with him." Trevor's voice was suddenly closer. Mallory watched his fingers gather the curtain and pull it back a bit. She lathered the gel over her arms as Trevor cocked his head to watch her. "Need some help?"

"I'm good," she answered with a grin. "So, some guy you went to school with just called out of the blue? What the hell? How'd he get your number?"

"No idea." Trevor shrugged. Mallory laughed at his struggle to keep his eyes on hers. "Before you moved in here, I hadn't watched a woman shower in years."

"And that was on TV, right?"

He grinned.

"Sure you don't need help?"

"Promise I'm good." She nodded. "Okay, so did you ask the guy—Sam?" When Trevor nodded, she continued, "did you ask him how he got your number?"

"Um." Trevor frowned. "I did. But he didn't answer me."

He scratched the back of his neck and then stood up straight, interest piqued anew, when she turned the taps to stop the water and reached for her towel.

"Mmm." He nodded his approval.

"What time do you work?"

"Go in at five."

Mallory sighed. "That sucks."

He nodded. Backed up a step to give her some room.

"So. What'd he want? I mean, why did he call?"

Trevor raised his eyebrows and shrugged. "That's the really weird thing. He said they were going to get together.

Like go out for drinks one of these nights. Asked if I...if we... wanted to go."

Mallory wrapped her towel around her chest and picked up her comb from the sink.

"Go out. Seriously? Like who's they?"

"The old gang."

"The old gang wants you to go out, and you're telling me you don't know them that well?"

"Eh. I knew them. I mean...I was like...I was friends with this guy named Davis Buckley. And so, I ended up around them because Davis hung out with them."

"Hmm." Mallory nodded. She wouldn't admit it to Trevor, but she was curious about this gang. She'd been living with Trevor for a few months, sleeping with him for a few months, and she didn't know much about him. Sure, she knew he liked salami and mustard. He was a movie guy, and he wasn't big into sports. He read now and then, so he said, and he was an artist. Usually good in bed, though Mallory was ready for the dreams and distractions to go away, so they could make love without the heaviness, the darkness always surrounding them.

What she didn't know was what music he'd listened to in high school. If she asked now, he'd list fifteen bands he liked. But he worked in a music store, for God's sake. She didn't know if he'd been a Boy Scout or who his first crush was. If he'd hung out with his dad a lot when he was a kid or if he had brothers and sisters.

"*Hmm.*" Trevor shook his head. "What does that mean?"

"I wanna go," she answered simply.

"What?"

"I wanna go."

"Why?"

Mallory squeezed past him into the bedroom. Trevor turned and watched her from the doorway as she stepped into clean panties. Dropped the towel and reached back to hook her bra.

"Well, because it's so out of the blue, don't you think?" She opened the closet door, and Trevor was suddenly out of her line of sight.

"They're assholes, Mal," Trevor announced. "Jesus, Sam was such a dick back then. I don't think you grow out of being a dick."

"Maybe you just become a bigger dick." She pulled a blouse from a hanger and started to put it on. Decided she better wait, or it would end up sticking to her before she left the apartment. Not that it would matter. It would stick to her on her walk to the bus stop. And on the bus. By the time she got to the library, it would look like it had been painted on.

"Probably." Trevor was propped in the bathroom doorway. She tossed the blouse on the bed and then slipped back by him. "So why would you wanna go?"

"Maybe I wanna see a big dick." She grinned at him in the mirror. Trevor laughed.

"You really wanna go?"

"I do."

"Wow. I thought I'd tell you this, and we'd laugh about how ridiculous it was and then forget the phone call ever happened."

"Well, now we can go out and laugh about the assholes and the big dick and forget any of it ever happened." Mallory turned from the mirror again, eyeliner pencil in hand, and stepped closer to him. Trevor stood up straight when she cupped him in her hand. "And then you can show me your big dick."

He nodded. "I like that part."

"Trev?"

"Hmm?"

"Any chance we can look at a different apartment? This place is killing me."

"Mm." He grinned as she slipped her hand inside his shorts. "I see what you're doing."

She laughed.

"Yeah." He nodded. "But the money tree's kinda bare…"

Mallory pulled her hand away. She kissed him—little peck on his lips—and backed away quickly when he reached for her.

"Money," she reminded him. "Work."

"Yeah, yeah." He nodded. She ducked out the door and watched him wander through the bedroom to the living room. Really, she wanted to get him out of this apartment because she thought it was killing *him*. What would Trevor Gerhardt be like in a different setting? At the moment, she felt stifled. As a person. As a couple. She liked Trevor. A lot. But they weren't going anywhere, and that bothered her.

"Set it up!" she yelled.

"Yep."

She grinned. Figured she'd just lost him. He would spend the rest of his day, before he went to work, stewing over the sketches and the paintings.

Chapter 21

PEYTON

Bellamy had lingered tonight long after they'd locked the doors. Tom was long gone, and Peyton had assumed Bellamy had gone, too. She'd stayed late, enjoying the quiet in the workroom. And she always enjoyed designing new pieces. She'd started playing with this idea, this line quite some time ago. Because she hadn't wanted to go home and regret what she'd done with Brion because she'd regretted what she'd done with Bellamy, tonight had seemed as good a night as any to stay later and work.

But she couldn't concentrate. Not even after she'd walked out to the showroom to make sure Bellamy had put all the trays away and locked the cabinets and the doors. Not even after she'd double-checked the parking lot to make sure Bellamy was really gone. And she'd felt stupid for that. Wasn't like she was in a movie. Bellamy might still be making moony eyes at her, but she wasn't stalking her, for God's sake.

She'd turned on some music in the workroom. First, she'd tried some Bob Seger, but she definitely wasn't in the mood for that. She'd changed it to Florence and the Machine, and while she liked it, she wasn't really in the mood for that, either. Finally, she'd switched the music off again and worked in silence for a while.

That didn't work, either.

Her mind kept wandering. To Hanna White. Neelie Collins. But mostly to Eden. Peyton knew Hanna still thought about Eden a lot; she'd seen her blog. She used to read it, but she'd quit when she realized Hanna's words always depressed her. Whether she was talking about an aunt who'd died or a guy who'd been eaten by a bear somewhere in the wilderness hundreds of miles away, Peyton always felt deflated and sad after she'd read the blog posts. And then she'd find herself thinking about Eden and everything that had happened and high school in general, and that usually made her drink. She didn't need someone else giving her reasons to drink. She found plenty on her own.

Frustrated with herself, with Hanna, Peyton leaned backwards in her chair. Dropped her head back and closed her eyes. She'd gotten better with this. In fact, mostly, she'd gotten pretty good at tucking Eden away. Forgetting those days in general. Sure, she still drank a lot, too much according to Brion, and Brion knew everything so he had to be right, but she drank to Eden without really acknowledging it.

With an exaggerated sigh—wasted, as no one was around to appreciate how put out she was—Peyton reached for her cell. Chewed on her lip as she scrolled through her text messages. Nothing new. Checked Facebook. Nothing new. She hadn't posted in a few years, other than to change her profile picture or cover photo. But she still stalked people. Sort of. Lurked. Maybe she just lurked and read other people's stuff.

Stalked.

Call a spade a spade, Peyton.

With a deep breath, she went to her contacts list and scrolled until she found Hanna's name. She only had her in her phone because her cell was connected to her Facebook account.

She stared at the screen for a moment. Realized her hands were shaking. Definitely time to close up shop for the night. She couldn't cut metal or set stones with shaking hands. She set her phone down and climbed to her feet. Jesus, was she really going to do this? After all this time?

She paced the workroom, lost in thought. Wondered what Eden would do now if she were here, and Peyton were dead and gone. Or if Hanna was gone. No, technically there was no rule against the rest of them getting together. No cops had warned them apart. No parents had suggested it best that they never see each other again. In fact, they'd all gone to the funeral. Of course.

No. No rule about not seeing each other again. Still felt wrong to her, though, to even consider it.

Peyton pushed her hair off her shoulders and rolled her head on her neck as she came back to the table. She picked up her phone. It was after seven-thirty. Hanna wouldn't answer anyway. She'd be busy putting her princess to bed. If Peyton knew Hanna and Bowie at all, and she did, they probably put the kid to bed by seven. Fed her juice and vegetables and considered candy a four-letter word.

She stared at her phone again as if waiting for a sign. She'd call. Hanna wouldn't answer. She wouldn't leave a message. That would be that.

Hanna might call back. But that left things in Peyton's control. If Hanna called, Peyton would ignore it. Simple.

She touched Hanna's name. Squeezed her eyes closed as the phone made its musical beeps to dial and then started ringing. Eyes closed, she saw Hanna's wedding picture on her Facebook page. *Talk about a princess.* Jesus, if Peyton ever got married—that was funny, right there—she'd so wear something sleek and elegant. Hanna had blown it with her wedding dress. God, the woman was like an amazon. She would have *rocked* a mermaid style dress.

Her mind jumped to Hanna in cut offs and a bikini top. A wine cooler in one hand, lit cigarette in the other. She wondered how Hanna and Bowie dealt with the past. Had they had a ceremony? Buried it? Signed a contract to pretend none of it had happened? Shook on it and then set about carving out their *perfect, healthy, in-your-face* life?

"Hey."

Peyton ducked her chin to her chest when she heard Hanna's voice in her ear. *Shit.* She'd been so sure Hanna wouldn't answer, and then she could tell herself she'd tried to contact her, and it hadn't worked out, and so she could just forget this and go back to her real life.

Such a good life.

Life, though. More than Eden had.

"Are you busy?"

"No." Hanna spoke quietly. Peyton wondered if she was in her little girl's room, tucking her in. Or if she was in the kitchen and Bowie was nearby and she was trying to hide from him the fact that she was talking to Peyton.

"Meet me at Bloody Mary's." She threw the words out before she could stop herself. The bar was actually called *Mary's*, but when they were kids, they'd all called it *Bloody Mary's*, and the guys had always tacked on countless tasteless jokes, and even now, twelve years later, Peyton could hear them all in her head. It wasn't even *Mary's* anymore. In fact, there'd probably been at least four owners in between Mary and whoever the hell ran the place now. Peyton didn't care. To her, it would always be *Bloody Mary's*.

She shivered a little in the workroom. Kind of summed up the years they hung out together.

"When?"

"Fifteen."

She heard Hanna clear her throat. Waited and wondered if she'd say no. If Bowie would flex his muscles and distract her.

"'k."

Peyton sighed and lowered her phone. Stared at it again, as if it had betrayed her and called Hanna without her help. Maybe she hadn't started this, but she'd just waded in and broken her own rules. She turned the lamp over her work table off. Told herself she'd had to do it. Hanna had come in three days ago. Peyton had been so distracted since then, she was still working on the same bit of metal that was supposed to be the bracelet that she'd been working on over the weekend. She'd had enough to drink the past three nights alone. Why not drink *with* someone for a change?

Unless, of course, the virtuous Hanna White had quit drinking.

She hesitated as she locked the door and then she wandered into the break room to get her purse. Didn't matter. She had to see Hanna again, at least, to figure out a way to exorcise the ghost.

Ghosts. Just because Eden was the only one who'd died didn't mean she was the only one to haunt Peyton.

Chapter 22

Hanna

She hadn't lied to Bowie. Not exactly. She'd told him she was meeting Peyton at Bloody Mary's. Or whatever the hell the place was called now. But she hadn't exactly been truthful about why Peyton had suddenly called, seemingly so randomly. She'd avoided his eyes, and she'd mumbled something about bumping into her the other day. Left out the coffee and donuts and bumping into her only because she'd purposely gone into Peyton's place.

Hanna chuckled again as she drove. *Peyton's Place*. No one else would think it was funny, and mostly, Hanna didn't, either. But she was desperate for a distraction from what she was doing, what was about to happen. Did Peyton have something specific to say to her? Or was she, like Hanna, drowning in memories now that the flood wall had been breached?

She hadn't been thrilled to see her; Hanna had known the cold she'd felt in the jewelry store the other day wasn't just an efficient central air unit. Peyton's hug had been a little stiff, she hadn't believed Hanna about being there to get something for Sylvi, and she'd said flat out that she didn't want to see anyone. Hell, she'd admitted that she saw Hanna and Bowie now and then and never spoke to them.

So, what the hell did she want now?

Hanna played with her iPod as she drove.

Better question. What the hell was Hanna doing? So, Peyton had called. And Hanna, rather than saying *hey, sorry, no, I can't meet you*, had jumped.

Mary's was a cavernous bar on a corner lot in what Hanna's parents would have described as the wrong part of town back when she lived at home. She'd seen that look on Bowie's face earlier, when she'd told him she was coming here. Stood for a moment, head cocked, ready for him to argue, to say she couldn't go.

Luckily, he hadn't. He'd only nodded, kissed her goodbye, and told her to be careful.

There were several cars in the lot, but the place was big enough that Hanna didn't worry it was crowded. Besides, who cared if it was? She looked around as she pushed the door closed and locked it. Tried to imagine which vehicle was Peyton's. She couldn't. There were half a dozen really nice cars in the lot, but just because Peyton's family owned a jewelry store didn't necessarily mean she drove a BMW.

Country music spilled out the door when Hanna stepped inside. Mary's had always been country, and as kids, they'd spent enough time here to know the words to Conway Twitty and George Jones songs. They'd come here because Davis had known a guy who would serve them even when they were only seventeen. He'd only served the guys, but he'd turned a blind eye to the guys giving their drinks to the girls and going immediately back for more.

Hanna supposed that had probably changed. The law was a little bit harder now on underage drinking violations and drinking and driving.

A Merle Haggard song played now, and Hanna wondered if the jukebox, if the music available on the box, was the same as had been played twelve, thirteen, even fourteen years ago. God forbid. It had been old then.

Dressed in jeans and boots and a sleeveless blouse, she felt at ease as she walked behind the blue-collar guys bellied up to the bar. She had a twenty tucked in one pocket, her cell in the other, and her car keys in hand. No one paid her a bit of attention, and she wondered if that was because she didn't particularly pay attention to any of them. Mary's had been her stomping ground, and she realized as she spotted Peyton in a booth near the back of the joint, she almost felt like she was coming home.

Would they come here? If the lot of them went out together, would they go somewhere trendy? Go out to eat? Or would they just come here and let it all hang out? Hanna wasn't sure which would be worse.

"Twenty-two." Peyton watched her slide into her side of the booth.

"I was coming from—"

"I know where you live."

Hanna stared at Peyton silently. Took in the harsh, negative vibes. Wondered again why she'd called.

"No waitresses," Peyton told her as she wrapped her fingers around her half-empty bottle of beer. There'd never been waitresses here, but Hanna had wanted to find Peyton first, before going after something to drink.

"Why'd you call?"

Peyton sat back in the booth. Worried the label on the bottle with perfect red fingernails. Hanna took in the wide silver band on her right ring finger, the skinny stacking bands on her right index finger and the big gold and green accent ring on her left hand. She skimmed over her black blouse and met her eyes.

"Why'd you come to the store?"

Hanna stared at her blankly. Had Sam called Peyton, too? She'd figured he would. Maybe that's why Hanna'd gone to the jewelry store to talk to Peyton. She certainly hadn't gone because she'd been excited about the possibilities and wanted to be the one to get everyone together. Maybe she'd just wanted to warn Peyton that Sam might call.

Peyton watched as Hanna hauled herself out of the booth again. She felt her eyes bore into her as she crossed the warped wooden floor to the bar. She asked for two beers, deciding it might be good to buy one for Peyton. Paid with the cash, dropped a buck in the jar on the counter and went back to the booth. She was unnerved to find Peyton still watching her.

Hanna noticed the tiny nod of her head as she set the beer down in front of her.

"What were you doing?"

"What?" Hanna took a long drink of her beer. She pulled her phone from her pocket and put it on the scarred table. "Hurts my butt."

Peyton snorted. "When I called. What were you doing?"

"Um." Hanna sighed. "Bowie was watching a documentary about some athlete."

"You." Peyton shook her head.

"I was reading."

Hanna decided she wouldn't tell her she was reading an essay about the Holocaust.

"What time do you put your little girl to bed?"

"Eight…eight thirty."

Peyton stared at Hanna for such a long, drawn out moment that Hanna squirmed in her seat.

"I was working." Peyton cleared her throat. "Designing a new line of metals…um…bangles…" She shrugged. "Can't concentrate."

Hanna tapped her fingers on the back of her phone. When they were kids, Peyton had wanted to be a model. When they were sixteen, she'd wanted to be a doctor. She'd been adamant that she wouldn't work with her dad. That she'd leave that to her brother.

"What happened to med school?"

Peyton stared at her silently for a moment.

"You're kidding, right?'

Hanna shrugged and shook her head. "You couldn't wait to get away."

"Like I could have handled med school." Peyton's voice was so quiet, Hanna had to lean forward to hear her. "After all of that…"

"Bowie got his degree in sports medicine."

"I'm not Bowie."

Hanna wondered what exactly she'd done to Peyton to deserve the attitude. They'd all parted company. Well. Sort of. But none of them had ever really exchanged harsh words.

"Look." Peyton rested her elbows on the table. She took a moment, rubbed her forehead and then her face and then buried her face in her hands. "I just…I don't like this. If I'd never seen you or talked to you again, I'd have been fine with that. I think about Eden, just the same as you do, and it hurts—"

"What do I have to do with Eden? With how much that hurts?"

"You just do, Hanna." Peyton rested her chin in her hand and stared at her boldly. "You all do. And I know you feel it, too. Because I've read your blog, and there've been times when I walked away from my computer thinking maybe I should just slit my wrists and end it all, because according to you, there's no hope."

"Pey—"

Peyton shook her head. "I get it. It's…how you deal. It's

your coping mechanism. Okay. Got it. I don't wanna do this. I don't wanna be sitting here with you. I don't wanna meet your kid. I don't wanna see Neelie. Don't wanna know what they're having, when she's due. I don't wanna see Davis. This is a bad idea. A really bad idea."

"I agree with you," Hanna answered simply. She saw the confusion on Peyton's face, in her cold eyes.

"Then why did you come to me?"

Hanna took a deep breath. "I don't know. I spent the weekend with Sam and Neelie, being someone I'm not anymore. Or trying to be someone I'm not anymore. And instead, I was just this half-assed version of myself, some-where between then and now. And I don't like that me. I don't like what's going on. Bowie and I are fighting about it. And I don't know if I wanted to warn you that Sam would be calling you. Or if I was looking for an ally."

"I'm not your ally."

"But we agree that this is a bad idea."

Peyton's nostrils flared a bit as she took a deep breath and then dabbed at her eyes with her fingertips. Hanna hated to see her makeup job ruined, but the tears brought Peyton down a notch.

"Does it bother you?"

Hanna pressed her lips together and turned her head just enough that she was looking at the red vinyl booth and not at Peyton.

"I mean…okay, Eden's dead, and we're not. But do you ever think about it? About that night?"

"Yeah."

"I just keep wondering…" Peyton drained her first beer. "If we're doing right by her by staying away from each other. Or if being together is the right thing to do."

"I don't wanna do right by Eden, Peyton. I don't want anything to do with this. With a reunion."

"And Bowie does?"

Hanna raised her eyebrows. "Yeah. He's made up his mind. He's in with or without me."

"Does he even know?"

Hanna bit her lip. Shook her head.

"We've never talked about it."

Chapter 23

MALLORY

They looked normal. She hadn't known what to expect. As much as she liked Trevor, she hadn't known what to expect his old friends to be like. She'd had a moment of uncertainty, well, honestly, she'd had a lot of those since the plans had been finalized. But she'd been looking forward to meeting them all too much to think too much about the fact that she would be the only outsider. The anticipation had trumped the anxiety, right up until the moment Trevor had pulled the door of The Winner's Bracket open, and she'd walked inside in front of him.

The Winner's Bracket was a trendy bar and grill; she and Trevor didn't frequent the place, but they had eaten here. Mallory's eyes jumped from the TVs around the dining area and the bar—the Cubs were on—to the patrons at the bar and then over the salad bar and finally to a table for eight, where four people were sitting and four empty chairs waited.

A blond couple—Mallory thought they looked straight out of Hollywood, with their long, shiny hair and summer tans—sat on one side of the table. The two across from them didn't appear to go together, but then how the hell would Mallory know?

The blond woman noticed them first. She offered them a tentative smile and then a half-wave and then the other woman—dark hair that fell in long, kinky curls over her shoulders—turned to look, too. That woman grinned, and Mallory felt something shift inside her. She wasn't sure if it was her stomach dropping or her stomach pushing her heart up into her throat. Didn't matter, same effect. She had a huge empty pit inside, and she felt like the women at the table could see through her now.

"Trevor?" The blonde pushed her chair back and slowly stood up. Mallory watched her unfold, stunned at how tall she was.

"Hanna."

Mallory looked up at Trevor—taller than Mallory, but shorter than the woman he'd called Hanna. She was glad she'd insisted he dress nice. He'd have refused anything dressy; Mallory wasn't sure he *owned* anything dressy. But he'd worn his best pair of jeans. New gray Vans.

Mallory watched the blonde's hands slide over Trevor's shoulders as she hugged him. Felt a tiny stitch of jealousy. Was it possible this woman knew things about Trevor that she didn't? Mostly, though, she was proud of Trevor; she liked the way his shoulders filled out the gray knit shirt he wore. The way his jeans accentuated his build. A little on the skinny side, sure, but he had six-pack abs and a nice ass.

"Where have you been for the last twelve years?" The woman drew back from him and turned to Mallory with a smile that nearly blinded her. "I'm Hanna White."

"Hanna, this is my girlfriend, Mallory." Trevor reached for her and settled his hand on her lower back. "And I've been here for twelve years."

"Hi." Hanna shook Mallory's hand enthusiastically.

Mallory wanted to like her; she seemed genuine. But again, what the hell did she know? "It's nice to meet you."

"You, too." Mallory nodded.

"You've lived here? Since graduation? Really?" Hanna looked back at Trevor. The three of them inched closer to the table. And then Mallory was being introduced to the others, and her head was swimming, and she decided she wanted a drink.

The guys did that guy thing, the half hug and half thump each other on the backs, and when the waitress appeared to get their drink orders, Mallory felt the other woman—the dark-haired one—watching her. Trevor ordered for her, and they sat down, and Mallory found herself next to Hanna. Hanna and Bowie. Married nine years. And the couple across from them—Sam and Neelie—had been married for three years. Mallory wondered if they'd all been paired up in high school. And if so, whom had Trevor dated? And why had these couples lasted, if Trevor and his girlfriend hadn't?

Mallory found herself studying Sam. She was careful about it. It was rude to stare, and she'd only just met him. Wasn't so much that he was good-looking—he was—because Bowie was, too. She was curious about Sam, though, because he'd been the one to call and ask Trevor to come.

"So, what do you do?" Bowie leaned around Hanna to ask Trevor. Mallory watched his big hand wrap around his beer bottle. Mallory sort of wished Trevor could say he was a graphic designer or that he worked in marketing at a big firm. The thought made her feel guilty; Trevor had a job. It just bothered her that he was overqualified to sell vinyl record albums.

"I work at Rewind," Trevor answered.

Hanna cocked her head and narrowed her eyes at him.

"Where's that? Is that a music shop?"

Trevor nodded. "Yeah. I do some cartooning, too. Some artwork."

"Artwork?" Neelie repeated.

Mallory felt a little puff of pride. Trevor was good; with a little ambition, he could be brilliant.

Trevor nodded again. He looked up as the waitress appeared with the bottled beers he'd ordered for himself and Mallory.

"That's so cool." Neelie raised her eyebrows. "Sounds like more fun than Human Resources."

Mallory took a healthy swallow of her beer as Neelie told Trevor she worked at a hospital near Springfield. Mallory was intrigued by the Whites, the fitness center they owned. Wondered about joining, because she felt like a puddle of lazy blob most days at the apartment she and Trevor shared. Decided she wouldn't mention that for a while.

"Where's Davis?" Trevor directed his question to Sam.

"He said he'd be a little bit late." Sam took a peek at his phone. "Had to drop his son off at his ex's on the way here."

"Son?" Hanna shook her head. "I didn't know he had a kid. I didn't know he was ever married."

"Divorced." Sam shrugged. "He and this girl had the kid when they were nineteen. They were together for a while. Broke it off. Davis still sees the kid."

Mallory noticed the frown, the troubled look on Hanna's face, though it was there and gone quickly.

"So, Davis has a ten-year-old son?"

Sam picked up his glass and stared at the contents for a moment. Mallory guessed it was Captain and Coke. He took a sip and then nodded.

"Yeah."

"He sees him a lot?" Hanna asked. She seemed concerned, but Mallory wasn't sure if it was concern for their friend or the kid.

"Yeah. Davis has partial custody. The kid's name is Connor."

"Hmm." Hanna pursed her lips. "I can't picture that."

"Tell me," Neelie agreed with a smirk. "I always thought he was gay."

"Davis?" Bowie snorted.

"Yeah." Neelie looked up quickly. "Didn't you?"

Mallory felt Trevor stir beside her. She glanced at him. He gave her a tight-lipped smile, but he didn't say anything. She reached under the table and rested her hand on his thigh. She'd only just met them, but she found it hard to connect them to the Trevor she knew.

"Um." Bowie groaned out loud. "No? I didn't...get that vibe. Did you?"

All eyes turned to Hanna.

"No. But then..." She shrugged. "Does it matter?"

"No!" Neelie laughed softly. "Not at all. I just...was surprised to hear he had a son."

"Where's Peyton?" Sam asked and again all eyes drifted to Hanna.

"Um." Hanna moved her head from side to side. Mallory shivered when she heard her neck pop. "I dunno, Sam. I don't know if she'll come. She wasn't sold on this."

"Why not?"

Mallory watched Hanna curiously. Why wouldn't Peyton be sold on hanging out with old friends? Mallory didn't know her, either, but she wondered why one of the gang wouldn't want to see the rest of them.

Hanna shot Sam a look as if to say *really?*

Sam sighed, obviously frustrated.

"Are we all gonna run from that the rest of our lives? Seriously?" He shook his head. "Would she want us to?"

Mallory jumped at the clink of glass on glass. She turned

to see Trevor reaching to set his bottle upright. A splash of beer puddled on the table between his bottle and glass.

"Hey!"

All of them looked up at the rowdy holler. A stocky guy with a receding hairline and a chip-toothed grin approached the table. He dropped his gaze to Trevor first, and before Mallory could ask if Trevor was okay, he stood up and exchanged the bro hug with the new guy.

Must be Davis, she decided.

"The gang's all here, huh?" Davis looked around at all of them and then turned to Sam with a frown. "Where's Peyton?"

"Right here."

Another long-legged, dark-haired woman appeared from behind Davis. She wore jeans that appeared to cost more than Mallory's paycheck, a black blouse, chunky silver jewelry and a look that said *let's get this the hell over with*.

"The gang *is* all here." Davis nodded appreciatively. "This is great, guys. Why the hell did we wait twelve years to do this?"

Peyton dropped into the empty chair beside Neelie. No happy hellos, no hugs, no smile. In fact, she looked miserable. Mallory looked up as Trevor sat down again and Davis shook Bowie and Sam's hands and then sat down next to Peyton.

"I'll drink to that." Sam picked up his glass again.

"Hell no!" Davis laughed. He looked around Neelie to Sam. "You gotta let me and Peyton get a drink first!"

Chapter 24

PEYTON

Dinner was awkward at best, but apparently only for her. Everyone else seemed completely at ease with each other. Peyton wasn't sure if anyone here was that good of an actor, or maybe it was more that no one else cared about what had happened when they were eighteen.

Neelie and Hanna kept up a steady stream of conversation, though Peyton would have to admit that Neelie did the majority of the talking. Job stuff. House stuff. Ob-gyn stuff. All crap Peyton would have bet money on *never* hearing come out of Neelie's mouth. If she'd had to guess back when they were eighteen what Neelie would end up doing with her life, she'd have laid money on drug-addicted run away or Vegas pole dancer. The Neelie Homemaker chattering away beside her gave her a headache.

Trevor didn't seem terribly comfortable, either, but he did talk. Mostly to Davis. Though the guys all got involved in conversation a couple of times about old times. Sam brought up the day their sophomore chem class had almost blown up the school. That had apparently tickled Trevor's funny bone, because he'd barked a pretty hearty laugh and then he'd explained to his girlfriend what had happened.

Peyton wasn't sure what to make of Trevor's girlfriend. If she'd had to predict Trevor's future back then, she'd have guessed he'd be a lifelong bachelor—he'd been a loner back then, even when he was with the group—and she might have said he'd be the guy to go postal some day and shoot up his workplace or an elementary school.

Mallory was pretty, and she talked. A lot. Happy. Well-adjusted. Not what Peyton would ever have expected for Trevor. She worked at the library, and she wrote grants and directed an adult outreach program—Peyton wasn't clear on what that involved—and she was researching starships or stars or something that involved space. Peyton had missed the explanation on that, too, and the reason for her research, but she didn't plan to ask for more information.

Her goal tonight was simply to make it through the evening and go home. And get drunk. She'd told herself she'd play it cool while she was out with the gang and reward herself when she got home. But she was already on her third beer, and she'd only nibbled at her burger, and she was going to need a lot more than three beers just to get through a few hours with these people.

Guilt warming her cheeks, she took a quick look around the table. Maybe they weren't so bad; maybe she'd built them up to be monsters in her memories. But they were part of the past, and they were connected to Eden and bad things, and she wanted nothing to do with them. *Any of them.*

"I didn't think you'd come."

She met Hanna's eyes over the table. The guys had all wandered together to the pool tables, and now she and Hanna were left at the table with their drinks. She wondered where Neelie and Mallory had gone, but she didn't want

Hanna to know she'd been zoned out for the past hour, so she didn't ask.

"I didn't, either." She leaned her elbow on the table and then propped her chin in her hand.

"What made you change your mind?"

Peyton blinked at Hanna. No idea what to say. Even if she had a reason she'd changed her mind,—and she didn't—she wouldn't share it with Hanna anyway. Finally, she shrugged.

"Can I ask you something?" Hanna leaned forward now, rested her forearms on the table. Her salad plate was pushed away to her left. Two empty beer bottles set in front of her. Peyton wondered if their waitress had gone home.

Hanna would ask even if she said no. Rather than give her a straight answer, Peyton decided to play it cool.

"What?"

"Why are you so angry with me?"

"I'm not angry with you."

"Nice try." Hanna smirked. "I felt it coming off you in waves at your store the other day."

"Maybe it's not anger, but dislike," Peyton suggested.

Hanna considered her answer and finally nodded as if to say that was okay.

"Still. We used to be friends. Didn't we?"

"Sure, Han."

"Then why the intense dislike now?"

"I told you I had no desire—"

Hanna interrupted her with a headshake. "I get that. I told you I agree with that. But this is personal. Between you and me. I can feel it."

Peyton looked around, lifted her eyes when Bowie approached the table. He leaned over to Hanna and said something quietly. Hanna rolled her eyes and shrugged. Peyton watched him walk away.

"That. Right there."

"Bowie?" Hanna snorted. "You're jealous because I married Bowie?"

"No. Been there, done that." Peyton took a drink of her beer. Reveled at the uncertainty in Hanna's eyes. "Just…your life. You. Married. Beautiful house. A little girl. Your own business."

Hanna pursed her lips. She dragged her eyes away from Peyton and studied her fingernails.

"Nice." She nodded. Her eyes met Peyton's, but she looked away immediately. "You feel the same way about Neelie?"

"I could give a fuck about Neelie." Peyton shrugged.

"What does that mean?" Hanna frowned and shook her head. "What—no. Never mind."

"Yeah? Backing down?"

Hanna sighed. "Where do you live?"

"In a loft apartment downtown."

"Sounds nice."

"It is," Peyton agreed.

"But you're unhappy?"

"I didn't say I was unhappy."

"No, but you hate me because of the life I have?"

"I don't know that I hate you, Han. I just have no desire to pick up where we left off. We have nothing in common but a bunch of dirty little secrets. We're not gonna just resurrect our friendship here over beer and salads."

"You didn't eat a salad."

Peyton laughed softly. "I do have a question for you."

Hanna waited for her to ask. Peyton twisted her bottle in circles on the table.

"What do you think Bowie would do right now? If he knew?"

Hanna took a deep breath and tried to let it out slowly, as if she wanted to hide from Peyton that her question had upset her.

"I don't really think it's that big of a deal, Peyton."

"Really?" Peyton nodded. "That's what you tell yourself? And you believe it now?"

Hanna met Peyton's eyes. The question, the memory had shaken her up. Peyton didn't care.

"This is what I'm talking about, Hanna. This is why none of us should ever spend time together again. And if you think for one second that I believe—"

"They're like overgrown boys over there," Neelie announced as she dropped into her chair beside Peyton. "Betting. They're wagering on their game of pool. I don't know about Bowie, but Sam hasn't played pool in years. They're betting quarters."

Peyton stared at Hanna, long after Hanna averted her eyes.

"Where's Mallory?" she asked Neelie.

"She was watching the guys. She's talking to someone on the other side of the bar now." Neelie shrugged. "What do you think of her?"

Neelie looked from Hanna to Peyton.

Without a word, Peyton climbed to her feet, surprised to realize she was shaking. She walked away from the table and headed in the direction of the ladies' room. Glad to find it momentarily empty, she used the first stall and then hurried out to wash her hands.

She caught a glimpse of herself in the mirror above the sinks. Still reasonably attractive, though she most definitely looked older than thirty. She huffed out a quick sigh. Wasn't so much that she hated Hanna for her life with Bowie. Just that she hated that she seemed to be the only one who hadn't been able to adjust after what had happened. Hanna wrote a blog about death, so yeah, she was maybe a little bit obsessed with death and that had to come from the accident and Eden. But Hanna had a healthy marriage and a child and *love*. Jesus, it made Peyton sick to watch her with Bowie. Even Neelie and Sam seemed happy. And Trevor had a normal girlfriend.

Why was it only Peyton who was unhappy? They'd all been there. They'd all been part of it. If she was scarred, they should be, too.

Chapter 25

TREVOR

He knew now. It had clicked into place in his gut first and then his brain. The minute Sam made that comment. When he'd asked Hanna if they were *all gonna run from it* and *would she would want them to*. He'd known exactly where the dreams were coming from, and the mystery was suddenly how he'd forgotten. How had he possibly buried that? The same way they'd buried Eden. Jesus, he should've gone to a shrink like Mallory had suggested. Probably could have been a one-shot session.

Trevor had felt like the world had just stopped when Sam asked Hanna that, when he was irritated that Peyton wasn't sure she wanted to come. In his head, everything had just stopped. The whole bar had gone silent, and his gut had twisted inside him, and his heart had sort of faltered, like it was thinking about quitting, and he'd been amazed that no one else had even noticed it. He'd nearly knocked his beer bottle over, and Mallory *had* noticed that, but then Davis had come in and the world had kicked back to life, and Trevor had thrown himself into the conversation.

And wondered what the hell it all meant. So, Eden was dead. She'd been dead for twelve years. It had been an accident.

Hadn't it?

Something about that, though, something about Eden and the accident had hung over him the rest of the night. Like darkness in his peripheral vision sliding in to blind him. Smother him. No one else seemed to notice that, either. No one else lingered on thoughts of Eden. The girls had talked house stuff; Neelie had rattled nonstop about the nursery Sam was doing for the baby. Trevor's disbelief over the whole Sam and Neelie thing had tamped down some of the lingering dread over the past, the accident, though even then, it was always just out of reach, hovering. Threatening.

The games of pool had been a little rowdy, the guys catching up. Bragging rights. Shared memories. There hadn't been time to worry about Eden, but Trevor had taken his shots with a monster at his back. He'd simply ignored it, figured it would come back to get him later in the night. He might remember Litchfield Lake now. He might remember the drunken nights there and that Fourth of July weekend, but there was something not quite right about it. The way the story was told. Something felt just a bit off, like retelling a movie plot and leaving out the twist. There was a reason his brain had been hammering at him with the dreams. Remembering Litchfield Lake wasn't suddenly going to make the nightmares go away.

The whole thing had given him a hell of a headache. Add in the beer he'd drunk, and he'd had to pull his pillow over his head this morning to block out the glare from the shaded window. He'd reached for Mal but found her side of the bed cold and empty. That had given him pause. Had he said something last night to upset her? He didn't remember arguing with her; in fact, even though he'd felt like he was dragging an iron anchor up the steps last night when they'd come home—an anchor with Eden's name on it—they'd been laughing. They'd messed around in the kitchen, just inside the door, and they'd made it half way through the living room, and then they'd stripped down to nothing and gone at it on the floor.

Fun. Playful.

He'd stretched then and rolled to his back. Heard her then. Out in the other room. He'd smelled coffee, so he'd finally braved the daylight, crawled out of bed, and ducked into the bathroom. That taken care of, he'd wandered out to the kitchen for coffee and stood watching Mallory, tapping away at the keyboard.

He'd sipped the black coffee as he crossed the living room and stood behind her. Watched her for a few moments. She'd been surfing dream interpretation sites, and so Trevor had known that she understood, too, that there was so much more to the dream and the black water.

Rather than stew over the paintings, over the sketches, Trevor had suggested they go for a walk. Mallory had agreed, decided it might be a good way to jog his memory. Get him away from the pressure to remember, from the bed he slept in when the nightmares got him, away from the canvases, away from the sketchbooks. Trevor hadn't told her he'd simply wanted to get away from it and get some fresh air. To hell with whether or not it helped jog anything loose.

They'd finished the coffee she'd made and then dressed in shorts and tees and tennis shoes. And they'd walked. They'd spent the morning walking hand in hand, though now and then one of them let go because it was just too damned hot and sweaty to touch each other. They'd gone west on Maine and looped around Tamarack Square. Watched little kids squeal and run through the fountain as their moms looked on. Slowed to walk through the farmers market, eyed home-made soaps and rugs and homegrown tomatoes and radishes. Trevor had almost suggested they buy something. The thought of a BLT with real tomato made his mouth water. But the thought of cooking in that horrid little kitchen in their horridly hot and soul-sucking apartment had kept his mouth shut. Mallory was right. They needed to do something. They needed to find a new place. Something a little less dingy but still low rent.

Hell. He should probably look for a real job. He had a college degree. Might not find something to bring in the big money, but it was probably time to buck up and get a real job and stop playing around at the music store.

"Did you like them?" He surprised himself when he spoke.

Mallory sipped from her soda glass. Eyed him thoughtfully for a moment. They'd stopped at Pop's, a corner pizza joint with delicious piping hot pizza and truly frigid air conditioning. Trevor grinned when he saw the goose bumps on Mallory's arms.

"I did." She nodded, but Trevor heard something else in her words.

"But?"

She lifted a shoulder lazily. Looked around the old building. Her eyes drifted over the small flat screen on the wall—baseball game and Mallory was anything but a sports fan—and then back to him.

"They just…" She pursed her lips. "They didn't strike me as people you'd hang out with."

"It was twelve years ago," he reminded her.

She shrugged again. "Still."

"I wasn't really that close with any of them. Maybe Davis. He and I had a few classes together. And he was tight with Sam. I hung out with them a lot, but I wasn't tight with any of them."

"Were they like that in school?"

"Like what?"

"Coupled. Like..."

Trevor watched her fidget with the napkin dispenser at their table.

"Were Sam and Neelie a thing?"

"No." Trevor shook his head. He studied the pizza between them. Three pieces left. He could kill it. Just wasn't sure how the last three pieces would ride in his gut on the walk back to their apartment. If anything, it had only gotten hotter outside since they'd come in here.

"Hanna and Bowie?"

"Nope."

"So, you were all just friends?"

Trevor pushed his glasses up on his nose and met her eyes.

"Friends...maybe with some benefits."

"Like?" Mallory raised her eyebrows. "What does that mean? Did you hook up with any of them?"

"Um." Trevor shook his head slowly. "Sort of. I know Neelie and Bowie had a really short thing."

"Wait." Mallory sat back and stared at him in surprise. "What?"

Trevor narrowed his eyes, watched a biker fly by the floor to ceiling windows at the front of the place.

"There was kind of a lot of that," he said quietly. "We drank a lot. Partied a lot."

"Does Hanna know?"

Trevor grinned and rolled his eyes. "How would I know?"

"What about Eden? What happened to her?"

Trevor frowned. He rested his elbows on the table and shoved his hands up under his glasses. Shook his head.

"Did she drown? In Litchfield Lake?"

It didn't sound right. Something about that didn't sound

right to him. But what the hell did he know? Why the hell couldn't he remember?

"I guess?" He shrugged.

"You guess?" Mallory repeated.

"I don't..." He shook his head and then rubbed his eyes. Took a deep breath and then moved his hands and looked at her, not surprised to find her watching him, studying him. "I don't...know."

"Wait." She cocked her head. "Someone died. But you don't remember...how."

"Yeah." He nodded. "Yeah, I guess."

Mallory narrowed her eyes at him, and finally, she pushed her chair back and hauled herself to her feet. They'd already paid for their lunch, but he didn't know what the sudden rush was.

"What? What're you doing?" Trevor scrambled to follow her lead.

"How far away is it?'

"Is what?" He watched her push her chair in.

"Litchfield Lake. How far is it to get to Litchfield Lake?"

"Half hour?" he mumbled. "Forty-five minutes?"

"Okay." She nodded. "Let's go."

"Go where?" he asked as he hurried after her. She pulled the heavy glass-paned door open, and Trevor followed her back into the thick heat. Within two steps, the chill of the frigid air on his skin was gone and his skin was sweat-slicked and hot.

"To the lake, Trevor. We're gonna borrow a car and plan a trip to Litchfield Lake."

Chapter 26

PEYTON

Peyton had done a mental run-through of Saturday night at least four times by Monday. Maybe it hadn't been *that* bad. In fact, she'd kinda had fun with Hanna. Not so much with Neelie, but then Peyton had never been a big Neelie fan. They had had fun when they were kids, but Neelie had been a little too rough around the edges for Peyton even then.

At any rate, she wasn't in the mood to be at work today. She definitely didn't want to have to deal with Bellamy. She didn't want to have to fire her, but she was tired of the sidelong glances and the sad, wistful little sighs Bellamy made sure she heard from time to time. Peyton stared at the metal in her hand, surprised to remember she'd almost told Hanna about Bellamy. Thank God she hadn't had any more to drink or she probably would've dumped the whole sordid story on Hanna, and then instead of sitting here thinking about Eden, she'd be regretting her confessions.

Hanna didn't seem that happy, though. Peyton was curious about that but not enough to care. Instead, she'd watched Hanna fidget with the saltshaker while she listened to Neelie talk about how perfect her life was with Sam. Peyton sure as hell didn't believe that.

Neelie and Sam lived in Springfield. To hear Neelie describe their house, it sounded like a cute little McMansion smack in the middle of a neighborhood of other cute little McMansions. Just like Hanna and Bowie's house. Okay, so Neelie hadn't said so exactly, but that's what Peyton had heard. She couldn't fathom that Neelie was married with a baby on the way and she was still single, still flailing around with single life, making the same damned mistakes she'd made when she was younger. Part of her hoped Neelie would fail, that she and Sam would split up, and that Neelie would prove to be a horrid mother. And part of her felt horribly guilty for thinking such a thing about someone she'd once considered a friend. Especially if she only felt that way because she was a failure herself and didn't want to be alone *in failure*.

Still, Neelie had been adamant when they were younger that she didn't want this life. She didn't want to be married, and she sure as hell hadn't wanted kids. And the fact that she married *Sam* really blew Peyton away. At least with Hanna and Bowie, Peyton got it. Sure, she was jealous of their life together, but not like Hanna assumed. She didn't want Bowie, she didn't necessarily need a husband, but she wanted *that life*. Someone to talk to when she came home at night, someone who paid attention to her when she did talk, unlike Brion.

Davis had aged; Peyton almost hadn't recognized him. When they were in high school, Davis had had long hair, and even though he hadn't been drop-dead gorgeous, there had been something about him that made a girl want, *need* to take a second look. Now he had a receding hairline, and he had that *spare tire* sort of look going, and he tended to repeat everything he said at least twice. But still, Peyton had kind of been glad to see him. Not like she really talked to him that much on Saturday, but it had been kind of cool to see who he was now.

She wasn't sure what to think about Trevor. She'd never known him that well when they were in school. He was Davis' friend, and he'd always been on the edge of their group, but she wasn't sure any of them—other than Davis— really knew him. Even if Hanna had made out with him at the lake, that didn't really mean anything. She wasn't even sure Hanna *had* made out with him. Eighteen-year-old Hanna White had always been somewhat of a goody two shoes, so making out with Trevor might have been just a kiss behind the house.

Trevor's girlfriend was pretty, and though Peyton hadn't really talked to her much Saturday night, she seemed nice enough. Peyton had sort of thought Mallory appeared too good for Trevor, too pretty or smart *or something* for Trevor, but then to be fair she didn't know Trevor at all these days. So, who was she to judge?

Really though, who was she to judge any of them? So what if she thought Sam and Neelie were fake? So what if she thought Davis had put on twenty pounds since high school, and that it was probably mostly from drinking, and so what if she thought Bowie was a bit heavy-handed with Hanna? Peyton lived alone, and within the last month she'd fucked Bellamy and Brion both, as a way to chase both of them out of her head. She was no expert on relationships. She could set you up with the right diamond ring, but she was pretty damned short on marital advice.

The bracelet was flawless, though Peyton had no memory of doing anything after cutting the metal. She studied it carefully as sounds of Kenny G's sax filled the workroom. She wondered what Tom and Bellamy would say, what her customers would say if she changed the easy-listening music to something harder. Something screamy and dark that would match how she felt inside right now.

She set the silver bracelet on the table and then pushed her stool back far enough to stand. She'd been at it for well over two hours, and the crick in her back hurt when she stood up straight.

It bothered her, though, that no one had talked about Eden. No, there wasn't any easy way to slip her name into the conversation. No one wanted to put a damper on the night out and say *hey, remember our dead friend*? But *shouldn't* someone have done just that? Shouldn't someone have *mentioned* her, said her name a few times? Even if they didn't talk about what had happened—and sometimes Peyton wanted to know *exactly what had happened*—shouldn't they at least remember her? She'd been a little bit like Trevor, just sort of on the periphery of their group. She'd sort of strad-dled them, the line they'd drawn around themselves. Some days she seemed to like being around them, seemed to want to be included. Some days, she'd appeared self-absorbed and too busy for them.

As the person who'd introduced her to the group, Peyton felt responsible for remembering her. Which was a long way from feeling guilty for her death, and Peyton had shoul-dered that for a long time after it had happened. Several thousand dollars and hours and hours wasted with a shrink, she'd finally had to forgive herself and move on. Her father had made it clear the money stopped when she'd turned twenty, and so Peyton had folded up the guilt and swal-lowed it. Chased it with the first of many swallows of alcohol.

If only she'd known then that it would creep back up her throat—the guilt and the heartache—how often she'd have to swallow it, to chase it with wine or sometimes even whisky, and that no matter who held her when she slept, she was always going to dream about her friend drowning in Litch-field Lake.

Her shrink had suggested more than once that perhaps Eden had taken her own life. Her death had been ruled an accident, but neither explanation made any sense to Peyton. How did a person just walk into a lake and drown? When human instinct was to fight? To survive? Suicide was a hard business; Peyton had tried it once or twice, and no matter how resolved she thought she was to end it, she always fought her way back to life. Couldn't imagine Eden just deciding that particular Fourth of July was the right time to do it and then walking into a lake and breathing in and dying.

Chapter 27

HANNA

They'd kissed and made up after Saturday, since it was over. Except in her head, Hanna reserved the right to still be pissed off, because how can something be over when it was really just beginning? Hanna knew Bowie had talked to Sam since Saturday, and much to her surprise, Peyton had texted yesterday. It had been a harsh text about Neelie and the baby and how Neelie would handle the two AM feedings, and Hanna had laughed even though she'd wondered at the same time what Peyton might have said about her behind her back.

She didn't want to think that. She and Peyton had been best friends in high school, and even though they'd lost touch through the years, whenever Hanna thought of a best friend —the *concept* of a best friend—she automatically thought of Peyton Kelly. Maybe that was stupid, immature on her part. Maybe married people didn't have best friends except for their spouses. Wasn't that what the rules said, married people were supposed to be best friends with their spouses?

She wondered, though. About Peyton. What sorts of nasty things Peyton had said about her and Bowie. She wondered, too, about that comment Peyton had made at the bar Saturday night. About Bowie. *Been there done that.* What the hell did that mean? *Peyton and Bowie? Seriously?* Why had Peyton never told her that? She wasn't sure she believed it, but if she decided to, she wasn't sure what she was going to think about it. She thought it was probably going to bother her.

As much as she'd enjoyed playing hooky last week when she and Bowie had been at odds with each other, as much as she'd enjoyed that little bit of freedom, she was back at work now. Back in the room with her spin class. With the same people she'd been hanging with every weekday morning for the past couple of years. Sure, she got new people in now and then, and of course, she lost a few to other forms of exercise and other gyms, and some just plain quit working out. She saw those people sometimes at the movies or the grocery store. It amused her the way some of them tried to duck and hide from her, as if she was going to scold them for quitting. Some of them didn't dodge her; instead, they were almost aggressive with her, in her face explaining why they'd stopped coming.

Hanna liked some of them, and she missed some of them, but she wasn't one to rail at anyone for skipping spin or aerobics. She wasn't going to berate anyone for the extra butter on their popcorn or for deciding the fitness center was too expensive. That was Bowie's gig.

Mostly, it felt good to be back on the bike. It felt good to feel the burn in her legs and to rev her heartbeat up and feel something other than the all-consuming dread that she'd been mired in since Bowie had first told her Sam had called. The class was a great excuse to pound the music loud, and she'd put together a new playlist Monday night, gone with some new hard rock, and that felt really good. It was nice to talk to Marj Kassidy, whose daughter was getting married in

October, (that's why Marj was faithful about coming to class. Had to look good in the mother of the bride dress!) and it was fun to talk to the college girls who came to class looking a little bit like they hadn't showered after the last class they'd come to, and Hanna wouldn't admit it to Bowie or anyone, for that matter, but she kind of liked flirting with Jarret Bridges, the retired cop who had become a regular in her class. She didn't care if he was in his sixties, he was sexy like Sam Elliot, and it was obvious he liked flirting with her, too.

She was just as bad. As Bowie. And Sam. She wanted nothing to do with any of this, and yet, when Peyton had called her last week, she'd dropped everything and gone to meet her at Bloody Mary's. She'd clicked on the links Neelie had sent her and then emailed back and *oohed* and *awed* appropriately at the baby furniture and bedding. She'd answered Peyton's text yesterday with a simple LOL, because talking behind Neelie's back felt even more ridiculous and immature than referring to Peyton Kelly as her best friend when they were thirty years old and should be above junior high behavior.

She found herself watching Bowie more closely now. Wondering if he'd been with Peyton at some point in their teenaged lives. Okay, so they hadn't dated when they were younger. They hadn't become involved until after high school, and they'd both agreed that none of that mattered. They'd both been involved with other people, and it was all in the past. Except if he'd fucked her best friend and neither of them had told her, that kind of mattered.

Of course, when she thought about it, when she obsessed over it in the middle of the night, in the middle of sex, it was the now Peyton and Bowie she was seeing in her head, not the teenagers. That made it worse. Hell yes, that made it worse. And yeah, okay, she'd sort of messed around with

Trevor, but she hadn't actually done it with him. And besides that, Trevor and Bowie weren't best friends.

Sam. That was a whole other story, and not one Hanna ever cared to tell Bowie. But it was different.

"What's wrong?" Bowie asked without lifting his gaze from the iPad between them.

"Hmm?" Hanna stirred to life and picked up her juice glass. She drained it in one more swallow and then slid off her tall chair.

"You've been staring at me since we sat down. Like I'm reading an article on the benefit of fatty oils, and you're reading me."

Hanna opened the dishwasher and set her glass in the top rack. She looked back at Bowie, surprised to find him watching her. With a frown.

"Nothing's wrong," she lied. Lying was becoming easier. She didn't like it. She hated it, really, but more than lying, she hated fighting. And if she brought it up again, the whole Sam thing, or if she asked him about Peyton, chances were, she'd start a fight. They'd had a nice evening with Sylvi, and the morning had been calm, and she didn't want to throw things off and start another day badly.

"You sure?"

"Yeah." She nodded. Washed her hands at the sink and then walked over to him as she dried them on a maroon dishtowel. She leaned in and kissed him.

"I read your last blog post," he told her. Her heart sort of dropped a bit. She'd been careful to avoid an argument and now he was diving in headfirst, surely to piss her off.

"Yeah?" She lowered her gaze from his eyes to the towel in her hands. "And?"

She felt his shrug; she was pressed up against his side, and she flicked her eyes up to meet his and then looked away quickly.

"I liked it." He sounded surprised. Maybe as surprised as she was.

"Really?"

"Yeah. Life after death is interesting, I think."

"Do you?" She backed away from him and tossed the towel back to the counter. "Sylvi. You ready, sweetie?"

"Just a minute, Mommy!"

Hanna glanced at her daughter. She was on the sofa, leafing through a picture book.

"I don't know if I believe in it, but I think it's interesting to think about," Bowie told her.

"So, you might think that everyone who dies is just... dead? Forever? Forgotten?"

Bowie tapped the home button on the iPad and stood up. They had to be at the center in a half hour. Bowie liked to be there early. Like twenty-eight minutes before they had to be there, if at all possible. On Thursdays, the doors opened at seven, and his first class started at seven thirty.

"I dunno." He pursed his lips and flipped the cover of the iPad closed. Hanna wanted to look at him, to watch his face. But that sort of felt belligerent, like she was challenging him. She hated that. Used to be they could look each other in the eye when they talked, but lately, it felt wrong, and Hanna always thought she saw amusement or anger in Bowie's eyes, and apparently, he saw something he didn't care much for in hers. He lifted his leg and propped his foot on his seat. Tied his shoe. "You really think people go to heaven or hell? You think Eden's up there watching us?"

She bit her lip because she wanted to tell him to fuck off. Bowie hadn't ever been sold on Eden. True, she'd only just started hanging out with them and none of them knew her that well. But that didn't mean her dying was okay. That they should all make a joke of it, of her.

"Okay, Mommy." Sylvi appeared at her side, the picture

book dangling from her left hand. She slipped her free hand into Hanna's and peered up at her with a smile. "I'm ready to go."

Hanna nodded. She wanted to ask Bowie what he would think if his mother passed away. Would she just be a dead body, decomposing in a grave six feet under in St. Luke's cemetery? Or would his beloved mother live on in another realm? What if, God forbid, something happened to Sylvi? Would he go through the process of a funeral and a burial and then just dismiss her? Or would Sylvi be a sweet little angel?

Why did he have to say that? Why had he plucked Eden's name from nothing and thrown it in her face that way?

"Why do you have to be such a dick about her?" She thought she spoke quietly, but Sylvi tugged on her hand. Hanna saw a flash of emotion on her husband's face—she was surprised that it looked more like guilt than anger—and then she looked down at Sylvi.

"What does it mean that Daddy is a dick?"

Hanna felt a whoosh of her own guilt flare inside. She was glad Bowie turned away from them. He headed out of the kitchen through the back door. Hanna squatted down in front of Sylvi and met her big eyes.

"That was a really bad thing for Mommy to say," she told Sylvi. "And I'm sorry."

"Are you mad at Daddy?" Sylvi's eyes grew wide with fear, Hanna supposed. Sort of made her feel good that she and Bowie fought so rarely, it scared Sylvi to see or hear something so mild. Kind of made her feel bad for scaring her little girl.

"I'm kind of sad at Daddy," Hanna answered simply.

"Why?" Sylvi leaned into her. "Why, Mommy?"

Hanna smiled, in spite of the bad feelings, the dread that

had just slipped back through her stomach. She kissed the tip of Sylvi's nose and shook her head.

"Nothing for you to worry about, Sylvi," she promised.

"Is it because Daddy didn't brush his teeth this morning?" she whispered dramatically.

Hanna grinned. "Yep. That's it."

"I brushed mine," Sylvi swore. Hanna stood and then leaned over to pick Sylvi up. She tossed her over her shoulder and carried her to the door. Bowie was waiting in the driver's seat of the SUV. "So, you can't call me something bad, Mommy."

Chapter 28

PEYTON

At least she'd had a few minutes to change after work before she'd heard the knock on her door. It irritated her. It was the only thing she didn't like about her apartment; people could come in off the street and come upstairs unannounced. Sure, the door had a deadbolt, and when she was home, Peyton kept the deadbolt flipped. But still. Who knew what sort of person might wander up the steps one day?

Like Brion.

Well, *not like Brion*. He was a pain in the ass, and he'd been coming around again after the other night. But a stranger. Any stranger could walk up those steps and knock on the door.

She should check the peephole. She didn't. It was five-thirty. Broad daylight. Not that women weren't assaulted or worse in broad daylight. But she couldn't be bothered to worry about it now. Glass of wine in hand, she flipped the deadbolt and turned the knob, assuming it was Brion and wondering if she would send him away empty-handed again or if she'd fuck him first.

"Hanna."

Curious that she hadn't made up her mind about what she would tell Brion and now she was staring at Hanna and feeling a knife of regret that it wasn't him. She didn't even like him. *Did she?* She liked his body; she'd always liked his body. But he wasn't particularly nice, and things had gotten so bad between them.

"Is this a bad time?" Hanna sounded uncertain.

Peyton considered saying yes. Just to make her squirm. Just to see what she would do. But she shrugged and took a step back.

"No."

Hanna, dressed in denim capris and a gray tank with a red blouse over it, hedged inside, as if she thought Peyton might close the door on her and smash her leg or her ass.

"I wasn't sure you'd be home."

Peyton raised her eyebrows. "How'd you find me?"

"Phone book." Hanna shrugged.

"We close at five."

Hanna nodded. She looked around the spacious room. Peyton noticed her eyes lingering in certain spots. The kitchen bar. The sofa. The window. The ugly view.

"It's nice."

"Does this mean I get to show up unannounced at your house?"

Hanna cut her eyes back to Peyton.

"Like you'd want to."

Peyton blinked. With her hair pulled back in a tight ponytail, Hanna looked all of eighteen right now. Just a touch of makeup. Big-ass diamond and wedding ring on her finger.

She sighed and led Hanna to the kitchen bar.

"Wine?"

"Please." Hanna set her purse on the counter. Peyton glanced at her hands, watched her set her keys next to her purse. Wondered where her phone was. No one went anywhere without a phone anymore. The nail on her index finger was considerably shorter than the rest, though it was painted the same responsible gray as the rest of them.

Hanna wrung her hands and then stopped suddenly and dropped them to her sides when she realized Peyton was watching her.

"I hate this."

Peyton looked away, guilty to be caught staring. She picked up the bottle of cabernet and then turned her back to her.

"What?" Peyton asked. She cleared her throat. "What do you hate?"

She reached to get a wineglass out of the cabinet but looked over her shoulder when Hanna didn't answer right away. Their eyes met, and Peyton quickly turned back to the wine. Wine, she could handle. People not so much.

"Coming here."

Peyton laughed softly. She pulled the cork from the bottle and poured the wine.

"Then why are you here?" she asked as she turned and handed Hanna the glass. Her fingers brushed Hanna's. The skin to skin contact sent a weird jolt through her. Not sexual. More like a flash of nostalgia. No particular memories, just the feeling of rainy days and popcorn and best friends.

Hanna sighed. Gulped some wine and then stared at Peyton silently for a moment. Peyton waited her out.

"A month ago, I was happily married." She shrugged. "A month ago, I was all about Bowie and Sylvi. I liked the gym. I love the people who come to our gym."

"No, you weren't." Peyton gave Hanna a tiny shake of her head. She slipped past her and moved to stand by the picture window.

"Excuse me?"

Peyton leaned on the window. Wondered if it bothered Hanna. If watching Peyton by the window gave her vertigo. It had driven Bellamy to distraction. She ignored the view. The alleyway. Searched the dry red for what to say. For words to send Hanna running. For the reason why she hadn't already done so. The wine offered her nothing, so she turned her back to the window and watched Hanna watching her.

"What about the blog?"

"What?"

"You can't sell me on your perfect life. Not when you write a blog about death."

Hanna waited for her to go on, but Peyton only stared at her.

"But it was perfect enough." Her words were little more than a whisper. "It was just right for me."

Peyton bit her lip. Let the wave of hatred roll over her.

"Lucky you." She pursed her lips. Took another drink and looked back at the window. It was cloudy; rain had threatened all day, but so far, the streets and sidewalks were dry. It was miserably hot. The humidity of August had come early this year. Peyton figured Hanna's lush green grass would be dry and brown long before July rolled around.

"And now…" Hanna tossed her hands up, barely managing to keep from spilling her wine.

"And now what?" Peyton moved again. She put her glass on the coffee table and then knelt on the sofa. Leaned against the back of it and watched Hanna. "Trouble in paradise?"

"You'd like that, wouldn't you?"

Peyton considered Hanna and Bowie. In a way, she understood what Hanna was saying. Life hadn't been perfect here in her loft apartment, but it had been *her life*. And now her life was connected again to the gang, and it felt ugly and mismatched, and she hated it.

She shrugged in response to Hanna's question. Honestly,

she didn't give a fuck about Hanna and Bowie, one way or
another.

"There's just this…" Hanna paced the length of the room.
"Bad vibe…under everything. Now. Like…Bowie and I
can…" She shrugged helplessly. "Ride to work together, same
as always. Fix dinner. Talk about our day over dinner. Talk
about a movie we want to see. Worry about the bills or pick
up groceries or read to Sylvi at night, but there's just something…bad…in the house. And I feel like I'm more attuned to
that than I am to my family."

"That's a little dramatic, don't you think?" Peyton arched
an eyebrow at her.

Hanna perched on the edge of the couch. She reached
over to set her glass down and then propped her elbows on
her knees and rubbed her forehead.

"I don't want…Sylvi…" She looked at Peyton. "To know.
About…us. About what Bowie and I used to be."

"You don't want Sylvi to know you were teenagers once?
That you smoked and you drank? That you listened to rock
and roll, and you got high and you slept around? Is that what
you're saying?"

Hanna sighed impatiently.

"Because you're the paragon of virtue. Right?" Peyton
lifted a shoulder suggestively. "You really think you're the
only parent out there who feels that way? You really think
your parents were perfect when they were kids?"

"What about Eden?" Hanna's voice was sharp.

"It was an accident." Peyton felt a niggling sensation at the
back of her neck. She hated herself for saying it.

"Was it?"

Peyton looked quickly at Hanna, only to find her staring
out the window. She wasn't waiting for an answer.
Thank God.

"This is familiar," Hanna whispered. "I didn't wanna do

this at all. And now here I am…coming to you…because you're familiar. Again." Hanna glanced at her. "Already."

Peyton, pinned in place by Hanna's stare, finally gave in with a small nod.

"I know."

"I don't want to…need this," she continued. "It's been Bowie and me and Sylvi for a long time. I don't want that to change."

Peyton drew her knee up to her chest and circled her arms around her leg.

"I've been alone for a long time, Hanna," she mumbled. "It's really hard to…" She shook her head.

Hanna looked around again. Picked up her glass and settled back into the sofa.

"You live here alone?"

Peyton nodded.

"I assumed…" Hanna raised her eyebrows.

"I lived with a guy for a few years." Her lips were moving before she could stop herself. "And then I realized I didn't want…" She glanced at Hanna, wide-eyed, and shrugged. "I didn't want to be with him. I don't love him. I don't know that I ever did."

"Who was it?"

"You don't know him." Peyton avoided a direct answer. "His name is Brion. Uptight. Pretentious. Eye candy."

Hanna winced.

"You weren't married?"

"No." Peyton rested her chin on her knee. "I don't need marriage. This…" She looked around the living room. "This is good. I like it here."

"It's beautiful."

"Do you…." Peyton took a deep breath. She couldn't believe she was about to ask this. Because she wasn't sure she cared, and if she did, she wasn't sure why. And because

Hanna might tell her to fuck off. "Do you have pictures? Of your daughter?"

Hanna looked up from her examination of her fingernails and stared at Peyton. She blinked. Nodded. Peyton sat frozen in place, waiting for Hanna to tell her to go to hell.

"Yeah." She cleared her throat. Nodded again. "Um." She climbed gracefully to her feet, and Peyton had a flash of memory. Of Hanna on her stomach on a blanket, propped on her elbows. Climbing with ease to her feet and rushing the lake. Shrieking with delight as she jumped from the dock and then laughing outrageously as she hit the cold water.

She wondered what *Spin Class Hanna* looked like.

"Bowie…" She said it as if she were beginning a long story. Peyton twisted on the sofa to watch her go after her purse and then carry it back to the sofa with her. She unzipped it—a black Coach bag—and pulled an iPhone from an inside pocket. "Thinks we need to have another baby."

"And you don't?" Peyton asked.

Hanna pressed her lips together as she scrolled through the photos on the phone.

"I did," she admitted. "I mean…I do…but…" She looked at Peyton suddenly, making her feel almost naked. Peyton made a face, hoping to indicate unmeasured levels of disdain for the whole conversation. "I don't wanna do that…while *this* is going on."

"This," Peyton repeated.

"This. The *let's all go out and have a drink* thing." Hanna sighed. "And then I sort of feel like now that this is happening, it's not gonna end."

"So." Peyton took the phone from Hanna when she stretched her hand out. "None of us…are good enough…to be around your precious kid."

Hanna's eyes were a little bit glassy.

"It's not about you being good enough." She shook her head.

"Then what is it about?"

"You all know my secrets," Hanna whispered.

Peyton studied the picture of the little girl with big blue eyes and big curly hair.

"Oh my God." She swallowed hard. The kid was adorable. "Those secrets have been buried twelve years, Hanna."

Hanna nodded. "I know. But we're all back together. All we gotta do is buy the shovels."

"So she finds out you aren't perfect." Peyton shrugged. "She is. She's…cute."

"I don't want her to make the same mistakes I did."

"She will," Peyton answered simply. "It's what people do. Fuck up. Start over."

Maybe there were other pictures of the kid on the phone. Maybe other friends would scroll through them. Peyton handed the phone back to Hanna and let her hand fall to the couch.

"Yeah. People do?" Hanna looked around the apartment pointedly and then turned back to Peyton. She cocked her head and shrugged her eyebrows. "What kinda mistakes do you make to get this life?"

Chapter 29

TREVOR

"I don't wanna do this." He shook his head.

"Of course, we're doin' this." Mallory shrugged and gestured to the car. "I borrowed a friend's car for the day. We're doing this."

"What'd you tell her? Karla? Why we needed her car?"

"That we were going to have a picnic."

"A picnic?" Trevor laughed. He shook his head again and eyed the Monte Carlo like it was a vicious animal, and it posed a threat to his and Mallory's security. "A picnic. You didn't tell her we were driving to Litchfield Lake to investigate the root cause of your boyfriend's nightmares?"

Mallory laughed and rolled her eyes. "C'mon. That sounds so dramatic." She pulled the keys from her pocket. "You wanna drive? Or do you want me to?"

Trevor frowned and hung his head. He rubbed his neck for a second and then shrugged. "You can."

"Yeah? Okay." Mallory hurried out into the street and opened the driver's door. "I'm kind of excited about this. I haven't taken a road trip in ages."

"A road trip to a lake where someone died."

"A lot of people have probably died in a lot of lakes around the country, Trev. C'mon."

Trevor sighed. He looked around again. Wondered how in the hell Mallory had gotten off work on a Friday. On a Friday when he wasn't scheduled to work. He crossed the sidewalk and then leaned over to open the passenger door.

"It's too hot for a picnic," he complained.

"We don't have to picnic," she told him. "Quit whining."

"Mal. I don't know if this is a good idea."

In the car, Mallory turned to him and stared at him silently for a moment.

"You're really upset about this."

"I thought we could go look at this apartment I read about in the paper yesterday." He shrugged. Reached out to fiddle with the stereo. When she didn't answer him, Trevor glanced at her.

"I thought you wanted to get to the bottom of this. Get past the dreams. The obsessive drawing."

"'s not obsessive," he argued half-heartedly. Sighed and dragged his eyes away from hers. "I do, Mal. I'm just..."

"It's okay to be scared."

"Not scared..." He watched two older guys wander down the sidewalk, paper coffee cups in hand. Wondered who they were. Where they were going. "Just...uneasy."

"I mean, you might...remember...something bad." From the corner of his eye, he saw her shrug. "I don't know how you could remember something that isn't bad. The way this is bugging you—"

"'s not bugging me."

"Trev. The dreams have been going on over a month now. That's like a giant red flag that something bad happened at that lake. And if someone died, then I'm guessing that something bad had to do with that girl's death."

Trevor leaned back on the passenger seat and closed his eyes.

"Sounded like a really nice apartment."

She laughed softly.

"That's not fair."

"I liked her."

Mallory started the car, mumbled a thank you to her coworker and friend, Karla Simmons, when it fired up instantly. They were both dressed casually. Shorts and tees. Flip flops. But it was still hot, and the interior of the car was hotter, and Mallory looked in the rearview mirror. Trevor figured she was checking to see if her makeup was melting off.

"The girl? That died?"

Trevor nodded.

Mallory adjusted the air conditioning vents and then reached back to put her seatbelt on.

"Like…she was cool? Fun? Or you liked her…like a girl?"

"Like a girl," he admitted. He opened his eyes and rolled his head on the seat to find her looking at him again.

She nodded. Looked away. Put the car in gear and then looked over her shoulder before pulling out into the sparse traffic.

"You hooked up with her?"

Trevor heard the strained nonchalance in her question. Wanted to reassure her that nothing had happened. And nothing *had* happened with *Eden*. He'd been pushing himself since last Saturday, trying to remember everything about that Fourth of July weekend. Trying to remember what had happened to Eden. He knew nothing had happened between them. She'd hardly given him the time of day. And he remembered being with Hanna. Messing around with her. Thinking maybe it wasn't so bad, because she was pretty hot, and she had great tits, and she'd been more than willing to let him put his hands on them. And that even when he was touching Hanna, he'd wanted Eden.

"No."

"But someone."

"Does it matter?"

He winced. No reason to growl at Mallory about any of this. None of it had anything to do with her.

"You know what? I wasn't a virgin the first time we had sex, Trev. I had a life, too."

"What's that supposed to mean?"

"I just don't get why you're being all secretive about it. Like you have this past to hide. So, you were doing it with someone from high school out at that lake." She shrugged. Cut her eyes at him and then looked back at the street. She'd rounded Tamarack Square, and she was now ready to turn left onto Fifth Street to head to Broadway. "Not telling me about it makes it seem like it was a big deal to you."

Trevor raised his eyebrows when she looked at him again.

"Was it?" she asked when he didn't say anything.

"Was it what?"

"A big deal?"

"No." He lifted his hands and scrubbed them over his face and then over his hair. "No. I hooked up with Hanna, Mal. We messed around."

He watched out his window as the light turned green and Mallory waited for a gap in traffic to make her left turn. People were scattered over the downtown sidewalks; some dressed for business and some dressed as casually as he and Mallory. He wondered where they were all going. Wondered why he'd let himself become such a waste. He had a college degree that he'd worked his ass off to get, and he worked part time in a record shop. He played for money, and just a little bit of money at that. Mallory was right. He had to get this lake thing figured out. No matter if it was a huge mystery or just something little nagging at him, he had to get it figured out and then he had to grow up.

Without looking, he turned the stereo up a bit. Nodded along to the beat of a Carly Rae Jepson song. Finally realizing Mallory hadn't said anything about his confession, he whipped his head around to look at her.

"What?" She kept her eyes on the road.

"What?" He shrugged. "You didn't say anything."

"About what?"

"About Hanna. You ask, and so I tell you, and now you're pissed."

"I'm not pissed."

"You're something."

"I'm not."

"Mallory."

She sailed through several green lights, all the better to ignore him and keep her eyes on the road. Finally, at Twenty-Fourth, she slowed at a yellow light and turned to look at him.

"She's gorgeous."

She looked away quickly, but Trevor heard it in her voice. The little twinge of green. The insecurity. If Trevor were painting it, he'd make that a shade of yellow.

He shrugged. "She's pretty. I'm not with her. I'm with you."

"So, did you guys—? Did you have sex?" Mallory drove with her right hand on the bottom of the wheel.

"No."

"No?"

"Um." He cleared his throat. "She didn't want to."

"But she gave you a blowjob. Right?"

He refused to answer her.

"So, this gorgeous blond chick gave you a blowjob, and she's not even who you wanted to be with that weekend."

"We were eighteen, Mal."

"Does her husband know?"

"How the hell would I know? I swear to you; I haven't seen any of them since that weekend. I didn't even sit with them at Eden's funeral."

"How'd she die?"

"She drowned."

"Like…what? She didn't know how to swim?"

Trevor dropped his head back on the seat and shrugged. "I don't know. We were all in the lake early that day. Swimming. So, yeah. She knew how to swim."

"Then how did she drown?"

"I don't know."

Mallory licked her lips. "We should've looked at that apartment."

Trevor twisted around in the seat to look at her.

"Seriously? You're mad. You're mad at me for telling you what you wanted to hear."

"She's intimidating, Trev!" she snapped. "They all were."

"They don't mean anything to me, Mallory. You do."

Chapter 30

MALLORY

She wasn't mad. Not really. She just didn't want to think about Trevor messing around with Hanna White. She kind of thought it wouldn't bother her if he'd admitted to hooking up with Neelie or Peyton, but she knew better than that. It was one thing to think of his past relationships when they were just nameless, faceless girls. Something else entirely when the relationships—even if they lasted thirty minutes or less—had faces, bodies, like Hanna White's.

It was stupid to get worked up over it, and she knew it. She fought the gnawing feeling in her stomach as she drove. Trevor didn't need this right now. He was pale and sweaty, even with the air conditioning vents blowing right at him. It was possible, even likely, that he might remember something bad when they were at the lake. Or that the visit would jog something loose and he'd remember it later tonight, when they'd come home. He needed her support now, not a jealous, whiny girlfriend.

He punched the stereo buttons constantly, and the abrupt changes in music made her crazy. But she counted each time he did it—sometimes she didn't make it past two—and watched the scenery out the window. A hot and humid Illinois June didn't make for beautiful scenery, but at least it kept her relatively calm.

When she slowed the car and turned onto a hard-packed gravel road somewhere outside of town—she'd lost track of where they were and let Trevor direct her, though he kind of seemed to be on auto-pilot, too—he sat up straight, as if his spine was made of steel. Swung his hungry gaze back and forth, apparently swallowing the details of their surroundings.

Remembering.

He didn't say anything, but Mallory took a peek at him a time or two as she eased the car farther down the gravel road. A thick canopy of trees hung over the one-lane path, shading them from the sun. Mallory eyed the thick undergrowth at the side of the road suspiciously. What if there were snakes out there? She shivered, hoped Trevor didn't notice.

"So." Her voice was loud in the car; Trevor had turned the music down, which was testimony to how freaked out he was. Trevor bled sound; he needed music to live. "Whose lake is this? I mean, there's a house here. So, I assume it's private property?"

Trevor, leaning forward now, ducked to see out from under the sun visor he'd flipped down at some point on the drive. Sweat beaded on his upper lip and his neck. Mallory had been hot when they'd first taken off, sure, but she was fine now. Actually, she was cold. Her bare toes were numb. She wished she had socks and tennis shoes on.

She glanced out her window again, peered at the underbrush. Of course, there were snakes out there. Perfect environment for snakes. She curled the toes of both feet, dreading the moment she had to get out of the car.

"Yeah." Trevor nodded without looking at her. "It's...um. Sam's uncle. Or his great uncle. Or something."

Mallory pursed her lips.

"You ever meet him?"

"No." Trevor rested his elbows on his knees. Shoved his glasses up from his nose and rubbed his eyes. "There was never anyone out here but us."

"So, no one's gonna greet us with a shotgun? When we get outta the car?"

Trevor snorted. "Well, I hope not."

"Yeah, me too," she mumbled.

"Here."

"What?"

"That road."

Mallory slowed the car to a stop. She eyed the *road* Trevor had pointed at and looked back at him.

"That's a road?"

"Mm-hmm."

"You're sure?"

"Yes. It's the fourth left from the first turn off. I've been counting."

"Trev, I'm not sure a skateboard would fit on that...road. I'll scratch the hell out of Karla's car if I try to drive through all that."

Trevor dropped his hand on her thigh and leaned over to see out her window.

"Mm." He made a *tssk* sound as if to show his irritation with the landowner for the lack of upkeep. "You wanna walk?"

She opened her mouth to tell him hell no, she wasn't going to walk. For one thing, she had cheap flip flops on. Trevor, at least, wore sportier, sturdier flip flops. His feet might last a little longer than hers.

But if she said no, they'd turn around and go home.

They'd have put a bunch of miles on a borrowed car—granted, it wasn't a Rolls Royce, but it belonged to Mallory's friend—only to chicken out and leave any answers they were looking for here, untouched.

"Sure." She shrugged.

Trevor, still leaning over her, turned his face to her and arched his eyebrows.

"Really?"

"Yeah. Let's do it."

He took a deep breath. Dropped a quick kiss on her mouth and then moved back to his side of the car.

"Okay." He attempted enthusiasm, but Mallory could still see the terror on his face. She eased the car over, halfway off the gravel road. Turned the keys and pulled them from the ignition. She stared at her door handle, aware that Trevor had opened his door and was turned to climb out of his seat.

"What?" he asked her.

She shook her head without looking at him. Of course, she'd pulled to the wrong side of the road, so his side was to the road and she was going to step out into tall, thick grass and weeds.

She cleared her throat and chirped *nothing*, and then she opened the door and climbed out before she could talk herself out of it. She hurried through the weeds to the narrow side road Trevor had told her to take.

At least it hadn't rained lately, so they weren't going to slosh through any mud puddles. Small comfort. Trevor reached for her hand as they walked, and she tried to hide a shiver of dread as she snuggled up to him.

"You feel like an ice cube." He looked at her with a small grin.

She answered with a one-shouldered shrug.

"So." Their eyes met, but she looked away quickly.

Glanced at their feet. Coast was clear so far. "Did you guys come up here a lot?"

"Mmm." He sighed. "Yeah, I guess. We'd come up here and just...hang out. Most of the time, it was just us guys. We'd cut seventh hour and grab a cooler of beer and come up here. The girls came up a few times. And then we were all here that one weekend."

"Special occasion?"

"I don't know. Just the summer after graduation. Kind of one last fling."

"And your parents? They were just all okay with it? With all of you hanging out up here? Drinking? Hooking up?"

"Mine were," he answered. His eyes moved constantly, surveying the land, the trees. She doubted he was worried about snakes. Maybe he was seeing ghosts. "I mean....they didn't know we packed a cooler every time we came here. I'm sure they suspected we were drinking. I don't know about anyone else's parents."

They walked without talking for a few minutes, the only sound their breathing which grew ragged the longer they walked. Mallory practically lived in flip flops; she had a pair in every color. But the gravel and the heat and the walking and walking and walking nonstop was already beginning to make her feet hurt.

"Did you ever do this?"

"Define this." She looked up at him curiously.

"Party weekends with friends."

"Drunken orgies?" she clarified.

He grinned sheepishly.

"Yeah. Not at a remote lake." She swallowed hard and looked around. "Where there might be...critters...around to party with us."

"No bears out here," he promised her.

She nodded. Flashed him a smile and rolled her eyes. "Thanks, Trev."

"Frogs. Lots of frogs." He laughed. "There was a frog in Peyton and Eden's room."

"In their room? Like…in the house?"

"Well." He winced. "It might have had help getting into their room."

"Eeww!" She shivered in disgust. "That's so mean."

Suddenly, the trees opened in front of them to reveal a spacious yard. A rambling house hovered at the far end of the lot, hidden partially from view by another grove of trees. From where they stood, the house looked old. Maybe not quite abandoned, but certainly neglected. The white siding was dingy. A gutter on a front window hung a little bit crooked. To Mallory's relief, there were no vehicles around. No new pickup trucks. No rusting piles of metal missing a tire or two. Nothing. It appeared she and Trevor were completely alone.

"Where's the lake?"

"Behind the house."

"Is it big?"

"Well, it's no Lake Eerie, but it's bigger than a pond." He shrugged and tugged on her hand to hurry her along.

She wondered what he was thinking as they walked. Apparently lost in thought, he didn't seem to notice her high-stepping through the ridiculously tall grass. He didn't seem troubled the way he sometimes did when he woke from the dreams. Just alert.

"Remember anything?" she finally asked, tired of trying to read his facial expressions.

"Sure." He shrugged and nodded. "But nothing…that would make me have that damned dream."

He hated talking about the dream. The nightmare. She got it. Made him feel emasculated.

"Tell me."

"What?" He glanced at her, but he was quick to look away. To sweep his eyes over the yard, the curving gravel drive, weeds grown up through the center of the tire paths.

"What do you see? What do you remember?"

She saw his eyes grow wide behind his glasses. He let go of her hand and swiped at sweat or a bug on the back of his neck. She hadn't thought about that. Bugs. Gnats. She held in a groan. Didn't want him to know she might already be regretting this. What if they went home with nothing more than a few bug bites? A frog or a snake sighting? Trevor's memories of hooking up with Hanna dragged back to the surface? That'd be great.

And then what if he *still* had the dream? Because what if it really had nothing to do with this lake, and it was that an uncle on his mom's side had fondled him or invited him to take part in a ritualistic sacrifice when he was thirteen?

"Um." He twisted his mouth in an almost ugly sneer and then shrugged and sighed and plunged into his memories. "We got here on a Friday. Like around noon. Because we ate…lunch…out back."

They had a picnic lunch, Mallory thought. And he'd sounded put off by her mention of it earlier today.

"Sam drove. The guys. We rode with Sam. Davis and I rode in the back of his truck—"

"That's illegal."

"So's everything else we did that weekend." He shook off her objection like she was a pest, a fly buzzing at his head. "The girls were in Neelie's car. She had an old Grand Prix or something. We ate lunch and started drinkin'. They all took their clothes off when we were eating. All of them had bikinis on. It was…surreal. We all knew we'd get some. All of us guys knew they were all gonna put out. Just a matter of who got what."

Mallory watched her feet clear the weeds as they walked. She'd just painted her toenails last week. Now she'd probably need to redo them. At the very least, they'd feel gross when she got home. The thought of showering in that hellhole of an apartment shot a jolt of revulsion through her. She almost retched. Stumbled a bit.

"You sure you wanna hear this?" Trevor apparently noticed. Thought his confession was bothering her.

Was it?

Hanna probably had a perfect pedicure. Twenty-four seven. A perfect *spa* pedicure.

"Would it bother you if I told you about the weekend I graduated from high school?"

Trevor eyed her wearily. "I don't know. What'd you do?"

"Drank a lot."

He sighed.

"What else? Do you remember?" Mallory asked to distract him.

"Um." He shook his head. Looked away again. "The girls… went inside. Picked rooms. We hit the lake. Drank all day. Davis…" Trevor laughed quietly.

"Davis?" she coaxed him.

He shook his head, lost in thought.

"Did you have a boat? Water skis?"

"Nah. Lake's not that big."

"So, you just spent the weekend swimming."

"Swimming. Lounging. We all crashed around like…five or six. Slept for a few hours. Started again later."

She nodded.

"So." Trevor reached for her hand again. "You just got drunk. On your graduation weekend?"

"Mm." She raised her eyebrows. "Hung out."

"And?"

They were close to the house now. Close enough to see

the torn screen in the door and years of dirt built up in the corners of the porch.

"Who did you room with?" she asked him.

"Davis." They walked slowly, heads craned to see the second story windows of the house. "We were in that room. Sam and Bowie were in that one." He pointed to the second window. "The girls were across the hall."

She saw the lake as they neared the back of the house.

"But…" Trevor squeezed her hand. "Like. Who were you hanging out with?"

"Friends," she answered vaguely.

"Are you playing hard to get?"

She laughed, lunged at him. He put his arm around her shoulders.

"No." She shrugged. "Probably not a good idea to get into details."

"You pretty much know my details."

"You wanted Eden. And instead you got some Hanna." She raised her eyebrows at him. "That about it?"

"Kinda."

"Like, did you get it both nights? More than once?"

"What friends were you with?"

"Just friends from school, Trev." She frowned. "We were drunk. There was a lot of liquor involved. A lot of skin. Condoms."

"Condoms," he repeated.

"Yep."

They rounded the house, and Mallory eyed the deck. The huge expanse of backyard. The rickety-looking wooden dock down by the lake.

"Where'd you do it? You and Hanna?"

"Um." He nodded back toward the front yard. "Front porch."

"Mm."

"Where'd you do it?"

"Um. In my friend's basement...first...and then upstairs in his bedroom."

"Twice." Trevor nodded. "Same guy?"

"Guys," she agreed.

"You were with more than one? Guy? At a time?"

"So..." Mallory waved his question away. "What else? What else do you remember?"

Trevor stood facing her, but he looked out at the lake.

"The ambulance. I...think I must have gone to bed. Because an ambulance woke me up—"

"An ambulance?"

"Yeah. Sam and Bowie found her." Trevor frowned. "I think."

"And she just...drowned?"

"Mmm."

"They recovered her body?"

"Yeah." Trevor nodded.

"It was Saturday. Same stuff as Friday. All day. Drinking. Talking about school." He shrugged. Glanced at her. "Teachers. The ones we hated. The ones we liked. College..."

"Was she drunk?"

Trevor started to answer; Mallory could swear she saw the yes on his lips, but he stopped himself.

"I don't know. I just remember...I just..." He shook his head. "I was. Upset. I was upset about something. And I went to bed."

Mallory stepped closer to him and nudged him.

"Trev." She slid her hands up over his arms. "Babe, I think it was probably just an accident."

He shook his head. Looked down at her. Mallory felt a pinprick of fear when their eyes met. Trevor squeezed his eyes closed. She let her eyes roam over his pale face. Closed her fingers around the back of his neck and touched his sweat-slicked skin.

"I don't think so," he whispered. "I don't think so, Mal."

"But you don't remember…anything bad happening."

"I don't remember it, but I feel it."

Chapter 31

HANNA

Hanna blinked. Stared at Bowie silently, his words repeating in her mind.

...the lake...Fourth of July...old times.

"What?" She shook her head and propped her elbows on her bent legs. The gray exercise mat under her was cold, and her sweat-soaked clothes were stuck to her skin, and she needed a drink. And now, after Bowie's suggestion—proclamation was more like it—she needed an adult drink and maybe miles of beach and clear blue water and her husband out of her sight.

"Sounds like fun, doesn't it?"

He wasn't out of her sight, unfortunately. He was on his knees in front of her, his hands on her feet. At home, if he held her feet while she did sit ups, they'd end up making out. No matter that she was hot and gross from her workout, he'd kiss her each time she sat up and finally, kissing him like that would drive her crazy, and they'd start rolling around and end up naked.

"Fun." She rubbed her face and her neck and then rubbed

her hands on her spandex shorts. Didn't do any good, because she was sweaty all over. "No, Bowie. It doesn't sound like fun."

"We keep saying we need to get away. We'll get someone to cover the desk for us. To cover the classes for the weekend. Mom will take Sylvi. We can hang out on the lake all weekend. No worries."

Hanna grabbed her hand towel and climbed to her feet. Bowie shot up immediately to follow her.

"Sounds thrilling." She wrapped the towel around the back of her neck and crossed the gym floor. It was late, after nine, and they should have left hours ago. Sylvi was in the playroom, and probably having a good old time, watching kids' shows and playing with the toys they'd put there. Hanna hated it when they stayed here this late. It wasn't normal for Sylvi. She should be at home. She should have had dinner in their kitchen, instead of on the counter at the gym. She should have been outside for a walk or to play on the swing set.

"What does that mean?" Bowie called.

Hanna let the gym door close behind her, but Bowie banged it open and followed her out through the short hallway to the counter. Hanna dried her face with the ends of her towel and then turned to face him.

"When we talked about getting away for a while…for a weekend," she leaned her elbow on the counter and stared at him boldly, "I meant Destin. Or Myrtle Beach. Not Litchfield Lake. I meant you and me. Maybe Sylvi. Not Sam and Neelie. Not Peyton and Trevor and Davis—"

"We can still take Sylvi to Florida. We can do that anytime. This just came up. With our friends. I don't get why this is such a big deal—"

"Because they aren't our friends anymore!" she yelled. The fitness center was closed. Only she and Bowie and Sylvi were there. Still. She hated arguing in front of Sylvi. Which is all they seemed to do anymore. "We haven't seen them since we got married. *Why* are they important to us again suddenly?"

Bowie huffed out an angry breath. He stalked around the counter and picked up his keys.

"How do friends just walk away? They were important to us when we were kids. How can you not feel anything for them now? This should be fun."

"I don't wanna be that person again, Bowie! I don't wanna be someone whose top priority is having a good time! I don't wanna be that party girl again—"

"Then don't." Bowie shrugged and shook his head.

"What?" Hanna turned to him, rested both elbows on the counter now. "Are you suggesting that I stay home? And you'll go without me?"

Bowie rolled his eyes and dropped into the chair behind the counter. It felt weird for her to be looking down at him. He scrubbed his hands over his sweaty hair.

"No. I'm not suggesting that at all." He spoke slowly, like he was trying to make a point, and she was too slow to follow him. "I'm just saying going back to the lake doesn't mean we have to be those people again. We're *not* those people, Han. We're not kids anymore."

Hanna bit her lip and took a deep breath. Exactly what she'd been trying to tell him since Sam had called the first time.

"But that doesn't mean we can't go and spend a weekend at the lake with friends. That we can't enjoy ourselves. Adults do that too, ya know? We don't have to be stupid about it."

Tired of this fight with Bowie, tired of every fight with Bowie (they'd happened so rarely before), Hanna felt herself giving in. She ducked her chin and rested her forehead on her hand. Maybe she was jealous. Bowie and Sam had reconnected seamlessly. Hanna's best friend had made it clear that she wanted nothing to do with her. Even after Hanna admitted to coming back to her for the familiarity. For a sense of home.

"Okay." She shrugged. "We go to the lake with them for the Fourth. Then what? Is it over then? Do we go back to our lives then?"

"Maybe we go back to our lives and our friends remain a part of our lives. The way it should be."

Bowie stood up suddenly. Hanna jumped at the shrill growl of the chair as he pushed it under the desk. She lifted her head and watched him toss a pen down on the desk calendar.

"What do you have against Sam anyway?"

Hanna snorted. What did she have against Sam? She wondered what Bowie would say if she told him just exactly what she had against his best friend. She met his eyes. Thought about telling him. Her skin still prickly cold, she felt chills break over her arms and legs. Her stomach felt leaden and her lungs frozen, and she couldn't breathe, let alone speak.

She'd put this behind her. She'd put that whole nightmare —a whole different thing than Eden—behind her, and damned if she'd drag it out now just to make Bowie get it.

"I'll get Sylvi," he announced as he walked away. Hanna watched him pull the door to the playroom open. She heard the singsong voices from a kids' show, and then she heard Sylvi chattering away at Bowie.

Chapter 32

TREVOR

They'd looked at a couple of apartments. Mallory had loved the first one, liked the second one. Trevor liked that they were both on the east side of Twelfth Street, and he liked that they were both ground floor apartments, and both appeared to have air conditioning units that actually cooled rather than moved hot air around the rooms. The first one, on Maine, was pretty high rent, and unless he landed a job as a CEO or they won the lottery, it was more than doubtful. The lease at the second one, on Frost, wasn't so bad. He'd been working the numbers when Sam texted.

Since they'd gone out that Saturday night, he'd been in touch with them. Texted a little bit here and there with Davis and Sam. The girls hadn't texted; Trevor was glad about that. Mallory hadn't said much about what he'd confessed about Hanna, but he knew she was a little bit bothered by it. After all, he'd been thinking about Mallory's graduation party since she'd shared the vaguest of details with him out at the lake.

Sam's text was about getting together again at the lake,

and just reading the words had made Trevor sick with dread. He'd sort of glanced at his phone, and his eyes had sort of jumped over the text and picked up the words *lake* and *again*, and he'd shoved the phone away without even actually reading the whole text. So, Sam had called him.

Trevor had been frustrated at first. He was in the middle of trying to make a huge life change. He wanted to find a better apartment for Mallory. For both of them, actually. A fresh start, something newer and maybe a bit bigger. He didn't know if this place would drive her away, but suddenly it seemed possible to Trevor. They were living near squalor, really, and for no reason. He wanted to make the change for the better, for her, to give their relationship a healthy home. And if he was going to do that, he needed to get a new job and commit to real responsibility, and hells bells, Sam was bugging him about this damned trip to the lake.

He didn't want to go. He wanted to put the lake, even the trip the other day, behind him. He wasn't proud of his high school self, wasn't proud about too much of anything about himself, but he knew he could do better. But he didn't need Sam sandbagging his efforts.

He let the call go to voicemail, but he knew even then that Sam would call back. Maybe if this was all Bowie's doing, he'd take no for an answer. He'd invite Trevor and Mallory along, and Trevor would say *thanks, but no thanks,* and that would be that. But it was Sam, not Bowie. Sam was a bit of a bully, always had been. Sam wanted them all to go to the lake together again, so as much as Trevor fought it, he knew in a few weeks, he and Mallory would most likely pack up and go back to Litchfield Lake.

Mallory came home while he was still crunching numbers on leases. She'd groaned when she'd come in to find him hunched over a notepad in his lap, pencil scratching the page. She probably assumed he was obsessing over the lake. He'd drawn it all again the night they'd come home from their little impromptu, secret trip out there.

Had to keep it a secret. Had to keep this whole thing a secret. Actually, he sort of wished he could have kept it a secret from Mallory.

He'd gone to sleep on the sketchpad that night. The dreams had been darker, though the lake wasn't the focus this time. Eden. The dreams that night had been about Eden. He hadn't shared that with Mallory. He hadn't shared the pictures he'd drawn after the new dream, either.

When she'd come home and found him running numbers, he'd turned to look at her over his shoulder. Flashed her a smile and told her to join him. She'd tossed her purse on the counter as she moved through the open living space, and then she'd joined him in the living area in front of the couch, and slowly eased to her knees beside him. He loved the way her face lit up when she realized he wasn't drawing but was still looking at apartments and what they could and couldn't afford.

And then Sam called again. And Mallory had picked up his phone and looked at it with sharp eyes. She'd handed it to him with an enthusiastic nod that he should answer it. He wondered what she would say when he told her what Sam wanted.

He hadn't listened to Sam's voicemail earlier. Sam referenced the voicemail and the texts that Trevor had left unanswered. Trevor simply claimed he was busy and hadn't seen the texts or had a chance to listen to the message.

Trevor hooked a finger under his glasses as Sam talked and slid them down his nose. He rubbed his eyes with his fingertips. Sam even had the details worked out. They'd meet at the lake as close to ten a.m. as they could. His uncle still owned the property, and though no one had used it lately, his uncle had assured him that the house was still in good shape. Still had electricity and running water.

Mallory leaned into him as he listened. Trevor wasn't sure if she was trying to hear Sam, too, or if she was staking her claim, or if she was just tired. Sam suggested each couple bring their own drink choice, but he actually had the grocery list divided up so that no one doubled up on snack items. Trevor turned his head to look at Mallory and rolled his eyes.

When Sam finally finished talking, Trevor told him he wasn't sure if they could make it. That he would talk to Mallory and get back to him. Sam had hesitated, and in that tiny space between Trevor's half-ass blow off and Sam's response, Trevor had a flash of memory. And it had nothing to do with Eden and everything to do with Sam.

Not used to being told no, Sam had dug in deep for a manly laugh and told Trevor to get out the big guns to talk Mallory into it, and then Sam had promised he'd call back the next day to finalize the plans. Trevor ended the call wondering what Sam considered the big guns.

Kind of hard to be romantic in the dump where they lived.

Trevor had tossed his phone down and looked around the living area, ready to get back to the numbers and his and Mallory's future. Or the possibility of their future, at least. Mallory, who had been so excited to realize he was doing that when she'd first come in, had slipped her arm through his and asked him what Sam wanted.

"I wanna go," she announced.

Trevor nudged her off him and turned back to the numbers. As far as he was concerned, they could talk about the trip later. This was more important.

"Really?" He tapped the pencil on the paper. "I think...we could swing that second place. I mean...I guess I could just pick up another part time job, if I can't find anything better. But—"

"Trev."

He looked at her at the same time he pulled his glasses off. Rubbed his eyes again.

"Why? Why do you wanna go?"

"Well." She shrugged. "I wanna get to know them better."

"Really?" He nodded. "You wanna get to know them?"

"I do." She cocked her head to study him. "And besides, maybe this will bring things to a head. Maybe you'll remember whatever it is…you've forgotten."

Trevor stood quickly and took a few steps away from Mallory. He was careful not to look at her, but he could feel her eyes on him as he paced the room.

"I think I know…"

"You remember?"

"No. But I think…"

"What?"

"Mal, I think I killed her." He stopped pacing. Propped his hands on his hips and lifted his head to meet Mallory's eyes.

Chapter 33

PEYTON

Bellamy wanted to say something. Peyton could tell. She watched with frantic eyes as Peyton folded a pair of jeans and a couple pairs of shorts and put them in her bag. Flip flops. Two t-shirts and a couple of tank tops. She probably wouldn't need half of what she'd thrown in the bag, but what did it hurt to have it just in case?

"Who're you goin' there with?" Bellamy asked as Peyton yanked her top dresser drawer open. Peyton grabbed a handful of underwear, two bras—one strapless—and tossed them in the open bag on the bed.

"Friends from school." She was deliberately vague. Bellamy had shown up uninvited with Chinese takeout, and though Peyton had been hungry and ready to find something for dinner, she'd been pissed to open her door and find her employee there.

Maybe she'd hoped it would be Brion. Not really, though. Maybe Hanna. Maybe, like Hanna had said a few weeks ago when she'd dropped in, Peyton was gravitating toward the familiar. And there was no one more familiar to her than

Hanna White.

Aware of Bellamy's agitation, her jealousy, as she watched her pack for a trip that involved hot girls like Hanna and Neelie (she'd never actually seen Neelie)—and the jealousy was pointless anyway, because Peyton wasn't interested in either of them, or any woman, for that matter—she pulled her swimsuit from the drawer and eyed it critically. She needed to put it on and check herself in the mirror. After all, who gave a damn what the suit looked like; it was what she would look like with it on. She wasn't particularly interested in turning anyone on at the lake. It was more about keeping up with Hanna. Which was ridiculous, because Hanna looked like a fitness queen, and no one could keep up with her.

And Mallory. Peyton had actually been surprised to find out Trevor and Mallory were going. She was glad; she hadn't had much of a chance to talk to either of them that night they'd all gone out, but she decided she wanted to. But still. Mallory was younger than the rest of them, and she was gorgeous with the dark blond hair and the golden eyes.

She almost laughed as she put the suit in the bag. Bellamy would croak if she'd seen Mallory and Neelie, too. So, she would pack the suit, but she might go to the mall before she left tomorrow and see if she could find anything on the clearance racks. Not likely, but it wouldn't hurt.

"Like…what friends, though?" Bellamy asked now.

Peyton lifted her eyes from her open bag and blinked her into focus. How did it matter what friends, because Peyton never discussed *any* of her old friends with Bellamy?

"Just friends I ran around with in high school, Bellamy," she said quietly.

"Are they all taking someone?"

"Well, Hanna and Bowie are married, and Sam and Neelie are married. Trev's bringing his girlfriend. That leaves me and Davis. No idea if he even has a someone, let alone if he's bringing her." She shrugged. "I heard he has a kid now."

"Let me go with you." Bellamy grinned, as if she was trying to sound cute. But Peyton heard the desperation in her words.

"No way."

Bellamy wasn't happy; her slouched shoulders and the pout she wore on her face gave her away, but at least she didn't hammer away at it, beg her to take her.

"How long will you be gone?"

"I dunno." Peyton dragged her fingers back through her hair. "I don't know, Bellamy. I don't answer to you. Remember?"

Bellamy cleared her throat. From the corner of her eye, Peyton saw her glance through the door to the kitchen.

"Want more wine?" she asked hopefully.

Peyton said she did, even as she wondered if Bellamy wanted to get her drunk. Again. She tucked her hair behind her ear and studied the contents of her bag again. She threw in another tank and a pair of old worn shorts to sleep in. Satisfied for the moment, she wandered back out to the kitchen just as Bellamy set the wine bottle down and someone knocked on the door.

"Who's that?" Bellamy asked quickly. "Are you expecting someone?"

Irritated—again? still?—Peyton shrugged and shook her head. She wasn't expecting anyone, and a random knock on her door irritated her on the best days. She ignored the glass Bellamy held out to her as she crossed the room and flipped the locks.

"Peyton—" Bellamy started to warn her against just opening the door, but before she could say more, Peyton pulled the door open. She grinned when she saw Brion's smile, the hopeful look in his eyes. Just because Bellamy was here and *maybe* because it had been a while—again—Peyton gestured for Brion to come in.

"Busy?" he asked as he stepped around her to come inside. He hadn't noticed Bellamy there in the kitchen, and Peyton was tempted to let him talk. To see just what he said after walking into her place with that look on his face. Maybe it would be good for Bellamy to hear it.

"Just had dinner," she told him. "You remember Bellamy, don't you?"

Now she wished she'd taken that glass of wine Bellamy had offered her. She nodded over her shoulder toward the kitchen. Brion followed her gaze and shot her a quick look before smiling at Bellamy. Part of her regretted telling him about her, about what had happened, but maybe now she could use that to get Bellamy out of here quicker.

"I was gonna ask if you wanted to get some dinner." Brion wandered into the kitchen. Peyton noticed the death glare Bellamy gave him when he picked up Peyton's wineglass and took a drink. She managed to stifle her laugh as she joined them, standing close to Brion at the counter.

Elbows on the bar, Brion turned only his head to look at Peyton. She was startled to feel a jolt of desire when their eyes met. Didn't think that had anything to do with Bellamy standing there watching them.

She remembered suddenly, as she stood a little too close to him at the counter, laughing uncontrollably, leaning into him, and trying desperately not to spill her beer. They were at a party on someone's patio, and Brion's friend, Steve, had fallen into the swimming pool fully clothed. It hadn't been a disaster; Steve knew how to swim. Still it had been funny when he lost his footing, tossed his drink, and fell in. She and Brion had laughed themselves sick and then they left the party, holding hands on the way to their car, and they'd gone home and snuggled on the couch.

The memory came out of nowhere, and Peyton was uncomfortable, and she glanced at Bellamy, wishing she would leave. Peyton didn't love Brion, did she? Sure, maybe at some point she'd been in love with him, but they'd fallen out of love, hadn't they? Had she moved out of Brion's place just because she wasn't crazy for him the way she used to be?

She dragged her eyes away from his face and tried to take a deep breath without calling attention to herself. She didn't know what to think, where this confusion was coming from, but it was certainly inconvenient right now. She needed Bellamy to leave, obviously, and she wasn't sure she wanted Brion here, either. Not with the lake thing tomorrow. She needed to be alone. To think. To prepare herself mentally.

The thought made her laugh softly. *Why* had she agreed to a weekend at Litchfield Lake if she felt like she needed to mentally prepare herself to go?

Still.

She glanced at Bellamy again. The kid looked miserable, leaning on the opposite end of the kitchen bar. Chin propped in one hand and the fingers of her other hand wrapped around the stem of her glass, she looked back at Peyton with big eyes.

Peyton had liked her before they'd ended up in bed together. Now Bellamy's attention had become heavy and unwanted, and even though Peyton had tried to explain to Bellamy it had only happened because she'd had too much to drink, the girl wasn't taking no for an answer.

"I was gonna—"

Peyton tore her eyes from Bellamy and over Brion's face and then over her shoulder when someone knocked on her door again. She sighed, excused herself, and went back to the door.

"Hey!' Hanna flashed her a big grin. "Whatcha doing?"

A flash of relief ripped through her, followed closely by

surprise, maybe even shock. She was happy to see *Hanna*? Hanna was her *rescue*?

"Packing," she answered with a small smile.

"I came by to see if you wanted to have a drink."

Peyton stared at her silently. If Hanna and Bowie were going away for the weekend, wouldn't they, wouldn't *she*—at least—want to spend tonight with their daughter?

"Um." Peyton raised her eyebrows. "Come on in."

Hanna was dressed down tonight in workout clothes. But rather than look gross and sweaty, like she'd just left the fitness center, she looked cute and athletic, like she'd just done a photo shoot for an ad campaign.

"Hey." Hanna smiled a little uncertainly when she realized they weren't alone.

Peyton looked from Hanna to Brion and finally Bellamy, and it crossed her mind that Hanna was the only one here not looking for sex. She coughed to hide her laugh and led Hanna to the bar.

"Han, this is Brion Mitchell." Peyton met Hanna's eyes and saw that Hanna recognized his name from that last conversation they'd had right here in her apartment. "And you met Bellamy at the store. Brion, this is Hanna White. Hanna and I went to school together."

Brion turned to Hanna and shook her hand.

"I've heard stories." He nodded, and Peyton laughed and shook her head. He *had* heard stories. She used to talk about the old days now and then. She'd shared plenty of stories about her friends, though she'd left out anything to do with the lake. And Eden.

She wondered when she'd stopped talking about her friends. Stopped thinking about her friends. Stopped thinking of them *as friends*. When had she started drinking too much? When had she closed herself off from everyone, including Brion? When had the demons grown too powerful, too fast to run from? Or had the distance from her friends allowed those demons to catch up with her?

Hanna appeared to have lost all her reservations about the lake reunion, about hanging out with the gang. She laughed lightheartedly in response to his comment, and the grin on her face appeared genuine.

"Ah, the stories." She nodded. Her voice was a little breathy, almost like she was nervous. She looked over Brion's shoulder and said hi to Bellamy.

"Did you guys really go cow-tipping?" Brion cocked his head at her.

Hanna barked a hearty laugh and cut her eyes to Peyton.

"Cow—oh my God!" She shook her head. "I totally forgot about that night. Yes." She looked back at Brion. "Yes. We tried, anyway."

"Sam got one down," Peyton reminded her.

"Whatever." Hanna rolled her eyes. "It was a calf."

"Was that the night Trevor ripped his pants doing the splits?"

Hanna looked at Peyton again with big eyes. She nodded slowly.

"Yeah." Her voice was soft, almost as if in disbelief. "It was. Wow."

"Why haven't we met before now?" Brion asked Hanna. He glanced at Peyton and then reached for her glass.

"She's married, Romeo," Peyton reminded him.

"Oh, I'm just thinking of the stories she could tell me about you." He shrugged and looked back at Hanna.

"Remember stealing the garden gnome from Mrs. Jenkins' yard? For the scavenger hunt?"

Peyton snorted. She moved around the back of the counter and picked up the bottle. Splashed a bit more in Bellamy's glass, suddenly feeling a little bit sorry for her.

Bellamy took a sip, and she wore a smile still, but Peyton thought it looked frozen and even a bit pained.

"I do." Peyton nodded slowly. "I haven't thought of that in years."

"Me neither," Hanna admitted.

Peyton wondered if this was why they were going. Why they'd all agreed to go back to the lake. What if they'd all let Eden's ghost haunt them through the past twelve years? So things hadn't always been perfect, but for a while, they'd been damned good. Maybe they'd all let Eden's ghost push them apart, so they'd all feel isolated.

Would she do that, though? Would Eden want them to be alienated from each other? Didn't seem likely. Then again, Peyton couldn't fathom the *majority of people* she knew turning into vengeful spirits when they died.

"We're going to the lake this weekend," she told Brion. "The old gang."

"Yeah?" He sounded interested, though Peyton had never talked about the lake.

"Yeah. Kicking back and hanging out. You should come with," Hanna told him. Peyton blinked and looked at Hanna quickly. It was one thing to invite Brion—she didn't *want* him there—but completely another thing to invite Brion in front of Bellamy, whom she *absolutely* did not want there.

"What lake?" he asked.

"Litchfield Lake," Peyton told him. "Just a place Sam's uncle owns."

"Any boating?"

"Nah." Peyton shook her head. "Not big enough for that."

"When do you leave?" He threw back the last of the wine and set the glass down.

Jesus. Was he considering it? Peyton studied his face as he watched Hanna. What the hell? Was he planning to hit on her? Even if she was married? Or did he want to be with

Peyton? And *why* were they having this conversation in front of Bellamy?

"Tomorrow." Peyton took the now empty bottle—Brion had drained the last of the wine into his—her—glass and rinsed it out. Set it in the sink.

"Gotta work." He sounded disappointed.

"Drive up Saturday," Hanna suggested. "How about you, Bellamy?"

Peyton felt a jolt of pressure in her mouth and realized it was her heart beating up her throat. She looked up at Bellamy with just her eyes.

"I work all weekend." The frozen smile melted back to demure, maybe, and she threw in a little shrug, as if to add on *darn it*.

"Peyton." Hanna propped her hands on her hips and shook her head.

"Hey. I need the best looking after the shop when I'm gone, don't I?"

She meant it, really. Bellamy could sell ice in Alaska if she wanted to. Besides that, if Bellamy went, Peyton would stay home.

Bellamy smiled. She took another sip of her wine and then set her glass down.

"I should go."

Peyton thought maybe she should argue. Throw out something like *oh come on, so early?* But she didn't want to. She needed Bellamy to leave.

"Thanks for bringing dinner by." She offered Bellamy what she hoped was a sincere smile as the girl picked up her keys and her purse from the bar stool at her end of the counter.

"You're welcome."

Peyton followed Bellamy to the door, a little bit relieved that Hanna and Brion were engaged in conversation again and a little bit worried about what that conversation might be about.

"Have a good weekend," Bellamy said quietly.

Peyton nodded and stepped back a bit when Bellamy leaned in. Rather than kiss her cheek, as she'd been about to do, Bellamy only touched her shoulder.

"Thanks." Peyton cleared her throat. Tolerated the touch but didn't return it. "I'll see you Monday."

Brion looked up at Peyton as she closed the door and turned back to them. She folded her arms over her chest and thought three was a crowd, but she wasn't really sure which of the two left she wanted to leave.

"Okay." Hanna shook her head and shivered as if she'd been suddenly chilled or maybe a black cat crossed her grave. *Interesting thought.* Peyton thought again of Eden and bit her lip. "We don't need to be going out for a drink tonight, anyway, right?" She flashed a grin at Peyton. "I should go home and fix Sylvi dinner."

Peyton arched her eyebrows, wondering why this thought had just occurred to Hanna.

"Do you wanna…" Hanna hesitated. "Do you wanna ride with us tomorrow?"

"No," Peyton answered quickly. No way in hell she'd ride with anyone. She needed her own car, so she could escape at the first sign of trouble. Which Peyton knew would most likely be inside herself and completely invisible to anyone else.

"Okay." Hanna looked back at Brion. "It was nice to meet you."

"You, too," Brion called as she headed to the door.

Peyton said goodnight and then locked the door behind Hanna. Turned back to Brion, jittery with nerves and need. Something she hadn't felt around him for a long time.

"Can you stay for a while?"

Chapter 34

MALLORY

She didn't believe Trevor had killed his friend, the girl named Eden. Trevor wouldn't kill a mouse, for God's sake, and she'd gotten in his face about that on more than one occasion. Yet another reason she desperately wanted to find a new apartment.

Didn't seem to matter to him, though, that she didn't believe he'd had anything to do with that girl's death. Even now, in Karla's borrowed car again—Mallory sort of wanted to talk to Trevor about buying something used (She'd buy it herself, but that might cut into her portion of rent money, and she wasn't sure what he'd think about that. Which is why she was waiting until after the lake weekend to bring it up.)— he seemed adamant that he'd done something wrong. Bad.

He kept saying that. *Something bad happened*, and he was sure it was his fault. Mallory really couldn't imagine anything sinister going on with the people she'd met the night they'd all gone out together. If Eden drowned in the lake, that was *bad*, wasn't it? Didn't have to take on deep, mysterious undertones. Death was bad. Accidental deaths were bad. Accidental deaths that occurred during a weekend of drunken partying involving underage drinkers were really bad. End of story.

Trevor insisted there had to be more to it than that. He'd pulled a memory from his dreams, and when he'd first told her that—when they were packing for the trip—she'd been a little bit on edge. But the memory was something about Sam. Wasn't really even concrete. Just a flash of Sam on the dock. Late at night, elbows on the rails, staring out over the lake.

Mallory had reminded him that he'd told her he'd been in bed when he heard the ambulance come to take Eden away. That he couldn't possibly have done anything bad if he was that far away from the lake where the girl died. Trevor hadn't looked convinced. Mallory had gone to him then, slipped her arms up over his shoulders, and rested her forehead against his chin. She hadn't said she loved him, even though she thought she might, but she'd kneaded her hands into his tight shoulder muscles and promised him it would be okay. That they'd use the weekend as an opportunity to snoop around the house, the lake, other people's memories, and just see what they could find.

He'd been placated by that, but Mallory noticed he was agitated again today. He was driving this time, and she was working a crossword puzzle in one of those puzzle books. She wanted to put her feet up on the dash, but she felt weird about doing that since it wasn't her car, and besides, she'd read a news story recently about a girl who'd been sitting like that and had been severely injured in an accident.

She chewed on her pencil now and considered the clue.

"Hit me," Trevor said over Zella Day's voice and "Seven Nation Army". Mallory lifted her eyes to watch him tapping out the beat of the song—Mallory thought it was hard to find a beat in her version—on the steering wheel. His left leg bounced, too, and Mallory sort of wanted to launch herself over his lap to make it stop moving.

"Five letter word for short and stout."

"Short."

She rolled her eyes.

"Five letters," he mumbled defensively.

"It's also part of the clue." She laughed and shook her head.

"What's it start with?"

"I dunno. But it ends in y."

"Fugly."

"Hey!" She snorted and lifted her chin to stare at him with feigned anger. "I'm short!"

"You're not stout, though."

"You don't think short, curvy women are attractive?"

"I do, actually," he argued. "But when you say stout, it makes me think of a dude. Like a middle-aged business dude. With a graying buzz cut. And fat, square hands. And chronic bad breath."

"That's oddly descriptive and gross." She shook her head. "And I don't think *fugly* is a real world."

He looked back at the road, but she knew he was smiling.

"Did you like that new Tori Amos CD?"

Used to be his random questions startled her, but she was used to it by now. She used to think it was because he was always lost in his own little world and had to work hard to catch up with everyone else, every conversation going on around him. Didn't take long before she changed her mind and decided that maybe it was actually that he was brilliant, and he was always ten steps ahead of everyone else and juggling at least five ideas in his head at the same time and now and then, something random just popped out.

"It's not new," she reminded him. "Came out in May."

He leveled a *really?* look at her.

"But I just brought it home last night."

Mallory grinned and leaned away from him when he tried to drop his hand on her thigh. He squeezed her leg, and she squealed and jumped.

"I haven't listened to it much," she answered.

"Shoulda grabbed it. Coulda played it now."

"You don't like my conversational skills?'

"Not when they're about fugly dudes with chronic halitosis."

Mallory laughed and dropped the puzzle book to the floor of the car.

"Okay. Prepare to be dazzled."

"Did we pack any grapes?"

"We did. Even though Sam told us exactly what to bring, we broke the rules and packed some grapes." She nodded when Trevor looked at her. "However, they're in the cooler. Which is in the trunk."

"Damn." Trevor fiddled with the radio volume. Mallory watched his long, slender fingers. Dropped her eyes from his hand to his leg. It was rare to see Trevor in shorts; in fact, it was early July, and he had no trace of a tan.

"Did we get the sunscreen?"

"Yep." He nodded. Checked the rearview mirror and then looked at his side mirror.

"Find anything in the classifieds last night?" Mallory had noticed lately that Trevor brought a paper home from work and studied the classified ads. She was proud of him for wanting to make this change, and she was excited for him, too. But she sort of felt like he wasn't just going to find the perfect job in the newspaper. These days, it was more about knowing the right person.

"Mm." He shrugged his lips. "Not really. I mean, there were a couple things I might check out, but not actual graphic design stuff." He turned to her and grinned. "Gotta be something out there that pays more than selling records."

"I hate that you have to give that up, though."

Mallory watched him reach to take her hand.

"Eh. Not giving up music, just selling the records." He rubbed his thumb over the back of her hand. "It'll be worth it if we can get a better place."

Mallory lifted their hands and pressed her grin to his fingers.

"Can we get a dog?"

Trevor laughed and shook his head.

"One thing at a time, woman."

Mallory rested her head on the seat and yawned.

"Mal?"

"Hmm?"

"Sam's not a bad guy."

Chapter 35

HANNA

It looked the same but different. Hanna figured it was all the same—the land, the house, the lake with a few years of dirt and neglect added to it—and that it was the way she'd remembered it for twelve years that was different.

The house smelled musty, and when Bowie pulled the screen door open for her, she heard Sam sneezing. The kitchen was smaller than she remembered, but big enough. They wouldn't be indoors much anyway. Someone—most likely Sam—had turned the air conditioner on, but the window unit had had a hell of a time keeping up with things twelve years ago. Hanna prayed that, at least, had been replaced since they'd been here last. Neelie wore a cute little white apron over her shorts and tank, and Hanna froze in her tracks to take it in. She watched Neelie putting drinks and small tubs of potato salads and applesauce and yogurt in the refrigerator and decided she'd never worn an apron in her life, and she wouldn't be caught dead in something like that with all the ruffles on the sides.

That thought made her uncomfortable. The last time

they'd been here, someone had been found dead, and Hanna still hadn't made peace with that part of coming back here.

"Hey." Neelie looked at her and Bowie over her shoulder and flashed them a big grin. Hanna was overwhelmed with déjà vu, except it wasn't really déjà vu, was it? If they'd really been there before? She remembered Neelie, head in the fridge, lit cigarette in hand, barefoot, Daisy Dukes riding up her butt when she'd leaned over. "Isn't this exciting?"

Hanna wondered how exciting it could be for Neelie since she was pregnant. The heat would have killed Hanna. She hadn't minded her pregnancy with Sylvi. Hadn't minded eating healthy and giving up alcohol for nine months. But she couldn't imagine getting through this weekend without it. Then again, Neelie seemed to have done a one eighty, and she was calm and collected, and maybe later, they'd all find her on the dock singing "Kumbaya".

"Yeah." Hanna nodded, a little belatedly, but Neelie didn't seem to notice. She went back to emptying their cooler into the fridge, and Hanna heard Sam sneezing again.

"The dust was pretty thick," Neelie said with a sweet, little laugh.

"Has anyone been here? Since we were?"

"Yeah." Neelie nodded. Cooler emptied, she swung the door of the refrigerator closed and stood up. Dried her hands on the apron and turned to Hanna and Bowie. "Sam's cousins have come and gone. But I do think it's been a few years since anyone's used the house."

"Got room for more?" Bowie stood behind Hanna, cooler in his hands. Hanna had forgotten he'd carried it to the deck. He must've grabbed it as Hanna came inside. She stepped aside quickly, guilty for not moving back to get the door for him.

"Of course." Neelie grinned. She moved and nudged their

cooler out of the way. "Is everybody coming? Did you talk to Peyton?"

Hanna set her purse on the butcher block kitchen table. She pushed her sunglasses up on her head and looked around at the room again, taking in the way the sun painted the kitchen as warm and homey. In her mind, for the past twelve years, everything about this house, the property, had been foreboding and scary.

"Yeah. I went by her place last night."

"You did?" Bowie paused in the act of emptying the cooler, a tub of guacamole in one hand and a small bag of apples in the other. "You didn't tell me that."

Hanna, aware of Neelie watching them, nodded and shrugged. "Yeah. Went by before I got home from the gym."

"I thought you went to the grocery store."

"I did." Hanna fought the urge to roll her eyes. Did he really want to make a scene over something so stupid right here in front of Neelie? "I asked her if she wanted to ride with us."

"Oh." Neelie grinned. She put her hands on the counter behind her and hoisted herself up to sit there. Hanna had to admit she was radiant. She'd always been cute, but there was something about her now that glowed. Of course, it would be *Neelie* to be the embodiment of a glowing pregnant woman. "She didn't want to?"

She needed a beer already. She wouldn't open one; it was too early, but dammit, she needed one. She'd been hurt that Peyton had said no to her offer, and yet, she understood, didn't she? She wouldn't have wanted to come up with someone else. Been at someone else's mercy as to when she could get the hell out of here.

"No. She wasn't sure when she could get away today." Hanna dismissed Peyton's refusal like it wasn't a big deal.

"Something about running into the shop before she could head out."

Neelie nodded and turned her eyes to Bowie. She had a great view of his ass and his back at the moment, and Hanna watched with amusement as she looked her share. She'd lied for Peyton. *Interesting.* Even more than that, she'd lied for Peyton to *Neelie.* Sure, there'd been squabbles among them when they were younger, and yes, she'd known Peyton longer, but they'd never told each other lies back in the day. They'd been equals, and their friendships had all been the same.

What made that different now? What made Hanna lie to Neelie for Peyton?

"I'm just glad she's coming." Neelie kicked her feet and let her heels gently thud against the cabinet. "Sam talked to Davis last night. He was with his son. Hanging out last night since he wouldn't see him again until Sunday."

"Ever find out who the kid's mom is?" Bowie asked Neelie.

"Sam knows her name. No one we know."

"We should do this again in, like, five years—"

"Five years, hell." Sam scratched his neck and looked over his shoulder as he joined them in the kitchen. "I think I got the air set so it should cool off in here pretty quick," he said to Neelie and then turned back to Bowie. "I think we should make this a yearly tradition."

Finished with the cooler, Bowie stood up and shook Sam's hand.

"Fine by me," Bowie said with a shrug. "I just meant we should bring the kids out. I think Sylvi's too little now."

"She is not," Sam argued good-naturedly. He yanked the fridge door open and grabbed an aluminum bottle of beer. "Does she swim?"

"Yeah." Bowie nodded. Hanna cringed when he followed Sam's lead and reached for a beer. "Like a fish."

"She'd love it," Sam announced.

Hanna stared at Bowie in disbelief. She'd bring Sylvi out here over her dead body. She shivered again. What was it with that line of thinking? Still. She meant it this time. She didn't want Sylvi in this house. In the lake outside. None of the above.

"How about we just consider this a test run?" she said quietly.

Bowie arched his eyebrows. He'd heard her. If they were at home, no doubt they'd blow up in a huge argument right about now. He wouldn't do that, though, in front of Sam.

"Hey." Sam crossed the room and leaned in to brush a kiss over Hanna's cheek. She swallowed hard and stepped back, but she kept a blank face. "We don't need a test run. We've always been awesome."

Voice gone, Hanna smiled uneasily and nodded. Sam looked back at Bowie and then the two of them walked out the back door. Hanna moved to the back of the kitchen, looked out back through the wall of windows. The guys sat at the round patio table, already involved in conversation.

"You don't want Sylvi out here."

Hanna looked back at Neelie.

"Hard to…" she shrugged helplessly.

"I know. I dreamt about her last night."

"Sylvi?" Hanna yelped.

Neelie watched her carefully as she eased off the counter. "No. Eden."

"Oh." Hanna laughed softly. She watched Neelie open the fridge. Prayed she wasn't going for a beer. She sighed in relief when her friend took the guacamole from the top shelf and then grabbed a bottle of water from the door.

"Do you ever visit her grave?" Neelie carried the guacamole and water to the table, set them down, and then went back to the counter. Hanna watched her dig around in a black reusable shopping bag and finally pull out a bag of bite-sized rice cakes.

"Really?" Hanna couldn't hold back the shiver of disgust. She hated rice cakes, no matter what she put on them.

Neelie grinned sheepishly. She pulled the head chair out from under the table and dropped into it. Propped her feet on the chair at her right.

"I did a few times," Hanna dragged her eyes away from Neelie, "right after...it happened. And then I quit." She shrugged. She'd had her reasons, and she'd needed to put it behind her. "But I did...last night."

"Before or after you went to see Peyton?"

Hanna heard a tiny little note of doubt in Neelie's voice. She looked at her quickly. Wondered if she'd seen through her lie earlier. About Peyton.

"After." She curled her fingers around another chair and pulled it out to sit down. "Someone put...artificial flowers... in the little vase thing." Hanna shaped her hands like a vase. "On the side of her headstone. I hate that."

"Artificial flowers?" Neelie twisted the guacamole open.

"On a grave." Hanna nodded. "Feels like someone saying *I don't have time to replace fresh flowers on a regular basis, so you're gonna have to deal with this.*"

Neelie stuck her finger in the green goop and then licked it.

"Jesus, Neelie, that's disgusting." Hanna turned her nose up.

"I like beets, too," Neelie admitted.

Hanna blinked and looked away.

"Maybe artificial flowers say *it's July and people wilt, so fresh flowers wouldn't live from the car to the vase, and you deserve to always have flowers here, so I'm leaving these for now.*"

Their eyes met. When Hanna didn't answer her, Neelie arched her eyebrows in question.

"Maybe," Hanna mumbled.

"How much weight did you gain with Sylvi?"

"Um." Hanna hung her head back and stared at the ceiling. "Maybe fifteen to twenty pounds."

"Was it hard to lose it? After she was born?"

Hanna laughed. "Are you kidding me? I'm married to a fitness Nazi."

Neelie grinned and poked her finger in the guacamole again.

Someone pulled the screen door open suddenly, and it crossed Hanna's mind that they should close the storm door. Sam had the air going, but if they left that door open, it would take longer for the house to cool.

"Hey." Trevor's girlfriend appeared first. Hair piled in a messy bun on top of her head, Nike shorts and a sporty tank, she looked ten years younger and cuter and a hell of a lot less hassled than Hanna. What would it be like coming here with a house full of strangers? With no bad memories and no ghosts packed in the bags?

"Hey, Mallory." Neelie finally reached to open the pack of rice cakes. "You look adorable."

Mallory, arms loaded down with grocery bags, hesitated at the counter. Neelie didn't see it, but Hanna did. Trevor had told her. Trevor had told his girlfriend the things she'd done with him here the summer they were eighteen. What a dumbass. Everyone knows you don't tell current girls or guys about past sexual encounters.

"Your word for the weekend is sunscreen," Hanna told her. Mallory moved again, and Hanna hoped that meant she was okay, and this wasn't going to be a miserable weekend for her. That she wasn't going to spend the entire weekend jealous about something stupid that had happened twelve years ago. That her jealousy wasn't going to feed Hanna's unease.

Neelie dipped a rice cake in the guacamole and took a bite. She seemed completely unaware of the moment, of Mallory's slight hesitation at her words, but Hanna wondered. Neelie hadn't been that oblivious when they were younger.

Hanna watched Mallory set the bags on the counter.

"I know." She laughed now as she turned to Hanna and Neelie. "Trev and I aren't out in the sun much. He looks worse than I do."

Hanna thought Mallory looked good. Her skin looked healthy. She thought about saying that to Mallory but decided against it in case the girl took it the wrong way.

"Where is he?" Hanna twisted around in her seat, but Trevor wasn't lurking anywhere in the kitchen.

"Talking to the guys." Mallory rolled her eyes.

Hanna and Neelie both laughed.

"Have a seat," Hanna offered.

"Thanks." Mallory chose a chair across the table from Hanna.

"Let's wager. Who's gonna show up last?" Neelie crunched another bite of rice cake. Hanna laughed out loud when she saw the look on Mallory's face.

"Rice cakes…" Mallory nodded slowly. "And guacamole."

Neelie shrugged, but she smiled.

"Peyton." Neelie announced as she turned back to Hanna. And though Hanna agreed with her, she didn't want to. So, she simply shook her head and said *Davis*.

"Loser gets KP duty?" Neelie suggested.

"Sure."

Chapter 36

PEYTON

She saw the look Hanna and Neelie exchanged when she walked in, but she didn't know what it meant. And to think she'd almost been looking forward to this on the drive up. She didn't want to deal with those sidelong glances that seemed to convey whole conversations; weren't they too old to do this? They'd never done it in high school. Why start now?

"Hey." Neelie flashed her a belated grin.

Peyton grunted at her and hoped Neelie took it as a hello. She carried her plastic grocery bags to the counter and set them down with obvious relief.

"Davis out there?" Hanna asked as Peyton turned to look at them. Mallory was reading the back of an open package of something—rice cakes?—and Neelie was fiddling with the lid on her water bottle.

"He pulled up just behind me." Peyton spun around to open the refrigerator door and ducked in. She reappeared a moment later, twisted open a beer. Hanna blinked at her in surprise. "Don't judge. I owe your beer gods one."

Hanna shrugged and laughed.

"He said he'd carry my cooler in for me."

"Davis did?" Neelie, slumped in her seat and still twisted around sideways to prop her feet on the chair to her right, looked over her shoulder at Peyton.

"Yep." Peyton stepped away from the counter and then opened the cabinet under the sink. She dropped the cap into the garbage can and turned back to the table as the door banged open and Davis lugged her cooler inside.

"Were you the last one here?" Hanna gushed the words out quickly and looked at Neelie with her eyebrows raised.

"Yeah." Davis carried the cooler over to the fridge and leaned over as he set it down. "Lucky me. Got suckered into carrying this eight-hundred-pound cooler for Peyt."

Peyton met Hanna's gaze. She wanted to be mad. No one had called her *Peyt* since they'd left this damned place last time. But Hanna was losing the fight with the smile on her face, and Mallory had put down the bag of rice cakes to look at her, and Peyton felt laughter rumbling in her stomach.

"Jesus, Davis." She rolled her eyes. "*Peyt?*"

"Huh?" He opened the refrigerator and grabbed an apple. Polished it on his shirt and then bit into it as he turned around to look first at Peyton and then Hanna and Neelie. "What's wrong with calling you Peyt?"

"I grew up."

"Well, we all did. We all got old." Davis patted his stomach as he chewed the apple. "You're hitting the alcohol already? Five o'clock somewhere blah blah blah?"

"No idea." She shrugged. "I needed a beer."

Davis took the beer from her and took a swig.

"Ew. With apple?" Hanna scrunched down and rested her head on the back of her chair. "That's disgusting. You guys are so gross."

Davis handed the beer back to Peyton and watched with

mock outrage when she wiped the lip of the bottle off with her shirt.

"Dude. Really?" Davis shook his head.

Peyton laughed softly.

"I don't know where you mouth has been in the last twelve years," Peyton reminded him.

"So, anyway." Hanna sat up again and leaned forward to rest her arms on the table. "Peyton was here before you, Davis?"

"Are we establishing a timeline? For alibis later or what?" Davis joked. Peyton sucked in a quick breath and looked the other way. No one else seemed bothered by his comment, but Peyton saw a flash of red and blue light in her head.

"No." Hanna stood up. She dropped a casual hand on Neelie's shoulder as she walked by her. "Neelie and I had a bet on who would show up last."

"And?" Peyton squeezed her eyes closed. The red and blue lights hurt her eyes. She rubbed the bridge of her nose. "Who won?"

"I did." Hanna stepped around the cooler and pulled the refrigerator door open. She leaned in to grab an apple.

"Copycat," Davis mumbled.

"Lame." She pointed at him and then turned her attention to Peyton. "I bet on you getting here before Davis."

"Thanks." Davis tapped the back of her knee with the toe of his silver running shoe.

"Is your Brion driving up tomorrow?"

Peyton snorted and took a drink of her beer.

"You have a Brion?" Neelie put her feet on the floor and turned completely around in her chair. "What's he like?"

"I have an ex-Brion," Peyton answered. She moved to the table and sat down where Hanna had been sitting. Glanced at Mallory. "How'd you get suckered into this? You didn't have to come."

"An ex-Brion?" Hanna turned the water on at the sink and rinsed the apple off. Took a paper towel from a roll someone had set out on the counter and wiped it dry. "Man, why? He's hot."

"So's Bowie," Peyton shrugged, "but I wouldn't want to date him, either."

"Do we need to talk about that?" Hanna bit into the apple and then wiped juice from her chin with the paper towel she still held in her hand.

"About what?" Neelie looked from Hanna to Peyton.

"The fact that there are four women in this room, and three of us have slept with my husband."

Mallory opened her mouth, and Peyton watched her, curious as to what she had to say. She laughed when the girl shook her head and got up without saying a word. They watched her round the end of the table, pop the screen door open, and walk outside.

"Good job." Peyton cocked her head at Hanna.

"I've never slept with Bowie," Davis told Hanna. "And on that note, I'll be outside."

"You—?" Neelie looked at Peyton in disbelief. "I mean, I didn't—"

"You did," Hanna argued. She pushed herself from the counter and crossed the room to sit where Mallory had been sitting. "Peyton and I saw you guys, Neelie."

"You saw us?" Neelie's eyebrows jumped comically. Peyton snorted.

"Yeah. On the dock. I wanted to watch to see if you got splinters."

Neelie giggled.

"Does Sam know?" Peyton asked her.

"I didn't tell him." Neelie shrugged and shook her head.

All eyes turned toward the door when they heard it open again. Mallory reappeared, open bottle of beer in hand.

Peyton lifted her own beer to tap Mallory's bottle as she slipped past her to sit down.

"Five o'clock somewhere, right?" Peyton asked with a grin.

"I dunno." Mallory shrugged and took a long drink. "I needed a beer."

Peyton looked back at Hanna and Neelie. "I like her."

"Why didn't you ever tell me?" Hanna leaned her elbows on the table and propped her chin in her hand. Closed her eyes. Peyton tucked a stray strand of hair behind her ear and then checked her ponytail.

"I dunno."

"When?"

"Hey!" Peyton stood up. "Hang on." She rushed out of the house and over the deck. She'd left her duffel in the car, so she jogged out now to get it. Her feet slid around in her flip flops, and she scraped the sides of them on loose pieces of gravel in the driveway. At her car, she reached into the back-seat and grabbed the bag. Closed the door again and considered locking it. Not like anyone was going to get into anything out here, but maybe better safe than sorry? She locked it and then headed back toward the house. The guys were still gathered around the table on the deck; it sounded like Trevor was talking about a movie.

"What was that about?" Hanna asked when Peyton walked back into the house and dropped her bag to the floor. "Because I'm not gonna forget—"

"We were sixteen." Peyton shrugged impatiently and unzipped the bag. "You'd never said anything about him at that time."

"So. Was he your first?" Neelie asked quickly.

Peyton started to answer that yes, Bowie had been her first, but it hit her then that it would bother Hanna. Of course, this was going to bother Hanna. She reached into her bag as she dropped back into her chair. Looked up first at Neelie and then finally dragged her eyes to Hanna.

"Was he?" Hanna watched her expectantly.

She took a deep breath and nodded. Dropped her eyes to the bag. Her fingers curled around the frame. She pulled the picture out and set it on the table.

"What is that?" Neelie leaned forward to see it better.

"I thought you said Cole Reese was your first."

Peyton met Hanna's eyes again and shrugged. "I lied."

"Why?" Hanna took the last bite of her apple and then got up to toss the core in the garbage can. Peyton watched her wash her hands and then dry them with another paper towel, but she looked away when Hanna turned back to them.

"Because I liked Cole." Peyton shrugged. She took a drink as Neelie half crawled up over the table to see the picture better. "I guess it was wishful thinking."

From the corner of her eye, she saw Hanna go to the refrigerator and grab a beer.

"Are you mad?"

"Wow." Neelie touched her fingertips to the glass frame. "Look at us."

Hanna sat down again and met Peyton's eyes over the table.

"No." She sighed.

Peyton raised her eyebrows, surprised by Hanna's answer.

"What is this?" Hanna reached for the frame. "Oh my God. Peyton. I didn't even know we had pictures."

Trevor's girlfriend leaned in closer to Peyton, so Peyton took the frame from Hanna and turned it around so she and Mallory could look at it together. Peyton had almost thrown the film away after that weekend. They'd all gone home with their parents after Eden's body had been pulled from the lake. Peyton had no idea who'd called them all, or who had been the first to call home and start a chain reaction. But before the ambulance had pulled away with Eden zipped in a black bag, their parents had shown up.

Her parents had been disappointed in what was obviously a party weekend. Peyton had lied and told them just she and the girls would be at the lake. She had no idea what anyone else had told their parents. She'd been in trouble, of course, though her parents hadn't exactly punished her. Her friend's death had been a lot to handle, though it hadn't *crushed* her with grief. She hadn't been that close to Eden. The depression had crept up on her, almost like quicksand climbing over her legs and then her chest and finally her head.

She'd argued with herself about the film, but in the end, she'd had it developed. Mostly the pictures had been out of focus or too dark or too dumb to save, and she'd thrown the majority of them away. She'd saved a couple group shots: one of all the girls and the other the whole group. They'd gathered in front of her camera, and they were young and care-free and tan and happy. The smiles in that *one* picture had haunted her for years.

Chapter 37

HANNA

She wasn't mad, but she couldn't pretend like it just didn't bother her. *Well*, she had been pretending all day, since Peyton had admitted that she'd been with Bowie, that he'd been her first. Maybe, Hanna mused to herself, it wouldn't seem like such a big deal if Peyton had told her back when it happened.

Hanna watched Davis do a cannonball off the dock out in the lake and then shriek as he hit the water. It had been kind of cold when they'd first jumped in, but by now, they were all used to it, and Hanna was actually over it. She checked the red polish on her toes as she wiggled them, glad she'd had a fresh pedicure for the weekend. Her butt hurt from sitting on the dock, so she tried to shift her weight a bit without calling attention to herself.

Mallory and Trevor were further out in the lake, hanging off the side of a blow-up raft. Hanna kind of liked watching them; they seemed younger and more carefree than the rest of them. To hear Mallory tell it, that wasn't necessarily the case. She hated their apartment, and they'd recently started looking to move. But Trevor was working part time selling records, and there was no money there. So now, he was looking for a *Real Job*. Hanna had noticed the way Mallory had flinched when she said that. Neelie had asked about his art, if it was good enough to do a show, but Mallory said she had no idea.

Hanna liked that she wanted to believe in him. That Mallory saw Trevor through stars in her eyes, and that she was proud of his art, and that she hated that he would have to quit a job he was passionate about just so they could move.

While they were talking in the kitchen, the guys had trooped inside together and scrounged through the coolers and refrigerator and assembled big cold cut sandwiches and added chips to their paper plates. Except Bowie. He put together an impressive looking sandwich, yes, but he had a container of yogurt and some carrot sticks with his. The guys had teased him, and Hanna noted that Sam had started the razzing about health food, and she heard her name come up and assumed Sam was suggesting she kept Bowie on a tight leash as far as nutrition and exercise. She was irritated that Bowie didn't argue, that he let them all believe that was the case, and she felt a wave of irrational anger, fear even, over what this weekend might mean.

Sam had the power to change her husband. To wear him down and make him the immature, arrogant kid he used to be. When he was with Sam. Hanna hated that about Sam. Bowie didn't know the half of it. She hated that side of Bowie, too. It scared her to think before the night was over, that might be all that was left of him for the weekend. Someone she could hate.

Davis had noticed Peyton's group photo first. He'd been on his way back out the door to the deck, and he'd stopped and kind of laughed and leaned over the table. He'd squinted a little bit while he looked his fill at the smiling, sun-kissed faces, and then he'd stood up and nodded and gone on outside. Sam noticed it next, and he'd studied it for a moment and then shivered like it gave him the willies.

"Jesus, that's creepy," he'd muttered as he followed Davis outside.

"Creepy?" Peyton repeated. "Hey!" She'd shouted at him, but he'd ignored her and so then Bowie had taken a turn to look at the picture. Only Hanna didn't think he'd really looked at it, and Hanna had remembered Eden's funeral and how Bowie hadn't ever gone close to the casket to pay his respects.

When they'd asked him about it, later, he'd sort of shrugged them off and yanked at his tie and mumbled that it just freaked him out. In the following years, Hanna had learned that Bowie was terrified of death. The concept. He'd never experienced death is his life before Eden.

Trevor had studied the picture with hungry eyes. He'd even set his paper plate down and picked up the photo for a better look. He didn't smile; in fact, Hanna thought he looked haunted when he'd finally put the photo down and then he'd looked at Mallory. Hanna had dragged her eyes away from Trevor to look at Mallory, and she'd seen the girl arch an eyebrow at him in question. He'd only shrugged and gone out to join the guys again.

"I just thought…" Peyton had cleared her throat. "I thought she should be here. Too."

Hanna and Neelie had agreed, and they'd had a brief *remember-when* session, and then they'd all grabbed something for lunch and finally gone out to join the guys.

And now here they were.

Hanna watched Bowie and Sam as they raced across the water. Bowie's body was solid and muscular, and he was a strong swimmer. Ordinarily, she'd be proud of him, but it made her sick to see him sink back to this stage of his life.

Sam Collins was an asshole, and Hanna worried that whatever wore off him on this trip would stick to Bowie and change him.

So things had been rough lately—since Sam Collins had called—but she and Bowie had a good marriage. She loved him. She just wasn't sure she could love him if he went back to being Sam's sidekick.

"Who's got Sylvi this weekend?"

Peyton's skin was a weird mix of cold and wet and hot when she nudged Hanna. Next to her on the dock, Hanna turned her head to look at her. Peyton kept her eyes on the lake. Hanna wondered what she was thinking.

"Bowie's mom."

"Yeah?" Peyton finally glanced at her, but Hanna couldn't see her eyes behind the dark sunglasses she wore. "Does she like that? Being with grandma?"

"Yeah." Hanna laughed and shrugged. "Why wouldn't she? She gets cookies and ice cream at Grandma's."

Peyton smiled. "And you guys don't let her have that stuff?"

"Not very often."

"Why is that?"

"What?" Hanna shook her head. "What do you mean?"

"Did your parents give you ice cream and cookies when you were a little kid?"

"Well, yeah—"

"And did you stay up all night sometimes, reading or giggling, talking to friends?"

Hanna didn't answer Peyton, because Peyton had been one of those friends on many occasions.

"And um….let me see…did you drive over the speed limit when you turned sixteen? Forget to wear your seatbelt sometimes?"

"Are you seriously criticizing—"

"You did all those bad things, and so your friend Eden died. Is that it? So, you and Bowie think that if you deny Sylvi sugar and TV time and iPads, she'll grow up safe, and her friends will be safe, and no one's ever gonna die?"

Hanna opened her mouth to argue, but she closed it before she could say a word. That was Bowie's thinking, exactly. She was torn between needing to defend him and defend herself. No. None of the above would guarantee Sylvi or her friends a long, happy life. But Bowie seemed to think it would. Bowie seemed to think the three of them could ward off unhappiness and most importantly, death, if they denied themselves a lot of what they'd both had as kids.

Except apparently Bowie had paused that lifestyle for the weekend. Okay, sure he ate carrot sticks instead of Doritos, but he'd already downed three beers and Hanna had heard him cut loose with the f word—*fuck*, not *fiddlesticks*—a dozen times, and she was pretty sure he'd been checking out Trevor's girlfriend's boobs when she'd come outside in her black and white bikini.

Hanna couldn't blame him. She was cute; her boobs looked great. But she wondered now if the guys were discussing Mallory's features or if they were swapping dirty jokes or if they were talking about the girls they'd done back in school.

"What?" Hanna gave herself a mental shake when Peyton climbed to her feet. She looked up—Peyton looked great, too, still with those long, sexy legs, and the red bikini and the gold rings on her fingers—but the sun made it hard to see Peyton's face. Hanna put her hand up to shield her eyes since her sunglasses weren't doing their job. "Where are you going?"

"Beer run," Peyton said simply. "Want one?"

She didn't. But the thought of sitting on this damned

dock for hours and watching everyone else drink was as appealing as the idea of a hot bath right now.

"Sure." She nodded and turned back to the lake in time to see Davis jump from the other dock in the center of the lake again. Hanna was curious about Davis. Everyone else looked pretty good with the previous twelve years added to their faces and their stomachs and their butts. But Davis hadn't aged as well.

Mallory let out a squeal and then a roar of hearty laughter, and Hanna watched Sam lean closer to Bowie and mumble something. They'd climbed onto the dock Davis had just jumped from. Both of them watched Trevor and Mallory, now kissing, hanging off the side of the raft.

Hanna felt a heavy weight in her stomach, and she realized it was *more* than not liking the teenaged Bowie White. She didn't like herself much either. She didn't like that she'd once been part of that kind of scene—the drinking to get drunk part, the making out with Trevor part, the watching part. Now she was ashamed of herself and disgusted with herself for being jealous. Not of Mallory and Trevor, but it bothered her that Bowie was watching them. That Sam was probably saying things, immature things, about what Trevor should do with Mallory, and Bowie was probably eating it up.

Peyton appeared at her side and handed her an open beer.

"Neelie's out," she announced as she sat down. Hanna glanced to her right where Neelie was stretched out on a lounge chair in the shade. Sweet, pregnant Neelie in her demure navy tank suit. Kind of made Hanna feel slutty in her bikini, though she knew she still had the body for it. Bowie had made sure of that.

"I wouldn't wanna be here if I was pregnant," Hanna mumbled. She took a drink of the cold, refreshing beer and decided she'd needed it after all.

Peyton looked over at Neelie again, but she didn't answer Hanna.

"Would you—"

"Be here if I was pregnant?" Peyton cut her a look that said she must be insane. Hanna laughed softly.

"Do you want kids?"

Now Peyton lowered her sunglasses to look at Hanna.

"I'm sorry." Hanna looked away. "None of my business."

"It's not," Peyton agreed, "and I don't know."

"You don't know?"

"I don't know what I wanna be when I grow up," Peyton admitted. She flicked her eyes up to meet Hanna's, but she looked away just as quickly. Turned her attention to the lake. "I know. Believe me, I know. I'm thirty years old. It's time to grow the hell up and do something with my life. And really, Hanna White, all I can think to do with my life is drink it away."

Hanna licked her lips. She wanted to say something. Something profound. Helpful. She didn't have a clue what it would be.

"I'm sorry."

"For what?" She turned her head to look at Peyton.

"What I said about Sylvi. It's not my business."

Hanna took a deep breath. "You weren't wrong."

Peyton nodded to acknowledge she'd heard her. She looked around the lake again and then cleared her throat.

"We all...dealt with it. Differently." She shrugged. "You guys went health Nazi. I went hell-bent on alcohol, thinking it might kill me quicker."

"You're still here." Hanna elbowed her gently.

Peyton nodded. "I'm still here. Epic fail, huh?"

"What about..." Hanna was going to ask about Brion, but she hesitated. Not her business.

"What?" Peyton cocked her head at her. "What about what?"

"Brion. What about Brion?"

Peyton bit her lip. Looked away. She was quiet long enough that Hanna decided she wasn't going to answer her.

"I don't know," she finally mumbled.

"What happened?"

"I dunno. We lived together for a couple of years. And then I decided he was an ass, and he's arrogant, and he's unbearable. And I moved out. And I don't know…"

"Do you miss him?"

Peyton's nod was slow to come, but Hanna saw it.

"You know that girl that was at my apartment?"

"The one who works for you?"

"Yeah."

"Yeah." Hanna nodded. She looked back at the lake to investigate the loud splashing and laughing. Trevor was trying to dunk Mallory now. "What about her?"

Peyton pursed her lips. Seemed to be considering what to say, maybe how to say it.

"I slept with her…a few weeks ago."

"You slept with her," Hanna repeated. "What? Like…when we were kids? She stayed over and you guys stayed up—"

"No." Peyton ducked her chin to her chest. Hanna stared at her fingers wrapped around her beer bottle. "As in we got drunk…and she kissed me…and the next thing I know, we're in my bed, and I'm having lesbian sex, and we woke up together, and now she's creepy as hell like she's stalking me."

Hanna stared at Peyton silently. As loose as they'd all been back the summer they'd graduated, the weekend they'd spent here at the lake, nothing like that had happened.

"How was it?"

She grinned when Peyton looked at her quickly.

"Mm." Peyton lifted a shoulder lazily. "It was great, but that doesn't mean—"

"Really?" Hanna lifted an eyebrow. "I'm curious. It was really good?"

"Yeah. She's apparently...pretty experienced, and I was drunk enough that...yeah, Hanna, I liked it. But. I don't want to keep doing it."

"Better than sex with a guy?"

"No."

"Hmm." Hanna considered that. She looked out at the lake again, but this time she looked for Bowie. Found him spread eagle on the other dock. Sam had jumped back in.

"She won't leave me alone. Thinks we would be great together, and we should have a relationship."

"What're you gonna do about it?"

"Well, right now, I'm doing Brion again," Peyton said with a laugh.

"Mmm." Hanna nodded her approval. "Does he know?"

Peyton answered with a tiny nod. "Yeah. He came by one night. Looking for something. And I just...jumped him. To prove to myself—"

"That you aren't a lesbian."

"That I don't..." Peyton shrugged helplessly. "Yeah."

"I'm sure he didn't mind."

Peyton shot Hanna a look of anger, but Hanna laughed out loud. Peyton grinned.

"He didn't."

"Did he stay last night?"

Peyton nodded. "Yeah. He did."

"It's not a big deal." Hanna swung her legs back and forth and took another drink of her beer.

"What?"

"I mean...don't...feel bad about it."

"Sleeping with Bellamy or using Brion like mouthwash?"

"Trying to get that bad taste out of your mouth?"

"Hanna White!" Peyton snorted.

Hanna laughed and dropped her hand on Peyton's thigh.

"I did not mean that, and you know it!"

Peyton took another long drink and shook her head.

"I'm gonna need a keg now."

"I'm just saying…" Hanna shrugged.

"I know." Peyton nodded her head from side to side. "I know. But now…Brion…and you guys. And there's still Bellamy. And I kind of want to fire her, but that's not gonna fly. That's the last thing I need—"

"What do you mean?"

"I don't need her slapping me with a sexual harassment suit."

"Oh, man." Hanna winced. "I never thought of that."

Peyton sighed. "I'm sorry—"

"Are you in love with him?"

"I don't know."

"What changed?"

"What?"

"When you were with him? What changed? You loved him once, right?"

"I changed." Peyton shrugged. "Again."

Chapter 38

MALLORY

She felt eyes on her as she walked out of the water. More than just Trevor's. Hanna and Peyton were on the end of the dock, feet dangling over the water, deep in conversation, but they called to her to join them. The water was cool, and even though they'd had an audience, it had been fun to play with Trevor that way. Splashing and dunking. Hanging on the side of the raft and kissing. It had crossed her mind that they were behaving like horny teenagers, but Trevor had kept his hands in sight, and nothing had gotten out of hand.

Mallory held her hand up to ask for a second and went in search of the beach towels she and Trevor had brought along. She found hers on the deck, dried her face off and then wrapped the towel around her neck and found a bottle of water in their cooler. A beer sounded good, but she decided it might be a bad idea with the heat and humidity and the fact that she hadn't eaten a whole lot earlier.

Peyton scooted over to make room for her to sit with them. Mallory sat down, hoping she didn't look as clumsy as she felt, and decided it was a little bit weird sitting here in swimwear this close to someone Trevor had messed around with when he was a kid. Thank God, she wasn't sitting right next to Hanna.

"You're getting pink."

Mallory looked down as Peyton poked her shoulder. They watched her skin turn from pink to white.

"Mm." Mallory winced. She didn't want to burn, but she was enjoying the day and she didn't want to go inside.

"We could move the party to the shade tree," Hanna suggested.

"We might wake Neelie up," Mallory argued. "I'm fine."

"Go get your sunscreen," Peyton told her. "Put more on."

Mallory considered that, decided it would be wise to reapply, and nodded. She started to stand, but Trevor swam toward the dock. When he reached the shoreline, he stood up and walked out of the water, pushing his hair back off his face.

"Whatcha need?" he asked Mallory.

"I was gonna get the sunscreen."

"I'll get it," he told her as he walked by her.

"Nice." Peyton nudged her and wiggled her eyebrows.

Mallory laughed out loud.

"You girls need anything?" Trevor called over his shoulder.

"No, thanks!" Hanna answered.

"Peyt?"

Hanna leaned forward to look at Mallory around Peyton. They both grinned when Peyton rolled her eyes.

"I'm good!"

Peyton sighed.

"What?"

"I don't hear anyone calling you Hanna Banana."

Hanna shrugged. "Thank God."

"How long have you and Trevor been together?" Peyton turned to Mallory.

"Um…a few months. I moved in with him in April."

"Where do you guys live?"

"I told you, at the corner of hell and fire." Mallory took a drink of her water and then screwed the cap back on the bottle. Hanna and Peyton laughed, but Mallory shook her head. "Not kidding. That apartment is horrible. It's upstairs. On Maine. Downtown. Hellhole. I don't wanna nag Trev, but God, I hope we can find something new."

"You live on Maine? I live on Maine."

"In a much nicer place, I'm sure."

"You should see her place," Hanna agreed. "It's so cool."

"And your McMansion isn't?" Peyton cocked her head at Hanna. "Really?"

"I didn't say that." Hanna smacked Peyton's leg. "I just like your apartment."

Mallory took the bottle of sunscreen when it appeared over her shoulder. She looked up at Trevor with a smile and told him thanks.

"Here." He reached to take it back, but Peyton shook her head and shoved his hand away.

"We don't need any of that going on right here," Peyton told him.

He grinned as he took the bottle back from Mallory.

"I can behave."

Peyton arched her eyebrows at him and looked the other way at Hanna.

Mallory leaned back on her hands as Trevor squatted behind her and squeezed lotion over her shoulders.

"That's cold," she mumbled.

"Feel good?"

"See? Don't do that." Peyton looked back at Trevor. "Don't say that stuff."

"Did anyone bring any charcoal to fire up the grill?"

"Fire up the grill," Hanna repeated.

Mallory laughed and looked up at Trevor. He rolled his eyes.

"Sam told Bowie to bring charcoal. Sam brought the meat."

Trevor nodded in response to Hanna. He looked out at the lake and frowned.

"Wonder what time it is."

"We just ate," Mallory reminded him.

"It's been a couple of hours." He shook his head. "And a charcoal grill takes longer to warm up."

"Are you seriously hungry?" Mallory twisted around to look at him.

"I will be." He nodded. Leaned toward her and kissed the tip of her nose.

Mallory watched him curiously as he walked back up to the deck and then went inside. Hard to reconcile this laid-back guy with the man who had been having nightmares for the past month. Especially when the nightmares involved this group of people and this lake.

Peyton said something, but Mallory didn't hear her clearly. She wondered what Trevor was doing, but rather than draw attention to her worries or Trevor himself, she turned back to Peyton.

"What?"

"Is he always this sweet?"

"Um." Mallory pursed her lips. "Most of the time."

She laughed with Peyton and Hanna. Wondered if he would always be this sweet if they got past this lake issue. Remembered him telling her when they were packing that he thought he'd killed Eden.

What a bizarre thing to say. Why would he even think something like that? Unless maybe he *had* done something to

Eden.

Mallory looked away from the two women beside her and drew in a deep breath.

He wouldn't. Trevor Gerhardt wasn't the killing kind, *was he*? How the hell did she know? She wasn't well-acquainted with any killers. Still, it would go a long way toward explaining the nightmares.

"So, who appointed Sam as the boss, anyway?" Peyton asked. Mallory knew she was talking to Hanna, but she turned her face to them again, anxious to hear Hanna's answer.

"Sam's Sam." Hanna shrugged. "You don't change who you are."

"I did."

"You think you did." Hanna stared at Peyton for a moment. "You're as much Peyton as Sam's still Sam."

"So, you're saying when I was eighteen, I was already a depressed, good-for-nothing, borderline alcoholic?"

Mallory looked from Hanna to Peyton. Wondered if she should give them some privacy.

"The alcohol's a crutch," Hanna said dismissively. "You're still you."

Mallory flinched, but Peyton only sighed.

"Like your blog is yours?"

"Yeah." Hanna nodded. "Yeah. Exactly like that."

"Hanna writes a blog about death," Peyton explained to Mallory.

"We're not that different, Peyton."

"Right." Peyton nodded slowly. "You live in a great house, and you have a great husband and a beautiful little girl. You guys have your own business."

Hanna, head turned away from both of them, shrugged.

"And I have nightmares about Eden. And I pretend I

don't. Bowie doesn't allow any discussion about her. Bowie runs my life. Maybe like alcohol runs yours."

"I thought you were madly in love with him."

"I do love him," Hanna said simply. "Doesn't mean my life is perfect."

"I have nightmares about her, too," Peyton admitted. "Now and then."

"I still don't get it." Hanna drained her beer and then made a face. "Yuck. That got warm fast."

"What don't you get?"

"You. And Brion."

"Why do you care?"

Hanna finally looked at Peyton. Mallory felt the heat in her glare. She looked away, again thinking she needed to move to give them privacy. But Hanna climbed to her feet and walked up the dock toward the house.

"What's not to get about a breakup?" Peyton looked at Mallory. "People split up all the time."

Mallory shrugged.

"Can I ask you something?"

"What?" Mallory nodded. She was watching Peyton, but she was wondering about Trevor. And Hanna. And what they might be doing in the house right now.

"Did Trevor want to do this? Come to the lake?"

Mallory considered her words carefully before she opened her mouth to answer Peyton.

"Mmm." She took a deep breath. She couldn't tell Peyton that Trevor had totally blocked all of them out of his mind. That he didn't remember the lake or what had happened here. Or maybe he did on a subconscious level. Trevor could tell them if he decided to, but it wasn't Mallory's place to share Trevor's strange dreams and drawings. "You know, he didn't say much. Maybe it was just…good timing for us. I think we were both going a little stir-crazy in that apartment."

"You'd make a good politician." Peyton arched her eyebrows and laughed softly. "Did he want to come? Did he wanna see everyone that night we all went out?"

"Yeah. He was okay with that," Mallory answered honestly. "I wanted to meet you guys."

Peyton snorted. "Yeah, we're great company."

Mallory cleared her throat. "What happened to Eden?"

"Trevor didn't tell you?"

When Peyton looked at her skeptically, Mallory simply shrugged, hoping Peyton would share the story from her point of view.

"I don't know," Peyton said quietly. "She drowned. But."

"But how does a person who knows how to swim drown?"

Mallory and Peyton looked up as Neelie joined them on the dock. She yawned and rubbed her eyes.

"God, I totally crashed." She rolled her head on her shoulders and rested her hands on her belly.

"They found her over there," Peyton told Mallory. Mallory followed the direction Peyton's finger was pointing. Tried to imagine a girl's body floating to the surface of the lake and tangling in the weeds and grass on the shoreline. It wasn't a big lake by any stretch of the imagination, but it was big enough that Eden's body could have been lost. That they could have had to drag the lake.

"When I was twelve," Mallory bit her lip, "a guy drowned in a lake…like this. Some teenagers. Hanging out. They ruled it an accident."

"You don't think it was?" Neelie leaned forward to look at Mallory around Peyton.

Mallory shrugged. "My friend's brother knew the kid. They all thought it was suicide."

"Wouldn't that be the hardest way to commit suicide?" Peyton mumbled. "How could you do it? How could you walk into water, when you know how to swim, and fight the instinct to survive?"

"You lose those instincts, though, don't you?" Neelie said softly. "When you decide to kill yourself?"

Peyton shrugged.

"I don't think Eden killed herself. It was an accident. We were all pretty stupid that weekend."

Mallory breathed a sigh of relief. She hadn't known how badly she needed to hear someone else say it was just an accident until Neelie did just now.

Chapter 39

TREVOR

He wandered through the first floor of the house slowly. The gang was still outside; he'd left Mallory with Peyton and Hanna. He was glad to see Mallory fitting in with the girls, even Hanna. There was nothing between him and Hanna, never had been. They'd made out when they were eighteen. End of story. But Eden. He'd liked her. Hadn't ever had the guts to tell her that, to ask her out. They'd talked only a little before the accident. Trevor remembered now that he'd been thinking about asking her out when the weekend was over.

Except…

He stopped walking now, chin dropped to his chest, hands propped on his waist. Except what? What was he thinking?

The drapes were pulled, so the living room was dark with just a shaft of pale daylight slicing through the hall from the kitchen. He squeezed his eyes shut and tried to pull it back, whatever it was he was thinking. He'd planned to ask her out when they all got home from the lake. Away from everyone else.

He'd told Hanna.

Jesus, had he really? Had he told Hanna he was going to ask Eden out? Or was his brain making that up? Would his brain make up false memories? *Could it?* Hell if he knew.

"Hey."

He dropped his hands to his sides and turned to find Hanna in the hall. Staring at him. Okay, so there hadn't been anything between them other than two friends who made out one night twelve years ago. But suddenly, it felt awkward, with just the two of them standing in the shadows of the living room.

"Hey." He nodded at Hanna. Sighed in frustration. Maybe if he'd had a few more minutes he could have at least pulled that thought back.

"Whaddaya doing in here by yourself?" She propped her shoulder on the wall and watched him. The frigid, stale air in the living room licked his skin and shot a chill up his back. His trunks were still wet, though he didn't think he was dripping on the old brown carpet.

He shrugged.

"Came in to use the bathroom," he told her. He had. And then he'd been drawn to the living room for some reason.

"She's really cute," Hanna announced suddenly, and Trevor was so deep in thoughts of Eden, he thought for a moment that Hanna was talking about her. He nodded slowly, and it hit him then that she meant Mallory, and he nodded again with more enthusiasm.

"Yeah." He grinned. "She is."

"Gonna marry her?"

"I have no idea." He took his glasses off—he'd grabbed them when he came inside—and rubbed his eyes. "It's a little early to say."

"Nah. If she's the one, you know by now."

Trevor thought Mallory might be the one, but he couldn't

ask her to make that commitment yet. Not until they figured out what the hell had happened at this place twelve years ago. Imagine what Mallory would feel like if they got hitched and then a day after saying *I do*, he remembered that he had killed Eden.

"Can I ask you something?" Trevor turned his back to Hanna and wandered further across the room. He stood almost directly in front of the window unit now, and his body shook with the cold.

And nerves.

"What?"

"Did I tell you…" He hesitated. Straightened a lampshade, though it was dark enough maybe he'd only just made it worse. He couldn't be sure.

"What?" She sounded interested now.

"When we were here. Before."

She didn't say anything, so Trevor took a quick breath and rubbed his hands over his black trunks. New. He'd had to go buy new trunks for this trip. He hadn't set foot in a swimming pool or lake or river in years. Did that mean something? Did it mean maybe he'd killed an innocent girl and developed a fear or hatred of water? Or did it just mean he got busy and interested in other things and hadn't wanted to do any water fun?

"Did I tell you I was going to ask Eden out? When we got back?"

Hanna sighed. Trevor turned to look at her, but he kept his distance. Seemed like he and Hanna had ended up on the front porch almost by default. And they'd talked for a long time. They'd bared their souls to each other, maybe because they were embarrassed about what everyone else was doing and what was expected of them. Like they were nervous, maybe.

"Yeah," Hanna said softly. "Yeah, you did."

Trevor cleared his throat. He felt a funny little vibration in his stomach. Felt kind of weird to reference secrets told on that front porch since they had given in and ended up screwing around out there. Trevor wondered now who'd paired up with who of their remaining friends at the lake.

He squeezed his eyes shut again. Little flash of Sam. On the dock. Someone on her knees in front of him.

He didn't know what to say. About that flash of memory. About what he'd said to Hanna. About what they'd done and how she was married to Bowie now, who could pick him up and snap him in two if he wanted to. About the girlfriend he'd brought here with him.

"Sometimes I think I hear her crying," Hanna said quietly.

"What?"

She shrugged. "I guess it's always just a dream." She stood up straight. "Either that or it's Sylvi."

"Han?"

Trevor wanted to keep talking. To keep prying at the boards in his memory, the ones that were piled over the memories here at the lake. He wanted to dig through them and find the truth, and he wondered suddenly if Hanna could help him do that. But Bowie was in the house now, calling for Hanna, and Mallory was out on the dock, and he and Hanna were standing here in the dark and maybe the others were wondering what the hell was going on.

He almost laughed at that. It was a ridiculous thought. He wasn't interested in the Hannas and Peytons and Neelies of the world. Hadn't been all those years ago.

"Yeah?" She turned away from Trevor and disappeared down the hall to the kitchen.

He waited another few minutes after he heard them go back outside before he went back to the kitchen. Walked down the hall with his fingers on the walls, as if he could read the memories through his fingertips. He remembered

AC/DC. Sam had brought a boombox, and there was always something loud and hard blaring from it, mostly AC/DC.

Hanna was in the water with Bowie when he went back outside. The heat crawled over him, up over his face, and stole his breath. He saw Mallory on the dock with Neelie and Peyton. Wondered what would become of this group when they left the lake this time. Even without a tragedy, he wasn't sure he wanted to stay in touch. This was fun, but he wasn't sure he wanted to carry it any further than a big birthday bash for all of them.

He stopped on the deck, eyes going automatically to the spot where he remembered seeing Sam that night on the dock. It had been dark, no city lights, the floodlights on the back of the house had been turned off. Trevor hadn't been able to sleep, so he'd come outside thinking he'd walk around for a bit.

Sam had been standing there with one hand on the rail of the dock and his other hand in someone's hair.

"Cool off?"

Trevor gave himself a mental shake and looked at Sam as he skipped up the steps to the deck.

"Yeah."

"Whaddaya think? When should we get the grill going?"

Trevor took a deep breath and stretched. "I dunno. What time is it?"

"I dunno." Sam took a long drink of water and then recapped the bottle. "I think I'm gonna grab that lounge chair in the shade for a while."

"Sounds like a plan," Trevor agreed. He watched Sam watch Neelie for a few moments and then wander back off the deck and over to the lounge chair Neelie had been sleeping in.

Peyton climbed to her feet and acted like she was going to

push Neelie off the dock. Neelie screeched and then there were peals of laughter from the lake.

Eden's hair fanned out behind her as she fell.

"Hey." Peyton threw her hip at him as she passed him on the deck.

Chapter 40

PEYTON

The chill in the air gave her goose bumps, and she shivered as she slipped carefully through the living room to the bathroom. She flipped the light on, closed the door, and then leaned against the counter and looked at herself in the oval mirror over the sink. She looked okay from the neck down. Nice tan. Still in shape, sort of, though she wouldn't arm wrestle Hanna anytime soon. Though, probably, Sam would pay to see it and even pull strings to set it up.

She slid her sunglasses off her nose and cringed at the bags under her bloodshot eyes. She'd tossed the last of her last beer; nothing worse than swallowing it warm. Well, actually, maybe there was, but Peyton didn't particularly want to think about that now. She sighed. Set her glasses on the counter and used the restroom quickly. Washed her hands. Stood for a moment with her hands under the cold water, remembering she and Eden locking themselves in here and giggling like kids.

Sam and Bowie had chased them. Out of the water and across the deck. They'd hid in here for an hour, Eden sprawled on the pink shag carpet and Peyton in the white porcelain tub. Sam had pounded on the door, but eventually, he'd lost interest and gone back to the water and the beer. Peyton and Eden had talked. Eden had admitted she'd been accepted into all of her college choices, but she was too scared to pick one. To pack up and move away. Peyton had told Eden she wished she could travel. Not necessarily the grunge backpack trip across Europe, but something like that. She'd told her that her parents would never allow it, and Eden had agreed her parents wouldn't, either.

She jumped now when someone knocked on the door.

"Just a second."

She splashed a little water on her face and then patted it dry with the rose-colored hand towel folded on the sink. She glanced at the pink shag carpet and the toilet seat cover and decided it had been kind of gross twelve years ago, and it was just creepy now.

Davis was in the hall apparently studying a framed picture on the wall. To Peyton it looked like a discount store Monet print. Davis seemed to be finding the meaning of life in the colors.

"All yours."

He turned to her with a grin.

"Thanks" He patted his bald spot and nodded toward the bathroom. "I need to fix my hair."

She laughed softly.

"When'd that happen anyway? Your hair used to be longer than mine."

Davis stepped into the bathroom and looked with disgust at the pink carpet.

"I feel like this is what a girl's bedroom would have looked like in the seventies."

"Yeah, minus the balding grown man." Peyton nodded.

He grinned and shrugged. "Yep. True. I got it cut off a

month after…" He cleared his throat. "After the funeral. Went
to work—"

"Where at?"

"Simpson Industries," he answered.

"Where?"

"It was a factory about an hour north of town. We made
parts for appliances. Met Amy at work—"

"Amy?" She shook her head.

"My ex-wife," he answered simply. "We dated for a few
months and got married. Had one kid together. She left
when Connor was two."

Peyton bit her lip.

"That sucks."

"Yeah. I went bald, she left."

Peyton laughed and shook her head.

"Well, we fought a lot. That might have had something to
do with it."

"And the beer belly?" Peyton asked.

"Jesus, you're hard on a guy." He rubbed his belly that
Peyton decided wasn't that bad. Definitely not great when
you put him next to the other guys here, but Davis was okay.
She'd sure as hell rather talk to him than Sam.

"I've got one, too."

"Yeah, if I had a magnifying glass maybe I could see it."
Davis pretended to study her stomach. "Besides, you've got
boobs. Guys can look past anything if you've got boobs."

Peyton rolled her eyes.

"On that note," she took a step back, "don't let the Pepto
Bismol room swallow you whole."

"Dude, I've had nightmares," he mumbled as he pushed
the door closed.

Peyton laughed to herself as she made her way back
through the house. She wondered if he really had nightmares. Not about the room. But about Eden.

She realized as she walked down the hall to the kitchen that she'd left her sunglasses on the bathroom counter. Rather than go back through the dark house—kind of gave her the creeps—she decided to wait in the kitchen for Davis to come back out. She'd had plenty to drink, and she wasn't tipsy, and that set off a few warning bells. Hanna thought she was joking about being a borderline alcoholic. Peyton could function without it, but she found it interesting the amount of alcohol she could consume before she felt the effects.

That thought brought her back to Bellamy. She had to admit she was glad to be away from the girl for a few days. But, she missed Brion; she really did miss him. Why hadn't she asked him to come? Why had she moved out? What the hell was wrong with her?

She grabbed a bottle of water from the refrigerator and sipped on it. Found her purse on the chair where she'd been sitting earlier and pulled her phone from the middle pocket. She'd missed two calls from Bellamy, but she ignored them. Texted Brion and asked if he wanted to join them.

Chapter 41

MALLORY

As the sun moved over the roof of the house and the dock fell under shade, the group got sun-drowsy and quiet. Sam slept under the shade tree where Neelie had napped earlier. Hanna and Bowie excused themselves and went inside, presumably to choose their room for the weekend. Maybe to rest, maybe not. Peyton, Neelie, and Davis spread out on the dock, the one closest to the house, and talked about old times. Trevor and Mallory took a walk.

Funny that she'd been in the lake and walked out of the lake and through the yard barefoot, and now that she was wearing flip flops again and walking with Trevor, Mallory was worried about snakes. They held hands as they walked, though again, it was so hot, and they were sweaty, and it was almost hard to hold onto Trevor.

She did, though, because he looked upset. He hadn't said much; he wasn't angry with her, she knew that. But he was almost scowling as they walked, and Mallory wondered if he'd remembered something when he was inside the house or if he was just torturing himself trying to remember something.

She couldn't decide if she should wait him out or ask him what was going on. Her stomach rumbled a bit, and she hoped that when they got back from their walk everyone would stir and start dinner. Apparently, Sam had decided the menu. Mallory didn't really care what they ate, as long as they did it soon.

"What're you thinking about?" She barely breathed the words because she didn't want to disturb him, not if he was remembering something.

But he shook his head helplessly.

"I just get these little flashes of memory," he answered. "I mean...I remember being here now. But I couldn't go through a timeline of events for you."

"But you remember the ambulance waking you up?" She hoped he didn't notice how hopeful she sounded.

"No. Actually, I don't," he admitted. "I remember the ambulance. But not...I don't remember being up in the bedroom when I heard it. It's just there. In my head."

She sighed. Squeezed his hand.

"Trev, maybe it was what they all say it was. Maybe it was just an accident."

She watched him struggle with that. With the possibility that Eden's death had been an accidental drowning, just as his friends said.

"I remember...being out on the porch with Hanna—"

"Spare me the details—"

"No. I don't mean that." He shook his head, oblivious to Mallory's teasing tone. "We talked. Forever. Before anything happened. Ya know? When you're supposed to be hooking up with someone, but you're kinda..."

"Nervous about it?"

"Yeah." Trevor nodded. "Yeah. We talked. I remembered talking to her about Eden."

Mallory swallowed hard. Looked around as they walked. Trevor had led her away from the house, around the lake. Surely, there were snakes in this grass out here.

"What about her?" She curled her toes as she walked. Maybe she wouldn't get back in the water. Maybe once she and Trevor were back from their walk, she'd sit up on the dock or the deck, away from any possible snakes. Or frogs. How the hell had she forgotten all of that and waded right into that lake water? She'd been fine with that stuff when she was a kid, but she hated it now.

"I wanted to ask her out." Trevor's eyes swept the lake. "I liked her. A lot. But I didn't know her that well. She'd only started hanging out with us. She was Peyton's friend."

"So, you told Hanna you liked Eden?"

He flashed Mallory a sheepish grin now.

"Sounds pretty stupid now, doesn't it?"

"It's how it works, though, right?"

"How what works?"

"Life." She shrugged. "Boy meets girl. Or girl meets boy. Somebody likes somebody. Somebody's gotta have the balls to make the first move. Maybe it works out, and boy and girl get married and have a family. And they buy a house with an oven and drive vans and go to the beach and live happily ever after."

"Or?"

"Or maybe they don't. And it starts over. Until they do."

Trevor frowned and studied Mallory's face.

"What?" She laughed.

"That's..." He shook his head. "I don't even know. Over-simplified. Depressing as hell. They buy a house with an oven? I mean, why not a house with a home theater system?"

Mallory snorted.

"So, what happened?"

"Hmm?"

"When you told Hanna. What'd she say?"

Trevor sighed and shrugged. Tore his eyes from Mallory and looked out toward the lake again.

"She told me to do it. To just ask her."

"So, did you?"

"No." Trevor stopped walking. "No. I don't remember…I was going to. But something came up."

"What do you mean?"

"I feel like I saw her with someone." Trevor let go of Mallory's hand and dragged his fingers back through his hair. Mallory smiled, wished she could reach him to smooth his hair out. It had dried funny, sticking up in places, and now he'd made the rest of it stand on end.

"With someone."

He nodded. "I keep getting a flash of Sam. On the dock."

Mallory waited for him to go on.

"Someone was with him. It was the middle of the night. I couldn't sleep, so I got up, and I was out walking around."

"You think you saw Eden making out with Sam?"

"I don't know." He shook his head. "I don't…think. I don't think so. But why else am I remembering that?"

"I read a book once about someone planting false memories in someone's head."

"Who would be planting false memories in my head?"

"Were you jealous?"

"What?"

"When you saw Sam. Did you feel jealous?"

"No." Trevor squatted down and reached for something.

Mallory screamed and jumped behind him.

"What is your problem?" He chuckled and looked up at her.

"What're you doing?"

"Picking a beautiful weed for you," he answered as he stood up. He turned to her, a long green weed in his outstretched hand.

"Jesus, don't do that." She slapped her hand over her chest, felt her heart thumping. "What if that's poison ivy?"

"It's not." He dropped it and then stepped toward her and slid his arms around her waist. "And Mal?"

"What?"

"Don't let Sam know you're afraid of snakes."

"What? Why?"

"Because you'll find one down your swimsuit," he answered. "He thinks it's funny. I told you they—"

Mallory chewed on her lip and tilted her head to look at Trevor.

"I thought you said Sam was a good guy."

"Why do you say that?"

"I don't know, but I'm getting the impression that he's a jerk."

"You're getting that from me?"

Mallory shrugged and looked around. "From everybody."

"Really." Trevor frowned. He dropped his hands from Mallory's sides and took her hand again. They started walking back toward the house.

"I'm getting hungry."

"Me too." He nodded. "I think everyone probably is. Sam asked me earlier when I thought we should get the grill going."

"What's on the menu tonight?"

"Um." Trevor shrugged. "No idea. If Bowie planned dinner, I'd say tofu."

Mallory snorted and shook her head. "Hanna writes a blog. About death."

Trevor looked at her but said nothing.

"And Peyton drinks," she continued.

"Why are you telling me this?"

"I don't know?" She finally shook her head. "I guess...I want you to know they're all dealing...with this, too. So maybe..."

"Maybe your boyfriend isn't a killer?"

"Trev." She stopped walking again. "I don't believe that. You know I don't believe you would hurt someone."

He leaned into her and kissed her. Just a soft, sweet kiss.

"So, when this is over," he took a deep breath, "you wanna get hitched and buy a house with an oven and get a van and go to the beach?"

"Was that a marriage proposal?"

"If I'm not behind bars." He gave her a curt nod.

"You left out the family part."

"You'd wanna have a family with a crazy person?"

"There's no hurry," she reminded him. "I'm not going anywhere."

She put her arms around him. Hoped he wasn't thinking about Eden. Comparing her to Eden. Thinking he needed to hurry up and ask her to marry him before something bad happened to her.

"No," he agreed, "but someone just pointed out to me that if you're with the right person, you don't need a lifetime to figure that out."

Mallory arched her eyebrows and grinned. "That's deep. That's really deep, Trev."

"You haven't answered me."

"Well..." She rubbed her thumb over his lips. "Here's the thing. I like the guy in this story. But I don't like how he did it. I need some romance."

"Making out in Litchfield Lake isn't romantic?"

"No. I kinda feel like we're making a cheap movie about drugs and sex, to be honest."

"Well, there's always lat—"

"Huh-uh." She shook her head. "I want to be alone with you. And I want you to say you love me before you ask me to marry you, and I want a ring."

"What kind of ring?"

"Nothing fancy," she answered with a shrug. "But this…I assure you…does not count as romantic."

"Mal, I lo—"

"Huh-uh." She rubbed his lips again and then patted his face gently. "Not here. Let's figure this out first."

He nodded. Kissed her again. Lingered a little longer at her mouth this time. And then took her hand, and they started walking again.

"Mal?"

"Hmm?"

"I think someone pushed her."

Chapter 42

PEYTON

It was funny the way everyone woke up and started moving at the same time, almost as if someone pushed play. Peyton had dozed off on the dock, and now her back hurt like hell, and she wasn't sure she was going to be able to stand up. She sat up slowly and looked around, noticed Neelie and Sam under the shade tree. Sam was awake, and Neelie was sitting in his lap. It looked almost normal to Peyton, except for the fact that Neelie was wearing that tank suit, and they were wearing wedding rings, and it was *Neelie and Sam.*

As she watched, Sam dropped a kiss on Neelie's cheek, eased her off his lap, and stood up. Trevor and Mallory had come back from their walk. They were up on the deck talking to Hanna. Peyton wondered where Bowie was; she hoped he was inside finding food. Then again, if Bowie was finding food for dinner, that might mean they were eating vegetables and tofu. She dropped her gaze as Davis stirred on the dock beside her, watched him look around and zero in

on their surroundings. He yawned as he sat up, and then he
shot her a cute grin.

"I can finally say I slept with Peyton Kelly." The grin
turned lecherous, and he wiggled his eyebrows at her.

Peyton rolled her eyes.

"If you say that to somebody, I might just have to kill you."

"Harsh."

She watched him struggle to his feet, and then when he
turned away from her, she climbed to her feet also. As they
walked up to the deck, the screen door flung open, and
Bowie appeared empty-handed.

"Bowie? What the hell? Where's the food?"

Bowie looked at Hanna and shook his head.

"Gotta get the charcoal going first, Han."

"What about the salad?" Hanna, slumped in her chair at
the patio table, rolled her head on the seat to look toward the
dock. When she saw Peyton coming, her face lit up, and
Peyton almost missed a step as she walked. What was that
about? Why did she light up inside just because Hanna
smiled at her? God, had it been that long since she'd had
friends and enjoyed being around other people?

"Do we want the salad already?" Bowie frowned. Peyton
saw the look on Hanna's face when Bowie walked by her and
crossed the grass to stand by Sam. Davis went inside, but
Peyton joined Hanna, Trevor, and Mallory at the table. She
sat down across from Hanna and rubbed her eyes. Probably
the nap had been a good idea. On the other hand, maybe not.
Peyton was not a good napper. She always woke up with a
fuzzy head that turned into an all-out headache if she didn't
feed it either with alcohol or coffee. She wasn't sure she
needed more alcohol right now, but even with the sun on the
other side of the house, it was still hotter than hell out, and
coffee sounded terrible.

She watched Hanna boldly, a little bit amused by her

reaction to Bowie. Then again it would piss Peyton off too, if her husband ignored her and went to Sam for directions. She dragged her eyes away from Hanna, twisted in her chair, and glanced back at Sam, Bowie and Neelie, who saw her looking at them and grinned. Peyton answered with a halfhearted smile, but she wasn't feeling it. Sam Collins was a dick.

Apparently, Sam gave Bowie the go-ahead to light the charcoal. Peyton turned back to Hanna as Bowie marched off toward the grill. It was actually pretty amazing that everyone was content to sit back and let Sam run the show. Kinda one thing for them to do it when they were eighteen, totally different now that they were all adults.

The screen door opened, and Davis came out carrying a bottle of water.

"Dude. Ten bucks if you get me a bottle of water too," Sam called.

"Fuck you, buddy," Davis answered with a grin. "Get off your ass and get it yourself."

Peyton twisted around again to look at Sam, who was sitting in the lounge chair again. Neelie laughed and headed toward the house. Sam flipped Davis off.

"Damn, man. You used to be cheap labor." Sam stretched his arms above his head and watched Davis with a smartass smile on his face. "Remember that? Remember when you were my bitch?"

Peyton sensed a spike of tension. Still twisted in her chair, she looked at Hanna over her shoulder. Hanna met her eyes and shrugged almost imperceptibly. Bowie still stood with his back to all of them, poking at the charcoal briquettes in the grill.

"You can't afford me now," Davis mumbled.

"You weren't that good then, man." Sam shrugged. "Sure as hell wouldn't give you more."

"Did you say something about a salad?" Peyton turned

back to the table. She wanted no part in whatever was about to explode. Hanna nodded, but her eyes were still on Davis and Sam.

"Fuck you, Sam." Davis uncapped the water bottle and took a long drink.

"Bowie. You remember that?" Sam called, apparently disappointed when Davis didn't rise to the bait.

"What's that?" Bowie looked at Sam over his shoulder and then looked back at the grill. He stood for a moment longer, and then apparently satisfied that the fire was burning, he turned and wandered back across the yard toward Sam.

"Remember? When I paid Davis a hundred bucks to suck me off?"

The late afternoon stopped. All sound, all movement stopped. Peyton couldn't be sure what anyone else was doing, but she was looking at Sam. Shocked that he'd said what he had. Whether or not he'd actually paid Davis to do anything didn't enter her mind. She was simply shocked he'd said it in front of everyone but his wife. Davis was part of the crowd, had been since day one. Sam had just thrown him under a bus with the same nonchalance he might throw an apple core into the trees.

The door banged shut, and Peyton glanced over to see Neelie standing there. Peyton couldn't decide if she'd heard him or not. She didn't look shocked—under the surprise and the anger Peyton felt at Sam for what he'd just said, she couldn't deny that if it was true, *she was* shocked—but she didn't look particularly happy, either.

"Didn't take much, did it?" Davis asked Sam from his spot on the dock. "What? Maybe thirty seconds?"

Dread settled in Peyton's stomach. She wasn't sure she could eat now. She didn't really care what Sam and Davis might have done all those years ago—at least she assumed Sam was referring to something that had happened here at the lake twelve years ago—after all, she'd spent the night with a female employee not long ago. Unless Sam had only done it, had only paid Davis to do it to use against him someday. Like now.

Of course, that's what he'd done. God, Sam had been a one-man wrecking crew that weekend at the lake. Look at what he'd done to Hanna. Hanna would never forget what happened, and if Bowie ever found out, he'd be pissed. He'd play right into Sam's plans. Maybe it would wreck Hanna and Bowie's marriage. It would wreck Bowie and Sam's friendship.

Peyton doubted any of it mattered to Sam.

Why had he done this? Why had he arranged for this weekend at the lake? Just to drag up the bad vibes from the past? Just to parade everyone's skeletons in front of everyone else? Only a cold-hearted son-of-a-bitch would do that. Bring everyone here in the guise of friendship and celebration only to hurt every one of them.

Peyton lifted her gaze when she heard the crunch of tires on gravel. From the corner of her eye, she saw Mallory reach to touch Trevor's hand. Neelie walked barefoot to the chair where Sam was still lounging. Slowly, he rolled up and off the chair to stand. He settled his arms on Neelie's shoulders and moved with her as if they were dancing.

"Buckley," he called. "You bring the burgers?"

"In the fridge." Davis sounded unruffled. Peyton scooted her chair back and stood at the same time Hanna did.

"Who wants a burger and who wants a steak?" Sam asked. He kissed Neelie, rubbed his hand down over her side, and squeezed her butt. Peyton flicked only her eyes over to see Hanna. What the hell was going on?

"Oh, I'm havin' a steak," Davis announced as he turned and moved back up toward the house. "Trev?"

"Um." Trevor shrugged. "Whatever."

"Ladies? Who wants what?" Sam walked away from Neelie. He walked by Davis and Bowie, knuckled Davis and then disappeared into the kitchen.

"What the hell?" Hanna turned a frown to Peyton.

"I dunno." Peyton shrugged.

"Hey." Hanna's face lit up suddenly. Peyton turned to see what she was looking at. Felt her knees go weak as Brion Mitchell rounded the side of the house. He looked a little uncertain, but the tension drained from his body when he met Peyton's eyes.

Chapter 43

TREVOR

He wasn't sure what he'd thought would happen. If he'd thought Davis might throw a punch at Sam. He'd decided if he did, Sam would crush him. Maybe they were all twelve years older, and maybe none of them was as fit as they'd been the summer after graduation. But Davis had never been particularly strong; he'd never been one of those buff guys, and now he was older and slower, and Sam would probably have beat the shit out of him.

Hadn't happened, though. The tension had built until suddenly Sam was talking about dinner, and he and Davis were laughing, and then Peyton's boyfriend or ex or whatever had shown up and the moment was forgotten.

Except it wasn't. *Not really.*

Sam and Bowie trooped into the house, probably to get the meat for the grill. Trevor could tell Peyton and Hanna were both rattled, but Peyton rushed away from the table and greeted the new guy with a hug, and Hanna stood and wandered down off the deck, out toward the lake.

Trevor sort of watched Davis for a few seconds, but Davis

ended up heading into the house with Sam and Bowie. Uncomfortable with Peyton and her guy standing with their arms around each other, both of them talking quietly, Trevor turned his attention to Mallory.

"That was weird." She barely breathed the words.

He nodded. "Yep."

"You think he was just bullshitting him?"

Trevor shook his head slowly. He knew now that he'd seen Sam and Davis on the dock together the night Eden had died. Made sense. He'd seen the long hair, but he'd known it wasn't one of the girls.

"It happened?" Mallory glanced at Hanna and then let her eyes roam over Peyton and her boyfriend and finally, she looked back at Trevor.

"Yeah."

Mallory's eyebrows shot up quickly. "That's who you—"

Trevor nodded again as Peyton turned and led her guy to the table.

"Hey, guys."

Trevor eyed her friend curiously; Peyton appeared transformed since he'd shown up. She wasn't bouncing on her toes or doing cartwheels, but she was smiling, and Trevor wasn't sure he'd seen Peyton smile since they'd all reconnected.

"This is my friend, Brion Mitchell. Brion, this is my friend Trevor Gerhardt. Trevor and I went to school together."

Trevor stood up and shook Brion's hand. The guy seemed okay, good smile, strong handshake.

"And this is Trevor's girlfriend, Mallory."

"You made it just in time for dinner," Trevor announced.

"Oh." Brion nodded appreciatively. "Good. I'm hungry."

They laughed, and then Hanna joined them on the deck again and exchanged a hello with Brion.

"What can I do to help?"

"Um." Peyton cleared her throat. "We might need a referee later."

"What's that supposed to mean?" Neelie appeared behind Peyton.

"Nothing," Peyton mumbled. "We're just not the smoothest group, are we?"

Trevor had to hand it to Peyton. She'd obviously been referring to what had just happened between Sam and Davis, but she appeared so unaffected, Neelie only nodded, watched her curiously, and then slipped by them to go back in the house.

"Hey." Sam, on his way back out, did a smooth little dance step with Neelie—balancing a plate of raw meat in one hand. "Lighten up, people!" he called.

Trevor watched Peyton and Hanna exchange a look and wondered what they were thinking. He couldn't ask them now, obviously, but a glance at Mallory proved she was wondering the same thing. Bowie pushed the screen door open and came outside with a fresh beer in hand. Trevor noticed Hanna watching him closely, but he looked away before Hanna could catch him. Watched Sam and Bowie at the grill, carrying on a conversation about baseball.

Suddenly, Sam handed the meat plate to Bowie and crossed back to the deck. Trevor dragged his eyes from him and let them slide over Peyton, who was now sitting next to Brion, and Hanna, who looked a little bit pale.

"Let's go decide which room we're gonna sleep in," Trevor suggested to Mallory.

She nodded and climbed to her feet immediately to follow him to the door. Trevor pulled the door open and led Mallory through the kitchen to the staircase in the corner of the living room. Though he was dry now, the stale air was cold, and he shivered as he hurried up the dark steps. Above him, late afternoon sunshine reached through the bedroom windows and stretched lazily through the hallway.

Trevor was relieved to find the second floor warmer, but it might prove hard to sleep if it didn't get any cooler than this up here later. He reached back for Mallory's hand as the hardwood floor beneath his feet groaned.

The master bedroom was Sam and Neelie's. Didn't matter if they'd marked the territory or not; in Trevor's head, it was their room. He led Mallory down the hallway, glanced into each room as they passed, and remembered the scene twelve years ago. The guys all shacked up on one side of the hallway and the girls on the other. Bunk beds? Twin beds? Trevor squeezed his eyes closed as he looked into the room he'd shared with Davis. Bunk beds. He'd slept on the bottom bunk. Davis had snored and kept him awake.

No. Davis hadn't kept him awake. Trevor hadn't been able to go to sleep. He'd lain awake for what felt like hours, and Davis' snoring had finally driven him out of bed and down the stairs and out of the house. He'd thought he'd take a walk, just wander around in the dark and see if it would settle him down.

He gave himself a mental shake now. *Settle him down?* What did that mean? Why would he need to settle down?

"This is an old house," Mallory mumbled. Trevor watched her run her fingers over the dark paneled walls. "This the room you stayed in?"

"Yeah." He nodded. "Davis had the top bunk. He snored."

"So do you." Mallory leaned into him and pressed her grin to his lips. He slid his arm around her waist and rested his other hand on her hip. Kissed her again.

"That a deal breaker?"

"I'd prefer a garden variety snore to the nightmares."

"Don't." He shook his head. Moved his hand up to wrap around her neck and nuzzled his mouth under her ear.

"Don't what?"

He shrugged. "*Nightmare.* I just…I hate that word."

"What else would you call it?"

"I don't know, but it makes me sound like a pussy."

She laughed and stepped back.

"You want this room?" he asked her.

"Bunk beds?" She cocked her head at him and frowned.

"Not sure we're gonna find better."

Mallory shrugged. "Let's look."

She took his hand, linked her fingers through his and led him a few more steps down the hall.

"Someone already claimed this room," she announced. Trevor noticed the luggage at the foot of the double bed.

"Bowie and Hanna, I bet," he decided. "It's okay. We're not gonna have sex here anyway, Mal."

"Eww." She shivered and looked at him over her shoulder. "No. We're not. That's gross."

"So bunk beds aren't going to hurt."

She walked to the next open doorway, slowed, and kept walking when she realized it was a bathroom.

"No, but…" She looked into the next room and then turned to him. Raised her eyebrows suggestively. Trevor peeked into the room and nodded his okay at the small double bed.

"But what?" He grinned and settled his hands on her hips again. Pressed her up against the wall at her back. "You're not sure you can keep your hands off me?"

She laughed softly, but her eyes were serious.

"I just wanna sleep with you." She bit her lip. "With your arm around me. It's creepy here, Trev."

Trevor nodded. He thought so, and while it wasn't a good thing that Mallory thought so, too, he was glad to know he wasn't alone. That he wasn't just feeling the after-effects of those dreams.

"Why would he do that?" She spoke so softly, Trevor had to strain to hear her. Not sure if she was talking about Sam or Davis, he drew his eyebrows into a frown and shook his head.

"Davis?"

She shrugged and rested her head on the wall. "Davis? Sam?"

"Davis did it for the money," he answered simply. "Hundred bucks could buy a lot of beer."

Mallory took a deep breath and let it out slowly. "Would you do that? For a hundred bucks?"

"No." He shook his head. "But I'm not Davis."

"Just…" She shivered with distaste. "I mean…if that's…the way he swings, that's one thing. But just for money." She licked her lips. They heard the screen door open and close downstairs. "But why would Sam do that?"

Trevor shrugged. Sighed and shook his head.

"I dunno. He's just…"

"He's a bully, Trev."

"Maybe," he agreed.

"No maybe. He's running the show. I'm betting he was *the guy* when you were kids, and he's still doing it. You guys are all letting him do it."

"Do what?" Trevor snapped. A door closed downstairs. Trevor glanced at the shadowed staircase. Figured someone had gone into the bathroom and closed the door.

"He's made all the decisions. He's calling all the shots."

Someone else was in the house. Trevor heard footsteps downstairs. Voices.

"And I'll tell ya something else," Mallory whispered.

Trevor tore his eyes from the stairwell and looked at Mallory. Arched his eyebrows to urge her to keep talking.

"Hanna White can't stand him."

So, Mallory had seen that flash of hate, too. If looks could kill, Trevor thought maybe Hanna's stare might have reached back through the years and killed Sam the first time they were at the lake. He wondered, though, if Mallory had seen anything else. The way Hanna had blanched. Hatred didn't particularly turn a person sickly pale, did it? If anything, Trevor tended to get worked up, heated up around people he strongly disliked. Angry. Maybe even *red-in-the-face* angry.

"She looked—" He stopped talking when he heard the first step creak. No one could sneak up those steps. Every damned one of them creaked and groaned. Someone was coming. Rather than appear guilty for sharing secrets, Trevor leaned into Mallory and kissed her. A wet lingering kiss that he broke only to drop staccato kisses over her jawline. He tugged gently at her earlobe with his teeth and then cupped the back of her head in his left hand.

"Scared." Mallory's whisper brushed his ear and made him shiver.

The step creaked again. Trevor lifted his head and looked that way again.

"Think they heard us?"

"I dunno." He shrugged. "Let's go back out. I'll grab our bags and bring 'em up."

Chapter 44

HANNA

Neelie sipped from a small bottle of orange juice. Eyes wide with interest, she listened to Brion talking with the guys. Hanna was curious about Brion, she'd admit that to herself but maybe not anyone else, especially Peyton. He was good-looking, and he appeared to be crazy about Peyton, but Hanna knew anyone could put on a mask and play a part. The guys were comfortable with him, but at the moment, Hanna wasn't sure that was a good thing. After what had just happened with Sam and Davis, she felt like they'd hit rewind, and they were eighteen again. An immature eighteen.

Sam and Bowie had grilled the meat, and she and Peyton had taken care of the side items, which amounted to taking tubs of potato salad and coleslaw from the refrigerator and opening them. She was hungry, but her burger was a bit pink in the center, and the color and Sam handing her the plated meat with that typical Sam Collins flourish—as if she should be grateful that he'd grilled it for her—made Hanna think of raw meat and blood and violence, and so she'd only picked at it. When she'd realized Bowie was watching her, she'd made herself eat half of it. He wouldn't say much, though, because it was rare for them to eat red meat.

The tension of earlier had melted away, but Hanna still felt that unease, the makings of dread, in her neck and her stomach. Even if it had been a joke, it was tasteless and uncalled for. But then, that was Sam. He'd always operated that way, hadn't he? Why should she be surprised about it now? As Brion debated regular heat pumps and geothermal heat with Sam, Hanna let her eyes creep over the group assembled on the deck. Davis was sprawled in a lawn chair, sandwiched between Neelie and Bowie. He'd wolfed down his steak and two helpings of potato salad, apparently unaffected by Sam's comment earlier or already over it. Mallory had eaten a burger, no nibbling for her. Hanna wondered where she'd put it; as slender as she was, Hanna thought they'd be able to see the burger slide down her throat and into her stomach. Trevor, next to Mallory, had attacked his steak with relish, and Hanna decided they'd all been hungry, waiting on Sam to say it was dinnertime, and then she wondered why. Why did they allow Sam to run things, to make the decisions?

Hanna wasn't sure if Trevor was listening to Brion and Sam. His gaze was fixed on something on the deck or his bare feet, but the scowl on his face seemed pretty intense for a discussion about the most efficient home heat source. Mallory stroked her fingers over his wrist absently; Hanna wondered if she even realized she was doing it. If Trevor wasn't listening to the guys, what was he thinking about?

She let her gaze move from Trevor to Bowie. His eyebrows arched and his gaze on Brion, he was listening intently. He must have felt her looking at him, because he turned just slightly to smile at her. Hanna felt a jolt when she saw Sylvi in his face. Fingers of that unease wrapped itself around the front of her neck, over her windpipe. She coughed at the slight pressure she felt in her throat. If Sam was just dicking around with Davis, whether he thought it was funny or if it had happened as he'd said and he'd announced it as he had to embarrass Davis, did that mean he would do it again? Just announce something recklessly, without regard for who he might hurt? Or would he just tell Bowie? Would he play it off as harmless or would he twist the situation around to make himself look good?

"Excuse me," she said quietly as she stood up. She slipped around Peyton's chair and hurried inside. The beer and the heat and the pink burger and the thought of raw meat soured her stomach. She made her way through the kitchen and to the bathroom. Closed the door and leaned on it for a moment, almost certain that Bowie would follow her.

The cotton candy pink carpet only made her feel worse. She was glad for the flip flops she wore; she wouldn't want to stand on this carpet barefoot. Resting her head on the door at her back, she closed her eyes and breathed deeply. In and out. Once. Twice. Three times. The nausea passed, but she recognized a dull ache at the base of her neck.

Wrung out, she peeled herself off the door and shuffle stepped—cringed when her toes touched the carpet and for just a moment she was eight again and trying desperately not to touch the carpet because it was lava—and leaned over the sink. She propped her hands on the porcelain sink and hung her head. Stared at the dark, circular stain around the drain. Feeling the nausea again, the burger and the beer trying to creep back up her throat, she squeezed her eyes closed. How the hell was she going to make it through the rest of the weekend? The rest of the *night*?

Obviously, Bowie wasn't going to come and check on her. She huffed out a quick breath and then turned the water on. Let it run for a few seconds and then splashed her face a couple of times. The cold water felt good on her warm skin.

Finally, she stood up to look in the small mirror above the sink and brushed the water droplets off her face with her hands. Rubbed her hands over her bikini bottom and wished again she'd found a different suit to bring along.

She'd seen Sam eyeing her a couple of times, and other times, her skin had crawled like someone was watching her, staring at her, and she knew it could only be Sam. Davis had never looked at her as anything more than a friend. Trevor had put his hands on her body twelve years ago, but it hadn't meant a thing to either of them. He wasn't interested in her that way. And Bowie's stare wouldn't unnerve her that way.

In case anyone was in the hallway, listening, Hanna decided she'd use the restroom. Slipped her bikini bottom down and perched on the toilet seat. She laughed softly when she realized she did have to go, and then she rolled her eyes at her paranoia. In case anyone was in the hallway? What? Like someone had snuck inside and followed her to the bathroom?

The doorknob jiggled, and she shot up off the toilet, sure suddenly that she hadn't locked it. She flushed and washed her hands and then took a deep breath to calm herself before she opened the door. What if she opened the door, and she was face to face with Sam? What if he shoved her back into the bathroom? Everyone else was outside. No one would hear her if she yelled. If she screamed bloody murder—

The knob rattled again. A jolt of pain ripped through her chest, and suddenly, she couldn't breathe, and she wondered if she would die of a heart attack on this matted pink shag carpet before Sam could get the door open.

"Han?"

Peyton.

Hanna's body sagged with relief. She reached a limp hand to the knob and popped the lock. Her fingers felt weightless and dead, and she stared at the knob, heart pounding now, trying to remember how to wrap her hand around it to open it.

"Hanna?" The door opened, and Hanna sucked her breath in quickly, the terror fresh again, because what if Sam was standing just behind Peyton in the hall? "Hey. You okay?"

Hanna moved out of the way as Peyton pushed the door open and stepped inside.

"*Are* you okay?" Peyton leaned back to close the door behind her. "Jesus, Hanna." She dropped her hand from the knob and looked back at Hanna. "You look like hell."

Hanna blinked at her, but she couldn't find her voice. She swallowed hard, nodded once, and then turned away as the burger and the beer and the terror clawed its way back up her throat.

"Han?"

Back to Peyton, she nodded. Put her hand up to hold Peyton off for a second and closed her eyes. Breathed in and out again, deeply. Slowly. Forced herself to relax.

"Sit down," Peyton told her. Hanna jumped when she felt Peyton's hand on her back. Hanna had been hot when she'd come in, still unpleasantly warm just seconds ago, but now she was chilled and clammy—she could feel the sweat on her forehead and her neck and on her lower back—and Peyton's skin was warm on hers.

Peyton leaned over and put the toilet lid down, but Hanna shook her head. She couldn't sit on that pink cover. The thought made her gag again. Instead, she turned and sat on the side of tub.

"What happened?" Peyton squatted in front of her, and again, Hanna felt like the past twelve years had never happened, and Peyton was still her best friend, and on top of the nausea and the terror which was every bit as real now as it was twelve years ago, she felt a stab of loss so sharp, Peyton might have sliced a knife through her body.

Feeling foolish, for all of the above—right now more for her reaction to Peyton's concern than anything else—Hanna shook her head. Regretted it instantly.

"I'm okay," she mumbled.

Peyton glanced at the toilet and then back at the sink and then finally, she looked at Hanna again.

"Did you get sick?"

"No." Hanna rested her elbows on her knees and leaned over to put her face in her hands. "God, I need a shower." She smoothed her hands over her forehead and back through her bangs. Even her hair was wet again with that nervous sweat.

"We all do," Peyton said with a small laugh.

"I thought I was gonna get sick," Hanna explained. She took a deep breath.

"Too much heat?"

"All of it, I think." Hanna dropped her hands and stared at Peyton boldly.

"Any chance you're pregnant?"

"Would I drink like that if I thought I could be pregnant?"

Peyton shrugged and shook her head. "Could I *not* drink if I thought I might be pregnant?"

"Yes, you could." Hanna rolled her eyes. "And no, no chance I'm pregnant. I just got overheated. And I'm not used to eating red meat. Pink red meat."

Peyton's lips twitched. "Right. Tofu…beans—"

"Don't be a bitch, Peyton." Hanna cringed when she heard the whine in her own voice.

"I'm sorry." Peyton nodded.

Hanna breathed deeply again. Wondered if she should tell Peyton. If she should tell her she'd just come undone because she was scared it was Sam rattling the doorknob.

"He hasn't changed," she said instead.

"No." Peyton rocked backward gently and dropped her butt to sit on the floor.

"Eeww. Gross." Hanna reached for her hand.

"What?" Peyton asked as Hanna linked fingers with her and tugged her back to her feet.

"Don't sit on that carpet. It's disgusting." Hanna shivered. "Especially in a bikini."

"Where'm I supposed to sit then? In the tub?"

Hanna laughed, let go of Peyton's hand, and waved her to sit on the toilet.

"Oh. Yeah." Peyton nodded, dropped to sit, and looked at the pink lid cover between her thighs. "This is so much better."

Hanna smiled and then shrugged apologetically.

"I hate this house," she whispered.

"Me too," Peyton agreed. "You shouldn't be here."

"None of us—"

"Han, you shouldn't be here. Why are you doing this to yourself?"

Both of them jumped when someone pounded on the door. Hanna dragged her eyes from Peyton. She took a deep breath again, flexed her fingers.

"Hanna? Are you okay, babe?"

Bowie.

"Yeah, I'm fine."

She couldn't decide if she should be happy Bowie had finally decided to check on her or if it should bother her that Peyton had been the first to realize she'd disappeared and come to look for her.

"What're you doing?"

Peyton stood up and leaned as far as she could to reach the door. She pulled it open, and Bowie stuck his head in through the small V.

"You okay?" he asked again.

"Yeah. Just got a little overheated, I think."

He stared at her suspiciously for a moment and then looked at Peyton.

"Girl talk, Bo," Peyton told him with a grin.

"You guys still do that?" He frowned and shot Hanna another quick look.

"Yep." Peyton hitched her butt up against the sink. "Why? You got something to be nervous about? She gonna tell me you're into role playing or something? Like, you're—"

"No." Bowie frowned at Peyton uncertainly and then looked back at Hanna again.

"Neelie's got some cookies—"

Hanna shook her head quickly. "Nope. Can't."

He nodded. "Mm-kay. I'm probably gonna…" He hesitated. "Get back in the water. If you're okay."

"Yeah, Bowie, I'm fine."

He moved and then pulled the door closed, the only sound the bottom of it dragging over the thick carpet. Peyton turned her head to look at her.

"Why don't you just tell him?"

Hanna swallowed hard. She'd never told a soul. Except Peyton. Who would believe her? Not even her own husband would believe her.

Chapter 45

PEYTON

Brion tugged gently at the elastic in her ponytail until it was loose, and he slid it down the length of her hair and watched her curls fall loose around her shoulders. She looked at him sideways and then looked back at the dock. The sun was falling on the other side of the house, and the scene before them—the dock, the lake, the trees beyond the lake—was cast in shadow, and Peyton found it almost easier to look at in shades of gray.

Neelie and Sam were in the water, but Peyton didn't care to guess what they were doing out there alone by the dock. She was okay with this, right now, sitting with Brion on the deck and watching her friends at play. But not Sam. Her hatred for him grew with each passing minute; a couple of times, she'd nearly climbed to her feet, overcome with the need to move. To act on that hate.

And do what? she'd asked herself each time. Do what, Peyton? Tell him? Like he'd care? Should she leave? Get in the Juke and drive back to town and forget any of this had happened? As much as she hated Sam, she had to admit she didn't want to do that. She was surprised to realize she liked Trevor and Mallory. Surprised to remember she liked Davis. And more than surprised to find herself reconnecting with Hanna. All of it felt okay except Sam.

Even Brion, thigh pressed up against her, even though there was all kinds of room on the deck and he didn't have to be touching her, was okay. Trevor and Mallory were under the shade tree, where Neelie and then Sam had napped earlier. Mallory had spread out a blanket, and the two of them were flopped on it, heads huddled together over an iPod Touch, talking and laughing. Peyton heard snippets of music, and half of her wanted to holler at them. Tell them to come to the deck and share the music—she was curious what Trevor the record sales associate listened to—but she didn't want to interrupt them, either. They weren't doing anything inappropriate, nothing kinky. Just having fun, and Peyton was loathe to break their vibe.

She glanced at Brion again. Watched him raise his beer bottle to his lips and take a drink. She'd quit. After finding a deathly-gray looking Hanna in the bathroom earlier, she'd switched to water. Just because. Whether she felt like Hanna might need her to be sober or if it was just because seeing Hanna look so squeamish had upset her stomach, she didn't know, but she'd quit, and now she was sipping water and sitting with Brion.

She didn't want to holler at Trevor and Mallory because she didn't want to interrupt this moment between her and Brion, either. In fact, she wanted to scoot closer to him. She wanted his arm around her. She looked away from him so he wouldn't see the desire on her face when she realized she wanted him to make love to her. Not the way they'd been going at it lately. Crazy. Violent. Desperate. She wanted to touch him and see if she could find what she'd lost.

It wasn't him.

She knew that now. Whatever she'd lost, whatever she believed she'd suddenly seen in him—arrogance, conceit— was her doubt, her *self-doubt*, her fear, and she'd projected it all at him to make him ugly and unappealing. If it was him, she was free to walk away and not look back and not be plagued with guilt over one more thing.

Hanna and Bowie had walked away earlier, hand in hand, and Peyton had watched them round the bend in the lake. She'd wished her friend would find the courage to talk to Bowie, but only half-heartedly, because Peyton was no better at relationships and honesty, and so who was she to judge anyone else?

"It was me," she said now to Brion. Her voice was gruff, and she glanced to her left to where Davis was sitting, cell-phone to his ear, talking to his son. Coverage out here was spotty at best, and Davis had tried and dropped several call attempts already.

"Hmm?" Brion played with her hair, and then he skimmed his fingers up over the back of her head. She closed her eyes, wished it was only the two of them here. Wished she had a beer or a bottle of wine. Without either, she felt small and a little bit stupid for the mistakes she continued to make, and confession had always frightened her. Priests and other religious people had always made her feel guilty, though she belonged to no religion, and cops made her nervous, though she'd never had a run in with any other than the night Eden's body had been found in the lake.

"I'm sorry." Her words were quiet, because they were meant only for Brion and not Davis, no matter if she liked him or not.

She held her breath, worried that Brion would try to make more of it, of what she'd said, and though she meant it, she wasn't ready to go any further. Not right now. This was good. The shadows. The breeze. Her friends nearby. Brion's leg pressed up against hers, his fingers in her hair.

She chanced a quick peek at him and froze when he looked at her and their eyes met. Brion drew his fingers from her hair, and Peyton tried to hide her disappointment, but then he stroked his hand down her arm and covered her hand with his.

Chapter 46

MALLORY

She wasn't thinking about snakes anymore, hadn't even worried about them earlier when she and Trevor had sprawled out on the blanket and speed-listened to the new songs he'd downloaded to his iPod Touch before they'd left. Maybe she'd finally had enough to drink that she had the courage to face a snake and make it stand down, or maybe she was just numb enough that it didn't matter anymore, or maybe she'd just been caught up in the moment with Trevor. It had been fun, a nice timeout from the group, just her and Trevor talking and laughing and listening to music. Music had always been important to Trevor, so naturally, it was an integral part of their relationship.

Now, slouched in a lawn chair on the deck, bare feet propped up on the railing and her head back against the chair, she was drowsy and comfortable and the whole idea of snakes or frogs or bad memories was foreign to her. She'd forgotten how much she liked being outdoors. No, she wasn't ready to sell her belongings and head for the hills to live off the land, but since she'd moved in with Trevor, she'd allowed this part of herself to be buried. It had still been chilly when she'd first moved in, and so she'd been agreeable to hanging out inside, watching TV or listening to music. She'd enjoyed playing Trevor's video games with him; she'd even beat him a few times at some of the games.

When it warmed up, he'd already been sucked into the black hole of the dreams and the lake, and they'd been overwhelmed. Still there, still trying to figure out why Trevor had the bad vibes about the place, being out here made Mallory realize there was so much more to life than what she and Trevor had experienced in the last few months. Definitely time for a change. No, they couldn't afford a house like Hanna and Bowie. Not now, maybe never, only time would tell. But they could find a different place. They could escape that soul-sucking crap apartment with the mice and the permanent sour smell in the staircase.

They could find a small place, a one-bedroom ground floor unit. Maybe even something with a small backyard and a patio. She closed her eyes now and pictured the two of them outside, maybe burgers on a small Weber grill, a couple of cold beers. A tiny patch of grass and maybe a couple of plants, if Trevor wouldn't let her have a dog. He wouldn't have to give up music, his love of music, to find a new job. Mallory would never ask that of him. She'd even be agreeable to him keeping the sales job at Rewind, because she suspected just a few hours a week there would make him happy.

But the thought of being outside with him, watching the sunset and feeling the breeze in her hair, made her happy. Made her anxious to get this damned lake mess figured out so they could move on. She opened her eyes. The whole group was gathered on the deck now, quietly musing over their high school days. Only she and Brion had nothing to add to the conversation, though both of them were entertained by the stories about food fights at lunch and the sixth hour algebra II teacher getting pissed when she realized some of the students were changing the time on the wall clock every day before class.

Hanna was stretched out with her legs in Bowie's lap. Her eyes were closed, though Mallory knew she was awake, because now and then she added to the conversation. Stretched out as she was, she still looked tense. Her shoulders were hunched as if she was cold, and Mallory knew she couldn't be cold, because even now just before ten o'clock, it was hot and sticky. Her forehead was drawn in a deep frown. She'd disappeared earlier when they were eating, and when she'd come back, she'd worn such a haunted look on her face, Mallory had actually looked over her shoulder to see if there was a ghost following her.

As the day had gone on, Mallory had decided that maybe something bad had happened here at the lake twelve years ago. Not just *bad*, because she still believed that Eden's drowning was bad and that alone could have caused Trevor's nightmares, but something *sinister*. Something *sinister bad* and it was like an electrical current that still flared to life around them now and then.

Then again, maybe she was just getting that vibe because of Sam. No matter what else might be going on, Sam Collins was a conceited, abrasive dick, and Mallory found she couldn't look at him and harness the dislike enough to hide it. So, she'd been working hard at *not* looking at him.

The rest of them were okay. She wasn't sure about Neelie, but it seemed that a woman who could be intimately involved with an overbearing guy like Sam surely wasn't someone Mallory wanted to know better. Then again, Sam seemed to tone it down when Neelie was by his side, and that only spoke volumes about how much of a dick he was.

Peyton was a little bit caustic, but Mallory could handle

her brand of snark. She had a beautiful smile once a person cut through the smoke and mystery around her. And though Peyton was quiet, Mallory recognized the give and take between her and Hanna as that of an age-old friendship.

Mallory found herself hoping she and Trev would leave here Sunday and stay in touch with his friends. Maybe they could go out with them now and again. Hell, if they ever got a new place—something nicer and more inviting—they could invite people over and entertain. It startled her to realize as much as she wanted to be with Trevor, she needed this inter-action with other people, too. It would go a long way toward fighting the dreams and the moods in which Trevor awoke.

Davis had apparently talked to his son earlier, and he was talking about him now. Something about a swim meet, and Mallory wondered if she'd ever be a mother. If she'd ever want to have a child. She glanced at Trevor. They hadn't really talked about it, about the future. About a family. Before meeting his friends, she would probably have said no. No to a family with him. But now, after seeing him interact with them, seeing that he contributed to the dynamics and noticing that his friends could change him for the better—her Trevor, the one from before, hadn't known how to have fun—she thought maybe it was possible.

Trevor must have felt her watching him, because he turned his face toward her and winked. She felt something stir inside, something other than desire and a little bit like happiness or belonging.

"Oh, man." Neelie yawned and stretched her arms up over her head. "I am beat. I'm gonna go up and go to bed."

"Mmm." Sam nodded. "Need me to tuck you in?"

"Nope. I'm good."

"Need me to—"

"Sam." Neelie shook her head. Mallory noticed Peyton glance at Hanna, but Hanna's eyes were still closed. Neelie leaned over and dropped a quick kiss on Sam's upturned face. She moved too quickly for his groping hand to find purchase, and he closed his fingers into a fist as she slipped away.

"Night, guys," she called as she pulled the screen door open.

The deck erupted in a chorus of *night, Neelies*, and the hair on the back of Mallory's neck stood on end. The door banged shut softly behind Neelie, and Mallory turned back to the table to find Sam staring at her.

Chapter 47

TREVOR

"Look." Davis cleared his throat and shrugged in an attempt to look casual. "I did it."

"What?" Trevor swallowed a mouthful of beer and then let the bottle dangle from his fingertips. Feet crossed on the rail of the deck, he stared up at the sky and tried to count the stars. Wondered if he was drunk, because who the hell tried to count stars except angsty teenaged girls and drunk guys?

After Neelie had gone to bed, the girls had decided they were ready to go up, too. Trevor had kissed Mallory good night when she'd leaned over him, smoothed his hand up over her hip and had a flash of regret that they'd only be sleeping tonight in the bed they shared. It was after ten, probably closer to ten thirty, and he was tired. He could turn in. Might be that he'd sleep well right here in the belly of the whale. Then again, he might dream and wake the house in a rage, trying to tear the pieces of this damned nightmare out of his head.

Probably, the girls hadn't gone to bed anyway. They were probably upstairs getting ready for bed and talking and laughing about something. Men, most likely. Bowie and Sam had jumped back in the lake for a near midnight swim, and Trevor could hear them yelling at each other.

"Sucked him off," Davis mumbled.

Trevor rolled his head on the chair to look at Davis. He didn't particularly give a damn what Davis had done, except that he remembered now that Sam was a prick, and even if Davis had a thing for guys, why Sam?

No idea what to say to that, he looked away when their eyes met.

"Hundred bucks, man."

He saw Davis shrug from the corner of his eye. Wondered if maybe *he* was drunk, because who made these late-night confessions other than angsty teenage girls and drunk people admitting to love or lust.

"I mean. Whatever, right?"

"Yeah, man," Trevor agreed. Because who cared what Davis had done twelve years ago? "Not a big deal."

"Only as big a deal as I make it," Davis said quietly.

Trevor nodded.

"You ever done it?"

"No."

"Nasty." Davis cut loose with a wicked laugh.

Trevor snorted and shook his head.

"I think you might wanna lay off the sauce there, big guy."

"Shoulda bit it off."

Trevor blinked, wondered if he'd heard Davis right.

"Fucking cocksucker."

"Wouldn't that be you?" Trevor took another drink of his beer.

Davis howled with laughter. Trevor watched him double over in his chair, eyes scrunched closed.

"Sometimes, I think that's what came between me and Amy."

Unnerved by the sudden somber tone in Davis' voice, Trevor looked at him again.

"Sam's dick?"

Davis shrugged his lips. "I thought about it a lot, man. After. Like I made myself sick over it. Ya know? You ever do anything you regret?"

Trevor didn't want to think about Davis and his ex and what he'd done to Sam, but he didn't particularly want to think about the way he'd been treating Mallory, either. The way he'd manhandled her after the dreams.

"Yep." He heard the clipped tone in his voice and hoped that Davis had had enough to drink that he wouldn't.

"I hate myself for that. Hundred bucks." He made a *tssking* sound and shook his head. "Perspective, man. At eighteen, that hundred bucks was a lot. Now sometimes I feel like I sold myself out for that."

"What do you mean?"

"You know Sam." Davis tilted his bottle to his lips, but he swung it away with a sigh when he realized it was empty. "What do you think I mean?"

Trevor handed Davis his beer.

"Blackmail?"

"Not even that," Davis mumbled. "I knew as soon as I did it, he'd use it. Blackmail. Stand-up routine."

"You tell your ex?"

Davis was quiet for a long time. Finally, he shook his head.

"Could you do it? With her?"

"Could I get it up?"

Trevor nodded.

"Sure."

"Then let it go." Trevor shrugged. "Don't let him control you."

Davis stared at him silently as if he was considering

Trevor's advice. Finally, he sighed and caved backwards in his chair.

"Maybe it was because she cheated," he decided.

"Who cheated?"

"My ex."

"Did you love her?"

"Nope. Not at all."

Trevor laughed softly and shook his head when Davis let out another rip of maniacal laughter.

"That could have something to do with it."

"You love your girlfriend? Mallory?"

Trevor stared at Davis now, unsure what to say. He might. He might be in love with her. After all, the woman had put up with a lot from him, and she'd stuck. That was saying something, right? But that was saying something about her, not about how he felt about her.

"I do." He nodded and rubbed at his chest. Heartburn or guilt for telling Davis he loved Mallory before he told her?

"Cool." Davis tipped his hand-me-down beer at Trevor in a salute. "You ever tell her that?"

"No."

"You should." Davis pursed his lips. "I hear women like that."

Amused, but concerned about how Davis would feel in the morning, he pointed at the beer.

"I think that should maybe be it for you tonight."

Davis waved away Trevor's concern. Sat forward again.

"It's just that…" He rubbed his hand over his face again. "I have a son, man. I have a son. What if Sam told my son?"

Trevor felt a flash of panic. Of course, Sam would tell Davis' son what he'd done.

"He doesn't even know your son, Davis." Trevor was pleased that he sounded calm and unconcerned.

Davis nodded. "I know. But." He shrugged. "He's got a

way, man. He's got a way. Brought us all here again, didn't he?"

Trevor felt heavy and slow suddenly. Bogged down with that dread that had consumed him after the nightmares. What if he just *asked* Davis what happened that night? Okay, it was possible Davis was drunk, and he might not remember things any better than Trevor did, but if he was drunk, he might not remember tomorrow that Trevor had asked him tonight about Eden. Nothing to lose.

He tuned back into Davis' rambling about cutting Sam's dick off.

"Feed it to lions, maybe."

"Do lions eat processed food?"

Davis snorted. "I hate him—"

"Davis."

Davis turned to stare expectantly at Trevor.

"What happened that night?"

"What night?" Davis shook his head.

"When Eden drowned."

"She—drowned? In the lake."

"Where were you? When it happened?"

"Passed out. Up in the room. I came out of it when the ambulance came flying up with that goddamned wailing siren. Scared the fuck outta me, and I jumped out of bed and tripped at the top of the steps. Banged my head on the wall when I fell. Shit, I was so out of it, that at first I thought the ambulance was there because I'd hit my head, and then I realized I hadn't hit my head until I heard the ambulance."

Trevor nodded, disappointed that he wouldn't get anything more from Davis.

"I'm gonna go on up," he announced.

Davis settled back into his chair again. Trevor glanced back at him before he opened the door, a little bit worried about him. What if he was so drunk, he wandered down to the lake and fell in? And drowned?

She hadn't fallen. Trevor scrunched his eyes closed and gave himself a mental shake. He'd thought earlier that someone had pushed her, and he'd seen her hair fan out behind her as she fell in to the lake. The fact that he'd made up the memory filled him with rage. He had a hard enough task ahead, figuring out what the hell happened. Sure as hell didn't need to fight his conscious self now, too.

"Davis?"

"Hmm?" Head on the lawn chair, Davis didn't lift it to turn and look at him.

"You cut off his dick?"

"Hmm?"

"Find a meat grinder."

"Will do."

In the darkness—the girls had turned the floodlights off when they'd gone inside—Trevor could barely make out Davis' nod. He lifted his gaze to the lake, the black water where Sam and Bowie were swimming now and thought about the dream.

Chapter 48

MALLORY

His hand was cold, and she hunched her shoulders to get away from him. Oblivious to her discomfort, he continued to rub her neck, and then suddenly, her bikini top fell away and he put his hands on her breasts. She jumped back, away from him, ready to give him hell for touching her. Fear unfurled inside her and replaced the anger—

She gasped and opened her eyes as she pushed herself up on her elbows. Confused by the pitch black everywhere she looked, Mallory blinked to make sure she was truly awake. Still nothing. She rolled her head on her neck and noticed a tiny sliver of gray in the black. Felt for Trevor beside her and heaved a painful sigh, relieved when her hand found his arm at her side.

She sat up, kicked the damp sheets down out of her way, and struggled to calm herself. They were at the lake. She and Trevor were at the lake. It was only a dream.

"Trev?" she whispered.

He snored quietly; Mallory could picture him, lying on his back, left arm flung up over his head. Heart still racing, she considered snuggling close to him just to feel safe. The dream had rattled her. The cold fingers on her neck. Untying her swimsuit top. Those same fingers, his hands on her breasts. She hadn't seen a face, but she knew she'd dreamt about Sam touching her. Because of the way he'd looked at her earlier when Neelie had gone up to bed.

She traced her fingers over Trevor's arm, but he didn't stir, and she didn't want to wake him. Not now that he was actually sleeping. He was probably exhausted just from being out in the heat and humidity all day. Add in the beer and the stress he'd been under lately, and he had to be beat. She was, and the stress for her couldn't be anything like what Trevor was feeling. Still. Ironic that they'd come to the heart of Trevor's nightmares and she'd been driven from sleep with her heart pounding in her throat.

A cool shower sounded good, but she couldn't do that, either. She twisted on the bed and swung her feet to the floor. Looked back over her shoulder to make sure she didn't wake him. When he didn't move or say anything, she stood and shuffled slowly from the bed to the door. Touched it gingerly, as if the house was on fire and she was trying to find a safe escape route, her hands made their way to the doorknob. She turned it slowly and eased the door open, stopping when it creaked.

She slipped out to the hallway and padded barefoot toward the stairs. The darkness here was as thick as in their bedroom, and she turned back to slip into their room and grab her cellphone for light. She left the door open, inched across the hardwood back to her side of the bed and felt around on the small nightstand for her phone. Her fingers touched the lace doily under the lamp and then found the cord of her charger. She followed it to the base of the phone, pulled the cord out, and then retraced her steps back to the door.

With a glance over her shoulder, she eased the door closed again and then started back toward the stairs. She would just go get a drink. Some water. Sit in the kitchen for a minute. Or maybe sit out on the deck. Just to calm down. She passed the bedrooms she and Trevor had looked at earlier, doors closed now, and then slowed at the top of the steps. She wiped her hand on her shorts and then transferred her phone to the other hand and touched the home button. Rather than use the flashlight, she simply made her way down the steps by the light of the home screen.

The A/C unit had been chugging away all day, and it was still going. The humming sound was almost a comfort to her, but the air still felt stale and cold, and it chilled her clammy skin. She wished she'd have thought to put her flip flops on before she left the bedroom, but she wasn't about to go back now. Instead, she cringed with each step she took on the shag carpet. Once in the kitchen, she switched on the overhead light and looked down at her phone. Three nineteen. She yawned, wished she was still sleeping, though the thought of that dream, of it going any further traced a shiver up her spine.

Fingers curled around her phone, she pulled the refrigerator door open with her left hand and reached for a bottle of water. Her eyes caught the Ziplock bag of grapes she and Trevor had brought, so she snagged it between her ring and pinky finger. Turned and bumped the door shut and then surveyed the kitchen. The framed photo Peyton had brought still set on the table. Curious, Mallory crossed the room—surefooted now that she could see—and set the water and grapes down. She stretched to reach the frame and picked it up.

She took a moment to study each of the faces. Catalogued what time and memories had done to each of those smiles. They all looked happy. Sun-kissed, good-time graduates celebrating their last summer as a group. Mallory was particularly interested in Trevor, Eden, and Sam's faces, but there was no mystery. No shadows. No foreboding. Mallory could have been looking at a group photo from her partying days the summer after high school.

Defeated, she set the frame down, picked up the bottle and the grapes, and glanced at the light switch. Decided to leave it on, even though she wanted to sit on the deck. She didn't relish the idea of coming back inside in the dark. Not after the dream she'd just had. Not that she thought Sam would be waiting for her in the kitchen. Still. Dreams could be unsettling.

She sighed as she pinned the grapes against her body with her arm, so she had a free hand to unlock the back door. If this one dream rattled her this much, she couldn't imagine what Trevor had been dealing with for well over a month now.

She'd expected the night to be quiet; she'd forgotten night sounds the same as she'd forgotten the joys of being outdoors. The sky still wore its black hat, though it was studded with stars. She set the bottle and the bag on the table they'd gathered around earlier and then dropped into a chair.

No traffic. No horns honking. Just the sounds of animals in the trees. Birds? Foxes, maybe?

She uncapped the water bottle and took a long drink. Set it down on the table and then stretched. Ran her fingers through her hair and let herself sink into the disappointment she felt. Yeah, she was enjoying the weekend, and she liked Trevor's friends (most of them), but she'd had such high hopes that Trevor would get to the crux of the dreams and dig up the memory that was eating at him so they could move on.

They were no closer to an answer after fifteen hours at the lake.

She leaned forward and pulled another chair close, so she could prop her feet on it. Considered that what she'd suggested to Trevor earlier was the only answer they would find. Eden's drowning had been accidental. Trevor had told her when he'd come to bed that he'd changed his mind. No one had pushed her. He didn't even remember seeing her fall.

So maybe she'd had too much to drink, and she'd slipped into the water and drowned. Devastating to the rest of them —horrifying, really, because even though Mallory had never seen someone die, she imagined it would be horrifying to watch—and heartbreaking to Eden's family. But an accident.

The fact that Sam Collins was an ass didn't necessarily factor into anything. Except maybe the bizarre question of why Neelie married him. The fact that Davis had willingly given Sam a blowjob was no one's business but Davis' and the fact that Sam had shamed Davis by telling all of them— Trevor had told her that, too—pointed only to the fact that Sam was a bully, who still flexed his muscles at his friends' expense.

Mallory chewed on her lip. Considered Trevor. Maybe the fact that it was Trevor having the dreams, that he might have something he'd buried so deep inside he'd forgotten the lake entirely, suggested that he *had* done something. Something *bad*. But Mallory couldn't wrap her mind around that possibility. Sure, people misjudged other people. Happened all the time. People lived next door to serial killers and after the police dug up ten or twenty bodies, they might tell them the killer was the nicest man they'd ever met.

People could camouflage crazy. Hide their true selves. Pretend to be someone they weren't.

But that wasn't Trevor. *Was it?* Had she ever been afraid of him since she'd met him? He was rough with her, yeah, after the dreams. Cold, rough sex didn't mean anything, though. He'd never hurt her. She didn't love it that way, but he had never hurt her. Never raised a hand to her. And earlier, when she and Peyton and Hanna had gone upstairs and tiptoed by Sam and Neelie's closed door so as not to bother Neelie, they'd talked more.

Both of them spoke fondly of the times they'd hung out with Trevor. They smiled when they said his name. Neither of them spat his name out like it tasted bad, the way they seemed to do with Sam's.

What if there were no answers? What if she and Trevor got home and the dreams still plagued him and nothing changed? What then? A shrink? Should she insist? But what if she pushed that angle, and he went and some patrician guy with wire-rimmed glasses and a goatee and suits that cost more than all the rent she and Trev had ever paid on the apartment told him he was dreaming of the black water because a trusted family member had molested him when he was six? What if that same shrink said it was because Trevor had killed someone's puppy when he was nine?

What if that same shrink said the dreams pointed to a penchant for violence, and Trevor was contemplating something horrible?

The screen door squealed quietly, and Mallory jumped off the chair. She spun around to face the door, afraid she would find herself face to face with Sam Collins.

"Hey."

Chapter 49

PEYTON

Peyton raised her eyebrows when she realized she'd scared Mallory. She winced and held her hands up, palms out.

"Hey." Mallory smiled, but her voice shook, and she laughed as if embarrassed for Peyton to know she'd scared her.

"Sorry." Peyton crossed the deck to sit down at the table, in the chair to Mallory's right. "Didn't mean to scare you."

Mallory shook her head and mumbled that it was okay. She sat down again.

"I'm a little jumpy."

Peyton looked at her quickly. "Why? What happened?"

She watched Mallory closely, not with suspicion for Mallory, but maybe that something might have happened to make her jumpy.

"Nothing." Mallory raised her eyebrows and then rubbed her eyes. "Had a bad dream."

"Mm." Peyton didn't want to make Mallory uncomfortable, so she looked away. Toward the lake, though she couldn't see it in the darkness. She wanted to tell herself she could make it out, that the lake was inky and darker than the rest of the landscape, but in truth, she couldn't see a damned thing, and it was a little unnerving.

"Probably the heat."

She glanced at Mallory. Why was she shrugging away a bad dream because of the heat? Peyton felt the potential for bad dreams, the creepiness rolling off this house in waves. Totally possible Mallory felt it, too.

"Maybe." She refused to agree one hundred percent. She didn't want the house to hear her and think it had her fooled. She laughed softly and mumbled at herself.

"What?" Suddenly Mallory had light in her hands, and Peyton realized she was holding her cell phone.

"I wondered how you got downstairs without breaking your neck."

"You didn't break your neck."

"Stubbed my big toe, though." Peyton leaned back and stretched her legs out in front of her. "Hurt like hell."

"If you were one of my brothers, I'd tell you to call a tow truck."

Peyton snorted and rolled her eyes.

"If you think this place is creepy now—" Why had she said that? Mallory hadn't said anything about the house or the lake being creepy. "You should have seen it lit up when the ambulance was here, and they pulled Eden's…"

She stopped talking. Her throat ached, and her heart was hammering.

"Were you here?" Mallory asked. Before Peyton could answer, Mallory continued, "outside? When the ambulance came?"

"No. Hanna and I were upstairs….she was a—" She caught herself, this time unwilling to say more. No reason to tell Mallory Hanna was a wreck that night even before the EMTs had pulled Eden's body from the lake and zipped her up in that black bag. "We were talking. And just heard the siren. So...surreal out here..."

"Yeah." Mallory reached for a Ziplock bag of grapes on the table, but once she held the bag, she didn't move to open it.

"I don't even know why they called an ambulance...I mean...the EMTs didn't go wading in for her, ya know? Her body was right there, and you'd think Sam and Bowie would have known she was..."

"Sam and Bowie found her?"

"Yeah." Peyton swallowed again, rubbed her neck to ease the pressure in her throat. "I feel like it was my fault."

"What?"

Peyton dragged her eyes back to Mallory, away from the general direction of the lake.

"What?"

"You said." Mallory eyed her suspiciously. "You said you feel like it's your fault."

Peyton licked her lips. She hadn't realized she'd said those words out loud, because she'd thought them in her head so many times through the years.

"I'm the one who invited her. She was new. At school. Transferred in at the start of the second semester senior year." She blinked at Mallory and then looked away. "I introduced her to everyone."

"It's not your fault."

"You'd think a shrink and several thousand dollars spent would make me believe that."

"You saw a shrink?"

Peyton hesitated. Why did Mallory sound so interested?

"I'm sorry." Mallory shook her head. "God, that was rude. I'm just...concerned about...a friend. And I wonder if a shrink could help."

"Tell your friend to sit in front of a mirror and talk to herself. Tell her to say what's on her mind and then ask herself how that makes her feel."

Mallory sighed and lowered her eyes to the grapes. Peyton regretted the flippant answer. Maybe Mallory's friend did need a shrink. Maybe Peyton had needed one, and maybe hers had helped, because after all, she was still breathing, wasn't she?

"I never said this house was creepy," Mallory said suddenly.

"This house is creepy as hell, Mallory."

"What's up with Sam?"

"What?" Peyton yelped and then she felt stupid and exposed, and she tried to take a deep breath and hide it from Mallory, and then she wondered why she bothered.

"He's a bully."

"Did he do something?"

"What?" Mallory shook her head. "Like what? Did he do something like what?"

Peyton stared at her silently.

"I'm not sure what you're asking. I just think he's a dick, and the rest of you guys are…"

Peyton arched an eyebrow and cocked her head. "We're what?" she asked with a grin.

Mallory shrugged and shook her head. "Why do you put up with that?"

Why, indeed? Why had they all let him lead when they were younger? Why did they all follow him so blindly? He was popular, yes. Nice-looking. Funny, but cruel. Bowie White would have been better as their skipper. Just as popular as Sam. A hell of a lot better looking than Sam. And nice. Nice down to the bone. Bowie White didn't have it in him to be cruel to anyone.

"I don't know." Her voice sounded funny even to her own ears. "Doesn't every *it* guy or girl have that mean streak?"

Mallory stared at her with a frown, as if she was puzzling out what Peyton had said, thinking about her own life, her high school years.

"Yeah. I guess so," she mumbled. "But he seems worse than usual."

Peyton caught herself before she could tell Mallory she didn't know the half of what Sam Collins was capable of.

"So." Mallory seemed to remember she was holding the bag of grapes. She opened the bag, plucked a grape from a stem and popped it in her mouth. "What brings you outside at—?" She held up her phone again and hit the home button. "Three fifty-one in the morning?"

"Couldn't sleep." Peyton sighed. "I had this crazy hope that the fresh air would help that. A little outdoor activity. Fresh air. Sunshine." She shook her head. "No such luck."

"You always have trouble sleeping?"

Peyton met Mallory's eyes. "For the past twelve years."

"Why?"

"I don't know."

"I mean, do you lay awake thinking about this?" Mallory tossed her hand out, and Peyton assumed she meant to encompass the house and the lake and Eden.

"Not—"

"I'm sorry." Mallory interrupted her. "None of my business. It's just…" She hesitated. Refused to look at Peyton.

"Just what?"

Peyton watched her thinking, deciding if she should say what was on her mind or not.

"Trev. He's been having horrible dreams."

Peyton sat forward, as if she needed to be closer to Mallory for this conversation.

"What do you mean?" she asked quietly. "Dreams about what? Eden?"

Mallory groaned and put the bag of grapes on the table. She shook her head, finger combed her hair back from her face.

"Never mind. I shouldn't have said that. I shouldn't—"

"I'm not gonna say anything," Peyton promised, even though Mallory had no reason to trust her.

"The dreams." Mallory stood up. She turned her back to Peyton. In the golden shaft of light spilling out the kitchen door, Peyton saw her shoulders jump and then fall with her dramatic deep breath. "They're about the lake."

"What about it?"

"He doesn't know."

"Just the lake?" Peyton wondered what the hell that meant.

"The water. The dock. He's been…"

Peyton stared at Mallory's back and waited for her to go on.

"Hey. You're all in. Tell me."

"He sketches this lake. Over and over and over again. Trying to figure it out."

"Figure what out?" Peyton shook her head when Mallory turned to look at her.

"Whatever happened here. That he forgot."

Peyton started to answer her, but she closed her mouth when she realized she had no idea what to say.

"Why does he think something happened here?" she asked after a long silence.

"Because he keeps having that dream!" Mallory snapped.

Peyton climbed to her feet slowly, prepared to tell Mallory that was a circular argument; nothing had happened here. But when she heard her own voice, she was stunned at what she actually said.

"Nothing happened here, Mallory," she shook her head, "except that Sam raped Hanna. And nobody knows that but Sam and Hanna and me."

She flinched. Covered her mouth a little late to catch the secret. Rubbed her free hand over her stomach to soothe the guilt inside. What the hell was her problem? She'd just dumped her best friend's secret to someone she hardly knew.

Mallory blurred in her vision, and then warm tears slid over her face, and Peyton was stunned because she didn't cry often.

"Oh my God." She groaned out loud. "Shit. Please—"

Mallory shook her head. "I'm not gonna say anything."

Chapter 50

HANNA

Bowie didn't move when she slipped out of bed. The splash of sunshine through their window streaked his lower legs and feet, and he was snoring, and though he wasn't one to sleep in, she tiptoed across the bedroom, her bare feet almost sticking to the hardwood floor. She looked back at him as she pressed her hand flat against the door. On his stomach, he had his head half-buried under the pillow he'd slept on, left arm shoved up under the other side of the pillow. Even posed like that, not moving, she could see the muscles under his skin, and for just a second, she considered going to him. Waking him and undressing and sliding over the top of him to make love. They were parents of a little girl; they knew how to be quiet.

She laughed when he rolled back to his side and slid his right hand under the waistband of his tighty-whities. She saw him grin and wiggle his eyebrows as he lifted his erection to offer it to her.

"No."

"You were thinking about it."

"Maybe," she admitted. "But we're not gonna do that here."

"Why not?" He flopped over on his back. Stroked his hand down the length of his penis and gave her a suggestive smile.

"Bowie." She groaned. Yes, she definitely wanted to go to him, to climb on and ride. But the thought of doing it, even if they were quiet, here with their friends in the other rooms, made her blush. "I'm not doing that here."

He rolled his head on the pillow to look at her. She took a few steps closer to the bed.

"I don't particularly need you," he said slowly, "but it would be more fun with you."

She rolled her eyes.

"I'm going downstairs."

"We could make it quick."

She shook her head. "That's not really a selling point."

"C'mon, Han." He raised himself to his elbows and winked at her. "Quickies are fun."

"Not here!" She jumped back away from his touch when he sat forward and moved around to his knees to reach for her.

"We did it back then."

"No, actually, that was you and Neelie," she reminded him.

"Well, I meant all of us." He shrugged. "You know about that?"

"About you and Neelie?"

He nodded. Pulled his underwear up. Hanna eyed the bulge in his pants with a grin.

"Peyton and I watched you guys, Bo." She cocked her head at him. Saw the flash of panic in his eyes.

"You did?"

"Yep. It was kind of a turn on. You told me, anyway."

"Kind of?"

"Well. *Neelie*." She shrugged.

"She was kinky—"

"Spare me your version," she said quietly, but she wondered what he'd have said if she let him talk. What he'd have admitted to. Had he and Neelie done it more than once here, when she and Peyton had watched them? Or had they been together after that? "I'm going downstairs."

"Han?"

"Hmm?" She turned at the door to look at him again.

"Are you mad? About me and Neelie?"

"I've known since it happened. Why would I be mad now?"

"What about you?"

"No interest in fucking Neelie, thanks."

"Did you? Here?"

"Um." She rubbed her neck, partially to keep the sweeping panic at bay and partly in an attempt to hide the furious flush climbing her neck. If Bowie noticed, he might keep asking questions that she didn't want to answer. That she *couldn't* answer.

"Davis?"

"No." She shook her head. "I didn't…" She licked her lips. How could she tell him she'd come to the lake a virgin twelve years ago? That she'd lost her virginity and her innocence—two completely different things, although she hadn't understood that before that weekend—here at the lake?

"You didn't do anything?" He frowned. Didn't believe her, obviously.

"I messed around with Trevor—"

"You and Trevor did it?" His mouth dropped open. "Really? He seemed so—"

"No. We just messed around."

"Did he make you come?"

"Not really." She wouldn't tell him she hadn't known what

the hell she was doing, fumbling around with Trevor on the front porch. What she was supposed to do to Trevor. How to let go, how to enjoy Trevor's rough, inexperienced fingers.

"Think he could now?"

"What?" She shook her head. "Bowie, that's just…wrong."

"I wouldn't let him anyway," Bowie mumbled.

"I think you need more sleep." She turned the doorknob. "I'm going downstairs."

"Han?"

"What?"

"I love you."

She laughed softly. "Love you, too."

Not quite eight, Hanna was surprised to find Neelie in the kitchen. She offered her a smile, noticed she was eating the rice cakes again, but this time with peanut butter.

"Morning."

Thank God, Neelie had at least dialed back the gushiness. Maybe she still wasn't a morning person.

"I didn't think anyone would be up yet."

"I'm starved." Neelie shoved a rice cake in her mouth and laughed around it. "And Peyton and Brion went for a swim."

"Seriously?" Hanna, head in the refrigerator now, stood up straight and looked over her shoulder.

"Don't look. They're skinny dipping."

"Really?" Hanna looked at Neelie and arched her eyebrows.

"Yep."

Hanna grabbed a bottle of juice and moved to stand by the door. She saw Peyton on the dock in the lake, leaning back on her hands, legs stretched out in front of her. Not a stitch of clothing on. While she stood there, Brion climbed up the ladder and sat by her.

"Hmm." Hanna opened the juice and took a drink. "Can't see much from here. Looks pretty big."

Neelie snorted.

"Like you need something bigger than Bowie."

Eyes still on the lake, Hanna tried to put the lid back on the juice and missed. She looked at Neelie, turned, and walked back to the table.

"I don't." She shrugged. "But I'm surprised you're still thinking about it twelve years later."

"I've had both Sam and Bowie." Neelie winked. "I can compare and contrast."

Hanna could too, but she wouldn't share that with Neelie. Bowie's body was big, all muscle. But he was kind, gentle, and when things got crazy, Hanna was never afraid of him. Sam was smaller and wiry and vicious. He'd started with kissing her, and he'd ignored her when she'd said *no*, when she'd asked him to stop.

"Yeah? Well. Lucky you." Hanna rubbed her throat and her chest, trying to ease the juice and the horrible memories back down where they belonged.

"Mm." Neelie nodded, but she didn't elaborate, much to Hanna's relief.

"Anybody else up?" Hanna asked hopefully. She didn't want to sit here and talk to Neelie, not after that conversation with Bowie—because now she was wondering just what he'd done with her that was kinky, and not after Neelie said she could compare Sam and Bowie. But she couldn't go outside, not with Peyton and her boyfriend skinny dipping and maybe doing other things.

"Nope. Stuck with me."

Hanna sighed and pulled a chair out. She sat slowly, mind still reeling. She could go back upstairs, but if she did, she and Bowie would end up naked.

"So." She reached for the photo frame and scooted it closer to her. Rubbed her thumb over the edge and looked at

Neelie. "Do you want a boy or a girl? Really? Tell me the truth, now that Sam's nor around."

"A boy."

Hanna was surprised. Most expectant mothers, herself included, always answered with the standard *doesn't matter, as long as the baby's healthy* line. Hanna stared at Neelie silently.

"I wanna give Sam a son."

Hanna gagged and covered her mouth.

"You okay?" Neelie studied her curiously.

"Yeah." Hanna nodded, cleared her throat.

"I mean…" Neelie pulled another rice cake from the bag and slathered it with peanut butter. Hanna watched her lick the knife, glad she'd marked all of her food with a Sharpie. "I'd like to have a little girl, too. But I want a boy first. For Sam. Just in case…"

"In case what?" Hanna's whisper was gruff. Her throat felt raw. In case of future miscarriages? Is that what Neelie meant? Or in case someone found out her husband was a son-of-a-bitch? Well, no, that wasn't it, because certainly people knew Sam Collins was a son-of-a-bitch. That he was a rapist, maybe? Hanna stared at Neelie blankly. Wondered if he'd ever touched anyone else that way.

"What?" Neelie looked down at herself and then twisted around to look behind her. "What're you looking at?"

"Nothing." Hanna shook her head quickly. "What do you mean? In case what?"

Neelie darted her tongue out to lick the butter knife again. She lifted one shoulder in a shrug, apparently done talking.

"Have you thought about names?"

"Why don't you like him?"

"What?" Hanna's hands shook as she twisted the top off her juice bottle again.

"Why don't you like him? You guys all treat Sam like shit. What'd he ever do to you?"

Hanna heard voices outside. Peyton and Brion talking and laughing as they walked back up to the house. She hoped they'd worn clothes to get out to the lake.

"Maybe you should ask your husband that, Neelie." Hanna leaned heavily on the table, but she climbed to her feet and ducked out the back door.

"Hey, Han!" Peyton called to her. "Good morning."

Hanna glanced at Peyton and Brion. She noticed the radiant smile on Peyton's face, the way Brion's hair stuck up at the back, that they were indeed wearing bathing suits, and that they were holding hands. She barely nodded, hurried off the deck, and over to the north side of the house into a small copse of trees.

"Hanna?"

She groped for something to hold her up, hand smacking a tree trunk, the bark skinning her palm. Head hung over, she vomited. Juice. Not enough to make her feel better. Only enough to make her throat burn more.

"Hanna."

Peyton rested her hand on her back. Just like all those years ago.

"I'm okay." Hanna dropped the juice bottle and swiped the back of her hand over her mouth. She spit. Tried to stand up straight and wobbled on her feet. Peyton slipped her arm around her waist.

"What happened?"

"Nothing."

"Hanna."

"Nothing happened." Hanna took a deep breath and tried again to stand. Legs soft and weak, she sank to the ground. Peyton went down with her, dropped her beach towel on the ground to sit.

"Did he say something?"

Hanna shook her head. Sweat beaded her upper lip. She felt it gathered on the nape of her neck.

"I can't do this. I can't do another day of this, Peyton. I can't do it."

"Okay." Peyton nodded. "Okay. Let's go home. I'll drive you."

Hanna closed her eyes, concentrated on breathing. Deep, slow breaths. In. Out. She couldn't leave. Bowie didn't understand her hatred for Sam. He didn't know. She couldn't tell him.

"I can't."

"Why? Why can't you go home?"

"He'll ask why. He'll ask me why."

"So tell him, Hanna." Peyton grabbed her wrist and squeezed it gently. "Tell your husband what his best friend did to you."

Hanna sobbed. She shook her head. Refused to meet Peyton's eyes.

"What if he doesn't believe me, Peyton?"

"He goddamned better believe you, Hanna White. He's your husband."

Hanna swiped at her nose. "Sam'll twist it. He'll just say we had sex. He'll tell Bowie..." She swallowed hard and looked around. "He'll tell everyone that he fucked me that weekend, and he'll tell everyone that I was a virgin, and—"

"Are you serious?" Peyton hissed. "You were—"

Hanna nodded.

"Jesus." Peyton sighed. "This is ridiculous."

Hanna rubbed her eyes. She wrapped her arms around herself and looked at Peyton.

"You need to go back to Brion."

"I'm not gonna leave you here like this. God, he's a monster. Why didn't you tell me?"

"I did."

"That you were a virgin?'

Hanna shrugged. "Does it matter?"

"Yes. Of course, it does—"

"How?" Hanna asked quietly.

"What?"

"How does it matter?" Hanna shrugged. "How does it matter, because no one even knows?"

Peyton dragged her teeth over her bottom lip. "It matters," she said in a gruff voice, "to me."

"Yeah? You care now? Again? Suddenly?"

Peyton tilted her head and stared at Hanna long enough to make her uncomfortable.

"Tell me." She squeezed Hanna's wrist again. "Easier like this? Or just burying it all and walking away?"

Hanna nodded. Dropped her gaze.

"If I were you, I'd make his life hell."

"How?"

"Tell everyone. Bring a lawsuit against him. Tell his boss. Tell his wife."

"Too late," Hanna mumbled. "I don't wanna drag Sylvi through that anyway."

"She's three. She's not gonna get it, Han."

Hanna shook her head.

"Goddammit, Hanna, *do something*. Make him pay for what he did to you."

Peyton started to scoot closer to her, but Hanna shook her head. Peyton drew back as if she'd slapped her.

"I just puked there." Hanna rolled her eyes. Peyton groaned out loud and then sighed.

"I hated this for you…when he did it. I hate him. I hate him, and I hate her for loving him! Does she love him? How can she love him? He's a mean, hateful man, and I don't get—"

"Hanna?"

Hanna lifted her head when she heard Bowie's yell.

"Skinny dipping, huh?" She cut her eyes to Peyton.

"I..." Peyton seemed to be searching for words, but Hanna didn't need them. She could read Peyton's heart in her eyes. Maybe in five minutes, the cynical woman would click back into her body, but right now, Hanna stared at the real Peyton. The Peyton who cared about her, about her friends, and maybe was in love with Brion Mitchell.

Hanna nodded.

"Hanna?"

"I gotta go back to the house," she whispered.

"How're you gonna hide what you're feeling?"

Hanna stood slowly, held her hand out as Peyton climbed to her feet.

"I've been doing it for twelve years." She shrugged. "I'm pretty good at it, Peyton."

Chapter 51

TREVOR

"I think I like that suit better," Trevor, still on his back in bed with his head propped on his arms, watched Mallory toss her sleep shirt aside. She stood at the foot of the bed in only the mint green bikini bottoms and let him look his fill.

"Yeah?" She grinned.

"Definitely." He nodded.

"We should go skinny dipping sometime."

"Really?" He drew one arm out from under the pillow and rubbed his eyes. "Why?"

"I don't know. It's fun."

"You've done this?"

"Of course. It's just part of growing up, isn't it?"

"How old were you when you did this part of growing up?"

"Fifteen." Mallory picked up the top of the new bikini, but she didn't put it on yet. Stared at Trevor expectantly.

"Fifteen? Really? With a guy?"

"Yep. My brother's friend."

"Did you guys—" Trevor shrugged. He sat up when

Mallory moved to his side of the bed and rested her knee on the mattress. He traced her collarbone with his fingertip. "Do it?"

"No." She shook her head.

"You were naked, and nothing happened?" Trevor watched his fingers slide over her breast, around and under it to cup her. "Because I couldn't know you were naked and not—"

"I didn't say nothing happened. Just that we didn't do it."

"Did you like it?"

"Mmm." She raised her eyebrows. "Yeah. It was...fun. That's why I think we should do it. It was nice out there last night—"

"What?" Trevor raised his gaze from her breasts, where he was now rolling her nipple between his thumb and fingers. "Last night?"

Mallory looked down to watch his hand when he moved to her other breast.

"I couldn't sleep."

"You went out there? By yourself?"

She nodded. "I don't think..." She caught her breath. Watched him drag his hand down over her stomach, his palm rubbing, molding her skin. His fingertips playing, teasing at her bikini bottom. "I don't think you should start something we can't finish."

"I want you."

"I need a shower."

"We all do." Trevor shrugged. Mallory sighed when he moved his hand back to her breasts. "I don't like that you went outside by yourself."

"It was fine." Trevor's thumb stroked the under curve of her breast, and Mallory squirmed where she was perched. "Don't. I don't wanna do this here."

He nodded. But he only leaned forward and pressed his

open mouth on her. Licked the curve his thumb had just traced and then flicked the tip of it over her nipple.

"Trev." She pushed him away and stood up. "I thought you could hook this for me."

"No, you didn't. You wanna do this as much as I do."

"Yeah, I do, but not here."

"If we had kids, you'd have to stop doing that."

Mallory had paced across the bedroom, but she stopped at the wall and turned back to him.

"What?"

He shrugged. "The topless thing. If we ever…had kids… you couldn't lounge around like that all the time."

She looked down at herself and then back at him.

"Not that I don't like it." He hurried to promise her. "I love that you spend most of your time at home topless. But…"

"Who said we were gonna have kids?" She shook her head.

Trevor opened his mouth to answer her, but he hesitated. Finally, he sat up and reached for his glasses. Wiggled his eyebrows at her when he looked at her again, glasses on his face.

"Even better." He laughed when she rolled her eyes. "Just putting it out there."

Mallory answered with a slow nod. "Okay. If you and I have kids, I have to start wearing a bra—"

"Well, no," Trevor argued. "Not necessarily a bra. But you'll have to…" He motioned to his chest. "Cover up…with something."

"Yeah. That's what bras do."

"But so do shirts," he reminded her. "And then your boobs are…free…and I'll still see them sway—"

"Ohmygod." Mallory slipped her arms through the straps of the bikini and reached back to hook it. She looked at

Trevor. "What is it with men? Boobs are all you think about."

Trevor pursed his lips. "Not all. Because right now I'm thinking about how smooth your thighs—"

"Trevor!"

"Sorry." He gave himself a mental shake. "How long were you outside? Last night?"

"Mm. Less than an hour."

"Why didn't you wake me up?"

"I didn't want to. You don't sleep like that very often."

Trevor considered her words. "Weird, huh?" He stood up. Stretched. Rubbed his hands over his head and then scratched his way down his chest and over his balls and looked at Mallory when his dick saluted her inside the shorts he'd slept in. "That I'd sleep so sound here. I thought I'd be awake all night."

"You drank a lot."

Trevor shrugged. "Not really. I feel fine now."

"I think…"

Trevor watched her pull her hair back to put it up. She frowned, concentrated like she was working on some fancy hairstyle instead of a loose ponytail to swim in a lake all day.

"What?" He moved to the window and pushed the drapes aside. Squinted at the sunlight in his eyes. "Davis was fucked up last night."

"What do you mean?"

Trevor yawned again. Glanced at her and then back to the window. He leaned his forehead against the glass pane. Not much to see but trees.

"He was rambling. Told me Sam wasn't lying. He was totally freaked about his kid finding out what he'd done."

When Mallory didn't answer him, he turned sideways at the window to look at her.

"What'd you say? To him?" she asked quietly.

"That it wasn't worth...the worry. That he was letting Sam win. None of us care that he did it."

Mallory nodded. Chewed absently on her lip.

"But what about his kid?"

Trevor shrugged. "Sam doesn't know his kid. I don't think he has to worry about that."

Mallory spread her fingers out in front of her and studied her thumbnail. Trevor watched her pick at it and then try to smooth it down.

"What?"

"What what?" She lifted only her eyes to look at him, but even so, Trevor felt like she was stalling him. Putting him off.

"What aren't you telling me?"

"Nothing." She dropped her hands to her sides. Smiled.

"Mal?"

"I just. I think Eden's death was an accident. I really, really do."

"And the dreams?"

She sighed. "I get it. Bad vibes. Yeah. Sam's a prick. But I think..."

"Were you alone outside? Last night?"

"What?"

"Were you alone?"

"Um." She swallowed hard. "No. Peyton came out after I'd been outside for a few minutes."

"Did you say something to her?"

Mallory sucked in a quick breath. She started to shake her head no, but when Trevor raised his eyebrows as if to warn her not to lie, she nodded.

"Yeah. Are you mad?"

He shrugged. Turned back to the window. The lush greenery outside should have been peaceful. Yesterday, the lake had been inviting. Fun. The sun had lit the water and made it green, and yet now, in his head all he could see was the black water from the dreams.

He rested his forehead on the window and looked down. Watched Peyton and Hanna walk out from under the canopy of shade the trees provided.

"I dunno."

"Trev."

"Hmm?"

"Sam raped Hanna that weekend."

"What?" Trevor looked back at Mallory. "What?"

"Peyton told me that was the only weird thing that happened, and that she and Hanna are the only ones who know about it."

"Sam? Raped her?"

Mallory nodded.

"Son-of-a-bitch."

"So...maybe..." Mallory shrugged helplessly. "Maybe you just picked up on that feeling. That...energy."

Trevor grinded the heels of his palms into his eyes and huffed out a deep breath.

"No." He shook his head. "No. He didn't."

"What?"

He heard Mallory come closer and then she took his hands and pried them away from his face.

"He didn't. Sam didn't rape Hanna."

"How do you know? What the hell are you talking—"

"Wasn't her. It wasn't Han." Trevor shook his head.

"Trevor."

Trevor dropped his head back and groaned.

"Jesus. It just all gets more and more twisted in my head."

"But babe, you don't know what went on between Sam and Hanna. If she says—"

"No, no." He shook his head. Took Mallory's hands in his. "I don't mean that. I don't doubt Hanna. I don't—"

"Look." Mallory stepped closer. She put her finger over his lips. "I promised Peyton I wouldn't tell anyone this. I think it all just…slipped out. I mean. Imagine. Imagine being Hanna and being around him now. And she's upset. And Peyton's upset for her—"

Trevor nodded. "Yeah. I get it. I'm not gonna say a word."

He couldn't say a word, because it didn't add up. Nothing anyone said, nothing he sort of remembered, nothing he dreamt added up. He'd almost had a full memory a second ago, and then it was gone, and he knew Mallory was wrong. Peyton was wrong. Sam hadn't raped Hanna.

But what the hell did that mean? Jesus. What if *he'd* done it? What if he'd forced himself on her when they were on the porch?

Trevor looked up when he heard someone yell something. He glanced at Mallory, relieved when she nodded that she'd heard it, too.

"Let's go down," she suggested. "You're making yourself crazy trying to remember something that didn't happen."

Trevor hesitated. *Something happened.* But he nodded, let Mallory think he agreed. Time to let it go. Go down for something to eat. Jump in the lake for a swim. And quietly keep making himself crazy trying to remember.

If he'd raped Hanna White.

Before either of them could move, the floor outside their closed door creaked. Footsteps moved down the hall and finally silence. Trevor met Mallory's eyes. Someone had been listening to them talk.

Chapter 52

PEYTON

"I'm sorry." She bumped Brion's hip with hers as they walked. He was a nature buff, and Peyton had forgotten how much he enjoyed being outside, so she almost felt like she was sharing him with someone else on this walk. And yet, it was good to share with nature, because Brion was calm and happy. Maybe he got too caught up, too stressed on his job, and maybe when he'd come home after a bad day and she'd greeted him with that cool indifference, it had hurt him. Maybe she'd imagined half the slights he'd dealt her, because she was so caught up in the past and the alcohol that barely touched her aches and pains, and maybe she'd hurt him.

"For what?" He was slow to look at her, to look away from the lake. Around the bend, the house almost completely out of sight, the sun lit a fire on the lake, and Peyton suddenly hated herself for wasting twelve years. Life wasn't always beautiful, no. But then again, it wasn't always ugly, either. She'd forgotten that, too. And she'd actively chosen to live in the ugliest way possible.

"Bringing you out here."

"Are you kidding me? When did you and I last start off a Saturday skinny dipping and making love outside under the sun?"

Peyton narrowed her eyes at him.

"You think anybody saw us?"

"Making love?"

She nodded.

"Does it matter?"

"Kind of. We're not kids anymore. It's just…private."

"I think we're fine," he assured her. "And I'm glad you asked me to come."

They stopped walking. Turned to look back at the lake again. The house was gone from view.

"Yeah, but it's all so…" She shrugged and shook her head. "It's all so messed up."

Brion brushed a loose curl away from her face. "Maybe you guys needed to do this."

"Closure. Most overused word in the—"

"No. Just…a way to heal," he offered hopefully.

She considered it. Maybe. Maybe coming here had been a way for all of them to heal. She felt much more content, if not happier, than she'd been in a long time. But what about Hanna?

"I don't know, Bri. I don't think Hanna should have come."

She'd told him. About what had happened when they were here the summer after graduation. About Sam cornering Hanna outside, when dusk had fallen. About how he'd pulled her around the back of the house, into the trees by the lake. The way he'd kissed her just tender enough to confuse her. Hanna hadn't wanted it. Peyton knew that without Hanna telling her. But those first gentle kisses had been enough to make her doubt what had happened.

He hadn't hit her. Hadn't raised a hand to her. Hadn't cut her. Hadn't tried to strangle her. All those violent things bad guys do to girls in movies when they rape them. So, Hanna hadn't known to call it rape.

She'd tried to be cool, to be glamorous with the cigarettes and the alcohol. She'd had the mouth of a sixteen-year-old boy, and she'd been pretty and innocent, and Sam had taken advantage of that, and he'd raped her, and Peyton hated that she'd come now. She hated that Hanna had never told Bowie. Hated that Hanna didn't trust Bowie to believe her over Sam.

Brion nodded and stepped closer to her. He slid his arms around her and pulled her gently toward him. Dropped a kiss on her head.

"Maybe not."

"I'm sorry," she said again.

"You said that already," he told her. Pulled back to look at her.

"No. Just..." She shook her head. "I'm sorry for the way things happened between us. I think...it was me. I did it to us—"

"We both did, Peyton," he argued. "We both made mistakes. And neither of us wanted to admit it."

She nodded.

"I don't know..." She swallowed hard. "I don't know what happens. Tomorrow. When we go back to real life. But...I wish we could start over."

"We can start over." He traced her eyebrows. "If that's what you want."

"You want me? You wanna do this?"

"What about Bellamy?"

She hadn't forgotten Bellamy—she wasn't sure she could —but with everything else going on up here at the lake, she'd pushed her to the back of her mind.

"That was a mistake," she admitted. "Another mistake."

"What if she doesn't wanna let it go?"

"She'll have to, won't she? If we're back together."

"Some people don't take no for an answer." He stepped back and took her hand so they could walk again.

"Well, she's not gonna rape me." Peyton knew he was referring to Sam.

"No, but she's your employee. And if you fire her, she could cause you trouble."

"I know." Peyton nodded. "I know. I've kind of been ignoring it. Wishing it would go away. Wishing *she* would go away."

When Brion didn't answer her, she looked up at him and laughed softly.

"What I do best, right?"

"Hmm." Brion studied her with a somber look, and then he grinned and shook his head. "I can think of a couple of things you do better."

As the house came into sight again, Peyton felt the familiar tension thread through her shoulders and her neck. They were out on the deck, though from this distance, she couldn't be sure who was sitting around the table.

"You don't have to stay," she told him.

"Trying to get rid of me?"

"No." She shook her head. "Just. Sam's an ass. He's hard to take."

Brion nodded. "You think I wanna leave you alone up here with him?'

Peyton looked toward the deck and looked back at Brion. "I'm hardly alone."

"Hanna wasn't alone, either."

Peyton shrugged. "I don't think he'd do that again. I think he's getting his thrills with the verbal attacks. Lining us all up and taking a shot at each of us just when we least expect it."

"What's he got on you?"

"Nothing." She shrugged.

"That you know of."

"Well. Yeah. Nothing that I know of."

"He's got a good fifty pounds on you."

"Brion." She shook her head. "He's with his wife. Nobody's in physical danger out here."

Brion smiled. "Okay. I'll stay anyway. Cross my fingers for a repeat of this morning tomorrow."

Peyton grinned, but she ducked her head as they rounded the lake and neared the dock.

Hanna and Bowie sat with Neelie and Davis on the deck. Davis was munching on a Pop-Tart. Hanna and Bowie appeared to be eating yogurt and granola. Peyton decided the Pop-Tart looked more appealing.

"Morning."

She ignored the look Hanna gave her. To downplay the conversation they'd had in the trees before she and Brion had taken off for a walk. That and she was a little embarrassed to know Hanna had seen them in the lake. That Hanna knew what was behind her smile today.

Davis squinted up at her.

"Peyt."

Peyton shook her head and looked at Brion. He smiled, but he didn't comment on the nickname.

"Hungry?" she asked him.

"Yes."

"Let's find something to eat."

"Make some noise," Bowie told them as they crossed the deck. "Daylight's burning. We've got three people still AWOL."

"Two of them might be busy." Peyton tossed a wink at Bowie over her shoulder and led Brion inside.

How did Hanna do it? How did she sit at that table with her rapist's wife? Maybe Peyton had had it wrong all these years. Maybe Hanna's blog had nothing to do with Eden's death. And everything to do with accepting her own loss.

Chapter 53

TREVOR

The headache had started just before nine and become almost unbearable by ten. They'd razzed him, given him shit about a hangover. But compared to Davis, he was the poster boy for health. Wasn't the beer. It was the needling sense that something was off. The feeling of panic, of outright refusal to believe Sam had raped Hanna. Not because he thought Hanna had made it up. And not really because he worried he'd done it. Though that thought remained in the back of his mind, there was *something* else.

He and Mallory had come downstairs earlier to find the whole gang on the deck in various states of breakfast grazing. Davis had apparently been hung over, tossed his cookies first thing and then crushed three Pop-Tarts and an apple and then he'd disappeared inside, and the rest of them figured he was puking all of it back up. Trevor wondered for a moment who was going to clean up after him, but it wasn't a pleasant thought, so he refused to linger on it.

Bowie and Hanna had been the first to race over the dock and jump into the lake. Trevor had watched Hanna. Sad for her. Angry as hell if Sam had actually done it. If Sam had forced himself on her, he wanted to throttle the son-of-a-bitch for her. She'd greeted Trevor and Mallory with a wan smile, and Trevor suspected she was exhausted from a day of pretending everything was okay yesterday and not that she felt any rage or fear toward him.

Brion and Peyton had apparently already gone for a swim earlier—from what Trevor gathered, it had been a private swim, and that had made him think of the conversation he and Mal had had upstairs about skinny dipping and kids. He'd leaned on the deck rail for several long minutes, trying to recreate the conversation. To picture the look on Mallory's face when he'd mentioned kids.

Had she looked horrified? No. He didn't think so. She hadn't grabbed onto the idea and run with it, the way some girls seemed to when a guy mentioned marriage and a family. But she hadn't seemed repulsed by the idea. Hadn't said no.

He'd have to get a better job. Now, more than ever, he was ready to find something better. To do things the right way for her. He wanted that future; he had to make damned sure Mallory wanted it, too.

"Jesus, Neelie, don't."

Trevor turned now to find Neelie and Sam in a stare off. He looked around only to realize he was alone on the deck with them. Looked to the left, past the shade tree to an open stretch of yard and saw Peyton and Brion tossing a Frisbee back and forth. Where had Mallory gone?

He had no idea what Neelie had done to Sam to piss him off, but Sam stood suddenly and shoved his chair back out of the way. Trevor watched him go inside and then he looked back at Neelie.

"You okay?"

She sighed, but she nodded.

"Can I ask you something?"

"Sure." He shrugged. Moved back to the table to sit down with her. He'd never known Neelie that well. She'd scared him when they were younger. She moved fast and left a lot of people—girls and guys alike—in her path. She'd never dated anyone, but Trevor'd heard she'd fuck anyone. That she'd bruised some guys' balls because he'd dissed her and spent the night with someone else. He'd wanted nothing to do with her.

Maybe she *was* the perfect match for Sam.

"What does Hanna have against Sam?"

Trevor stared at her silently, aware of her reputation, and hoped like hell he walked away from this conversation intact. Especially his balls and his dick, because he'd need them to win Malloy over to the idea of marriage and a family after he got a new job. Besides, no way was he going to be the one to tell Neelie her husband had raped Hanna.

Had he, though?

Trevor rubbed the back of his neck.

"What?" he finally asked to stall for more time.

"I know none of you like him. You don't get him." She shook her head. Rubbed her thumb over the lip of her juice bottle. Trevor thought the blood red nails worked for her. "But she's over the top. Like she can't stand to be near him—"

"Why don't you ask her?" he suggested. Decided to play dumb. It wasn't even that much of a stretch.

"I did." Neelie lifted her chin and met his eyes.

"And?"

"She told me to ask him."

"So, why're you asking me?" He frowned, leaned forward.

"Because."

Trevor saw something in her eyes, fear? sorrow maybe?—but it passed quickly.

"I'm afraid of what he'll say."

He took a deep breath and looked around again. Afraid of what he'll say, so ask the wrong people and play it safe.

Is that what *he* was doing?

"He's your husband, Neelie. Ask him." He stood up.

"I know what he'll say," she mumbled. "I want the truth."

Trevor only shrugged his eyebrows at her and went in search of Mallory. She must have gone inside to use the restroom. He carried some of the garbage inside with him, Davis' Pop-Tart wrappers. The empty yogurt containers. Shuffled it all in his hands to open the door and stepped inside.

He heard muffled voices. Looked up but found the kitchen empty. He crossed the floor quickly, dropped the garbage to the counter, and went looking for Mallory.

"...I liked the other one better..."

Sam's voice.

Trevor was torn between needing to run and wanting to crawl. It felt familiar. Overhearing Sam trying to charm someone. *Déjà vu?*

"Made 'em perfectly round..."

Someone answered Sam, but it was a mumble and Trevor didn't hear it clearly.

"Mal?" he called. He found them in the hall outside the bathroom. Mallory lingering at the back of the hall, Sam not touching her, but clearly blocking her escape.

"Hey." Sam looked at him over his shoulder. "She's hot, Trev, but the bikinis that tie shape the tits better. Just told her that so she'd know which one you prefer."

"Leave her alone."

"What?" Sam shook his head. Tossed his hands up innocently.

"Leave her alone," Trevor repeated.

"Hey." Sam shrugged. "Just trying to help a friend out. We

like big round tits, Mal." He looked away from Trevor and turned toward Mallory.

"You say one more thing about my girlfriend's body and—"

"And what?" Sam sighed. Rolled his eyes at Trevor. "You've seen my wife, Trevor. She's a whore for me. I don't need your seconds."

Trevor lunged, but Sam ducked into the bathroom and closed the door.

"You okay?" he asked quietly. Mallory nodded. Trevor reached for her. Took her hand, but he wanted to put his arms around her. He wouldn't, though. Not here. Not where Sam would open the door and find them together.

"I'm fine," Mallory assured him as he dragged her to the staircase. "Trev. It's okay."

"I wanna kill him."

She shook her head. Touched his lips with her fingertips.

"Let it go." She kissed him, a quick peck on his mouth, and backed away. "C'mon. Let's go swim."

Trevor took a deep breath.

"Did he touch you?"

"No." Mallory tugged on his hand. "No. He was...flirting. He started out flirting. Like...harmless...it was just...gross."

"He's not harmless," Trevor warned her as she pulled him toward the kitchen.

Chapter 54

Hanna

The lake was warm today like bath water, and she decided when she'd gone inside to grab a bottle of water, she wouldn't get back in. Even though maybe it was just the same as it had been yesterday (as Bowie had told her when she'd complained to him about it), the way it had lapped at her shoulders and over the top of her suit when she and Bowie were treading water out by the dock made her feel grimy, almost defiled, she couldn't stand to think of spending another minute, let alone another day and night at this hellhole, and she wanted to pack their things up and go home. Leave this irresponsible, cocky side of her husband here with the other ghosts and go home and see Sylvi.

Sylvi was sweet and precious and innocent and everything Hanna was not and never would be again. Hanna would go home and unpack and wash their clothes and shower in water hot enough to scald her, to leave her skin shiny and pink, before she would see or touch her daughter.

She'd forgo the donuts and the coffee and the impromptu park or theater visits. She'd willingly fold herself back into the obedient, agreeable wife she'd been to Bowie, if it meant keeping Sylvi safe from any harm.

Bowie didn't want to leave.

Maybe it was her imagination, but she felt eyes on her like fingers ripping at her bikini and stabbing her, pinching her. When she'd looked, though, Sam had been hamming it up with Bowie, Sam on the air drums and Bowie the air guitar, and she was forgotten to them both, and only Neelie was watching her. Did that mean Neelie had talked to Peyton? Hanna knew Neelie wouldn't have said anything to Sam.

No one noticed when she went inside. The house was quiet and hot, though the A/C unit plugged away in the living room. Hanna shivered in the one spot of frigid air as she hurried through the living room to the stairs. Where was Davis? He'd come inside earlier, and he'd never come back out. The doors upstairs were all open, and the beds had all been made to one degree or another, hers and Bowie's maybe the most rumpled-looking. She stood for a moment at the foot of the bed, saddened by that and feeling stupid that it bothered her. Was it *really* Sam? Was it time spent with Sam that had rounded Bowie's sharp edges, blurred the precision with which he usually moved through life? Or was it as simple as a vacation, where everyone was allowed to be lazy?

She grabbed a t-shirt, one with the name of their fitness center on the back, and tugged it on over her suit. She considered shorts, but decided that might draw too much attention to herself, and anyway, the t-shirt fell below her swim suit. She shouldn't have to worry about this. Women shouldn't have to dress in ways to keep men under control. Then again, right now, she was sick of feeling like someone was looking at her, and she needed to cover her skin.

She looked in each room again as she passed, a little concerned about Davis. He hadn't had enough to drink to

kill him, had he? *Well, no.* Besides, he'd told them all he'd
prayed to the porcelain god earlier this morning. Maybe he'd
gone for a walk. Or maybe their paths had crossed, and he
was outside now with the gang.

Neelie was in the kitchen when she went downstairs.
Hanna hated that this morning had happened, because now
Neelie was aware of the awkwardness between them, and
Hanna couldn't fake her way through a conversation.

"Did Bowie tell you I gave him a hand job in physics lab?"

Hanna slowed her steps, but she didn't stop. No, Bowie
hadn't told her that, and she recognized this as Neelie's
attempt to assert herself. Her need to be in control because
she was scared of what Hanna wouldn't tell her.

"Nope." She shrugged.

"And he jack—"

"Neelie." Hanna stopped walking and turned to stare at
the other woman. Neelie wiped the kitchen counter down
and then turned to look at her. "I don't care."

"I think you do."

"I don't, though." Hanna shook her head. "Because in the
end, I win. I got Bowie. You got Sam."

"Sam loves me."

Hanna shrugged her lips and frowned. "Does he?" Neelie
sputtered in anger, but before she could speak, Hanna held
up her hand to stop her. "Good. For you. If that's what you
want."

She turned and walked out of the house, heard Neelie
throw something behind her, but she didn't look to see what
it was. Outside, she looked around for Davis. Felt her skin
itch just a bit, between her shoulder blades. Could be sweat.
Could be sweat and the lake water. And nerves.

Trevor and Mallory were walking up the dock, water
dripping off them. Sam and Bowie were sprawled in lawn
chairs on the deck, both of them drinking again already.

"Bowie." Sam twisted his leg on the deck railing and made a show of studying it. Hanna wondered if he'd been bitten by something. She wished he had, by a snake or something, and she looked away as immature laughter bubbled inside her. She *needed* to go home.

Peyton and Brion were stretched out under the shade tree, a blanket spread beneath them. That, at least, had worked out well, and whether or not she and Peyton stayed in touch when this weekend in hell was over, it made Hanna happy to think Peyton had decided to give herself a second chance.

"Dude." Bowie tilted the bottle to his lips and sipped. Sunglasses hiding his eyes, Hanna wondered what he was looking at. Trevor and Mallory grabbed the towels they'd slung over the deck rail earlier, still caught up in their own conversation.

"Did you know our little Trevor's grown some balls?"

Hanna's heart hurt, and she felt little stabs of ice in her wrists and her fingertips. The weekend had turned into a game for Sam, and only he knew the rules or when it was time to make a play, and Hanna envisioned all of them as tiny targets lined up for Sam to pick off one by one.

"Man." Bowie shook his head at Sam. "Don't."

"Don't. Really?" Sam snorted. "What? You get yourself some morals somewhere?" Sam craned his neck to look at Hanna. "You let her call the shots now?"

"Just let it go," Bowie mumbled.

"Trevor threatened me," Sam announced, obviously deciding to ignore Bowie. Hanna saw Peyton jump to her feet, Brion directly behind her. Mallory glanced at Peyton and then looked back at Trevor.

"Jesus, Sam."

"*Jesus, Sam.*" Sam mimicked Bowie. "I told him Mallory had nice tits, and he threatened me."

The screen door banged shut, and Hanna looked over her shoulder at Neelie.

"You like Mallory's tits so much, maybe you should be fucking her."

"I'd like to." Sam nodded.

"Fuck you." Neelie turned to go back inside, but she hesitated at the door.

Hanna's stomach twisted, and the yogurt she'd eaten was sour at the back of her throat. She needed Bowie. She was alone on the deck, and Sam kept looking at her, and each time he did, she felt his hips banging against hers, the tree bark scraping over her skin.

"Sam." Bowie sat up slowly, like an old-fashioned TV dad, slow to anger, but maybe reaching the boiling point. Hanna hoped he was pissed and ready to end this ridiculous charade so they could just go home.

"Shut the fuck up, Bowie." Sam remained in the chair, leg on the rail, beer bottle dangling from his fingertips. "Hey." He formed a gun with his fingers and acted like he shot Bowie. "I did fuck your wife, though. Jesus, she was hot. Tight little bitch—"

Bowie turned slowly to look at Hanna, shock on his face.

"You son-of-a-bitch!" Peyton tore free of Brion's hand on her shoulder. "You good for nothing, son-of-a-bitch, you raped her. You raped Hanna—"

"She wanted it." Sam shrugged. "All you little cunts want it, and then you all—"

"You—" Bowie took a step toward Sam. "You raped my wife?"

Sam lowered his shades to look at Bowie. "I popped her—"

"Shut up!" Neelie's voice was low and threatening.

"You raped my wife?" Bowie said again. Hanna watched

the emotions flash over Bowie's face. Disbelief. Rage. Betrayal.

"This cocksucker saw us," Sam told Bowie as he pointed at Trevor. Hanna dragged her eyes from Bowie to Trevor. What the hell did that mean?

"When did you do it? When—"

"She was a sweet little eighteen. Lighten up, White. Trevor stuffed it down her throat the night before. How the hell was I supposed to know she was a virgin?"

"Before or after?" Bowie grabbed a handful of Sam's hair to pull him out of the chair.

"Jesus, pussy." Sam shoved his hand away.

Hanna met Peyton's eyes over Bowie's shoulder.

"Did you rape my wife before or after Eden?"

"Eden?" Trevor repeated.

"You sure you wanna go there?" Sam stood up slowly. Raised his eyebrows at Bowie. "You sure you wanna bring her into it?"

"I covered for you." Bowie spoke so quietly, Hanna had to strain to hear him. His face was frozen in that same betrayal she'd glimpsed earlier. "I covered for you for the same damned thing you did to my wife?"

"Watch yourself." Sam reached out and pressed his knuckles to Bowie's chest. "Trevor knows what happened. You want everybody to know?"

"Bowie?" Hanna whispered. She cleared her throat. "Bowie? What's he talking about?"

"You son-of-a-bitch. I covered—"

"Fuck you!" Sam threw the beer bottle down. Hanna jumped when shattered glass and beer flew everywhere. She saw a piece of brown glass on the top of her foot. The bead of blood that bloomed under it. "Fuck you. You didn't *cover* for me, fuckwad. You helped me. You. *Helped.* Me. You got it?"

Hanna looked up when Sam threw a punch at Bowie.

Bowie put his arm up to block him and hit him in the ribs with a jab.

"You covered for me. I covered for you. Remember that? Remember?"

"Bowie?" Hanna sniffled. Swiped at her nose. The cut on her foot stung, and the beer puddle expanded to her toes. "Bowie, please?" The smell of yeast, of the beer, made her gag.

"You're disgusting," Neelie told Sam.

"Maybe," he agreed. "Maybe so. But so's Bowie White."

"Shut up." Bowie swung again, but Sam ducked out of the way.

"Ask Bowie how Eden died," Sam suggested.

"Sam?"

Hanna was scared to look away from them, from Bowie and Sam, but when she heard the desperation in Neelie's voice she dragged her eyes from them and turned to Neelie.

"Ask him." Sam looked at Hanna. Swept his eyes over the rest of them, except Trevor and Mallory, who were behind him. "Trevor can tell you. Trevor's not here to spend the weekend with friends, boys and girls. No, Trevor, who did have his dick down your wife's throat, by the way," Sam looked at Bowie pointedly, "has been having dreams about the lake. Mysterious dreams. He's here to solve the mystery." Sam twisted to look at Trevor. "Just a second, and I'll let ya pull the mask off the bad guys, *Scoob*...Yeah." Sam looked back at Bowie and then Hanna. "So, he'll solve the mystery, and then he and his bitch are gonna live happily ever after, where Mallory can't run around topless anymore, because Trev wants babies."

Hanna saw Trevor and Mallory exchange a look.

"Okay, Trev. You're on. Who killed Eden?"

Hanna leaned over, cupped her hand over her lips when

she threw up a little in her mouth. She turned away and spit over the railing of the deck.

Say Sam. Say Sam. God, please, Trevor, say Sam.

"Sam."

Hanna heard Neelie wail, like the siren all those years ago, and her knees went weak. She sank down to the deck, knees in the beer and the broken glass, and tried to breathe. He'd killed Eden. Jesus, if she'd have fought him, he might have killed her, too.

"And Bowie."

Chapter 55

Trevor

He felt their stares heavy on his shoulders. Heard the girls crying, Neelie and Hanna sobbing. Sam and Bowie breathing heavy.

...the floodlights were off, and he could only make out one shade of black against the night sky. Someone was crying. He had heard someone scream earlier, one of the girls. He moved quietly; maybe they wouldn't see him, but they might hear him.

"Just leave me alone."

Eden. *It was* Eden *crying.*

"Shut up." Sam.

"Man, just let her go. Why do you do this? Control yourself—"

"Shut up, Bowie. Lemme think..."

"Let me go!" Eden sobbed. "Please?"

"The bitch bit me." Sam again.

Trevor froze at the dock when he heard the scuffle. Was Sam gonna throw her down here and climb on top of her?

"You wanna turn?" Sam asked.

"Fuck no," Bowie snapped. "God, Sam. What the hell—stop it, Eden—"

*Another scuffle, Eden crying again and someone—Sam? Bowie?
—breathing heavy. Trevor heard a splash.* Someone had fallen in.
*He stood frozen, waiting for another splash. For someone to go in
after whoever had fallen into the lake.*

"Where'd she go?" Bowie's gruff voice.

"Fuck if I care," Sam answered.

"Sam."

"She'll find her way out."

"She's drunk. It's dark. She's never been up here before—"

*Trevor heard another splash. Had one of them gone in after
her? His knees went weak with relief, and he had to piss after
guzzling that bottle of water in the kitchen.*

"She's stuck," Bowie mumbled.

"She'll be fine—"

"Sam, she's gonna drown—"

"Then nobody's gonna know what happened."

"Sam."

"You weren't a Boy Scout, Bowie White. Fuck her."

Heavy breathing again.

"This sucks."

*"It was an accident," Sam said calmly. "She was drinking. She
fell in the lake. Her shorts got stuck on something on the dock. So
what?"*

"Sam, she's got a family—"

"We're family, Bowie. Right?"

"You let her drown." The words were bitter in Trevor's
mouth, and he spit, but couldn't get rid of the aftertaste. The
well of relief that had filled him then, when he'd thought
Bowie had gone in after Eden, was nothing to what he felt
now. He'd been ready to confess to Hanna's rape, to killing
Eden, and though it sucked to realize he'd witnessed it—sort
of?—he hadn't done anything. He hadn't killed Eden. "You
sons-of-bitches let her drown. So no one would know Sam
tried it with her, too."

"You—" Bowie appeared paralyzed with rage and maybe shock, maybe betrayal. "You made me let her drown? You suggested we were family, and that we'd keep our little secret, after you'd already raped Hanna?"

Sam shrugged. "You made your choice, Bowie. I didn't *make* you do anything."

Neelie lunged at Sam, but Peyton rushed the deck and grabbed for her. Hanna's legs, her heart, was too heavy to move. Trevor watched her for a moment. The screen door banged open, and Trevor moved sideways, knocking Mallory to the ground as Davis appeared, recklessly waving a handgun.

"Put the gun down!" Brion yelled.

"You're a worthless piece of shit—"

"Davis, put the gun—"

Peyton's yell turned into a sharp scream, but the roar of the gunfire drowned her out. Trevor felt something warm and wet on his back and his neck. Mallory writhed beneath him, sobbing, clutching at his shoulders, his back. He lifted his head to see what was going on, to find Davis.

Sam slumped on the deck, against the railing. Trevor saw the bullet hole high in his shoulder. Thank God, Davis was a shitty shot, or Sam might be dead. Not that Trevor cared what happened to Sam. Just Davis. And his son.

"You shot me, you son-of-a-bitch." Sam's mumble was high-pitched and whiney.

"I went…" Trevor, head still ducked over Mallory, struggled to breathe and talk. "I went in after you guys started to walk away. I went in after her. Tried to pull her to the side of the lake, but the pocket of her shorts had caught on a piece of iron on a dock leg. I pulled her away from it."

"You're not a hero, Gerhardt," Sam told him, but he was subdued now.

"No," Trevor agreed, "because you guys killed her."

"Where the hell did Davis go?" Peyton's voice rang out above the rest of them. "He's still got the gun. Davis!"

"Davis?" Trevor sat up on his knees, Mallory still lying in front of him. She linked her fingers through his.

"You went in?" she whispered. "You went in after her?"

Trevor nodded. "She was already gone."

"You pulled her out."

"Sam and Bowie must have heard me. They came back out...rushed out, like they weren't just there a minute before that, watching her drown."

Mallory nodded.

"Brion! Brion, no!" Peyton called. Trevor looked up and watched her run off the deck toward Brion, who was moving cautiously to the side of the house.

"You're disgusting," Neelie said quietly. "You. Disgust. Me."

"We're not so different, Neelie," Sam reminded her. His voice was low and gruff.

"I thought so, too," she answered. "That's why I married you. Figured I didn't deserve much better. At least I never..."

"Never what?" Sam asked.

Trevor helped Mallory sit up. Bowie knelt on the deck next to Sam, a wadded towel pressed to the bullet wound.

"Anybody call an ambulance?" Trevor suggested. "Because I'm not gonna let this son-of-a-bitch die."

When no one moved, Trevor climbed to his feet. Stumbled a bit as the world shifted. Once he was steady, he reached to help Mallory up. He looked at the table behind Bowie and Sam.

"Somebody call a goddamned ambulance!" he shouted. "Let's not do this again!"

"I betcha Trev was a Boy Scout," Sam mumbled to Bowie.

"Fuck you." Trevor hurried up to the deck and pulled Mallory into the house with him. He wouldn't leave her around Sam or Bowie now. Never again. "Where's your phone?"

"Upstairs."

"Okay. Get it. Please."

She was running before he got the words out. He stood in the kitchen, head back and eyes on the ceiling as he traced Mallory's footsteps above him. Nothing could get her. Nothing could hurt her. This was done. Mystery solved. But he wanted her back down here with him. And he wanted this phone call made.

And then he wanted to get the hell away from Litchfield Lake.

He heard her feet pound back down the stairs. Heard the musical tones that told him she was dialing.

Another gunshot cracked outside.

"Davis." Trevor hung his head.

Epilogue

MIDWESTERN SUMMERS WERE HOT AND HUMID, AND TREVOR remembered how the neighborhood yards were brown and dead before August was over, and how they'd go back to school and then get out early because of the heat, and he'd heard today the schools had let out an hour early. One-hour early dismissal seemed dumb to him, but what did he know? Just that the classrooms were most likely no hotter an hour later than they were at the time of dismissal, and the bus rides home were hot and miserable. But he wasn't a school superintendent or a teacher or a bus driver and he didn't even have kids, and so what the hell did it matter to him?

He did have a yard, though. Brown and wilted, but a yard, nonetheless. They'd just moved; in fact, they were still settling in, and Mallory's family had come down earlier in the week with more of her stuff, and they were living out of boxes.

But they had a yard.

And a house.

Smallish. Old. But clean. Central air. Little backyard and a patio that he could cover with his legs if he could do the splits. Mallory was happy, kept giving him those cheesy grins, and he liked the place, but he saw it as a stepping stone. The new job was also a stepping stone. He'd settled way too damned long at the old place, the old part of his life. He'd settled long enough to become stagnant, and he was loathe to slow down now that he'd taken that first step.

"Do you think they like chocolate chip cookies?"

Trevor turned to look at Mallory. She was leaning into the kitchen window; he could see her face pressed up against the screen.

"Who doesn't like chocolate chip cookies?" He shrugged.

"They'll be here. Like…in fifteen minutes."

"Okay." He nodded.

She was nervous. He got that. He watched her close the window. Pictured her in the kitchen, putting cookies in the oven. Decided that though he missed the topless stage, it was probably a good thing she'd taken to wearing clothes, if she was using the oven more often.

He turned back to the crumbling chiminea at the corner of the cement patio. Fed the fire another sketch.

He wouldn't admit it, probably not even to Mal, but he was a little anxious, too. They'd never entertained before, unless you called slapping bologna sandwiches together for her family when they'd come down earlier in the week entertaining. And he didn't.

Wasn't just that, though. Entertaining. Inviting old friends into their charming one-bedroom bungalow—that's how the real estate agent described the house. Old friends who lived in loft apartments and McMansions.

Wasn't that, either. Not really.

They hadn't seen much of each other since the weekend of the Fourth of July. It had been a somber, awful end to the weekend, and though they'd kept in touch—for example, Trevor knew that Hanna had asked Bowie to move out—they hadn't actually seen each other or spent time together. He and Mallory had decided to give this a shot, invite them over for a cookout. See how it played out. And go from there. Might be that none of them wanted a damned thing to do with each other anymore. Might be that tragedy brought them together.

Neelie had already filed for divorce, according to Peyton. Trevor didn't blame her, though he didn't like her, either. No one knew where Sam had disappeared to after being treated for the gunshot wound. He'd claimed it was self-inflicted, and there had been a bit of an investigation, but the same investigation had somehow turned up child pornography on Sam's computer and three separate sexual harassment suits filed against him on the job. Apparently, he'd managed to finagle his way out of each one; the good ole boys ruled the firm where he worked, and each time, the woman involved walked away with a small settlement, and Sam kept his job.

Trevor sighed and dropped another sketch into the fire.

"I wish you wouldn't do that."

He looked up as Mallory joined him on the patio. Took the beer she offered him with a smile.

"I have to."

"There's something wrong about burning your creation. Your art."

"You framed one of the paintings," he reminded her. He'd been livid when he'd first seen it. Yeah, artistically it was good. Better than good. And he wasn't even a painter. But every time he looked at it now, on the wall next to the framed sketch of his duck cartoon character he'd named Dooz, he felt the black water in his shoes. On his legs. Covering his waist as he'd tugged at Eden's body until her shorts ripped and he dragged her to shore. Dead. The painting haunted him, though only in his waking hours.

She'd left the back door open so both of them heard the doorbell ring.

"Ready for this?" he asked with a deep breath and a big grin.

"Yeah." She nodded. "I'll get it."

"Hey." He turned to watch her walk back to the house.

"Hmm?"

"We've got a house with an oven now." He lifted a shoulder suggestively.

"That's still not a good marriage proposal." She shook her head.

He smiled and watched her go inside. Turned back to the chiminea and set the whole pile of sketches in the flames. Wondered who would be here first? Peyton and Brion? Hanna?

"Hey."

Trevor turned as Davis and his son hurried out the back door.

"Man, that's cool!" Connor marveled at the chiminea.

"Davis." Trevor nodded at him.

"I like it." Davis looked around the yard and the patio appreciatively. Mallory joined them, handed Davis a beer, and held a bottle of root beer up in question. Davis nodded that she could offer it to his son.

"Here's to bad aim." Trevor clinked his bottle against Davis' and took a long drink.

Davis carried a gun in his truck. And he'd heard the scuffle on the deck. Snapped and gone after the gun, come back through the front of the house, and fired at Sam. They'd all agreed to mutual hatred, and that might prove to be an insufficient foundation for the newfound old friendships. But they were all relieved Davis hadn't killed him. Trevor thought that might be a plus.

The second shot, what Trevor had assumed was a suicide

shot, had been a shot fired into the trees. Sobbing and spine-less, Davis had dropped the gun then and rambled that he needed to die, but he didn't have the courage to turn the gun on himself.

"Here's to cowardice," Davis said with his same-old self-deprecating grin.

"That's not cowardice," Mallory corrected him. "That's the will to live."

Davis shrugged ambiguously and drank from his bottle. Trevor watched him sneak a peek at his son, who was mesmerized by the fire.

"You still seein' that guy?" Trevor asked quietly.

Davis snorted. Looked at Trevor as the back door opened and Hanna, Peyton, and Brion joined them.

"He's a shrink," Davis told Trevor. He said it slowly, as he did every time Trevor joked with him about *seeing someone*.

"I know." Trevor nodded. He watched Mallory hugging the girls, met Brion's eyes, and nodded. "Everything working out?"

Davis shrugged. "Still kicking."

Careful not to look at him, Trevor nodded.

"I'm glad."

"We'll call it bad aim." Davis held his bottle out again.

"I'll drink to that." Trevor tapped his bottle and took a long drink.

About the Author

Tracy is the author of the Lorelei Bluffs women's fiction series, the Williams Legacy, and several stand-alone women's fiction novels. She has recently dabbled in contemporary romance, as well.

Tracy's books have been called gripping, emotional, and timely, and readers describe her characters as real and relatable.

Go to www.broemmerbooks.com to learn more about Tracy and her books.

Also by Tracy Broemmer

Women's Fiction Novels:

Luther's Cross (Writing as Therese Kinkaide)

Luther's Cross 10th Anniversary Edition (Tracy Broemmer)

Fairytale (Writing as Therese Kinkaide)

Just Like Them (Writing as Therese Kinkaide)

Small Hours (Writing as Therese Kinkaide)

Picket Fences

Two Story Home

Green-Eyed Girl

Say Everything

Come Home For Christmas

Ever, Again

Safe as Houses

Damsel

Every Little Thing, Lorelei Bluffs, Book 1

Two A.M., Lorelei Bluffs, Book 2

Blind, Lorelei Bluffs, Book 3

Leaving July, Lorelei Bluffs, Book 4

Hesitation Marks, Lorelei Bluffs, Book 5

Four Letter Words, Lorelei Bluffs, Book 6

See Kate, Lorelei Bluffs, Book 7

Loved You More, Lorelei Bluffs, Book 8

A Lorelei Ending, Lorelei Bluffs, Book 9

I Do, Lorelei Bluffs, Book 10

Truth Is, The Williams Legacy, Book 1

Other People's Ugly, The Williams Legacy, Book 2

Omissions, The Williams Legacy, Book 3

Contemporary Romance Novels:

Destiny's Calling: Your Future Is Waiting

Wedding Day Shenanigans

Holiday Fling

The Kiss Off

Something Like Love

Love, Nashville, The Mississippi Queen Trilogy, Book 1

Forever, Duncan, The Mississippi Queen Trilogy, Book 2

Always, Jess, The Mississippi Queen Trilogy, Book 3

Contemporary Romance Novellas:

Indian Summer, A Novella

Dear Jaclyn Perris, A Novella

Contemporary Romance Short Stories:

Perfect Pictures, The Wine Tasting Series, Traminette

Coming Home, The Wine Tasting Series, Edelweiss

Save Me Every Dance, The Wine Tasting Series, Rosé

Marry Me, The Wine Tasting Series, Shiraz

Birthday Wishes, The Wine Tasting Series, Muscat

Dad Jeans, The Wine Tasting Series, Vignoles

Made in the USA
Monee, IL
27 July 2024

62198961R00215